DATE DUE			11/17
			PRINTED IN U.S.A.

COMPASS

COMPASS

Mathias Énard

Translated by Charlotte Mandell

A NEW DIRECTIONS BOOK

Originally published in French as *Boussole* by Actes Sud in 2015
Published by arrangement with The French Publishers' Agency

The photograph on p. 267 is © Service historique de la Défense, CHA/CAEN, 2747 x 4294, and the photograph on page 272 is © BPK Bildagentur/Museum Europäischer Kulturen, Staatliche Museen zu Berlin/Art Resource, NY. The other photographs are courtesy of the author.

Manufactured in the United States of America
New Directions Books are printed on acid-free paper
First published clothbound by New Directions in 2017

Library of Congress Cataloging-in-Publication Data
Names: Énard, Mathias, 1972– author. | Mandell, Charlotte, translator.
Title: Compass / Mathias Enard ; translated by Charlotte Mandell.
Other titles: Boussole. English
Description: New York : New Directions, 2017.
Identifiers: LCCN 2016039665 | ISBN 9780811226622 (alk. paper)
Classification: LCC PQ2705.N273 B6813 2017 | DDC 843/.92--dc23
LC record available at https://lccn.loc.gov/2016039665

10 9 8 7 6 5 4 3 2 1

New Directions Books are published for James Laughlin
by New Directions Publishing Corporation
80 Eighth Avenue, New York 10011

Die Augen schließ' ich wieder,
Noch schlägt das Herz so warm.
Wann grünt ihr Blätter am Fenster?
Wann halt' ich mein Liebchen im Arm?

Once more I try to close my eyes,
yet my heart beats strong and warm—
when will the leaves at my window turn green,
when will I hold my darling in my arms?

—Wilhelm Müller & Franz Schubert,
Die Winterreise

On the Divers forms of Lunacie in the Orient

We are two opium smokers each in his own cloud, seeing nothing outside, alone, never understanding each other we smoke, faces agonizing in a mirror, we are a frozen image to which time gives the illusion of movement, a snow crystal gliding over a ball of frost, the complexity of whose intertwinings no one can see, I am that drop of water condensed on the window of my living room, a rolling liquid pearl that knows nothing of the vapor that engendered it, nor of the atoms that still compose it but that, soon, will serve other molecules, other bodies, the clouds weighing heavy over Vienna tonight: over whose nape will this water stream, against what skin, on what pavement, toward what river, and this indistinct face on the glass is mine only for an instant, one of the millions of possible configurations of illusion — look, Herr Gruber is walking his dog despite the drizzle, he's wearing a green hat and his eternal raincoat; he avoids getting splashed by the cars by making ridiculous little leaps on the pavement: the mutt thinks he wants to play, so it leaps toward its master and gets a good slap the second it places its dirty paw on Herr Gruber's coat, despite everything he manages to reach the road to cross, his silhouette is lengthened by the streetlights, a blackened pool in the midst of the sea of shadows of the tall trees ripped apart by the headlights along the Porzellangasse, and Herr Gruber seems to think twice about plunging into the Alsergrund night, as I do about leaving my contemplation of the drops of water, the thermometer, and the rhythm of the trams descending toward the Schottentor.

Existence is a painful reflection, an opium addict's dream, a poem by Rumi sung by Shahram Nazeri, the ostinato of the *zarb* makes the window vibrate slightly beneath my fingers like the skin of the drum, I should go on reading instead of watching Herr Gruber disappearing under the rain, instead of straining my ears to the swirling melismata of the Iranian singer, whose power and timbre could make many of our tenors blush with shame. I should pause the CD, impossible to concentrate; pointless reading this offprint for the tenth time, I don't understand any of its mysterious meaning, twenty pages, twenty horrible, frosty pages, which reached me precisely today, today when a compassionate doctor may have named my illness, declared my body officially diseased, almost relieved at having given my symptoms a diagnosis—a deadly kiss—a diagnosis we'll need to confirm while beginning a treatment, he said, and following the disease's evolution, evolution, there it is, there we are, contemplating a drop of water evolving toward disappearance before it reforms itself in the Great All.

There is no such thing as chance, everything is connected, Sarah would say, why did I receive this article in the mail precisely today, an old-fashioned, stapled offprint instead of a PDF accompanied by a note hoping it "arrives safely," an email that could have given some news, explained where she is, what this Sarawak is where she's writing from, according to my atlas it's a state in Malaysia in the northwestern part of the island of Borneo, not far from Brunei and its rich sultan, not far from the gamelans of Debussy and Britten either, it seems to me—but the tenor of the article is quite different; no music, aside perhaps from a long dirge; twenty dense leaves that appeared in the September issue of *Representations*, a fine journal from the University of California for which she has often written. The article bears a brief inscription on the title page, without commentary, *For you dearest Franz, with love, Sarah*, and was mailed on November 17, two weeks ago — it still takes two weeks for a piece of mail to make the journey from Malaysia to Austria, maybe she skimped on the stamps, she could have added a postcard or some explanation, what does it mean, I went through every trace of her I have in my apartment, her articles, two books, a few photographs, and even a copy of her doctoral thesis, printed and bound in red Skivertex, two hefty volumes weighing three kilos each:

"There are certain wounds in life that, like leprosy, eat away at the soul in solitude and diminish it," writes the Iranian Sadegh Hedayat at the beginning of his novel *The Blind Owl*: the little man with round glasses knew this better than anyone. It was one of those wounds that led him to turn the gas on high in his apartment on the rue Championnet in Paris, one evening of great solitude, an April evening, very far from Iran, very far, with as his only company a few poems by Khayyam and a somber bottle of cognac, perhaps, or a lump of opium, or perhaps nothing, nothing at all, aside from the texts he still kept, which he carried off with him into the great gas void.

We don't know if he left a letter or a sign other than his novel *The Blind Owl*, finished long ago, which would earn him, two years after his death, the admiration of French intellectuals who had never read anything from Iran: the publisher José Corti published *The Blind Owl* soon after Julien Gracq's *The Opposing Shore*; Gracq would experience success after the gas on the rue Championnet had just had its effect, in 1951, and would say that the *Shore* was the novel of "all noble rot," the kind of rot that had just finished off Hedayat in an ether of wine and gas. André Breton defended the two men and their books, too late to save Hedayat and his wounds, if he could have been saved, if the sickness had not been, very certainly, incurable.

The little man with the thick round glasses was the same in exile as he was in Iran, calm and discreet, speaking softly. His irony and his malicious sadness led to his censorship, unless it was his sympathy for madmen and drunkards, maybe even his admiration for certain books and certain poets; perhaps he was censored because he dabbled in opium and cocaine, all the while making fun of drug addicts; because he drank alone, or had the defect of no longer expecting anything from God, not even on certain evenings of great solitude, when the gas calls; perhaps because he was miserable, or because he believed sensibly in the importance of his writing, or didn't believe in it—all disturbing things.

The fact remains that on the rue Championnet there is no plaque marking his stay, or his death; in Iran there is no monument to his memory, despite the weight of history that shows he cannot be overlooked, and the weight of his death, which still burdens his compatriots. His oeuvre lives on today in Tehran in the same way that he died, in poverty and secrecy, on stalls in flea markets, or in truncated reeditions, shorn of any allusions that might plunge the reader into drugs or suicide, in order to preserve the young people of Iran who suffer from those diseases of despair, suicide, and drugs, and who thus throw themselves into Hedayat's books with delight, when they can find them. Celebrated and under-read in this way, he joins the great names that surround him at Père-Lachaise, not far from Proust, just as sober in eternity as he was in life, just as discreet, with few visitors and without any ostentatious flowers, ever since that April day in 1951 when he chose gas and the rue Championnet to put an end to all things, eaten away by a leprosy of the soul, imperious and incurable. "No one makes the decision to commit suicide; suicide is in certain men, it is in their nature," Hedayat wrote in the late 1920s. He wrote these lines before he read and translated Kafka, before he introduced Khayyam. His work begins with the end. The first collection he published opens with *Buried Alive* (*Zendeh beh goor*), with suicide and destruction, and clearly describes the thoughts, it seems, of the man in the instant he abandoned himself to the gas twenty years later, letting himself fall gently asleep after taking pains to destroy his papers and notes, in the tiny kitchen invaded by the unbearable perfume of the nascent spring. He destroyed his manuscripts, braver perhaps than Kafka, or perhaps because he had no Max Brod close at hand, perhaps because he trusted no one, or because he was convinced it was time to die. And while Kafka faded away, coughing, correcting until the last minute the texts he'd end up wanting to burn, Hedayat left in the slow agony of heavy sleep, his death already written twenty years earlier, his whole life pockmarked by the wounds and sores of the leprosy that ate away at him in solitude, which we might guess is linked to Iran, to the Orient, to Europe and to the West, as Kafka in Prague was at once German, Jewish, and Czech without being any of those things, more lost than anyone or freer than everyone. Hedayat had one of those wounds of self that make you reel through the world; it was that crevice that opened up until it became a crevasse; in this there is, as in opium, or in alcohol, or in anything that splits you in half, not an illness but a decision, a will to fissure your being, until the very end.

By opening this article with Hedayat and his *Blind Owl*, we propose to explore this crevice, to go look inside the cleft, to enter the drunkenness of those men and women who have wavered too much in alterity; we are going to take the little man by the hand to go down and observe the gnawing wounds, the drugs, the elsewheres, and explore this between-space, this bardo, this barzakh, the world between worlds into which artists and travelers fall.

Sarah's prologue is a surprising one, these first lines are still, fifteen years after she has written them, just as disconcerting—it must be late, my eyes are closing over the old typescript despite the *zarb* and Nazeri's voice. Sarah had been furious, when she was defending her thesis, at being reproached for the "romantic" tone of her preamble and for her "absolutely irrelevant" parallel with Gracq and Kafka. Morgan, her thesis advisor, had tried to defend her however, albeit rather naively, saying "it's always a good thing to talk about Kafka," which had made the jury of vexed Orientalists and sleepy mandarins sigh. They could only be drawn out of their doctrinal snooze by the hatred they felt for one another: in any case they forgot Sarah's unusual introduction rather quickly to squabble over questions of methodology; that is, they didn't see how *walking* through the text (the old boffin spat out this word like an insult) could have anything scientific about it, even if one allows oneself to be guided by the hand of Sadegh Hedayat. I was passing through Paris, happy to have an opportunity to attend a "Sorbonne-style" thesis defense for the first time, and happy that it was hers, but once past the surprise and amusement of discovering the dilapidated state of the hallways, the room and the jury, relegated to the backwaters of God knows what department lost in this labyrinth of knowledge, where five authorities would, one after the other, display their utter lack of interest in the text that was supposed to be under discussion, all the while deploying superhuman efforts—like me in the audience—not to fall asleep, this exercise filled me with bitterness and melancholy, and when we walked out of the room (a dingy classroom with cracked, warped desks made of

chipboard, desks that held not knowledge but distracting graffiti
and stuck-on chewing gum) to let these people deliberate, I was
seized by a powerful desire to take to my heels, to go down the
boulevard Saint-Michel and walk by the water so as not to meet
Sarah and so she couldn't guess my impressions of this famous
defense that must have been very important to her. There were
about thirty people in the audience, a big crowd for the tiny hallway we were crammed into; Sarah came out with the attendees,
she was speaking to an older, very elegant lady, whom I knew
to be her mother, and to a young man who looked disturbingly
like her, her brother. It was impossible to move toward the exit
without passing them, I turned around to look at the portraits
of the Orientalists adorning the corridor, yellowing old engravings and commemorative plaques from a sumptuous time gone
by. Sarah was chatting, she looked exhausted but not dejected;
perhaps in the heat of scholarly debate, while taking notes to
prepare her replies, she'd had a totally different impression from
the audience's. She saw me and waved. I had come mostly to support her, but also to prepare myself, even if only in imagination,
for my own doctoral defense — and what I had just witnessed
was not reassuring. I was wrong: after a few minutes of delib-
eration, when we were readmitted into the room, she received
the highest grade; the famous presiding judge, the enemy of
"walking through the text," complimented her warmly on her
work and today, as I reread the beginning of this text, I must
admit there was something strong and innovative in these four
hundred pages on the images and representations of the Orient,
non-places, utopias, ideological fantasies in which many who
had wanted to travel had gotten lost: the bodies of artists, poets,
and travelers who had tried to explore them were pushed little
by little toward destruction; illusion, as Hedayat said, ate away
at the soul in solitude — what had long been called madness,

melancholy, depression was often the result of a friction, a loss of self in creation, in contact with alterity, and even if it all seems to me today a little over-hasty, romantic, to be honest, there was probably already an actual intuition there on which she based all of her later work.

Once the verdict was given, very happy for her, I went over to offer my congratulations, and she kissed me warmly asking: What are you doing here, and I replied that a happy coincidence had brought me to Paris, a white lie, she invited me to join her and her relatives for the traditional glass of champagne, which I accepted; we found ourselves upstairs at a neighborhood café where these sorts of events are often celebrated. Sarah suddenly looked dejected, I noticed that she was floating in her gray suit; her form had been swallowed up by the Academy, her body bore the traces of the effort made during the previous weeks and months: the four preceding years had all been building up to this moment, had no meaning except for this instant, and now that the champagne was flowing she was displaying the gentle, exhausted smile of a woman who has just given birth — she had dark rings under her eyes, I imagine she'd spent the night going over her paper, too excited to sleep. Gilbert de Morgan, her thesis advisor, was there of course; I had met him in Damascus. He didn't hide his passion for his protégée, he was gazing fondly at her with a paternal air that veered gently to the incestuous as he consumed more champagne: at the third glass, his eyes alight and his cheeks red, leaning alone at a high table, I caught his eyes wandering from Sarah's ankles to her belt, from bottom to top and then from top to bottom — at which point he let out a little melancholy burp and then emptied his fourth glass. He noticed I was observing him, looked fiercely at me before recognizing me and said with a smile, We've met before, haven't we? I refreshed his memory, yes, I'm Franz Ritter, we saw each other in Damascus with Sarah — oh of course, the musician, and I was already so used to this contemptuous mistake that I replied with a slightly moronic smile. I hadn't yet exchanged more than a few words with the graduate, she was being sought out by all of her friends and parents, and I was already cornered with this great scholar whom everyone, outside of a classroom or a department meeting, wanted ardently to avoid. He asked me all the conventionally approved questions about my own university career, questions I didn't know how to answer, questions I would rather not even ask myself; but he was in good form, chummy, as the English say, not to say bawdy or lewd, and I was far from imagining that I would see him again a few months later in Tehran, under very different circumstances and in a different state altogether, still accompanied by Sarah who, at this moment, was immersed in conversation with Nadim — he had just arrived, she must have been explaining the rebuttals and ins and outs of the defense, why he hadn't been there, I don't know; he too was very elegant, in a beautiful round-collared white shirt that lit up his olive complexion, his short black beard; Sarah was holding his hands as if they were about to start dancing. I excused myself from the professor and went to talk to them; Nadim immediately gave me a brotherly embrace that brought me back in an instant to Damascus, to Aleppo, to Nadim's lute in the night, intoxicating the stars in the metallic sky of Syria, so far away, so far, ripped apart not by comets now but by missiles, bombs, screams, and war — impossible, in Paris in 1999, with a glass of champagne in hand, to imagine that Syria would be devastated by the worst violence, that the Aleppo souk would burn down, the minaret of the mosque of the Omayyads collapse, so many friends would die or be forced to go into exile; impossible even today to imagine the amplitude of the damage, the scope of this suffering from a comfortable, silent Viennese apartment.

The CD's over. What strength in this piece of Nazeri's. What magical, mystical simplicity, this architecture of percussion that supports the slow pulsation of the song, the distant rhythm of the ecstasy to be attained, an hypnotic *zikr* that sticks in your ears and stays with you for hours on end. Nadim is a lute player who's internationally recognized today, their marriage had caused a big commotion in the little expat community in Damascus, so unexpected, so sudden it became suspicious to many, and especially to the French Embassy in Syria — one of the countless surprises so typical of Sarah, the latest being this particularly startling article on Sarawak: not long after Nadim arrived I said my goodbyes, Sarah thanked me at length for having come, she asked if I'd be staying a few days in Paris, if we'd have time to see each other again, and I told her I was returning to Austria the next day; I respectfully took my leave of the academic now entirely slumped on his table.

I walked out of the café and resumed my Parisian stroll. For a long time, with my feet scuffling through the dead leaves of the Seine quays, I went over the real reasons that made me waste my time like this, first at a thesis defense and then at the drinks that followed, and I caught a glimpse, in the halo of light that enveloped the brotherly arms of the Parisian bridges, pulling them out of the fog, of a trajectory, a promenade, whose goal or meaning might not appear until afterward, and which obviously has to pass through here, through Vienna where Herr Gruber is coming back from his walk with his filthy mutt: heavy footsteps on the stairs, the dog yapping, then above me, running and scratching over my ceiling. Gruber has never been a considerate neighbor but he's always the first to complain about my music, Schubert's fine, he says, but these old operas and all this, ahem, *exotic* music, it's not exactly to everyone's taste, if you know what I mean. I understand the music bothers you, Herr Gruber, I'm very sorry about it. However I would like to call to your attention the fact that I have carried out every experiment possible and imaginable on your dog's hearing, when you're out: I have discovered that only Bruckner (though only at sound levels bordering on the unacceptable) calms down his scratching on the floor and manages to quiet his shrill barking—which the entire building complains about for that matter—something I plan on developing in a scientific article on veterinary musical therapy which will without a doubt earn me the congratulations of my peers, "On the Effects of Brass Instruments on Canine Moods: Developments and Perspectives."

He's lucky I'm tired, is Gruber, since otherwise I'd happily put on another loud blast of *tombak* drumming, some exotic music for him and his dog. Tired out from this long day of remembering in order to escape—why hide from the truth—the prospect of illness, tired already this morning when I came back from the hospital and opened the mailbox, I thought the padded envelope contained those wretched medical exam results the lab is supposed to send me a copy of: before the postmark set me straight I hesitated to open it for several long minutes. I thought Sarah was somewhere between Darjeeling and Calcutta, and here she is in a verdant jungle on the northern part of the island of Borneo, in the former British possessions of that bulbous island. The monstrous subject of the article, the dry style, so different from her usual lyricism, is frightening; for weeks we haven't exchanged any letters and at exactly the instant I'm going through the most difficult period in my life she reappears in this singular way—I spent the day rereading her texts, with her, which helped me avoid thinking too much, it took me out of myself, and even though I had promised myself I'd begin correcting a student's dissertation, it's time to go to sleep, I think I'll wait till tomorrow morning to dive into this student's observations, *The Orient in*

Gluck's Viennese Operas, because fatigue is making my eyes close, I have to abandon all reading and go to bed.

The last time I saw Sarah, she was spending three days in Vienna for some academic reason or other. (I had obviously offered to put her up at my place, but she had refused, arguing that the organization that had invited her was offering her a magnificent, very Viennese hotel she didn't want to pass up for my *sagging* sofa, which had, I admit, annoyed me no end.) She was in high spirits and had arranged to meet me at a café in the First District, in one of those sumptuous establishments where the abundance of tourists, lords of the place, confers a decadent air that she liked. She had quickly insisted we go for a walk, despite the drizzle, which had upset me, I had no desire to play at being holiday-makers on a cold, wet autumn afternoon, but she was bursting with energy and ended up persuading me. She wanted to take the D tram to its terminus, high up in Nussdorf, then walk a little along the Beethovengang; I retorted that we'd mostly be walking in the mud, that it was better to stay in the neighborhood — we strolled on the Graben up to the cathedral, and I told her a few anecdotes about Mozart's bawdy songs that made her laugh.

"You know, Franz," she said as we were walking by the lines of horse-drawn carriages near St. Stephen's Square, "there's something very interesting about people who think that Vienna is the gateway to the East," which made me laugh too.

"No no, don't laugh, I think I'm going to write about it, on the representations of Vienna as *Porta Orientalis*."

The horses' nostrils were steaming from the cold and they were calmly defecating into leather bags hanging under their tails so as not to dirty the extremely noble Viennese cobblestones.

"I can't see it, even though I'm thinking hard," I replied.

"Hofmannsthal's phrase, 'Vienna, gateway to the Orient,' seems to me very ideological, linked to Hofmannsthal's *desire* about the place of the empire in Europe. The phrase is from 1917 . . . Of course, we have *ćevapčići* and paprika here, but aside from that, it's more the city of Schubert, Richard Strauss, Schönberg, nothing very Oriental in that, in my opinion." And even in representation, in Viennese imagery, aside from the croissant, I had trouble seeing anything evoking the Orient even a tiny bit.

It's a cliché. I had conveyed my scorn for this idea, so worn out it didn't make sense anymore: "Just because the Ottomans have been at your gates twice doesn't necessarily mean you become the gateway to the Orient."

"That's not the question, the question isn't in the reality of this idea, what interests me is understanding why and how so many travelers have seen Vienna and Budapest as the first 'Oriental' cities, and what that can teach us about the meaning they give to the word. And if Vienna is the *gateway* to the Orient, to what Orient does it lead?"

Her search for the meaning of the Orient, endless, infinite — I confess I questioned my certainties and reconsidered them, and as I mull it over now, as I turn off the light, there may have been in the cosmopolitanism of Imperial Vienna something of Istanbul, something of the Öster Reich, the Empire of the East, but it seems remote, very remote today. It's been a very long time since Vienna was the capital of the Balkans, and the Ottomans no longer exist. The Hapsburg Empire was indeed the empire of the Middle, and with the calm and regular breathing that precedes sleep, listening to the cars gliding over the wet road, the pillow still deliciously cool against my cheek, the resonance of the beating of the *zarb* still in my ears, I have to admit that Sarah probably knows Vienna better than I do, more profoundly, not stopping at Schubert or Mahler, the way foreigners

know a city better than its inhabitants, who are lost in routine—
long ago, before we left for Tehran, after I had settled here, she'd
dragged me to the Josephinum, the former military hospital
where there's an absolutely atrocious museum: the exhibition
of anatomical models from the end of the eighteenth century,
conceived for the edification and training of army surgeons,
without having to rely on cadavers or their smells—wax figures
commissioned in Florence from one of the greatest sculpture
studios; among the models exhibited in the glass cases framed
in precious wood there was, on a pink cushion faded with time,
a young blonde woman with fine features, lying with her face
turned to the side, neck a little bent, hair down, a gold diadem
on her forehead, her lips slightly open, two rows of beautiful
pearls around her neck, one knee half-crooked, her eyes open in
a gaze that was more or less inexpressive but that, if you looked
at her for long enough, suggested abandon or at the least passivity: completely naked, her pubis darker than her hair and
slightly rounded, she was very beautiful. The figure was opened
up from chest to vagina: you could see her heart, her lungs, her
liver, her intestines, her uterus, her veins, as if she had been
carefully cut up by an incredibly skillful sexual criminal who
had made an incision in her thorax and abdomen and exposed
her like the inside of a sewing box or a very expensive clock or
an automaton. Her long hair unfurled on the cushion, her calm
gaze, her curled fingers suggested that she might even be taking
pleasure from it, and the whole thing, in the glass cage with its
mahogany posts, provoked both desire and terror, fascination
and disgust: I imagined, almost two centuries earlier, the young
doctors-in-training discovering this body of wax—why think
about these things before falling asleep, much better to imagine
a mother's kiss on your forehead, that tenderness you wait for
at night that never comes, rather than anatomical mannequins

opened up from clavicle to abdomen — what did these budding medics contemplate facing this naked simulacrum, were they able to concentrate on the digestive or respiratory system when the first woman they saw thus, without clothes, from high up in their tiered seats and from the height of their twenty years, was an elegant blonde woman, a fake female corpse to whom the sculptor had ingeniously given all the aspects of life, for whom he had employed all of his talent, in the fold of the knee, the flesh tint of the thighs, the expression of the hands, the realism of the sex, in the blood in the spleen veined with yellow, the dark, alveolar red of the lungs. Sarah went into raptures over this perversion, look at the hair, it's incredible, she said, they've carefully arranged it to suggest nonchalance, love, and I imagined an amphitheater full of military medics exclaiming with admiration when a coarse mustachioed professor, pointer in hand, unveiled this model to count the organs one by one and to tap, with a knowing air, on the centerpiece: the tiny fetus contained in the pinkish womb, a few centimeters from the pubis with its blonde, shimmering, delicate hairs, so fine one imagines they reflect a terrifying, forbidden softness. Sarah pointed it out to me, look, it's crazy, she's pregnant, and I wondered if this waxy pregnancy was a whim of the artist's or stipulated by the commissioner, to show the eternal feminine from every angle, in all its possibilities; this fetus, once discovered, above the pale tuft of hair, added even more to the sexual tension the whole thing exuded, and an immense guilt gripped you, for you had found beauty in death, a spark of desire in a body so perfectly carved up — you couldn't help but imagine the instant of conception of this embryo, a time lost in wax, and wonder what man, of flesh or resin, had penetrated these perfect innards to impregnate them, and immediately you turned aside your head: Sarah smiled at my shame, she always thought me a prude, probably because she couldn't see that it wasn't the scene in itself that made me turn away, but the one that was taking shape in my mind, much more disturbing, actually—I, someone who looked like me, penetrating this living-dead woman.

The rest of the exhibit was similar: a body flayed alive rested calmly, his knee bent as if nothing were wrong, though he didn't have a square centimeter of skin left, not a single one, to show the whole colorful complexity of his circulation of blood; feet, hands, various organs lay in glass boxes, details of bones, joints, nerves, in other words whatever the body contained of mysteries great and small, and obviously I have to think about that now, this evening, tonight, when this morning I read that horrible article by Sarah, when I myself have had my own illness proclaimed, and while I'm waiting for these stupid test results, let's think of something else, let's turn over—a man trying to fall asleep turns over and finds a new point of departure, a new beginning—let's breathe deeply.

A tram rattles past my window, another one going down the Porzellangasse. The trams heading up are quieter, or maybe there are simply fewer of them; who knows, maybe the municipality wants to bring consumers to the center and couldn't care less about bringing them back home afterward. There's something musical in this clattering, something of Alkan's "Chemin de fer" but slower, Charles-Valentin Alkan the forgotten piano maestro, friend of Chopin, Liszt, Heinrich Heine, and Victor Hugo, Alkan who they say was crushed to death by his bookcase as he was grabbing a volume of the Talmud from a shelf—I read recently that it's probably not true, one more myth about this legendary composer, so brilliant he was forgotten for over a century, apparently he died crushed by a coat rack or a heavy shelf on which hats were kept, the Talmud had nothing to do with it. In any case his "Chemin de fer" for piano is absolutely virtuosic, you hear the steam, the squeal of the first trains; the locomotive gallops along on the right hand, and its coupling rods roll along on the left, which produces a rather strange increase in movement, one that I think is atrociously difficult to play—kitsch, Sarah would have ruled, very kitsch, this train business, and she wouldn't have been completely wrong, it's true that there's something outdated about "imitative" programmatic compositions, but there might be an idea for an article in that, "Train Sounds: The Railway in French Music," adding to Alkan Arthur Honegger's "Pacific 231," "Essais de locomotives" by the Orientalist Florent Schmitt, and even Berlioz's "Chant des chemins de fer": I could even compose a little piece myself, "Porcelain Trams," for bells, *zarb*, and Tibetan bowls. It's very likely Sarah would think this was the epitome of kitsch, would she deem the evocation of a spinning wheel, a running horse or a floating boat just as kitsch, probably not, I think I remember she appreciated Schubert's lieder, as I did, in any case we spoke of them often. Madrigalism is definitely a major question. I can't get Sarah out of my head, in the coolness of the pillow, the cotton, the tenderness of the feathers, why had she dragged me to that incredible wax museum, it's impossible to remember why—what was she working on at that point, when I moved here, when I felt as if I were Bruno Walter summoned to assist Mahler the Great at the Vienna Opera, a hundred years later: having returned victorious from a campaign in the Orient, in Damascus to be precise, I was sent for to assist my university professor and I had almost immediately found this lodging a stone's throw from the magnificent campus where I was going to officiate, a small apartment, true, but pleasant, despite the scratchings of Herr Gruber's pet, where the sofa bed, regardless of what Sarah said about it, was perfectly adequate, and as proof: when she had come for the first time, the time of that strange visit to the museum of cut-apart beauties, she had slept on it for at

least a week without any complaints. Delighted at seeing Vienna, delighted that I was showing her Vienna, she said, even though she was the one who dragged me to the most bizarre places in the city. Of course I took her to see Schubert's house and Beethoven's many residences; of course I paid a fortune (without admitting it, by lying about the prices) so we could go to the opera — Verdi's *Simon Boccanegra* full of swords and fury in Peter Stein the Great's production, Sarah had emerged enchanted, amazed, astounded by the place, the orchestra, the singers, the spectacle, though God knows opera can be kitsch, but she had surrendered to Verdi and to the music, not without pointing out to me, as was her habit, an amusing coincidence: Did you notice that the character who is manipulated throughout the entire opera is named Adorno? The one who thinks he's right, rebels, is mistaken, but ends up being proclaimed doge? What a funny coincidence. She was incapable of putting her mind to sleep, even at the Opera. What had we done afterward, probably taken a taxi to go up and dine in a *Heuriger* and enjoy the exceptionally warm spring air, when the Viennese hills smell of grilled meat, grass, and butterflies, that's what would do me good, a little June sun, instead of this endless autumn, this constant rain striking my window — I forgot to draw the curtains shut, in a hurry to go to bed and put out the light, what an idiot, I'll have to get up again, no, not now, not now that I'm in a *Heuriger* under a trellis drinking white wine with Sarah, discussing Istanbul perhaps, Syria, the desert, who knows, or talking about Vienna and music, Tibetan Buddhism, the trip to Iran that was looming on the horizon. Nights in Grinzing after nights in Palmyra, *Grüner Veltliner* after Lebanese wine, the coolness of a spring evening after the stifling nights of Damascus. A slightly awkward tension. Was she already talking about Vienna as the *gateway to the Orient*, she had shocked me by panning Claudio Magris's *Danube*, one of my favorite books: Magris is a nostalgic Habsburger, she said, his *Danube* is terribly unfair to the Balkans; the further into it he gets, the less information he gives. The first thousand kilometers of the river's course occupy over two thirds of the book; he devotes only a hundred or so pages to the next eighteen hundred: as soon as he leaves Budapest, he has almost nothing more to say, giving the impression (contrary to what he announces in his introduction) that southeastern Europe is much less interesting, that nothing important had occurred or was built there. It's a terribly "Austro-centrist" vision of cultural geography, an almost absolute negation of the identity of the Balkans, of Bulgaria, of Moldavia, of Romania, and especially of their Ottoman heritage.

Next to us a table of Japanese tourists was wolfing down some incredibly large Viennese schnitzel which hung over each side of the plates that were themselves huge, like floppy ears on a giant stuffed animal.

She became flushed as she said this, her eyes had gotten darker, the corner of her mouth trembled a little; I couldn't help but laugh: "Sorry, I don't see the problem; Magris's book seems scholarly, poetic, and even sometimes funny to me, a stroll, an erudite and subjective stroll, what harm is there in that, true, Magris is a specialist on Austria, he wrote a thesis on the vision of empire in nineteenth-century Austrian literature, but what do you want, you can't snatch away from me the notion that *Danube* is a great book, and what's more a worldwide bestseller."

"Magris is like you, he's nostalgic. He's a melancholy Trieste native who misses the empire."

She was exaggerating, of course, with the help of the wine, she was getting up on her high horse, speaking louder and louder, so much so that our Japanese neighbors sometimes turned to look at us; I was beginning to be a little ill at ease — and although the idea of an Austro-centrism at the end of the twentieth century seemed hysterically funny, entirely delightful, she had annoyed me by using the word "nostalgic."

"The Danube is the river that links Catholicism, Orthodoxy, and Islam," she added. "That's what's important: it's more than a hyphen, it's . . . It's . . . A means of transportation. The possibility of a passage."

I looked at her, she seemed to have entirely calmed down. Her hand was resting on the table, a little closer to me. Around us, in the inn's lush garden, between the vines on the trellises and the trunks of black pines, waitresses in embroidered aprons were carrying heavy trays loaded with carafes that overflowed a little as the girls walked on the gravel, their white wine so freshly drawn from the cask that it was frothy and cloudy. I had wanted to discuss our memories of Syria but instead I found myself holding forth on *Danube* by Magris. Sarah . . .

"You're forgetting Judaism," I said.

She smiled, a bit surprised; her gaze cleared up for an instant: "Yes, of course, Judaism too."

Was this before or after she brought me to the Jewish Museum on the Dorotheergasse, I forget, she had been outraged, absolutely shocked, by the "poverty" of this museum — she had even penned a *Supplementary Commentary on the Official Guide to the Jewish Museum of Vienna*, very ironic, rather hilarious. I should go back there one of these days, to see if things have changed; at the time the exhibit was organized by floor — temporary exhibits first, then permanent collections. The holograms displaying the eminent Jewish personalities of the capital had struck her as unutterably vulgar, holograms for a vanished community, for phantoms, what horrible obviousness, not to speak of the ugliness of those images. And she was still only at the beginning of her indignation. The top floor made her do nothing short of bursting out laughing, a laughter that changed little by little into a sad rage: dozens of glass cases overflowing with every kind of object, hundreds of goblets, menorahs, tefillins, shawls, thousands of pieces of Judaica piled up in no order whatsoever, with a summary and terrifying explanation: *articles despoiled between 1938 and 1945, whose owners never came forward,* or something like that, war trophies discovered among the debris of the Third Reich and piled up under the roof of the Jewish Museum of Vienna as if in the attic of a slightly chaotic grandparent, a stockpile, a heap of old stuff for an unscrupulous antique dealer. And there's no doubt, said Sarah, that it was done with the best intentions in the world, before the dust took over and the meaning of this hoard became totally lost and gave way to a shambles, or what the French call a *capharnaüm,* or *Capernaum,* which is the name of a town in Galilee, remember, she said. She kept alternating between laughter and anger: what a bizarre image of the Jewish community, what an image, I swear, imagine the schoolchildren visiting this museum, they'll think these vanished Jews were candlestick-collecting silversmiths, and she was probably right, it was depressing and made me feel a little guilty.

The question that haunted Sarah after our visit to the Jewish Museum was that of alterity, of how this exhibit eluded the question of difference to focus instead on "eminent personalities" who stood out from those who constituted the "same" and an accumulation of objects stripped of meaning that "watered down," she said, religious, cultural, social, and even linguistic differences to present the material culture of a brilliant and vanished civilization. It looks like the heaps of scarab fetishes in the wooden exhibit cases at the Cairo Museum, or the hundreds of arrowheads and bone scrapers in a museum of prehistory, she said. The object fills the void.

Great, I was happily in a *Heuriger* taking advantage of a magnificent spring evening and now I have Mahler and his *Kindertotenlieder* in my head, songs for dead children, composed by a man who held his own dead daughter in his arms in Maiernigg in

Carinthia three years after composing them, songs whose horrible dimension wouldn't be understood until long after his own death in 1911: sometimes the meaning of a work is atrociously amplified by history, multiplied, increased in horror. There is no such thing as chance, Sarah would say steeped in Buddhism, Mahler's grave is in the cemetery in Grinzing, a stone's throw from that famous *Heuriger* where we spent such a beautiful evening despite our Danube "dispute," and these *Kindertotenlieder* are set to poems by Rückert, the first great German Orientalist poet along with Goethe, the Orient, always the Orient.

There is no such thing as chance, but I haven't closed the curtains yet and the streetlight on the corner of Porzellan is bothering me. Take heart; it's annoying for someone who's just gone to bed to have to get up again, whether you've omitted a natural need that your body suddenly reminds you of or whether you've forgotten your alarm clock far away from you, it's a bitch, speaking vulgarly, to have to push back the duvet, search for your slippers — which shouldn't be far away — with your toes, decide fuck the slippers for such a short trip, then leap over to the curtain cords, resolve on a rapid detour to the bathroom, urinate sitting down, feet in the air, to avoid prolonged contact with the freezing tiles, carry out the reverse journey as quickly as possible to finally rejoin the dreams you should never have left, still the same melody in the head that you rest, relieved, on the pillow — as a teenager, it was the only piece by Mahler I could bear, and even more, it was one of the rare pieces that was capable of moving me to tears, the cry of the oboe, that terrifying song, I hid this passion like a slightly shameful defect and today it's very sad to see Mahler so debased, swallowed up by cinema and advertising, his handsome thin face so overused to sell God knows what, you have to keep from detesting this music that encumbers orchestra programs, the bins of record dealers, radio stations, and last year, during the centenary of his death, you had to block your ears because Vienna oozed Mahler even through the most unsuspected cracks, there were tourists wearing T-shirts with Gustav's effigy, buying posters, magnets for their fridges, and of course in Klagenfurt there was a crowd to visit his cabin by the Wörthersee — I never went, that's an excursion I could have suggested to Sarah, to go journey through mysterious Carinthia: there is no such thing as chance, Austria is between us in the middle of Europe, we met there, I ended up returning, and she never stopped visiting me here. Karma, Fate, whatever name you want to give these forces in which she believes: the first time we saw each other was in Styria, on the occasion of a conference, one of those High Masses of Orientalism organized at regular intervals by the leading figures of our field who, as is the custom, had accepted the presence of a few "young research fellows" — for her, for me, a baptism of fire. I made the journey from Tübingen by train, via Stuttgart, Nuremberg, and Vienna, taking advantage of the magnificent journey to put the finishing touches on my talk ("Modes and Intervals in the Musical Theory of al-Farabi," an entirely pretentious title, given the lack of certainties contained in this summary of my research) and especially reading *Small World*, a hilarious book by David Lodge that comprised, in my opinion, the best possible introduction to the world of academia (it's been a long time since I reread it, hmm, that's something that could enhance a long winter evening). Sarah was presenting a much more original and polished paper than mine, "The Marvelous in *The Meadows of Gold* by Masudi," drawn from her doctoral thesis. As the only "musician," I found myself placed on a panel of philosophers; she, strangely, was taking part in a round table on "Arabic Literature and Occult Sciences." The conference took place in Hainfeld, the home of Joseph von Hammer-Purgstall, first great

Austrian Orientalist, translator of the *Thousand and One Nights* and of Hafez's *Divan*, historian of the Ottoman Empire, friend of Silvestre de Sacy and of anyone that the little band of Orientalists counted as members at the time, designated sole heir of a very aged Styrian aristocrat who had bequeathed him her title and this castle in 1835, the largest *Wasserschloss* in the region; Hammer-Purgstall, teacher of Friedrich Rückert, to whom he taught Persian in Vienna, and with whom he translated extracts from Rumi's *Divan-e Shams*, a link between a forgotten château in Styria and the *Kindertotenlieder*, which joins Mahler to the poetry of Hafez and the Orientalists of the nineteenth century.

According to the conference program, the University of Graz, our host in this illustrious palace, had done things right: we would be housed in the nearby little towns of Feldbach or Gleisdorf; a *specially chartered* bus would take us every morning to Hainfeld and bring us back in the evening after dinner, *served in the castle inn*; three rooms in the building had been prepared for the discussions, one of them being Hammer-Purgstall's own splendid library, whose shelves were still stocked with his collections and—the cherry on the cake—the Tourist Office of Styria would constantly offer on-site *tastings and sales of local products*: it all seemed particularly "auspicious," as Sarah would say nowadays.

The place was entirely surprising.

Surrounded by ornamental moats, it was a two-story building with dark-tiled, gabled roofs, nestled between a modern farm, a forest and a marsh. The building enclosed a square courtyard fifty meters long on each side—so strangely proportioned that, from the outside, and despite the wide corner towers, this castle seemed much too low for such broad dimensions, as if crushed into the plain by a giant's palm. The austere external walls were losing their gray plaster, which had flaked off in large sections, revealing the brick, and only the vast entry porch—a long, dark tunnel with low ogival vaulting—had preserved all its baroque splendor and especially, to the great surprise of all the Orientalists who crossed this threshold, an inscription in Arabic, in bold relief on stone in beautiful calligraphy, which protected the house and its inhabitants with its blessings: without the shadow of a doubt it was the only *Schloss* in all of Europe that brandished the name of all-powerful Allah in this way on its frontispiece. I had wondered, as I got off the bus, what this herd of academics could possibly be contemplating, noses in the air, before I was astounded in turn by the little triangle of arabesques lost in Catholic territory, a few kilometers away from the Hungarian and Slovenian borders: had Hammer-Purgstall brought this inscription back from one of his many trips, or did he have it painstakingly copied by a local stonemason? This Arabic welcome message was only the first of many surprises, the second was just as great: after passing through the entry tunnel, you suddenly felt as if you were in a Spanish monastery, or even an Italian cloister; all around the immense courtyard, and on its two floors, ran an endless series of arcades, arches the color of Siennese earth, interrupted only by a white baroque chapel whose bulbous dome bell tower stood out against the southern aspect of the whole. Any movement through the castle, then, had to be done through this immense balcony onto which, with a monastic regularity, the many rooms communicated, which was quite surprising in a corner of Austria whose climate was not known to be among the warmest in Europe in the winter but which was explained, I later learned, by the fact that the architect, an Italian, had visited the region only in the summer. So the valley of the Raab took on, provided you remained within this oversized *cortile*, a Tuscan air. It was early October and it wasn't very nice out the day after our arrival in the Styrian Marches, at the home of the late Joseph von Hammer-Purgstall; a little dazed by my train journey, I had slept like a log in a neat little inn in the heart of a village that had seemed to me (maybe because of the fatigue of the journey or the dense fog on the roads snaking between the hills coming from Graz) much more remote than the organizers had said, slept like a log, now's the time to think of that, maybe now I should also find a way to tire myself out, a long train trip, a hike in the mountains, or a visit to seedy bars to try to get my hands on a ball of opium, but in the Alsergrund it's not very likely I'll fall upon a band of Iranian *teriyakis*, opium smokers: unfortunately these days Afghanistan, victim of the markets, exports mostly heroin, an even more terrifying substance than the pills prescribed by Dr. Kraus, but I have high hopes, high hopes of finding sleep, and if not in time the sun will certainly get around to rising. Still this feeling of unhappiness in my head. Seventeen years ago (let's try with a flip of the pillow to chase away Rückert, Mahler, and all the dead children) Sarah was much less radical in her positions, or maybe just as radical, but more timid; I'm trying to picture her getting off that bus in front of the Hainfeld castle, her long, red, curly hair; her plump cheeks and freckles gave her a childlike look that contrasted with her profound, almost harsh gaze; there was already something indefinably Oriental in her face, in her complexion and in the shape of her eyes, which has become accentuated with age, it seems to me, I must have the photos somewhere, probably not from Hainfeld but many forgotten pictures of Syria and Iran, pages in an album, I feel very calm now, lethargic, lulled by the memory of this Austrian conference, of the Hammer-Purgstall castle, and of Sarah, standing in its forecourt, scrutinizing the Arabic inscription with a nod of her head and a dazzled look, that same head I have observed wavering so often between wonder, perplexity,

and indifferent coldness, the coldness she shows when I greet
her for the first time, after her lecture, drawn by the quality of
her text and, of course, her great beauty, the auburn curls that
hide her face when, a little moved during the first few minutes,
she reads her paper on monsters and miracles in *The Meadows
of Gold*: terrifying ghouls, djinns, *hinn, nisnas, hawatif,* strange
and dangerous creatures, magical and divinatory practices, half-
human beings and fantastic animals. I walk over to her by forg-
ing my way through the crowd of scholars swarming around the
coffee-break buffet, on one of those arcaded balconies opening onto the very Italian courtyard of this Styrian castle. She
is alone, leaning on the balustrade, empty cup in hand; she is
looking at the white façade of the chapel, where the autumn
sun is reflected, and I say excuse me, wonderful talk on Masudi,
how incredible all those monsters are, and she smiles kindly at
me without saying anything, watching me struggle between her
silence and my shyness: right away I realize she's waiting to see
if I'm going to bury myself in banalities. I make do with offering
to refill her cup, she smiles again, and five minutes later we are
in full conversation, talking about ghouls and djinns; the fascinating thing, she tells me, is how Masudi distinguishes between
pure inventions of popular imagination and creatures that are
attested and *authentic*: djinns and ghouls are very real for him, he
collects testimonies that are acceptable according to his criteria
for proof, whereas *nisnas*, for example, or griffons and phoenixes
are mythical. Masudi teaches us a lot of details about the life
of ghouls: since their form and instincts isolate them from all
beings, he says, they seek the wildest solitudes and are happy
only in deserts. In their bodies, they take after both man and
the most brutal animal. What interests Masudi the "naturalist"
is to understand how ghouls are born and reproduce, if they
are indeed animals: carnal relations with humans, in the middle

of the desert, are entertained as a possibility. But the thesis he privileges is that of the Indian scholars, who think that ghouls are a manifestation of the energy of certain stars at their rising.

Another conference-goer joins our conversation, he seems very interested by the possibilities of coupling between humans and ghouls; he's a pleasant enough Frenchman named Marc Faugier who presents himself humorously as a "specialist in Arabic coupling" — Sarah launches into somewhat terrifying explanations of these monsters' charms: in Yemen, she says, if a man was raped by a ghoul in his sleep, which can be detected by a high fever and troublesome pustules, a theriac is used composed of opium and plants that flowered when the Dog Star rose, along with talismans and incantations; if death ensues, the body has to be burned the night after death to prevent the birth of the ghoul. If the sick man survives, which is rare, a magic drawing is tattooed on his chest — on the other hand, no author, apparently, has ever described the birth of the monster . . . Ghouls, wearing rags and old blankets, sought to disconcert travelers by singing them songs, they are like the Sirens of the desert: while their actual faces and smells are indeed those of a decomposing corpse, they still have the power to transform themselves to charm a lost man. A pre-Islamic Arab poet nicknamed Ta'abbata Sharran, "The One Who Carries Unhappiness under His Arm," speaks of his amorous relationship with a female ghoul: "When dawn appeared," he says, "she presented herself to me to be my companion; I asked her for her favors and she knelt down. If you question me about my love, I will say it is hidden in the folds of the dunes."

The Frenchman seems to find this delightfully base; this passion of the poet and the monster seems rather touching to me. Sarah is unstoppable; she goes on talking, on this balcony, while most of the scholars return to their panels and studies. Soon we're left alone, outside, all three of us, in the evening that's descending; the light is orange from the last remnants of the sun or the first electric lights in the courtyard. Sarah's hair shines.

"Did you know that Hainfeld castle also houses monsters and wonders? Of course it's the home of Hammer-Purgstall the Orientalist, but it's also the place that inspired Sheridan Le Fanu to write his novel *Carmilla*, the first vampire story that would make British high society tremble, decades before *Dracula*. In literature, the first vampire is a woman. Did you see the exhibit on the ground floor? It's absolutely incredible."

Sarah's energy is extraordinary; she fascinates me; I set off to follow her through the hallways of the immense building. The Frenchman has stayed behind to devote himself to his scholarly activities while Sarah and I play hooky, searching, in the night of shadows and forgotten chapels, for traces of the vampires of mysterious Styria — the exhibit is actually in the basement rather than the ground floor, in vaulted caves decorated for the occasion; we are the only visitors; in the first room, several large painted wooden crucifixes alternate with old halberds and representations of burning pyres — women in rags burning at the stake, "The Witches of Feldbach," explains the accompanying text; the curator hasn't spared us sound effects — distant shouts drowned in fierce crackling. I am disturbed by the great beauty of these beings who are paying for their commerce with the Devil and whom the medieval artists show half-naked, flesh undulating in the flames, cursed undines. Sarah observes and comments, her erudition is extraordinary, how can she know all these stories so well, all these histories of Styria, when she too has just arrived at Hainfeld, it's almost unnerving. I begin to be frightened, I'm suffocating a little in this damp cellar. The second room is devoted to love potions and magical concoctions; a granite basin engraved with runes contains a black liquid, not very appetizing, and when you approach it a piano melody plays, in which I think I recognize a theme by George Gurdjieff, one of his esoteric compositions; on the wall to the right is a representation of Tristan and Iseult on a boat playing chess; Tristan is drinking from a large cup he holds in his right hand while a turbaned page pours love potion from a wineskin for Iseult, who is looking at the chess board and holding a piece between her thumb and forefinger—behind them, the maidservant Brangien is watching, and the infinite sea unfurls its waves. I suddenly have the feeling that we're in the dark forest near the granite fountain in *Pelléas et Mélisande*; Sarah amuses herself by throwing a ring into the black liquid, which has the effect of increasing the volume of the swelling, mysterious melody by Gurdjieff; I look at her, sitting on the rim of the stone basin; her long curls caress the runes as her hand plunges into the dark water.

The third room, probably an old chapel, is devoted to *Carmilla* and vampires. Sarah tells me how the Irish writer Sheridan Le Fanu spent an entire winter in Hainfeld, a few years before Hammer-Purgstall the Orientalist moved there; *Carmilla* is inspired by a true story, she says: Count Purgstall did indeed take in one of his orphan relatives named Carmilla, who immediately struck up a profound friendship with his daughter Laura, as if they had always known each other—very soon, they became intimate; they shared secrets and passions. Laura began to dream about fantastic animals that visited her at night, kissed her, and caressed her; sometimes, in these dreams, they transformed into Carmilla, until finally Laura wondered if Carmilla was actually a man in disguise, which would explain her agitation. Laura fell ill with a wasting disease that no doctor managed to cure, until the Count heard tell of a similar case, a few miles away: several years before a young woman died, two round holes in the upper part of her throat, victim of the vampire Millarca Karnstein. Carmilla is none other than the anagram and reincarnation of

Millarca; she is the one sucking out Laura's vitality—the Count would have to kill her and send her back to the grave with a terrifying ritual.

In the back of the crypt where large blood-red panels explain the relationship of Hainfeld to vampires there is a canopy bed, carefully made up, with white sheets and wood paneling hung with brilliant silk veils that the curator has lit up from below, with very gentle lighting; on the bed, the body of a young woman is lying, in a diaphanous dress, a wax statue imitating sleep, or death; she has two red marks on her chest, at the level of the left breast, which the silk or lace leaves completely uncovered—Sarah walks over, fascinated; she leans over the young woman, gently strokes her hair, her chest. I am embarrassed, I wonder what this sudden passion signifies, before feeling a suffocating desire myself: I observe Sarah's thighs in their black stockings rub against the light cloth of the white nightdress, her hands brushing against the statue's belly, I'm ashamed for her, very ashamed, suddenly I'm drowning, I breathe in deeply, lift my head from my pillow, I am in darkness, I am left with this last image, that baroque bed, this crypt that's both terrifying and gentle, I open my mouth wide to rediscover the cool air of my bedroom, the reassuring contact with the pillow, the weight of the duvet.

A great shame mingled with traces of desire, that's what's left. Such memory in dreams.

One wakes up without having fallen asleep, seeking to recapture the shreds of pleasure of the other in oneself.

There are recesses that are easy to shed light on, others that are darker. The dark liquid probably has to do with the terrifying article I received this morning. Amusing that Marc Faugier invited himself into my dreams, I haven't seen him in years. Specialist in Arabic coitus, that would make him laugh. Of course he wasn't present at that conference. Why did he appear there, through what secret association, impossible to know.

It was definitely Hainfeld castle, but larger, it seems to me. I feel a very strong physical loss, now, the pain of separation, as if I had just been deprived of Sarah's body. Love potions, caves, dead young women—as I rest I have the feeling that I myself was stretched out under that canopy, that I was ardently desiring Sarah's caresses, on my own deathbed. Memory is quite surprising, the horrible Gurdjieff, good grief. What was he doing in there, that old Oriental occultist, I'm sure that gentle, bewitching melody is not by him, dreams superimpose masks and that one was very obscure.

Who wrote that piano piece, I have the name on the tip of my tongue, it could be Schubert, but it's not him, a passage from Mendelssohn's *Romance sans paroles* maybe, in any case it's not something I listen to very often, that's for sure. If I fall immediately back to sleep I might rediscover it, with Sarah and the vampires.

As far as I know there was no crypt in Hammer-Purgstall's actual castle, neither crypt nor exhibit, on the ground floor there was a typically Styrian restaurant serving veal schnitzel, goulash, and *Serviettenknöndel*—though it's true that we took an immediate liking to each other, Sarah and I, even without any ghouls or supernatural couplings, we took all our meals together and spent a long time scrutinizing the shelves in the library of the surprising Joseph von Hammer-Purgstall. I would translate for her the German titles she had trouble deciphering; her Arabic, much better than mine, allowed her to explain to me the subject of books I could make nothing of and we stayed there by ourselves for a long time, shoulder to shoulder, while all the Orientalists had hurried to the restaurant, fearing there wouldn't be enough potatoes for everyone—I had just met her the day before and already we were side by side, leaning over an old book; my eyes must have been dancing over the lines and my chest contracting, I could smell the perfume of her curls for the first time, I was experiencing the power of her smile and her voice for the first time: it's strange to think that, without any special surveillance, in this library whose large window (sole accidental in the outer façade, which was so regular as to border on monotony) opened out onto a little balcony overlooking the southern moat, we had in our hands a collection of poems by Friedrich Rückert hand-dedicated to his old teacher Hammer-Purgstall—wide, sprawling handwriting, a complicated, slightly yellowed signature, dated from Neuses, somewhere in Franconia, in 1836, while below us trembled, by the water's edge, the sweet rush known as *calamus*, which long ago was used to cut reed pens. *"Beshnow az ney tchoun hekayat mikonad,"* "Listen to the *ney*, the reed, how it tells stories," begins Rumi's *Masnavi*, and it was wonderful to discover that these two Persian translators, Hammer-Purgstall and Rückert, were there together, while outside the rushes offered us a majestic synesthesia, evoking, in a gesture, the tenderness of Schubert and Schumann's lieder, Persian poetry, the aquatic plants used to make flutes over there in the Orient, and our two bodies, held motionless and barely touching, in the almost absent light—as it was long ago—of this library with immense wooden shelves bent by the weight of the years or the books, behind their fittings made of precious marquetry. I read for Sarah a few poems in this little collection by Rückert, and tried to translate them for her as best I could—it mustn't have been very brilliant, this sight-translation, but I didn't want the moment to pass, so I took my time, I admit it, and she didn't make any move to shorten my hesitations, as if we were reading an oath.

A funny oath, since odds are she no longer remembers that

time or, rather, that she never attached the same importance to it as I did — and as proof, this morning she sends me, without a word, this article, so out of character, which is giving me nightmares worthy of an old opium addict.

But now with my eyes wide open, sighing, a little feverish, I have to try to fall back asleep (some shivers running up my calves, the colder I feel the hotter I burn, so to speak, as in the Louise Labé poem) and forget Sarah. We've stopped counting sheep a long time ago; "*Go to your happy place,*" someone said to a dying man in an American TV episode, what would be my *happy place*, I wonder, somewhere in my childhood, by the edge of a lake in the summer in the Salzkammergut, at an operetta by Franz Lehár in Bad Ischl, or in bumper cars with my brother at the Prater, maybe in the Touraine at our grandmother's house, a region that seemed extraordinarily exotic to us, foreign without being so, where the maternal language we were almost ashamed of in Austria suddenly became dominant: in Ischl everything was imperial and shimmering, in Touraine everything was French, we murdered chickens and ducks, we picked green beans, we chased sparrows, we ate rotting cheeses rolled in ash, we visited fairy-tale castles and played with cousins whose slang we didn't entirely understand, since we spoke an adult French, the French of our mother and a few Francophones in our entourage, a Viennese French. I can see myself as King of the Garden, stick in hand, as captain on a barge floating down the Loire beneath the walls of Alexandre Dumas in Montsoreau, on a bicycle in the vines around Chinon — these childhood lands are making me feel a terrible pain, maybe because of their sudden disappearance, which prefigures mine, illness and fear.

A lullaby? Let's attempt a catalog of lullabies: Brahms who rings out like a cheap music box, whom all the children in Europe have heard in their beds, nestled in a blue or pink stuffed animal, Brahms the Volkswagen of the lullaby, solid and efficient, nothing puts you to sleep as quickly as Brahms, that mean bearded pillager of Schumann without any daring or whimsy — Sarah adored one of Brahms's sextets, the first one probably, opus 18 as I remember, with a theme — how to say it — that overwhelms you. The amusing thing is that the actual European hymn, the one that resounds from Athens to Reykjavík and leans over our charming blond heads, is that damn lullaby by Brahms, atrociously simple, just as the most effective sword blows are the simplest. Before him Schumann, Chopin, Schubert, Mozart, and *tutti quanti*, hmm, there might be an idea for an article in that, the analysis of the lullaby as genre, with its effects and its prejudices — not many lullabies for orchestra, for example, the lullaby belongs by definition to chamber music. To the best of my knowledge, there is no lullaby with electronic accompaniment or for player piano, but I'd have to check. Am I capable of remembering a contemporary lullaby? Arvo Pärt the fervent Estonian composed some lullabies, lullabies for choirs and string ensembles, lullabies to put entire monasteries to sleep, I spoke of them in my crushing paper on his piece for string orchestra, *Orient & Occident*: you can perfectly picture dormitories of young monks singing before going to bed, conducted by bearded priests. But I have to admit there is something consoling in Pärt's music, something of that spiritual desire of Western crowds, desire for simple music resounding like bells, of an *Orient* where nothing has been lost of the relationship that links man to heaven, an *Orient* brought close to an *Occident* by the Christian *credo*, a spiritual leftover, a husk for times of desolation — which lullaby for me, then, lying in the dark, here and now, when I'm afraid, I'm afraid, I'm afraid of the hospital and disease: I try to close my eyes but I'm worried about this confrontation with my body, with my heartbeats that I'll find too rapid, the pains that, when you pay attention to them, multiply into all the recesses of the flesh. Sleep will have to come by surprise, from behind, the way the executioner strangles or decapitates you, the way the enemy strikes you — I could take a pill, quite simply, instead of curling up like a petrified dog under my damp covers which I pull back, too warm underneath, let's go back to Sarah and to memory since both are inevitable: she too has her illness, much different from mine that's for sure, but an illness all the same. This Sarawak business possibly confirms my doubts, has she too become lost in turn, lost body and soul in the Orient like all those characters she has studied so?

The thing that actually sealed our friendship, after Hainfeld and our readings of Rückert, was the little thirty-kilometer excursion that we took at the end of the conference; she had suggested I go with her, I obviously accepted, lying about the possibility of changing my train ticket — so, after a slight lie, I took part in this expedition, to the great displeasure of the waiter from the restaurant who was driving the car and was surely planning on finding himself alone in the countryside with Sarah. It seems very clear to me now that this was no doubt the reason for my invitation, I had to serve as chaperone, remove any possible romantic character from this outing. What's more, since Sarah knew very little German and the driver-for-the-day had poor command of English, I was commandeered (as I soon unhappily realized) to provide conversation. I was reasonably impressed by what Sarah was eager to see, the reason for the excursion: the monument to the Battle of Saint Gotthard, or more precisely of Mogersdorf, an arrow's flight away from Hungary — what possible interest could she have taken in a battle in 1664 against the Ottomans, a victory of the Holy Empire and its French allies, in a village in the middle of nowhere, atop a hill overlooking the valley of the Raab, tributary of the Danube that flowed a few hundred meters away from the rushes of Hainfeld, I would find out before long, but first I had to suffer through forty-five minutes of endless talk with a young, not particularly forthcoming guy who was extremely disappointed at seeing me there next to him when he had pictured Sarah and her miniskirt — I myself was wondering why I had committed myself to all these expenses, train ticket, additional night in a hotel in Graz, just to chew the fat with this country waiter who, I'll admit, was not a bad guy. (I realize that Sarah, quietly sitting in the backseat, must have been having a good secret laugh at having managed to kill two erotic birds with one stone, the two suitors canceling each other out in one sad, reciprocal disappointment.) He was from Riegersburg and had gone to the local hotel school; on the way, he told us a few anecdotes about the *burg* of Gallerin, fief of the Purgstalls, an eyrie perched since the first century on top of a high peak that neither the Hungarians nor the Turks ever managed to capture. The Raab valley was unfurling its orange-hued autumn foliage and, around us, the hills and old extinguished volcanoes of the Marches rolled verdantly as far as the eye could see under the gray sky, forests and vines alternating on their slopes, a perfect *Mitteleuropa* landscape; all that was missing were a few layers of fog, the cries of fairies or witches as a sonorous background for the tableau to be complete — a fine drizzle had started falling; it was eleven a.m. but it could easily have been five in the afternoon, I wondered what on earth I was doing there, on a Sunday, when I could have been happily seated on my train headed for Tübingen instead of going to a lost battlefield with a stranger or near-stranger and a rustic waiter who must have only gotten his driver's license last summer — little by little I was turning sullen in the car; obviously we had missed a turn and had reached the Hungarian border, opposite the town of Szentgotthárd whose buildings could be seen beyond the customs barracks; the young driver was embarrassed; we turned back—the village of Mogersdorf was a few kilometers away, on the side of the promontory that interested us: the camp of the Holy Empire, marked by a monumental concrete cross a dozen meters high, built in the 1960s; a chapel made from the same material and at the same time completed the ensemble, a little further away, and a stone panel depicted the scenario of the battle. The view was clear; you could see the valley, which continued straight east, on our left, toward Hungary; toward the south, hills pleated the thirty or forty kilometers separating us from Slovenia. Scarcely had Sarah gotten out of the car than she became excited; once oriented, she looked at the landscape, then the cross, and kept saying over and over, "It's just extraordinary"; she kept walking back and forth across the site, from chapel to monument, before returning to the big engraved information table. I wondered (the waiter too, apparently, who was smoking and leaning on his car door, looking at me from time to time in a slightly panicked way) if we were witnessing the reconstruction of a crime, à la Rouletabille or Sherlock Holmes: I expected her to unearth some rusty swords or horse bones, for her to point out the position of such-or-such regiment of uhlans or Piedmontese pikemen, if there were uhlans and Piedmontese in this melee, facing the fierce Janissaries. I was hoping this would give me an opportunity to shine by adding my knowledge of Turkish military music to the battle and its importance for the *alla turca* style so common in the eighteenth century, Mozart being the most famous example—in short, I was waiting to ambush them near our carriage, with the coachman, not caring to dirty my shoes further along near the edge of the promontory, the information table and the immense cross, but five minutes later, once her circumvolutions were finished, Sarah the savage detective was still in mid-contemplation of the engraved map, as if she were waiting for me to join her: so I walked over, imagining a feminine maneuver to get me to join her, but maybe the memory of battles isn't actually propitious for the game of love, or else I just didn't know Sarah too well: I had the feeling I was disturbing her thoughts, her reading of the landscape. Of course, what interested her in this place was the way memory was organized, not so much the confrontation in itself; for her, the important thing was the big cross from 1964 that, by commemorating the Turkish defeat, traced a frontier, a wall, facing Communist Hungary, the East of that time, the new enemy, the new Orient that was naturally replacing the old. There was no place either for me or for Mozart's *Turkish March* in her observations; she took a little notebook out of her pocket and took a few notes, then smiled at me, obviously very happy with her expedition.

It was starting to rain again; Sarah closed her notebook and put it back in the pocket of her black raincoat; I must have reserved my reflections on the influence of Turkish military music and its percussions for the ride back: it's certain that in 1778, when Mozart composed his eleventh piano sonata, the Ottoman presence, the siege of Vienna, and this battle of Mogersdorf were already quite remote, yet his *Rondo alla turca* is quite certainly the piece of that era that bears the closest relationship with the *mehter*, the fanfares of the Janissaries; is this because of travelers' accounts, or simply because he had a genius for synthesis and deployed, magnificently, all the characteristics of the "Turkish" style of the time, no one knows and, to shine in this old car creeping along in the midst of Styria oozing of autumn, I didn't hesitate to synthesize (or rather appropriate) the work of Eric Rice and Ralph Locke, unsurpassed on the subject. Mozart succeeded so well in embodying Turkish "sound," the rhythms and percussions, that even Beethoven the immense with the *tam taladam tam tam taladam* of his own *Turkish March* from *The Ruins of Athens* just barely managed to copy it, or pay homage to it, perhaps. It's not the easiest thing in the world to be a good Orientalist. . . . I'd very much like to tell Sarah, now, to make her laugh a little, about that hilarious performance, recorded in 1974, of eight world-famous pianists interpreting Beethoven's *Turkish March* onstage, with eight massive pianos in a circle. They played this strange arrangement for sixteen hands first, and then, after the applause, they sat back down and played it again, but in a burlesque version: Jeanne-Marie Darré got lost in her score; Radu Lupu materialized a tarboosh from God knows where and plonked it on his head, maybe to prove that as a Romanian he was the most Oriental of them all, and he even pulled a cigar out of his pocket and played any old way, his fingers encumbered by the ash, to the great displeasure of his neighbor Alicia de Larrocha who didn't look as if she found it very funny, this concert of dissonances and wrong notes, no more than did poor Gina Bachauer, whose hands looked tiny compared to her enormous body: quite definitely the *Turkish March* is the only piece by Beethoven with which they could allow themselves this schoolboy farce, although we might dream of the exploit being repeated for a Chopin ballad or for Schönberg's *Piano Suite*, for example; it would be nice to hear what humor and slapstick could add to those works. (There's another idea for an article, on appropriations and irony in twentieth-century music; a bit broad in scope no doubt, there must already be studies on the subject, I vaguely recall a contribution — by whom? — on irony in Mahler, for example.)

What was fascinating about Sarah was how knowledgeable she was already, in Hainfeld, curious and erudite, greedy for knowledge: even before she arrived she had boned up (long before Google, in those already ancient times) on the life of

Hammer-Purgstall the Orientalist, so much so that I suspected her of having read his memoirs, and thus of lying to me when she said she knew very little German; she had prepared her visit to Mogersdorf, knew everything about this forgotten battle and its circumstances: how the Turks, superior in number, had been surprised by the cavalry of the Holy Empire hurtling down the hill when they had just crossed the Raab and their lines weren't yet formed; thousands of Janissaries stuck between the enemy and the river had attempted a desperate retreat, and many of them had drowned or been massacred from the shore, so many that an Ottoman poem, Sarah said, describes the mutilated body of a soldier floating all the way to Györ: he had promised his beloved to return and there he was, all bloated, his eyes pecked out by crows, relating the horrible outcome of the battle, before his head separated from his body and continued on its terrifying way at the Danube's mercy, to Belgrade or even Istanbul, proof of the courage of the Janissaries and their tenacity — on the ride back, I tried to translate this story for our driver who, I could see his eyes in the rearview mirror, was looking at Sarah next to him with a slightly terrified air: it's not very easy to murmur sweet nothings to a young lady who's telling you about battles, rotting corpses, and torn-off heads, even though she was relating these stories with real compassion. Before you can begin to think about beauty, you have to plunge into the deepest horror and go completely through it, according to Sarah's theory.

Our young guide was, all things considered, very nice, he dropped us off in Graz in mid-afternoon, with bag and baggage, not without pointing out (even getting out of the car to introduce us to the owners) a restaurant he knew in the old town, a stone's throw from the climb to the Schlossberg. Sarah thanked him warmly, as did I. (What was the name of that boy who had so kindly showed us around? As I remember he had a name usually belonging to a generation previous to his, like Rolf or Wolfgang—not Wolfgang, I'd remember that; Otto, maybe, or Gustav, or even Winfried, which had the effect of artificially aging him, creating in him a strange tension, accentuated by a mustache, wispy and juvenile, that sought to go beyond the corner of his lips just as vainly as the Turkish army did the fateful Raab.)

I could have gone to the train station and caught the first train to Vienna, but this young woman, with her stories of monsters, Orientalists, and battles, fascinated me too much to leave her so quickly, when I had the possibility of spending the evening alone with her rather than with Mother—not an unpleasant thing in itself, just too habitual; I had chosen to live in Tübingen precisely to be away from Vienna (too stifling, too familiar), not to come back to dine with my mother every Sunday. Six weeks later I was to leave for Istanbul for the first time, and the Turkish stirrings of this stay in Styria delighted me—hadn't the young dragoman Joseph von Hammer-Purgstall himself begun his career (albeit after eight years of interpreter's school in Vienna) for the Austrian legation on the Bosphorus? Istanbul, the Bosphorus, there's a *happy place*, a place I'd go back to right away if I weren't kept on the Porzellangasse by the doctors, I'd settle in a tiny apartment on top of a narrow building in Arnavutköy or Bebek and I'd watch the boats go by, I'd count them, observing the eastern bank change colors with the seasons; sometimes I'd take a water taxi to Üsküdar or Kadiköy to see the winter lights on Bagdat Caddesi, and I'd come home freezing, with my eyes exhausted, regretting not having bought gloves in one of those well-lit shopping malls, hands in my pockets, gazing fondly at Leander's Tower that looks so close in the night in the middle of the Strait, then back at home, high up, out of breath from climbing the stairs, I'd make myself a strong tea, very red, very sweet, I'd smoke an opium pipe, just one, and I'd gently doze off in my armchair, awakened from time to time by the foghorns of tankers coming from the Black Sea.

The future was just as radiant as the Bosphorus on a fine autumn day, was promising to be just as auspicious as that evening in Graz alone with Sarah in the 1990s, our first dinner tête-à-tête, I was intimidated by the romanticism this procedure implied (even though there was no pewter candlestick on the *Gasthaus* table), but not her: she spoke in the same way, exactly, and about the same horrible things as if we were eating, for example, at a university cafeteria, neither more quietly nor more loudly, whereas for my part the muted atmosphere, the low lighting, and the chic aloofness of the waiters led me to whisper, in confidential tones — I didn't quite see what secrets I could have confided in this young woman who was continuing her stories of Turkish battles, encouraged by our visit to Graz and the Landeszeughaus, the Styrian Arsenal, straight out of the seventeenth century. In that fine old house with decorated façades there were thousands of weapons in neat rows, carefully arranged, as if fifteen thousand men were about to line up tomorrow on the Herrengasse to take either a saber or a cuirass or an arquebus or a pistol and run to defend the region against an improbable Muslim attack: thousands of muskets, hundreds of pikes, halberds to stop horses, helmets to protect foot soldiers and cavalrymen, myriads of handguns, knives ready to be grasped, powder horns to be distributed, and it was rather frightening to see, in this orderly accumulation, that many of these objects had served their use: the armor bore traces of the bullets it had stopped, the blades were worn down by the blows they'd struck, and you could easily imagine the pain that all these inert things had caused, the death spread around them, bellies ripped open, bodies hacked to pieces in the fury of battle.

You could hear in this arsenal, said Sarah, the great silence of these instruments of war, their eloquent silence, she added, so much did this accumulation of deadly weaponry, having survived its owners, illustrate their sufferings, their fates and, finally, their absence: that's what she spoke about during our dinner, about the silence the Landeszeughaus represented, how she compared this silence to the many stories she had read, mainly Turkish ones, forgotten voices relating these battles — I must have spent the evening looking at her and listening to her, or at least I can picture myself, under her spell, bewitched by her talk, which mingled history, literature, and Buddhist philosophy; had I scrutinized her body, her eyes in her face as if I were at a museum, the two clouds of freckles on her cheeks, her chest which she often hid with her forearms by crossing her wrists under her chin, as if she were naked, in an unconscious gesture that has always seemed to me charming, discreet, and annoying at the same time, since it sent me back to the supposed concupiscence of my gaze upon her. Such a strange thing, memory; I'm incapable of rediscovering her face from yesterday, her body from yesterday, they vanish to make way for those of to-day, in the setting of the past — I had probably added a musical note to the conversation: there was indeed a musician in that battle of Mogersdorf, a forgotten Baroque composer, Prince Pál Esterházy, first of that name, the only great warrior-composer or great composer-warrior we know of, who fought countless times against the Turks, author of cantatas including the magnificent cycle *Harmonia Caelestis* and a great harpsichordist himself — it isn't known if he was the first to be inspired by that Turkish military music he heard so often, but I doubt it: after so many battles and so many disasters on his lands, he must have wanted above all to forget violence and devote himself (with success) to Celestial Harmony.

À propos military music: the stampede of Herr Gruber who's getting ready for bed. So it's eleven p.m. — incredible all the same that this gentleman *runs* to the bathroom, every night, every blessed night Herr Gruber rushes to his toilet at eleven o'clock sharp, making the floor creak and all my lights tremble.

Coming back from Tehran, I'd stopped in Istanbul where I spent three splendid days, alone or almost alone, aside from one memorable jaunt with Michael Bilger to "celebrate my liberation," since after ten months without leaving Tehran and an immense sadness I deserved a hell of a party, in town, in smoke-filled bars, taverns where there were music, girls, and alcohol, and I think that's the only time I've been drunk in all my life, really intoxicated, drunk with sound, drunk with women's hair, drunk with colors, with freedom, drunk enough to forget the pain of Sarah's departure — Bilger the Prussian archaeologist was an excellent guide, he took me from bar to bar through Beyoglu before finishing me off in a nightclub somewhere: I collapsed in the midst of whores and their colorful dresses, my nose buried in a little dish containing raw carrots and lemon juice. He told me the next day he'd had to carry me to my hotel room, according to him I was bellowing the *Radetzky March* at the top of my voice (how horrible!), but that I cannot bring myself to believe, why on earth (even if I was on my way to Vienna) would I sing that martial theme in the Istanbul night, I'm sure he was laughing at me, Bilger has always made fun of my Viennese accent — I don't think I've ever sung Johann Strauss at the top of my lungs, or even whistled the *Skaters' Waltz*, even back at school, waltz classes were real torture, plus the waltz is the curse of Vienna and should have been forbidden after the arrival of the Republic, at the same time as the use of titles of nobility: that would have spared us any number of frightful nostalgic balls and atrocious concerts for tourists. All waltzes, except of course for Sarah's little waltz for flute and cello, "Sarah's Theme," which was one of those mysterious, childlike, fragile little phrases that made you wonder where she could possibly have unearthed it, and which is also a good place to go back to, music is a fine refuge against the imperfection of the world and the failings of the body.

The next day in Istanbul I woke up in high spirits, as if nothing were wrong, so powerfully did the energy of the city and the pleasure of walking through it erase the effects of the alcohol I'd imbibed the night before, no headache, no nausea, nothing that didn't disappear all of a sudden, Sarah amid my memories, cleaned by the wind from the Bosphorus.

The little waltz is a powerful drug: the warm tone of the cello envelops the flute, there is something highly erotic in this duo of instruments intertwining each in its own theme, its own phrase, as if harmony were a calculated distance, a strong bond and an impassable space all at the same time, a rigidity that joins us to each other while preventing us from actually touching. A coitus of snakes, I think the image is from Stravinsky, but what was he talking about, certainly not a waltz. In Berlioz, in his *Faust*, in *Les Troyens* or *Roméo et Juliette*, love is always a dialogue between an alto and a flute or an oboe — it's been a long time since I've listened to *Roméo et Juliette*, its striking passages of passion, of violence and passion.

There are lights in the night, behind the curtains; I might as well go back to reading, I have to rest, I'll be exhausted tomorrow.

In Graz I must have slept poorly as well, after the tête-à-tête dinner, I felt just a bit depressed by the perfection of this girl, her beauty but especially her ease in holding forth, commenting, exposing with an extraordinary naturalness the most unlikely information. Was I already aware of our similar trajectories, did I have a premonition of what was about to start with this dinner, or did I let myself be guided by my desire, wishing her goodnight in a hallway that I can see again perfectly, walls covered in chestnut felt, furniture made of blond wood, lampshades dark green, as I can see myself lying afterward on the narrow bed with my arms crossed under my head, sighing and looking at the ceiling, disappointed at not lying beside her, not discovering her body after being charmed by her mind—my first letter will be to her, I said to myself thinking about my trip to Turkey; I was imagining a torrid correspondence, a mixture of lyricism, descriptions, and musical erudition (but mostly lyricism). I suppose I had told her in detail the goal of my Istanbul stay, European music in Istanbul from the nineteenth to the twentieth centuries, Liszt, Hindemith, and Bartók on the Bosphorus, from Abdülaziz to Atatürk, a project that earned me a research grant from a prestigious foundation I was not a little proud of, which would lead to my article on how Donizetti's brother, Giuseppe, introduced European music to the Ottoman ruling classes—I wonder what that article is worth today, not much probably, aside from its reconstruction of the biography of that singular, almost-forgotten character, who lived for forty years in the shadow of sultans and was buried in the cathedral in Beyoglu to the sound of the military marches he had composed for the Empire. (Military music is decidedly a point of exchange between East and West, Sarah would have said: it's extraordinary that this Mozartian music "rediscovered" in a way its point of origin, the Ottoman capital, fifty years after the *Turkish March*; after all it's logical that the Turks were charmed by this transformation of their own rhythms and sonorities, since there was—to borrow Sarah's vocabulary—the self in the other.)

I'll try to reduce my thoughts to silence, instead of abandoning myself to memory and to the sadness of this little waltz; I'll use one of those meditation techniques Sarah is familiar with, which she explained to me, laughing a little all the same, here in Vienna: let's try to breathe deeply, let our thoughts slide into an immense white space, eyelids closed, hands on stomach, let's mimic death before it comes.

11:10 P.M.

Sarah half-naked in a room in Sarawak, scantily clad in a tank top and cotton shorts; a little sweat between her shoulder blades and in the hollows of her knees, a bunched-up sheet, pushed down, reaching halfway up her calves. Some insects are still clinging to the mosquito net, drawn by the pulsing of the sleeper's blood, despite the sun that's already piercing through the trees. The longhouse is waking up, the women are outside, under the porch roof, on the veranda; they're preparing the meal; Sarah can vaguely make out the sound of the mixing bowls, muted as wooden gongs, and the foreign voices.

It is seven hours later in Malaysia, the day is dawning.

I managed what, ten minutes thinking of almost nothing?

Sarah in the jungle of the Brookes, the white rajahs of Sarawak, the dynasty of those who wanted to be kings in the Orient and became them, holding sway over the country for almost a century, among the pirates and decapitators.

Time has passed.

Since the Hainfeld castle, Viennese strolls, Istanbul, Damascus, Tehran, we are each lying down on our own, separated by the world. My heart is beating too quickly, I can feel it; I'm breathing too frequently; fever can provoke a slight tachycardia, the doctor said. I'll get up. Or get a book. Forget. Not think about these stupid exams, disease, solitude.

Ah, I could write her a letter; that would occupy me — "Dearest Sarah, thank you for the article, but I confess its content worries me: are you well? What are you doing in Sarawak?" No, too anodyne. "Dear Sarah, you should know that I am dying." A little premature. "Dear Sarah, I miss you," too direct. "Dearest Sarah, could old sufferings one day become joys?" That's good, *old sufferings*. Had I cribbed from the poets, in my letters from Istanbul? I hope she hasn't kept them — a monument to boastfulness.

Life is a Mahler symphony, it never goes back, never retraces its steps. This feeling of the passing of time is the definition of melancholy, an awareness of finitude from which there is no refuge, aside from opium and oblivion; Sarah's thesis can be read (I'm just thinking of this now) as a catalog of melancholics, the strangest catalog of adventurers into melancholia, of different kinds and from different countries, Sadegh Hedayat, Annemarie Schwarzenbach, Fernando Pessoa, to mention only her favorites — to whom she also devoted the fewest pages, constrained as she was by Scholarship and the University to stick to her subject, to *Visions of the Other Between East and West*. I wonder if what she was looking for, in the course of that scholarly life that completely took over her own, her quest, was her own cure — to conquer the black bile through travel, first, then through knowledge, and then through mysticism, and probably me too, me too, if you think that music is time thought out, time circumscribed and transformed into sound, if I am thrashing about today in these sheets, odds are that I too am stricken with this High Ailment that modern psychiatry, disgusted with art and philosophy, calls *structural depression*, even though the doctors, in my case, are interested only in the *physical* aspects of my illnesses, which no doubt are entirely real, but which I so wish were imaginary — I

am going to die, I am going to die, that's the message I should
send Sarah, let's breathe, breathe, turn on the light, let's not get
carried down that particular slope. I'll put up a fight.

Where are my glasses? This bedside lamp is truly awful, I absolutely have to replace it. How many nights have I turned it
on and then off again saying that? How slack. There are books
everywhere. Objects, images, musical instruments I'll never
learn how to play. Where are those glasses? Impossible to get my
hands on the proceedings of the Hainfeld conference where her
text on ghouls, djinns, and other monsters appears alongside my
speech on al-Farabi. I don't throw anything out, and yet I lose
everything. Time strips me bare. I realized that two volumes
of my complete works of Karl May are missing. No matter, I'll
probably never reread them, I'll die without having reread them,
it's an atrocious thought, that someday you'll be too dead to reread *Through Desert and Harem*. That my "Panorama of Istanbul
from Galata Tower" will end up in a Viennese antique dealer's
who will sell it explaining that it comes from the collection of
an Orientalist who died recently. So what's the use of changing
the bedside lamp? "Panorama of Istanbul . . ." or that drawing
by David Roberts lithographed by Louis Hague and carefully
hand-colored for the Royal Subscription Edition, depicting the
entrance to the mosque of Sultan Hassan in Cairo, he can't sell
it off, the antique dealer, I paid a fortune for that engraving.
The fascinating thing about Sarah is that she owns nothing. Her
books and pictures are in her head; in her head, in her countless
notebooks. Me, though — objects reassure me. Especially books
and scores. Or they worry me. Maybe they worry me as much as
they reassure me. I can easily imagine her suitcase for Sarawak:
seven pairs of knickers, three bras, the same number of T-shirts,
shorts, and jeans, loads of half-filled notebooks, and that's it.
When I left for Istanbul the first time, Mother had forced me

to take soap, laundry detergent, a first-aid kit, and an umbrella. My trunk weighed thirty-six kilos, which caused me trouble at the Schwechat airport; I had to leave some of the contents with Mother, who'd had the good taste to accompany me: I had halfheartedly left her Liszt's correspondence and the articles by Heine (I missed those later), impossible to slip her the package of detergent, the shoehorn, or my hiking boots, she said "But that's indispensable, you can't leave without a shoehorn! Plus it weighs nothing," why not a bootjack while I was at it, I was already bringing a whole assortment of ties and jackets "in case I get invited over by respectable people." For a time she would have forced me to take a travel iron, but I had managed to convince her that, if it was in fact doubtful that one could find good Austrian detergent in these remote lands, electrical appliances were abundant, even omnipresent, given the proximity of China and its factories, which had only very mildly reassured her. So that suitcase became my cross, thirty kilos of cross dragged with difficulty (the overloaded wheels obviously exploded at the first bump) from lodging to lodging in the terrifyingly steep streets of Istanbul, from Yeniköy to Taksim, and earned me quite a few sarcastic remarks from my housemates, especially for the detergent and the first-aid kit. I wanted to present the image of an adventurer, an explorer, a *condottiere*, and I was nothing but a mama's boy overloaded with diarrhea medicine, buttons, and sewing thread *just in case*. It's a little depressing to admit that I haven't changed, that journeys have not made an intrepid, brave, tanned man of me, but a pale monster with glasses who trembles today at the idea of crossing his neighborhood to go to the lazaretto.

Look, the light from the lamp is highlighting the dust on the "Panorama of Istanbul from the Galata Tower," you can hardly see the boats anymore, I should clean it and above all get my hands on those damn glasses. I bought this photochrome in a shop behind Istiqlal Caddesi, a lot of the filth must come from Istanbul itself, original dirt, when I was with Bilger the archaeologist—according to the latest news he's still just as crazy and alternates stays in the hospital with periods of terrifying exaltation when he discovers tombs of Tutankhamen in the public gardens in Bonn, before collapsing again, conquered by drugs and depression, and one wonders in which of these phases he is the most unsettling. You have to hear him shout, gesticulating wildly, that he is the victim of the pharaoh's curse and describe the scholarly conspiracy that keeps him from important positions to realize just how sick he really is. The last time, when I was invited to give a lecture at the Beethovenhaus, I tried to avoid him, but by ill luck he was not at the clinic—he was there in the audience, in the very first row if you please, and obviously asked an endless and incomprehensible question about an anti-Beethoven conspiracy in Imperial Vienna, in which everything was mixed up—resentment, paranoia, and the certainty of being a misunderstood genius—the audience was looking at him (rather than listening to him) with an absolutely appalled air, and the organizer kept giving me terrified looks. God knows, though, that we were close, once—he had a "promising future ahead of him" and had even directed, in an interim capacity for a few months, the office of the prestigious Deutsches Archäologisches Institut in Damascus. He was earning a lot of money, crisscrossing Syria in an impressive white SUV, going from international dig sites to untouched Hellenistic sites, lunching with the Director of Syrian National Antiquities, and associating with many high-ranking diplomats. We had gone with him once, on the Euphrates, to an inspection in the middle of the desert behind the atrocious city of Raqqa, and it was a wonder to see all those Europeans sweating blood in the middle of the desert sands to direct gangs of Syrian workers, real artists of the shovel, and show them where and how they should dig into the sand to make traces of the past come alive again. Starting in the freezing dawn, to avoid the midday heat, the natives in keffiehs would scrape the earth following the orders of French, German, Spanish, or Italian scholars many of whom weren't even thirty yet and came, unpaid usually, to benefit from practical experience on one of the tells of the Syrian desert. Each nation had its sites all along the river reaching as far as the gloomy lands of Jezirah on the borders of Iraq: the Germans had Tell Halaf and Tell Bi'a, which covered a Mesopotamian city answering to the delicate name of Tuttul; the French had Dura Europos and Mari; the Spanish, Halabiya and Tell Halula, and so on, they fought each other for Syrian concessions the way oil companies fight for oil fields, and were as little inclined to share their patches of rock as children their marbles, except when they had to take advantage of the money from Brussels and banded together, since everyone was in agreement when it was a matter of scraping, not earth this time, but the coffers of the European Commission. Bilger was like a fish in water in this milieu; he looked to us like the Sargon of these needy masses; he would comment on the sites, the finds, the plans; he called the workers by their given names, Abu Hassan, Abu Mohammed: these "local" workmen earned a pittance, but a pittance that was much more than what a local construction job would have made them, not counting the entertainment of working for these Franks in safari jackets and cream-colored scarves. This was the big advantage of "Oriental" campaign excavations: whereas in Europe they were forced by their budgets to dig themselves, archaeologists in Syria, like their glorious predecessors, could delegate the lowly tasks. As Bilger said, quoting *The Good, the Bad and the Ugly*: "You see, in this world there's two kinds of people, my friend: those with loaded guns and those who dig." So the European archaeologists had acquired an extremely specialized and technical Arabic vocabulary: dig here, clear there, with a shovel, a pickax, a small pick, a trowel — the brush was the privilege of Westerners. Dig *gently*, clear *quickly*, and it was not rare to overhear the following dialogue:

"Go one meter down here."

"Yes boss. With an excavation shovel?"

"Um, big shovel . . . Big shovel no. *Instead* pickax."

"With the big pickax?"

"Big pickax no. Little pick."

"So, we should dig down to one meter with the little pick?"

"*Na'am na'am.* Shwia shwia, *listen, don't go smashing in the whole wall to finish more quickly*, OK?"

"OK boss."

In these circumstances, there were obviously misunderstandings that led to irreparable losses for science: a number of walls and stylobates fell victim to the perverse alliance of linguistics and capitalism, but on the whole the archaeologists were happy with their personnel, whom they trained, so to speak, season after season: some were archaeological workmen from father to son for several generations, who had known the great ancestors of Oriental archaeology and had figured in excavation photos since the 1930s. It is strange to wonder, for that matter, what their relationship may have been to that past they were helping to restore; obviously Sarah had asked the question:

"I'm curious to know what these excavations represent, for these workers. Do they have the feeling that we're stripping them of their history, that Europeans are stealing something from them, once again?"

Bilger had a theory: he argued that for these workmen whatever came before Islam does not belong to them, is of another order, another world, which falls into the category of the *qadim jiddan*, the "very old"; Bilger asserted that for a Syrian, the history of the World is divided into three periods: *jadid*, recent; *qadim*, old; *qadim jiddan*, very old, without it being very clear if it was simply his own level of Arabic that was the cause for such a simplification: even if his workers talked to him about the succession of Mesopotamian dynasties, they would have had to resort, lacking a common language that he could understand, to the *qadim jiddan*.

Europe sapped Antiquity under the Syrians, the Iraqis, the Egyptians. Our triumphant nations appropriated the universal with their monopoly on science and archaeology, dispossessing the colonized populations by means of this pillage of a past that, as a result, they readily experienced as alien: and so brainwashed Islamist wreckers drive tractors all the more easily through ancient cities since they combine their profoundly uncultivated stupidity with the more or less widespread feeling that this heritage is an alien, retroactive emanation of foreign powers.

Raqqa is today one of the cities administered directly by the Islamic State of Iraq and Syria, which must not make it any more welcoming, the bearded cutthroats are having a great time slicing carotids here, chopping hands off there, burning down churches and raping infidels to their heart's content, customs that are *qadim jiddan*, madness seems to have taken over the region, an insanity that may be just as incurable as Bilger's.

I've often wondered if there were warning signs predicting Bilger's madness and, unlike the madness of Syria itself, aside from his extraordinary energy, his talent for handling people and his megalomania, I can't see many, but that's probably enough. He seemed remarkably stable and responsible; during our time together in Istanbul, before he left for Damascus, he was passionate and efficient — he's the one who introduced me to Faugier: he was looking for a roommate, while I was searching in vain through all the German-speaking institutions to find a lodging for the two months I had left to spend on the Bosphorus, having exhausted the kindness of the Kulturforum at the palace of Yeniköy, magnificent headquarters of the embassy and then of the Consulate General of Austria, high up past Roumeli Hisar, a stone's throw from the house of Büyükdere where my eminent compatriot Hammer-Purgstall had been housed. This palace was a sublime place whose sole inconvenience was being, in this city worn away by traffic jams, extraordinarily difficult of access: so my suitcase and I were very happy to find a room to rent in the apartment of a young French research fellow in the social sciences, who was working on prostitution at the end of the Ottoman Empire and at the beginning of the Turkish Republic, a subject that I obviously hid from Mother, fearing she'd picture me living in a brothel. It was a centrally located apartment, which brought me closer to my musical researches and to the ex-Italian Choral Society whose headquarters was a few hundred meters away. Faugier was indeed interested in prostitution, but in Istanbul he was "in exile": his real field of study was Iran, and he had been welcomed by the French Institute for Anatolian Studies while waiting to obtain a visa to go to Tehran, where I would in fact find him years later: there is no such thing as chance in the world of Oriental Studies, Sarah would have said. He was giving his adoptive institute the benefit of his expertise and was preparing an article on "The Regulation of Prostitution in Istanbul at the Beginning of the Republic," about which he spoke to me day and night—he was a strange erotomaniac; a Parisian rascal, rather elegant, from a good family but afflicted by a horrible outspokenness, which had nothing in common with Bilger's subtle irony. How and why he hoped to obtain a visa to Iran was a mystery to everyone; when he was asked the question, he would limit himself to "Ah ah ah, Tehran is a very interesting city, lots of seedy parts, they have everything there," without wanting to understand that our surprise stemmed not from the resources of the city connected with such research, but from any sympathy the Islamic Republic might grant to this rather bawdy branch of science. (Good Lord I'm thinking like my mother, *bawdy*, no one has used that word since 1975, Sarah is right, I'm an old-fashioned prude, hopeless, there's nothing for it.) Contrary to what you might imagine, he was extraordinarily well-respected in his field and wrote columns from time to time in the big French papers — it's funny he's inviting himself into my dreams, *specialist in Arabic coitus,* that wouldn't have displeased him, even though, so far as I know, he has no relationship with the Arabic world, only with Turkey and Iran, but there you go. Our dreams might be more knowledgeable than we.

That madman Bilger laughed a lot at having "set me up" with such an individual. At the time he was taking advantage of one of his countless scholarships, he'd made friends with all possible and imaginable *Prominenten* — and had even used me to get in with the Austrians, very quickly becoming even closer than I to our diplomats.

I was corresponding regularly with Sarah, postcards of the Hagia Sophia, seen from the Golden Horn: as Grillparzer said in his travel journal, "There may be nothing like it in the whole world." He describes, enthralled, this succession of monuments, palaces, villages, the power of this site that struck me fully too and filled me with energy, so open is this city, a wound in the sea, a gash engulfed by beauty; to stroll through Istanbul was, whatever the goal of one's expedition, a wrenching of beauty on the frontier — whether you regard Constantinople as the easternmost city in Europe or the westernmost city in Asia, as an end or a beginning, as a bridge or a border, this mixed nature is fractured by nature, and the place weighs on history as history itself weighs on humans. For me, it was the limit of European music, the most Oriental destination of the indefatigable Liszt, who had drawn its outlines; for Sarah it was the beginning of the land where her travelers had wandered, in both directions.

It was extraordinary, leafing through the pages of the *Journal of Constantinople—Echo of the Orient* at the library, to realize to what extent the city had always attracted (thanks, among other things, to the largesse of a sultan who, however, by the second half of the nineteenth century, was mostly ruined) whatever Europe contained in the way of painters, musicians, men of letters, and adventurers—it was absolutely wonderful to discover that, ever since Michelangelo and Da Vinci, everyone had dreamed of the Bosphorus. What interested me in Istanbul, to use Sarah's terms, was a variation of the "self," the visits and travels of Europeans to the Ottoman capital, more, really, than Turkish "alterity"; aside from the local personnel of the various institutes and a few friends of Faugier or Bilger's, I didn't have much contact with the natives: once again language was an insurmountable obstacle, and unfortunately I was far from being like Hammer-Purgstall who could, he said, "translate from Turkish or Arabic into French, English, or Italian, and speak Turkish as well as German"; perhaps I lacked those pretty Greek or Armenian ladies who could stroll with me, as they did with him, every afternoon by the Strait to practice the language. On this subject Sarah had a horrified memory of her first Arabic course in Paris: an authority, a renowned Orientalist, Gilbert Delanoue, had, from high up in his rostrum, delivered the following truth: "To have a good knowledge of Arabic, you need twenty years. This period of time can be cut in half with the help of a warm dictionary made of flesh and blood." "A warm dictionary made of flesh and blood" is exactly what Hammer-Purgstall seemed to have, and even several of them; he didn't hide that fact that what he knew of Modern Greek he owed to the young women of Constantinople to whom he whispered sweet nothings by the water's edge. That's how I pictured the "Faugier method"; he spoke Persian and Turkish fluently, a Turkish of the lower depths and a real gutter Persian, learned in the brothels of Istanbul and the parks of Tehran, on the job. His auditory memory was prodigious; he was able to remember and reuse entire conversations, but curiously he lacked an ear: all languages, in his mouth, sounded like an obscure Parisian dialect, so much so that you might wonder if he was doing it on purpose, convinced of the superiority of the French accent over native phonetics. The people of Istanbul or Tehran, perhaps because they'd never had the luck to hear Jean-Paul Belmondo jabber away in their idiom, were bewitched by the strange mixture of refinement and vulgarity that emerged from this monstrous association, a mixture of their worst, most down-and-out places and of a European scholar with the elegance of a diplomat. He employed the same coarseness in all languages, even English. The truth was that I was terribly jealous of his elegance, his knowledge, his outspokenness, as well as of his familiarity with the city — maybe too of his success with women. No, *especially* of his success with women: on this fifth floor, lost at the end of a back alley in Cihangir that we shared, whose view resembled that of the "Panorama," there were often soirées, organized by him, to which many desirable young people came; I even danced (I blush to remember) one evening, to a hit by Sezen Aksu or Ibrahim Tatlıses, I forget now, with a pretty Turkish girl (longish hair, formfitting bright-red cotton sweater matching her lipstick, blue eye shadow accentuating the eyes of a houri) who'd then sat next to me on the sofa, while we talked in English; around us, other dancers, holding beers; behind her stretched the lights of the Asiatic shore of the Bosphorus as far as the Haydar Pasha train station; they framed her face with its prominent cheekbones. The questions were banal, what do you do, what are you doing in Istanbul, and as usual I was tongue-tied:

"I'm interested in the history of music."

"Are you a musician?"

(Embarrassed) "No. I . . . I study musicology. I'm a . . . a musicologist."

(Surprise, interest) "How great, which instrument do you play?"

(Keen embarrassment) "I . . . I don't play any instrument. I just study. I listen and write, if you prefer."

(Disappointment, disappointed surprise) "You don't play? But you can read music?"

(Relief) "Yes, of course, that's part of my job."

(Surprise, suspicion) "You read, but you don't play?"

(Shameless lie) "Actually I can play several instruments, but poorly."

Then I launched into a long explanation of my research, after a pedagogical detour through the plastic arts (not all art historians or critics are painters). I had to admit that I wasn't too interested in "modern" music (or rather, technically speaking, I must have lied and invented a passion for Turkish pop, I know myself too well) but rather music from the nineteenth century, Western and Eastern; the name of Franz Liszt was familiar to her, but Haci Emin Effendi meant absolutely nothing to her, probably because I was pronouncing it terribly. I must have shown off by telling her about my investigation (which I found fascinating, breathtaking even) into Liszt's piano, that famous "grand piano, the large A-E-A model, with seven octaves, triple-strung, a mechanical piano with Érard double escapement, with all the improvements, in mahogany, etc." on which he had played for the Sultan in 1847.

In the meantime the other guests had also taken seats and

helped themselves to more beers, and Faugier, who till now had been lavishing his attention on another girl, began to focus on the young woman to whom I was painfully telling, in my English (which is always laborious, I didn't know how to pronounce "mahogany" for example, so like *Mahagoni* in German), about my pathetic little studies: in the blink of an eye and in Turkish, he made her burst out laughing, at my expense I'm sure; then, still in the same language, they talked about music, at least I think so, I understood Guns N' Roses, Pixies, Nirvana, then they left to dance; for a long while I contemplated the Bosphorus shining through the window, and the ass of the Turkish girl undulating almost under my nose, as she swayed against that smug fop that was Faugier — it's better to laugh about it now, but at the time I was pretty annoyed.

Obviously I knew nothing of the reality of the rift, the crack in Faugier that would become a rift — it wasn't until years later in Tehran that I discovered what was hiding behind this seducer's façade, the sadness and somber, solitary madness of this frequenter of the lower depths.

It was of course thanks to Faugier that I smoked my first opium pipe — he had brought back the passion and technique from his first stay in Iran. Smoking opium in Istanbul seemed to belong to another age, an Orientalist's whim, and precisely for that reason I let myself be tempted — I, who had never touched any illegal drug or any vice — by this opium, this "thebaic": very moved, frightened even, but with a fear filled with pleasure, the fear of children facing the forbidden, not that of adults facing death. Opium was, in our imagination, so strongly associated with the Far Orient, with faded color prints of Chinese men stretched out in opium dens, that one almost forgot it came from Turkey and India and had been smoked from Thebes to Damascus to Tehran, which, in my mind, also helped allay my apprehension: to smoke in Istanbul or Tehran was to rediscover a little of the spirit of the place, to take part in a tradition that we were not familiar with, and to bring back to light a local reality that colonial clichés had moved elsewhere. Opium is still traditional in Iran, where *teriyakis*, opium smokers, number among the thousands; you see stick-thin grandfathers, gesticulating and vindictive, mad until they smoke their first pipe or dissolve a little of the residue burned the day before into their tea and then they become gentle and wise again, wrapped in their thick cloaks, warming themselves near a brazier whose coals they use to light their *bafours* and soothe their souls and their old bones. Faugier told me all this during the weeks preceding my initiation, which would bring me closer to Théophile Gautier, Baudelaire, and even to poor Heinrich Heine, who found in laudanum and especially in morphine a remedy for his ills, a consolation in his endless agony. Faugier had used his contacts among the brothel-keepers and nightclub bouncers to get a few balls of the black resin that left a very particular odor on your fingers, an unknown perfume that reminded you of incense, but as if caramelized, sweet and bizarrely bitter at the same time—a taste that haunts you for a long time, returns to your sinuses now and then and to the back of your throat, on certain days; if I call it up now, this taste, I can find it again by swallowing my saliva, closing my eyes, as I suppose a smoker must be able to do with the horrible burnt-tar stench of tobacco, much different, for unlike what I thought before I had the experience, opium doesn't burn, but boils, melts, and gives off a thick vapor upon contact with heat. No doubt it's the complexity of the preparation that saves the European masses from becoming Iranian-style *teriyakis*; smoking opium requires traditional savoir-faire, it is an *art*, some say, which is much slower and more complex than injection—Jörg Fauser, the German William Burroughs, describes in *Rohstoff*, his autobiographical novel, the hippies in Istanbul in the 1970s who spent all the blessed day injecting themselves, on filthy beds in the countless *pensions* in Küçükayasofia Caddesi, with raw opium they dissolved in a rush in every possible kind of liquid, incapable of smoking it effectively.

In our case, the preparation was *à l'iranienne*, according to Faugier; I was able to verify later, by comparing his gestures to the Iranians', how well he had mastered the ritual, which was more than a little mysterious: he didn't seem like an opium addict, or at least he didn't have any of the symptoms one usually associates with drug addicts—slowness, thinness, irascibility, difficulty concentrating—and yet he was a past master in the preparation of pipes, according to the quality of the substance he had in hand, raw or fermented opium, and the material he had at his disposal, in our case an Iranian *bafour*, whose large clay bowl was gently warmed in a little brazier; with the curtains carefully drawn, like my heavy curtains now in cloth from Aleppo, red and gold, their Oriental motifs faded by years of poor Viennese light—in Istanbul we had to resign ourselves to hiding the Strait behind blinds so as not to be seen by the neighbors, but the risks were small; in Tehran you risked much more: the regime had declared war against the drug, the Revolutionary Guards clashed in veritable pitched battles with smugglers in the east of the country, and for anyone who might have doubted the reality of this fight, the day before Nowruz, the Iranian New Year, in 2001, when I had just arrived, the judges of the Islamic Republic organized a spectacle of extraordinary cruelty and broadcast its images across the entire world: the public execution of five traffickers including a thirty-year-old woman, hanged from cherry picker trucks, blindfolded, slowly raised into the air, ropes around their necks, legs kicking until death ensued, and their poor bodies dangled at the ends of telescopic arms; the girl's name was Fariba, she was wearing a black chador; her dress, swelled by the breeze, made her into a terrifying bird, an unfortunate crow who cursed the spectators with its wings, and I took pleasure imagining that the crowd of brutes (men, women, children), who were shouting slogans as they watched these poor devils raised up to death, would be stricken by her curse and experience the worst kinds of suffering. These images haunted me for a long time: they at least had the merit of reminding us that, despite all the charms of Iran, we were in a cursed country, territory of pain and death, where everything—even the poppies, flowers of martyrdom—was red with blood. I hurriedly tried to forget all that in music and poetry, because you still have to live, like the Iranians who are past masters in the art of oblivion—the young people smoked opium that they mixed with tobacco, or else took heroin; drugs were extraordinarily cheap, even in local currency: despite the efforts of the mullahs and the spectacular executions, the idleness of the youth was so great that nothing could prevent them from looking for consolation in drugs, parties, and fornication, as Sarah says in the introduction to her thesis.

Faugier examined all this despair as a specialist, an entomologist of despondency, abandoning himself as well to the most formidable excesses, in a kind of contagion of his object of study, eaten away by a galloping sadness, a tuberculosis of the soul that he tended, just as Professor Laennec tended his lungs, with formidable quantities of narcotics.

My first opium pipe brought me closer to Novalis, Berlioz, Nietzsche, Trakl—I entered into the closed circle of those who had tasted the fabulous nectar Helen served Telemachus, so he could forget his sadness for a while: "Then Helen, daughter of Zeus, had another thought, and right away, she poured into the wine they were drinking a balm, nepenthe, which makes one forget one's ills. Whoever drank this mixture could shed no tears for a whole day, even if his mother and father had died, even if his brother or beloved son were killed in front of him with a sword, and he saw this with his own eyes. And the daughter of Zeus possessed this excellent liquor that had been given her by Poly-damna, wife of Thon, in Egypt, fertile land that produces many balms, some salutary and others deadly. There all doctors are the cleverest of men, they are of the race of Paeon," and it is true that opium chased away all grief, all pain, moral or physical, and cured, temporarily, the most secret ills, even the very perception of time: opium induces floating, opens up a parenthesis in aware-ness, an inner parenthesis where you feel as if you are touching eternity, as if you have conquered melancholy and the finitude of being. Telemachus enjoyed two kinds of drunkenness, the one caused by contemplating Helen's face, and the other from the power of the nepenthe, and I myself, once, in Iran, while smok-ing by myself with Sarah, since she had no taste for hard or soft drugs, had the luck of being caressed by her beauty when the gray smoke emptied my mind of all desire of possession, all an-guish, all solitude: I could see her truly, and she gleamed like the moon — opium didn't disturb the senses, it made them objective; it made the subject disappear, and it's not the least of the contra-dictions of this mystical narcotic that it draws us out of ourselves, all the while making awareness and sensations keener, and proj-ects us into the great calm of the universal.

Faugier had warned me that one of the many alkaloids that composed opium could cause vomiting, and that a first opiated experience could be accompanied by violent nausea, which was not the case for me — the only side effect, aside from strange erotic dreams in mythical harems, was a healthy constipation: another advantage of the poppy for the traveler, always subject to more or less chronic intestinal irregularities that number, along with worms and various amoebas, among the travel companions of those who journey through the eternal Orient, although they're rarely mentioned in their memoirs.

Why opium has disappeared today from the European pharmacopeia, I do not know; I gave my doctor a good laugh when I asked him to prescribe me some—he knows, though, that I have a serious disease, I'm a good patient, and that I wouldn't abuse it, if in fact (and that's obviously the danger) it's possible not to abuse this panacea, but Faugier assured me, to dissipate my last fears, that you didn't develop a dependency by smoking one or two pipes a week. I can see his gestures now, as he was preparing the *bafour*, whose clay bowl had been warmed in the embers; he would cut the hard black paste into little pieces, which he would soften by bringing them closer to the heat of the brazier, before grasping the warm pipe—the waxed wood, ringed with brass, looked a little like an oboe or shawm without reed or holes, but with a gilded mouthpiece that Faugier would put in his mouth; then he would delicately pick up one of the burning coals with the help of a pair of tongs and would press it against the upper part of the bowl; the air he inhaled would make the ember turn red, his face would be covered in bronze glints; he'd close his eyes as the opium melted, producing a tiny crackling noise, and a few seconds later he'd spit out a light cloud, the excess his lungs hadn't managed to hold in, a breath of pleasure; he was an ancient flautist playing in the half-light, and the perfume of burnt opium (spicy, bitter, sweet) would fill the night.

My heart is beating as I await my turn; I wonder what effect the black gum will produce; I'm afraid, I've never smoked anything, aside from a joint in school; I wonder if I'll cough, vomit, faint. Faugier utters one of his horrible phrases, "What the fuck, sure doesn't suck," he hands me the pipe without letting it go, I support it with my left hand and bend over, the metal tip is warm,

I discover the taste of opium, remote at first, and then, when I breathe in as Faugier brings close to the bowl a white-hot coal whose heat I can feel against my cheek, suddenly powerful, more powerful, so powerful I can no longer feel my lungs — I'm surprised by the almost watery sweetness of this smoke, surprised by the ease with which it can be swallowed, even if, to my great shame, I feel nothing but the disappearance of my respiratory apparatus, a grayness inside, as if my chest were blackened by a lead pencil. Faugier watches me with a fixed smile, he becomes worried — So? I make an inspired face, I wait, I listen. I listen to myself, I look inside myself for new rhythms and accents, I try to follow my own transformation, I'm very attentive, I'm tempted to close my eyes, I'm tempted to smile, I smile, I could even laugh, but I'm happy to smile because I feel Istanbul around me, I hear it without seeing it, it's a very simple, very complete happiness that settles in, here and now, without expecting anything but absolute perfection from the suspended, dilated instant, and I suppose, at that instant, that the effect is there.

I watch Faugier scrape the residue of opium with a needle.

The brazier becomes gray; little by little the coals grow cold and are covered with ashes; soon we'll have to blow on it to rid them of this dead skin and find again, if it isn't too late, the flame that's still inside them. I listen to an imaginary musical instrument, a memory of my day; it's Liszt's piano; he's playing in front of the Sultan. If I dared, I'd ask Faugier: According to you, what might Liszt have played at the Çiragan Palace, in 1847, before the court and all the important foreigners the Ottoman capital had at the time? Was Sultan Abdülmecit as music-loving as his brother Abdülaziz would be, first Wagnerian of the Orient? Certainly his *Hungarian Melodies*, and certainly too his "Grand Galop Chromatique," which he played so often all over Europe and in Russia. Maybe, as elsewhere, his *Improvisations on a Local Theme* mixed with the *Hungarian Melodies.* Did Liszt take opium? Berlioz did.

Faugier shapes a new ball of black paste in the pipe's bowl.

I calmly listen to this distant melody, I look, from high up, at all these men, all these souls still walking around us: who was Liszt, who was Berlioz, who was Wagner and all the people they knew, Musset, Lamartine, Nerval, an immense network of texts, notes, and images, clear, precise, a path visible by me alone that links old Hammer-Purgstall to a whole world of travelers, musicians, poets, that links Beethoven to Balzac, to James Morier, to Hofmannsthal, to Strauss, to Mahler, and to the sweet smoke of Istanbul and Tehran, is it possible that opium is still accompanying me after all these years, that you can call up its effects as you do God in prayer—was I dreaming of Sarah in the poppy, for a long time, like this evening, a long, profound desire, a perfect desire, since it requires no satisfaction, no completion; an eternal desire, an endless erection without goal, that's what opium provokes.

It guides us in the shadows.

Franz Liszt the handsome boy arrives in Constantinople from Jasi, city of the bloody pogroms, via Galata on the Black Sea at the end of May 1847. He has just finished a long tour, Lemberg, Czernowitz, Odessa, all the concert halls in Eastern Europe, large or small, with all the noteworthy people, great or small. He is a star, a monster, a genius; he makes men cry, women faint, and it's hard for us to believe, today, what he writes about his success: five hundred students accompany him, on horseback, to the first relay post when he leaves Berlin; a crowd of young women showers him with flower petals when he leaves the Ukraine. There is no artist who knows Europe so well, down to its most remote borders, west or east, from Brest to Kiev. Everywhere he goes he sets off rumors, gossip that precedes him to the next city: he has been arrested, he's gotten married, has fallen ill; everywhere people wait for him and, the most extraordinary thing, he actually arrives everywhere, heralded by the appearance of his Érard piano, at least as indefatigable as he, which the Parisian manufacturer sends by boat or coach, as soon as he knows the destination of his best representative; hence the *Journal de Constantinople* publishes, on May 11, 1847, a letter from Paris, from the manufacturer Sébastien Pierre Érard himself, announcing the imminent arrival of a grand piano, in mahogany, with all possible improvements, shipped from Marseille on April 5. So Liszt is on the way! Liszt is coming! Despite extensive research, I can't find many details about his visit to Istanbul, aside perhaps from the name of the woman who was supposed to accompany him there:

> And that poor Mariette Duplessis who is dead . . . She is the first woman with whom I fell in love, who is now in who knows what cemetery, abandoned to the worms of the grave! She did tell me fifteen months ago: "I will not live; I'm a singular girl and I won't be able to cling to this life that I don't know how to lead and can no longer bear. Take me, lead me where you like; I won't bother you, I sleep all day, in the evenings you can let me go to the concert and at night you can do what you like with me." I had told her I'd take her to Constantinople, since that was the only sensible trip possible I could have her make. Now she is dead . . .

Sarah found that phrase extraordinary, "Take me, lead me where you like; I won't bother you, I sleep all day, in the evenings you can let me go to the concert and at night you can do what you like with me," a declaration of absolute beauty and despair, a total nudity — unlike Liszt I know where she is buried, the Montmartre cemetery, which Sarah showed me. The fate of the original, though, was more enviable than that of the Lady of the

Camellias; the younger Dumas has even, if we judge him by that phrase, tarnished her character a little: Verdi's adaptation of the life of Marie Duplessis, however, is indeed *musical*, but a little excessive in tragedy. *La Traviata* was created in Venice in 1853, things moved quickly at the time; seven years after her death, the little courtesan Marie Duplessis *alias* Marguerite Gautier *alias* Violetta Valéry is famous, with Dumas *fils* and Verdi, all over Europe. Liszt confides sadly:

> If by chance I had been in Paris during la Duplessis's illness, I'd have tried to save her at all costs, for she was truly a delightful person, and the habit that is called (and that may be) corrupting never stained her heart. Believe me when I say that I had conceived for her a somber, elegiac attachment, which, quite without my knowing it, had set me on the track of poetry and music. That was the last and only jolt I've felt in years. One must give up explaining these contradictions, the human heart is a strange thing!

The human heart is indeed a strange thing, Franz Liszt's artichoke heart didn't stop falling in love, even with God—in these reminiscences of opium, as I hear the virtuosities of Liszt that occupied me in Constantinople rumbling like death march drums, a *singular girl* also appears to me, over there in Sarawak, even if Sarah has nothing in common with la Duplessis or with Harriet Smithson ("Do you see that fat Englishwoman sitting in the proscenium," Heinrich Heine has Berlioz saying in his account), the actress who inspired the *Symphonie Fantastique*. Poor Berlioz, lost in his passion for the interpreter of "poor Ophelia": "Poor great genius, grappling with three-quarters of the impossible!" as Liszt writes in one of his letters.

You'd need a Sarah to be interested in all these tragic fates of forgotten women—what a spectacle, though, of Berlioz's, mad with love, playing the timpani in his own *March to the Scaffold* when the *Symphonie Fantastique* was performed in the great Conservatoire hall. This fourth movement is pure madness, a dream of opium, poisoning, ironic, grating torture, a march to Death, written in one night, a night of poppies, and Berlioz, writes Heinrich Heine, Berlioz from his timpani was looking at Harriet Smithson, staring at her, and every time his eyes met hers, he beat his instrument harder, like a man possessed. (Heine also notes that the timpani, or percussions in general, were instruments that suited Berlioz. Berlioz never traveled to the Orient, but was, at the height of his twenty-five years, fascinated with Hugo's *Les Orientales*. So there might be a *second* Orient, that of Goethe or Hugo, of people who know neither Oriental languages, nor the countries where they are spoken, but who rely on the works of Orientalists and travelers like Hammer-Purgstall, and even a *third* Orient, a *Third-Orient*, that of Berlioz or Wagner, which feeds on these works that are themselves indirect. The *Third-Orient*, there's a notion to develop. For instance, there are more things in timpani than are dreamt of . . .) The fact remains that this poor Ophelia that was Harriet Smithson, unlike the British troops, succumbed to the French percussions and married the artist. This marriage *forced by art* ended in disaster, sometimes music can't do everything, and Heine notes, a few years later, as the *Symphonie Fantastique* is being performed again at the Conservatoire, that "Berlioz is again seated behind the orchestra, at the drums, and the fat Englishwoman is still in the proscenium, and their gazes meet again . . . but he doesn't strike so hard on his timpani."

You have to be Heine to be able to outline in this way, in ten lines, the story of a defunct love; *the fine, witty Henri Heine*, as Théophile Gautier calls him, Heine who asks him, as the hashish-smoker is about to leave for Constantinople, in Paris at a concert of Liszt's, with his German accent full of humor and mischievousness: "How will you manage to talk about the Orient when you're actually there?" A question that could have been put to all travelers to Istanbul, so much does the journey diffuse its object, disseminating and multiplying it in reflections and details until it loses its reality.

Franz Liszt doesn't say much about this visit to Turkey, of which a commemorative plaque, in the little street that goes down to the French Consulate in Beyoglu, briefly reminds passersby. We know he was welcomed, as soon as he disembarked from his boat, by the music master Donizetti and the Austrian ambassador, whom the Sultan had summoned to form part of the welcoming committee; that he stayed at the palace of the composer Ali Rıfat Çağatay for a few days, invited by the Great Lord, and that he gave a concert there on that famous Érard piano; that he then spent some time at the Austrian embassy and then at the French embassy, where he was the guest of the ambassador François-Adolphe de Bourqueney and gave a second concert, still on the same instrument that followed him positively everywhere; that he met the ambassador himself at the end of his stay, since the wife of said ambassador had been ill till then; that he gave a third concert in Pera and rediscovered two old acquaintances there, a Frenchman and a Pole, with whom he went on an excursion into Asia; that he sent thanks by mail to Lamartine, great specialist in the Ottoman Empire, who had sent him a letter of introduction to the Minister of Foreign Affairs Reshid Pasha: that's pretty much all we can say for certain.

I can picture again my walks between sessions poring over archives and the newspapers of the time; my visits to specialists who might be able to inform me, always somewhat grumpy historians frightened, as so often in academia, by the possibility that a young man might know more than they or catch them in a mistake, especially if said young man was not Turkish, but Austrian, and worse, only half-Austrian, and that his research subject fell into a scientific void, a hole, between the history of Turkish music and European music: sometimes, which was a little depressing, I felt as if my thoughts were like the Bosphorus—a beautiful place between two shores, indeed, but one that, at bottom, was nothing but water, not to say wind. In vain I would reassure myself by telling myself that the colossus of Rhodes or Hercules had also in their time had one foot on each shore—the mocking gazes and acerbic remarks of the specialists still often managed to discourage me.

Fortunately there was Istanbul, and Bilger, and Faugier, and opium, which opened up the gates of perception to us—my theory on Liszt's inspiration in Constantinople arose from his *Harmonies poétiques et religieuses*, and mainly from the "Bénédiction de Dieu dans la solitude," which he composed not long after his stay in Istanbul, in Woronice; the musical "adaptation" of the poem by Lamartine answers the question of the first lines, "D'où me vient, ô mon Dieu! cette paix qui m'inonde? / D'où me vient cette foi dont mon coeur surabonde?" (Whence, oh my God! does this peace that is overwhelming me come? / Whence comes this faith with which my heart is overflowing?) and I was utterly convinced it had to do with Liszt's encounter with Oriental light and not, as commentators often described it, with a lover's memory of Marie d'Agoult "rehashed" for princess Carolyne zu Sayn-Wittgenstein.

After his visit to Istanbul, Liszt gave up his life as a wandering musician, renounced the fame of his brilliant years, and began, in Weimar, a long trajectory toward contemplation, a new journey that was opened up—even though some of these pieces had in fact been sketched out before—by the *Harmonies poétiques et religieuses*. Despite being massacred by all beginning pianists,

the "Bénédiction . . ." nonetheless remains not only the most
beautiful of Liszt's melodies, but also contains the composer's
most simply complex accompaniment, an accompaniment (and
this, to my beginner's ears, was what brought the piece closer
to an *illumination*) that one had to make sound like overflowing
faith, while the melody represented divine peace. That seems
to me today a slightly "teleological" and simplistic reading (music rarely being reducible to the causes of its composition), and
above all to be linked to my own experience of Istanbul—one
morning that was intensely blue, the air crisp with cold, when
the Prince Islands stood out in the oblique light beyond the Seraglio Point and when the minarets of old Istanbul streaked the
sky with their lances, their pencils to write the hundredth name
of God into the pure hollow of the clouds, there still weren't
many tourists or passersby in the strange little street (high,
blank stone walls, old caravanserai, and closed libraries) leading to the back of the Süleymaniye mosque, built by Sinan the
Divine for Süleyman the Magnificent. I pass the colored marble
peristyle; a few gulls flit between the porphyry columns; the
tiled pavement gleams as if it had rained. I have already been
inside several mosques, Santa Sophia, the Blue Mosque, and I
will see others, in Damascus, Aleppo, in Ispahan even, but none
will have this immediate effect on me, once I've left my shoes
in a wooden compartment and penetrated the prayer hall, a
wrenching at my heart, a loss of bearings, I vainly try to walk
and let myself fall where I stand, onto the red rug with blue
flowers, trying to collect my wits. I discover that I am alone in
the monument, alone surrounded by light, alone in this space
with its disconcerting proportions; the circle of the immense
cupola is welcoming, and hundreds of windows surround me—
I sit down cross-legged. I am moved to the point of tears but I
do not cry, I feel lifted up from the earth and I run my eyes over

the Izmit faïence inscriptions, the painted surroundings, everything glitters, then a great calm seizes me, a wrenching calm, a summit glimpsed, but very soon the beauty eludes me and rejects me — little by little I rediscover my senses; what my eyes perceive now indeed looks magnificent to me, but has nothing in common with the sensation I've just felt. A great sadness grips me, suddenly, a loss, a sinister vision of the reality of the world and all its imperfections, its pain, a sadness accentuated by the perfection of the building and a phrase comes to me: only the proportions are divine, the rest belongs to humans. As a group of tourists enters the mosque I try to stand up and my legs, gone numb after the two hours spent seated, make me stumble and leave the Süleymaniye like a drunken man, a man hesitating between joy and tears, and I flee, I fled more than left the mosque; the great wind of Istanbul finally woke me up, especially the cold of the marble in the courtyard, I had forgotten my shoes, completely disoriented, realizing that I had spent two hours motionless or almost motionless, two hours have gone by, nonexistent, recalled solely by my watch: I suddenly realize I'm standing in my socks in the middle of the courtyard and my shoes have disappeared from the rack where I had left them, there's something that brings you instantly back to the sufferings of the World — so I in turn stole a pair of thick blue plastic sandals, after a few fruitless attempts at discussion with a mustached concierge who struck his arms against his body as a sign of powerlessness, "*no shoes, no shoes*," but let me appropriate these lifeguard's flip-flops lying there, with which I crossed Istanbul like a dervish, my soul suffering.

And memory is such a sad thing, for I remember more clearly my shame walking through the city in socks in my worn-out navy-blue rubber slippers than the emotion that had overwhelmed me and the vanished hours in the Süleymaniye, the first spiritual exaltation I'd ever felt that didn't stem from music — a few years later, telling this story to Sarah, which she called "The Satori of the Shoe," I remembered this quatrain by Khayyam:

> *I went to the mosque and stole a rug there.*
> *Much later, I repented,*
> *And went back to the mosque: the rug was worn-out,*
> *It had to be replaced.*

Unlike old Omar Khayyam I never dared go back to the Süleymaniye, the last time I passed through Istanbul I stayed in the garden, to see the tomb of that architect, Sinan, who was, along with few other men, an intermediary between us and God; I addressed a brief prayer to him, and thought again of the loathsome sandals I inherited that day and had lost or thrown out since, without first verifying, man of little faith that I was, whether or not they were miraculous.

Stendhal syndrome or real mystical experience, I have no idea, but I imagined that Liszt the heavenly Gypsy had also been able to find there a release, a force, in these views and buildings; that perhaps a little of that light of the Orient he carried in him had been revived during his visit to Constantinople. That was no doubt an interesting intuition on the personal level but for scholarship, in view of the few commentaries we have by Liszt himself about his journey on the Bosphorus, surely an excessive aspiration.

What I did on the other hand manage to reconstruct was a pretty plausible description of the first Ottoman ensemble, the private orchestra of Abdülaziz, who played sitting on the ground on the seraglio rugs; we know that the Sultan was annoyed by the "Oriental" tics of his violinists when they performed Italian and German works, and that he had organized a chorus to provide private concerts of operas, especially *The Marriage of Figaro*:

the great man became enraged because his singers had difficulty singing any other way but in unison, and the virtuosic duos, trios, quartets, and octets of *Figaro* became a sonorous jumble that wrenched impotent tears from the music-loving monarch, and this despite all the efforts of the eunuchs with their angelic voices and the wise advice of the Italian music master. Istanbul, though, had already given birth, in 1830, to a great forgotten composer, August von Adelburg Abramović, whose existence I had patiently retraced: after a childhood on the Bosphorus, Adelburg became famous in Budapest for a "national" opera, *Zrinyi*, in which he tried to demonstrate that, unlike what Liszt asserted, Hungarian music was not of gypsy origin—there's something fascinating in this, that it's precisely a Levantine who made himself the champion of Hungarian nationalism through the intermediary of his hero Miklós Zrinyi, sworn enemy of the Turks; it's probably that intimate, profound contradiction that pushed him toward madness, a madness that was so serious that it would lead to his internment and his death, at the age of forty-three. Adelburg, the first important European musician born in the Ottoman Empire, ended his life in madness, in the rift of alterity; as if, despite all the bridges, all the links held out by time, a mixed identity turned out to be impossible, faced as he was with the nationalist pathology that was little by little invading the nineteenth century and slowly destroying the fragile footbridges constructed earlier, giving way only to the politics of domination.

My glasses were under the pile of books and journals, obviously, I'm so absentminded. At the same time, to contemplate the ruins of my bedroom (ruins of Istanbul, ruins of Damascus, ruins of Tehran, ruins of myself) I don't need to see them, I know all these objects by heart. The faded photographs and yellowing Orientalist engravings. The poetic works of Pessoa on a sculpted wooden book stand meant to house the Koran. My tarboosh from Istanbul, my heavy wool indoor coat from the souk in Damascus, my lute from Aleppo bought with Nadim. These white volumes, black silhouette with a rebellious forelock on the spines, are the journals of Franz Grillparzer—of course this cracked everyone up in Istanbul, that an Austrian was going around with his Grillparzer. Laundry detergent, fine, but Grillparzer! Germans are jealous, that's all. I know where the problem lies: Germans can't bear the idea (I'm not the one who invented it, it was Hugo von Hofmannsthal who affirmed it in a famous article, "We Austrians and Germany") that Beethoven left for Vienna and never wanted to go back to Bonn. Hofmannsthal the greatest librettist of all time has also written elsewhere a strange dramatic dialogue between Hammer-Purgstall the eternal Orientalist and Balzac the indefatigable, which Sarah quotes abundantly in her article on Balzac and the Orient; I confess I no longer remember very clearly what it's about, I fished the article out yesterday, it's here, look there's a little piece of paper slipped inside, a note, an old letter written on a torn-off page, with red margins and blue lines, a half-page from a school notebook:

Dearest Franz,

Here finally is the publication that has occupied me for the last few months. I'm a little far from my beloved monsters and other horrors, as you say, but it's only temporary. The Hainfeld conference has turned out to be quite fruitful, you can judge for yourself . . . And not just in academic terms!

I can never thank you enough for the picture of the castle and your translations.

I'm guessing you're about to leave Istanbul, I hope your stay there was beneficial. Many thanks for the "commission" and the photos! They're

*wonderful! My mother is delighted. You're really lucky, what a dream,
to discover Constantinople . . . Will you come back to Vienna or Tübingen? Please don't forget to let me know the next time you come through
Paris,*

    Soon I hope, with love,

                                            Sarah

    *P.S. I'm curious to know what you'll think of this "Viennese" arti-
cle — only good things, I hope!*

It's pleasant to rediscover by surprise this dear handwriting,
in ink, a little hurried, a little hard to read but tender and elegant — now that computers have taken over, we rarely see the
calligraphy of our contemporaries, perhaps handwritten cursive
will become a form of nudity, an intimate, hidden manifestation,
concealed from everyone except lovers, lawyers, and bankers.

Now I'm not sleepy anymore. Sleep has never really wanted
me, it abandons me very quickly, around midnight, after pes-
tering me all evening. Sleep is a selfish monster that does only
what it pleases. Dr. Kraus is an awful doctor, I should switch.
Dismiss him. I could offer myself the luxury of dismissing my
doctor, showing him the door, a doctor who talks to you about
getting enough rest every visit but is incapable of making you
go to sleep does not deserve the title of doctor. I have to admit,
in his defense, that I've never taken any of the rubbish he's prescribed for me. But a doctor who can't guess that you aren't going
to take the rubbish he prescribes for you is not a good doctor,
that's why I should switch. Kraus seems like an intelligent man
though, I know he likes music, no, I'm exaggerating, I know he
goes to concerts, which proves nothing. Only yesterday he said
to me "I went to hear Liszt at the Musikverein," I replied that he
was lucky, it's been a long time since Liszt played in Vienna. He

laughed of course, saying "Ah Dr. Ritter you're making me die of laughter," which is all the same a strange phrase, coming from a doctor. I still can't forgive him for laughing so much when I asked him to prescribe opium for me. "Ah ah ah, I can write you the prescription, but then you're going to have to find a pharmacy from the nineteenth century." I know he's lying, I checked in the *Official Journal*, an Austrian doctor has the right to prescribe up to 2 grams of opium per day and 20 grams of laudanum, so it must be out there. The absurd thing is that a veterinarian of the same nationality can prescribe up to 15 grams of opium and 150 grams of tincture, it makes you want to be a sick dog. Maybe I could beg Gruber's mutt to sell me a little of his medicine without his master knowing, so that dog could finally be useful for a change.

I wonder why I'm obsessing today over this question, I've never been drawn to drunkenness and I've smoked a grand total of five or six pipes in my life — years ago. Probably because of the text by Balzac that Sarah quotes in this yellowing article with its rusty staples, its dust that clings to your fingers:

They asked opium to make them see the golden domes of Constantinople, and to roll them on divans in the seraglio, in the midst of the women of Mahmoud: and then, drunk with pleasure, they would fear either the cold of the dagger, or the swish of a silk bodice; and, in the grip of the delights of love, they could feel a premonition of the pyre ... Opium delivered the entire universe to them!

And, for 3 francs 25 centimes, they could travel to Cadiz or Seville, climb onto the walls, stay there lying under an awning, occupied with seeing two eyes of flame—an Andalusia sheltered by a red silk tent, whose shimmer communicated to that woman the ardor, the perfection, the poetry of the figures and fantastic objects of our young dreams ... Then, all of a sudden, as they turned round, they found themselves face to face with the terrible face of a Spaniard armed with a well-loaded blunderbuss!

Sometimes they tried the rolling plank of the guillotine and woke up at the bottom of the trenches, in Clamart, plunging into all the sweetness of domestic life: a hearth, a winter evening, a young woman, charming children, who, kneeling, were praying to God, instructed by an old nurse . . . All that for three francs of opium. Yes, for three francs of opium, they rebuilt even the enormous concepts of Greek, Asian, and Roman Antiquity! . . . They conjured up the Anoplotherium lost and rediscovered here and there by M. Cuvier. They reconstructed Solomon's stables, the Temple of Jerusalem, the wonders of Babylon, and the whole Middle Ages with tournaments, castles, knights, and monasteries! . . .

For three francs of opium! Balzac is jesting, that's certain, but still, three francs, how much can that be in schillings? No, sorry, it would have been crowns at that time. I've always been bad at conversion. One has to give Sarah credit for having the wherewithal to come across the most incredible and forgotten stories. Balzac, who in theory felt passionate only about the French and their customs, writing a text on opium — one of his first published texts, at that. Balzac, the first French novelist to include a text in Arabic in one of his novels! Balzac the native of Tours who becomes friends with Hammer-Purgstall the great Austrian Orientalist, even dedicating one of his books to him, *The Cabinet of Antiquities*. There's an article that could have made a sensation — but nothing makes a sensation, in the Academy, in the human sciences at least; articles are isolated, lost fruits that no one or almost no one bites into, I know a little about that. But, according to Sarah, the reader who opened his second edition of *La Peau de chagrin* in 1837 found this:

LA PEAU DE CHAGRIN. 39

Il apporta la lampe près du talisman que le jeune homme tenait à l'envers, et lui fit apercevoir des caractères incrustés dans le tissu cellulaire de cette peau merveilleuse, comme s'ils eussent été produits par l'animal auquel elle avait jadis appartenu.

— J'avoue, s'écria l'inconnu, que je ne devine guère le procédé dont on se sera servi pour graver si profondément ces lettres sur la peau d'un onagre.

Et, se retournant avec vivacité vers les tables chargées de curiosités, ses yeux parurent y chercher quelque chose.

— Que voulez-vous? demanda le vieillard.

— Un instrument pour trancher le chagrin, afin de voir si les lettres y sont empreintes ou incrustées.

Le vieillard présenta son stylet à l'inconnu, qui le prit et tenta d'entamer la peau à l'endroit où les paroles se trouvaient écrites; mais quand il eut enlevé une légère couche de cuir, les lettres y reparurent si nettes et tellement conformes à celles qui étaient imprimées sur la surface, que, pendant un moment, il crut n'en avoir rien ôté.

— L'industrie du Levant a des secrets qui lui sont réellement particuliers, dit-il en regardant la senence orientale avec une sorte d'inquiétude.

— Oui, répondit le vieillard, il vaut mieux s'en prendre aux hommes qu'à Dieu !

Les paroles mystérieuses étaient disposées de la manière suivante.

40 LA PEAU DE CHAGRIN.

لو ملكتني ملكت آلكل
و لكن عمرك ملكي
و اراد الله هكذا
اطلب و ستنال مطالبك
و لكن قس مطالبك على عمرك
وهي هاهنا
فدكل مرامك ستنزل ايامك
اتريد فى
الله مجيبك
امين

qui voulait dire en français :

SI TU ME POSSÈDES, TU POSSÉDERAS TOUT.
MAIS TA VIE M'APPARTIENDRA, DIEU L'A
VOULU AINSI. DÉSIRE, ET TES DÉSIRS
SERONT ACCOMPLIS. MAIS RÈGLE
TES SOUHAITS SUR TA VIE.
ELLE EST LA. A CHAQUE
VOULOIR JE DÉCROITRAI
COMME TES JOURS.
ME VEUX-TU?
PRENDS. DIEU
T'EXAUCERA.
SOIT !

Whereas in the original 1831 edition, one found only the following text:

116 LA PEAU DE CHAGRIN.

— Que voulez-vous?... demanda le vieillard.

— Un instrument pour trancher le chagrin afin de voir si les lettres y sont empreintes ou incrustées...

Le vieillard lui présenta le stylet. Il le prit et tenta d'entamer la peau à l'endroit où les paroles se trouvaient écrites; mais quand il eut enlevé une légère couche du cuir, les lettres y reparurent si nettes et si conformes à celles imprimées sur la surface, qu'il crut, pendant un moment, n'en avoir rien ôté.

— L'industrie du Levant a des secrets qui lui sont réellement particuliers! dit-il en regardant la sentence talismanique avec une sorte d'inquiétude.

— Oui!... répondit le vieillard, il vaut mieux s'en prendre aux hommes qu'à Dieu!

Les paroles mystérieuses étaient disposées de la manière suivante :

LA PEAU DE CHAGRIN. 117

SI TU ME POSSÈDES TU POSSÉDERAS TOUT.
MAIS TA VIE M'APPARTIENDRA. DIEU L'A
VOULU AINSI. DÉSIRE, ET TES DÉSIRS
SERONT ACCOMPLIS. MAIS RÈGLE
TES SOUHAITS SUR TA VIE.
ELLE EST LA. A CHAQUE
VOULOIR JE DÉCROITRAI
COMME TES JOURS.
ME VEUX-TU?
PRENDS. DIEU
T'EXAUCERA.
— SOIT!

—Ah! vous lisez couramment le sanscrit?... dit le vieillard. Vous avez été peut-être au Bengale, en Perse?...

» — Non, Monsieur, répondit le jeune homme en tâtant avec une curiosité digitale cette peau symbolique, assez semblable à une feuille de métal par son peu de flexibilité.

Le vieux marchand remit la lampe sur la

92

Abstract
Among the many relationships that European authors and artists of the first half of the nineteenth century had with the Orient, many have already been explored. We are quite familiar, for example, with the modalities of that encounter in Goethe or in Hugo. However, one of the most surprising relationships between scholarly Orientalism and literature is the one Honoré de Balzac had with the Austrian Orientalist Joseph von Hammer-Purgstall (1774–1856), which not only led to the first inclusion of a text directly in Arabic in a work destined for a French audience but also quite certainly explains the meaning, until now obscure, of the conversation Hugo von Hofmannsthal portrays the two men having in Vienna in 1842 [*sic*], "On Character in the Novel and the Drama" (1902). Here we witness the formation of an artistic network that irrigates, starting from the Orientalist Hammer-Purgstall, all of Western Europe, from Goethe to Hofmannsthal, including Hugo, Rückert, and Balzac himself.

This summary is impeccable, I had completely forgotten this article, it is indeed *Viennese*, as she said—she had asked me to find the engraving of the Hainfeld castle that Hammer sent to Balzac in a letter soon after his stay. Sarah adds a French element to the theory (defended also by Hofmannsthal) that Austria is the land of encounters, a frontier land much richer in contacts and fusions than Germany itself, which, on the contrary, seeks to extirpate the *other* from its culture, to plunge into the depths of the *self*, in Sarah-like terms, even if this quest is bound to result in the greatest violence. This idea deserves to be studied—I must have received this article in Istanbul, then, judging from the little note that asks me if I'd "come back to Vienna or to Tübingen"; she thanks me for the photos she had requested, but I'm the one who should have thanked her: she'd given me the opportunity to visit a magnificent neighborhood in Istanbul where I would never have gone otherwise, far from tourists and from the usual image of the Ottoman capital, Hasköy the inaccessible at the bottom of the Golden Horn—if I look carefully I should be able to find the letter where she asked me to go photograph for her (today no doubt the internet makes this sort of excursion pointless) the school of the Alliance Israélite Universelle, which her maternal great-grandfather had attended in the 1890s, and there was something very moving in going, without her, to discover these sites from which she came, so to speak, but which neither she nor her mother had ever seen. I have absolutely no idea how a Jew from Turkey had ended up in French Algeria before the First World War, and Sarah isn't sure she knows herself—one of the many mysteries of the twentieth century, which often hide violence and pain.

It was raining over Hasköy, one of those Istanbul rains that swirl around in the wind and, even though it's just a fine mist, can soak you to the bone in a second at a street corner; I carefully sheltered my camera in my raincoat, I had two rolls of 36-exposure color film, 400 ASA, a real archaeology these words are today—are the negatives still somewhere in my box of photos, it's highly likely. I also had a map of the city, which I knew from experience was very incomplete when it came to street names, and an entirely Viennese umbrella with a wooden handle. Getting as far as Hasköy was quite something: you had to go around by the north via Shishli, or else follow the Golden Horn through Kasimpasha, a forty-five minute walk from Cihangir over the hills of Beyoglu. I cursed Sarah when a car spattered the bottom of my pants with mud as it rushed past me, and almost postponed indefinitely this expedition that was starting out in the most inauspicious way, already covered in filth, raincoat spotted, feet soaking, just ten minutes after emerging from the house where Faugier, observing the clouds darkening the Bosphorus, hung over from his raki from the night before, tea in hand, had kindly warned me: it's not a fit day to put an Orientalist out of doors. I decided to take a taxi, which I had wanted to avoid, obviously not out of stinginess, but simply because I didn't know how to explain to the driver where I was going: I settled for *Hasköy eskelesi, lütfen,* and after a good half hour of traffic jams I found myself by the water, on the Golden Horn, in front of a little, entirely charming harbor; behind me, one of those very steep colorful hills so peculiar to Istanbul, a precipitous street whose asphalt was covered in a fine layer of rain, a transparent stream that gently trickled down the slope to join the sea — this strange aquatic ascension reminded me of our amusements by the mountain waterfalls in Austria; I would leap from one side of the lane to the other according to the whims of this urban river, not too sure where to go; the inconvenience of having wet shoes was largely compensated for by the pleasure of the game. I imagine the passersby must have thought that a mad tourist afflicted with hydrophilia was mistaking himself for a trout in their neighborhood. After a few hundred meters and a fruitless attempt to unfold my map under my umbrella, a man of a certain age with a short white beard came up to me, looked me up and down from head to toe, and asked, in English: "Are you a Jew?"

Since obviously I didn't understand, I replied What? or How's that again?, before he explained his question, smiling: "I can do a good Jewish Tour for you."

I had been approached by a prophet who had just saved me from the flood — Ilya Virano was one of the pillars of the Jewish community in Hasköy, he had seen me lost and had guessed (as he himself acknowledged, the neighborhood wasn't exactly overflowing with tourists) that I was probably looking for something that had to do with the Jewish history of the neighborhood, through which he guided us, my camera and me, for the rest of the day. Mr. Virano spoke perfect French, which he had learned at a bilingual school in Istanbul; his native language was Ladino, whose history he explained to me: the Jews who had been chased out of Spain and had settled in the Empire had brought their language with them, and this Renaissance Spanish had evolved with them in their exile. The Jews of Istanbul were either Byzantine or Sephardic or Ashkenazic or Karaite, by their order of arrival in the capital (the mysterious Karaites were more or less the last to arrive, most of them having moved there after the Crimean War) and it was absolutely miraculous to hear Ilya Virano recount the high points of this multiculturalism, through the buildings in the district: the Karaite synagogue was the most impressive, almost fortified, surrounded by high walls enclosing little wood-and-stone houses, some of which were inhabited, and others threatened with ruin—my naïveté made Ilya Virano smile when I asked him if their occupants were still Karaite: it's been a long time since there were any Karaites here.

Most of the Jewish families of Istanbul have moved elsewhere, to more modern neighborhoods—Shishli or the other side of the Bosphorus—or else emigrated to Israel or the United States. Ilya Virano explained all that without any nostalgia, very simply, in the same way he initiated me into the theological and ritual differences between the many branches of Judaism during our tour, walking alertly through the steep streets, almost respectful of my ignorance; he asked the family name of this ancestor I was trying to trace: it's too bad you don't know, he said, there could still be some cousins here.

Mr. Virano must have been around sixty-five; he was tall, quite elegant, with an athletic build; his suit, short beard, and slicked-back hair gave him the look of a young film star on his way to pick up a girl at her parents' to take her to the school dance, in a slightly grayer version of course. He talked a lot, happy that I understood French: most tourists on the Jewish Tours are Americans or Israelis, and he had little opportunity, he said, to practice this beautiful language.

The old temple of the Jews expelled from Majorca, the Mayor Synagogue, was occupied by a little workshop for mechanical things; it had preserved its wooden dome, columns, and Hebrew inscriptions; its outbuildings served as warehouses.

I had come to the end of my first roll of film, and we hadn't yet reached the old lycée of the Alliance Israélite Universelle; it had stopped raining and, unlike my host, I felt an onset of slight melancholy, an inexplicable, vague sadness — all these sites were closed and looked abandoned; the sole synagogue still functioning, with its Byzantine marble pillars along the façade, was used only for special occasions; a quarter of the big cemetery had been removed by the construction of a motorway and had been taken over by weeds. The only mausoleum of importance, belonging to a great family, Virano explained — such a great family that it owned a palace on the Golden Horn, where some military institution is now housed — looked like an old Roman temple, a forgotten place of prayer, whose sole colors were the red and blue graffiti written on it; a temple of the dead that overlooked the hill where we had a bird's-eye view of the end of the Golden Horn, when it stops being an estuary and becomes again a simple river, in the midst of cars, factory chimneys, and large blocks of buildings. The gravestones looked as if they were thrown here and there down the slope (laid flat, as custom dictates, my guide explained), sometimes broken, often illegible — he deciphered the family names for me, though: Hebrew resists the passage of time better than Latin characters, he said, and I had trouble understanding this theory, but the fact is that he managed to pronounce the names of these dead and sometime find their descendants or relatives, without any apparent emotion; he climbed up here often, he said; ever since the highway was built there are no more goats, no more goats so fewer goat droppings but grass galore, he said. Hands in my pockets, strolling between the graves, I searched for something to say; there was graffiti here and there, I said *anti-Semitism?* He replied no, *love*, what do you mean, love, yes, a boy who wrote the name of his beloved, *To Hülya forever*, or something along those lines, and I realized that there was nothing here to desecrate that time and the city hadn't already desecrated, and that no doubt soon the graves, their remains and their slabs, would be moved and piled up elsewhere to give way to excavators; I thought of Sarah, I didn't take any pictures of the cemetery, didn't dare take out my camera, even if she had nothing to do with all this, even if no one had anything to do with this disaster that was all of ours, and I asked Ilya Virano to please show me where the Alliance Israélite school was, as a fine sun was beginning to shine on the waters of the promenade called the *Eaux-Douces d'Europe* and illuminate Istanbul all the way to the Bosphorus.

The lycée's neoclassical façade was dark gray, punctuated by white pilasters; there was no inscription on the triangular pediment. It stopped being a school a long time ago, Ilya Virano explained; today it's a retirement home — I conscientiously photographed the entrance and the courtyard; a few very old pensioners were taking the air on a bench under a covered porch; I thought, as Mr. Virano went to greet them, that they must have begun their lives within these walls, that they had studied Hebrew, Turkish, French here, that they had played on this patio, had loved here, copied poems, and argued over insurmountable trifles and that now, the circle closed, in the same slightly austere building with the immaculate tiled floor, they were gently ending their days, looking out the windows, from the top of their hill, watching Istanbul advance with great strides into modernity.

11:58 P.M.

Aside from this note found in the article on Balzac, I don't remember Sarah ever talking to me again about those photos of Istanbul snatched from the rain and from oblivion—I returned depressed to Cihangir, I wanted to say to Bilger (who was having tea at our place when I arrived) that archaeology seemed to me the saddest of activities, that I saw no poetry in ruin, or any pleasure in rummaging through disappearance.

I still know very little about Sarah's family, aside from the fact that her mother spent her childhood in Algiers, that she left and moved to Paris when Algeria became independent; I don't know if the great-grandfather from Istanbul was on that journey. Sarah was born a few years later in Saint-Cloud, and grew up in Passy, in the 16th arrondissement, which she referred to as a very nice neighborhood, with its parks and playgrounds, its old patisseries and noble boulevards—what a strange coincidence that we both spent part of our childhoods near a house of Balzac's: she on rue Raynouard, where the great man had lived for a long time, and I a few kilometers from Saché, the little Touraine château where he frequently stayed. It was almost an obligatory excursion every summer, during our vacation at Grandmother's house, to visit Monsieur de Balzac; this château had the advantage of being much less visited than the other ones in the area (Azay-le-Rideau or Langeais) and was a *cultural resource*, in Mother's words — I imagine that Grandmother would be happy to know that this Balzac whom she regarded a bit as her cousin (after all, they had both gone to school in Tours) had also come to Vienna, like her; she visited us once or twice, but, like Balzac, she didn't like traveling, and complained that she couldn't abandon her garden for long, any more than Honoré could his characters.

Balzac visited Vienna, where he met his great love, Mme Hanska, in May 1835. "On March 24, 1835," notes Hammer-Purgstall, "while returning from an evening in pleasant company at the home of Comtesse Rzewuska [maiden name of Ewelina Hanska], I found a letter from Captain Hall [we should note here that Captain Hall is none other than Basil Hall (1788–1844), navy officer, friend of Walter Scott, author of many travel accounts and especially of *Hainfeld's Castle: A Winter in Lower Styria*, which would inspire Sheridan Le Fanu to write his novel *Carmilla*][18] which informed me of the gravity of the state of health of my dear Baroness Purgstall, who was dying."[19]

We know, then, that it was through the intermediary of Mme Hanska that the great Orientalist knew Balzac's work, and that he had already been visiting the Countess and her friends for some time.[20] It was only when he returned to Styria, in April, after the death of the Baroness, that Joseph von Hammer learned that Balzac was coming to spend a few weeks in Vienna.[21] They visited each other, liked each other. Hammer even gives us some idea of the European fame of the novelist: one day, he writes, when he went to Balzac's Viennese domicile, he was told that Balzac was absent, and had gone to visit Prince Metternich; Hammer decided to join him at the palace, since he was supposed to be going there himself. He found a crowd in the antechamber, and the chamberlain explained to him that all these gentlemen were waiting for their audience, but that the Prince had locked himself inside with Balzac for over two hours already, and forbade anyone to disturb him.[22]

Incredible to think that Metternich himself was so enthralled by this debt-ridden man, who was living in Paris under assumed names, running around Europe pursuing the woman he loved, between writing novels. What could they have been talking about, for two hours? European politics? Balzac's opinions on the government of Louis-Philippe? *La Peau de chagrin*? Sarah's article especially foregrounds Mme Hanska's role as mediator between Balzac and the Orient; when Hammer finally gave Balzac the Arabic translation of the text that is included in *La Peau de chagrin*, he did so through Countess Rzewuska. Similarly, the interview with Metternich is certainly thanks to her. I imagine Balzac in Saché, holed up with his papers, pen, and coffeemaker, scarcely going out, and then only to wander around the park and stretch his legs; he *lived like an oyster*, as he said; he would go down to the river, collect a few fallen chestnuts and throw them in the water, before climbing back up to pick up *Le Père Goriot* where he had left off; is he the same man as the hopeless lover of Vienna, always rejected by the prudish Évelyne Hanska, turned down for fifteen years, that says a lot about Balzac's strength of character and patience. He ended up marrying her, in 1850, that's reassuring; just before dying five months later, which is less so. Maybe it was partly desire that kept this staggering man from falling, you get the impression that Balzac ruined himself in work and writing because he was staggering, because his life (outside of his sentences, where he is God) escaped him, that he tottered from creditor to creditor, from impossible love to unsatisfied desire and that only books are a world made to his measure, he who was a printer before being a writer. Three thousand pages of letters, that is the monument he built to his love, and often, he spoke to Évelyne about Vienna, about his future journey to Vienna, where he hoped to go to visit Wagram and the battlefields in Essling, since he had it in mind to write a story about a battle, a formidable battle story, which would take place entirely in the heart of combat, without ever leaving it, in one furious day; like Sarah in Saint-Gothard, I picture Balzac pacing up and down Aspern, taking notes, imagining the troop movements on the hills, the place where Maréchal Lannes was fatally wounded, locating the lines of sight, the trees in the distance, the shape of the hills, all things that he will never write, because he lingered in Vienna and this project may only have been a pretext: he will be too occupied, afterward, wrestling with *La Comédie humaine* to find the time to give substance to this idea — just as Sarah, as far as I know, never wrote in detail about her vision of the battle of Morgersdorf, mixing all the stories, Turkish and Christian, accompanied by the music of Pál Esterházy, if she ever planned to do so.

Oh look, in this article Sarah reproduces the engraving of Hainfeld castle that Hammer-Purgstall sent to Balzac after he went back to Paris, I must have visited all the antique shops in Vienna to do her this favor — Hammer-Purgstall sent an image of his castle to his friends the way we'd send a photograph today, that kind Hammer-Purgstall whom Balzac says is "patient as a goat straining at its tether" and to whom he will dedicate *The Cabinet of Antiquities*, to thank him for his knowledge of Orientalism. I suppose I was running around all the antique dealers in Vienna like Balzac behind Évelyne Hanska, madly, until I got my hands on this image, which she reproduces in the midst of quotations from the correspondence related to his stay in Vienna:

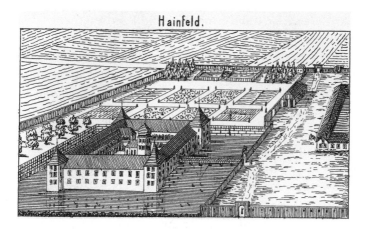

Hainfeld.

April 28, 1834: If I were rich, I'd enjoy sending you a painting, an Interior of Algiers, painted by Delacroix, which seems excellent to me.[31]

March 9, 1834: Between now and Vienna, there's nothing but work and solitude.[32]

August 11, 1834: Oh, to spend the winter in Vienna. I'll be there, yes.[33]

August 25, 1834: I truly need to see Vienna. I must explore the fields of Wagram and Essling before next June. I especially need engravings that show the uniforms of the German army, and I will go look for them. Have the goodness to tell me only whether or not they exist.[34]

October 18, 1834: Yes, I've breathed in a little of the Touraine autumn; I've imitated the plant, the oyster, and when the sky was so clear, I thought that was an omen and that a dove would come from Vienna with a green branch in its beak.[35]

Poor Balzac, what did he get in Vienna, a few kisses and some promises, if we are to believe these letters that Sarah quotes abundantly—and I, who so looked forward to her coming to my capital, to the point of buying new clothes and getting my hair cut each time she came, what did I get, another offprint I don't dare decipher—life ties knots, life ties knots and they're rarely those on St. Francis's cincture; we meet, we run after one another, for years, in the dark, and when we think we finally hold another's hand in ours, death takes everything away from us.

Jane Digby does not appear in Sarah's article on Balzac and the Orient, but she's one of the indirect links between the man from Touraine and Syria; the beautiful, sublime Jane Digby, whose body, face, and dreamy eyes wrought such havoc in nineteenth-century Europe and the Orient—one of the most surprising lives of the time, one of the most *adventurous*, in every sense of the word. A scandalous Englishwoman, divorced at twenty, banished for her "promiscuity" by Victorian England, then successively mistress of an Austrian nobleman, wife of a Bavarian baron, lover of King Ludwig I of Bavaria, married to a Greek nobleman answering to the magnificent name of Count Spyridon Theotokis, finally abducted (not unwillingly) by an Albanian pirate, Lady Jane Ellenborough née Digby ended up finding stability in love in the desert, between Damascus and Palmyra, in the arms of Sheikh Medjuel el-Mezrab, prince of the tribe of the Annazahs, a man twenty years her junior, whom she married when she was over fifty. She lived the last twenty years of her life in Syria, in the most perfect happiness, or almost— she experienced the horrors of war during the 1860 massacres, when she was saved by the intervention of Emir Abd el-Kader, exiled in Damascus, who protected many Syrian and European Christians. But no doubt the most atrocious episode of her existence took place much earlier, in Italy, in Bagni di Lucca, at the foot of the Apennines. That evening, Leonidas, her six-year-old son, whom she loved immensely, wanted to join his mother, whom he saw down below, in front of the hotel porch, from his bedroom balcony—he leaned over, fell, and was crushed on the terrace floor, at his mother's feet, dead instantaneously.

It was perhaps this horrible accident that prevented Jane from experiencing happiness anywhere else but at the end of the world, in the desert of oblivion and love—her life, like Sarah's, is a long road to the East, a series of stations that led her, inexorably, ever further toward the Orient in search of something indefinable. Balzac met this extraordinary woman at the beginning of her immense journey, in Paris at first, around 1835, when "Lady Ell" was cheating on her Bavarian Baron von Venningen with Theotokis; Balzac tells Mme Hanska that Lady Ell had just run away again with a Greek, that her husband arrived, dueled with the Greek, left him for dead and brought his wife home before having the lover treated—"what a singular woman," Balzac notes. Then, a few years later, returning from Vienna, he stops at the castle of Weinheim, near Heidelberg, to visit Jane; he relates these days by letter to Mme Hanska and we can legitimately suspect that he is lying, so as not to set off Évelyne's jealous rages, which we know were frequent, when he says "another one of those accusations that make me laugh." I wonder if Balzac was indeed seduced by the scandalous adventuress with the blue eyes, it's possible; we know she was partly the inspiration for the character of Lady Arabelle Dudley in his *Lily of the Valley*, Lady Dudley the conquering, the loving, the carnal. I read that novel a few miles from Saché, in those Touraine landscapes where Lady Dudley and that idiot Félix de Vandenesse galloped; I cried for the poor Henriette, who died from sadness—I was a little jealous, too, of the erotic pleasures the fiery Arabelle offered Félix. Already Balzac was contrasting a chaste, dull West with the delights of the Orient; you get the impression he's glimpsing—through the paintings of Delacroix, which he so appreciates, and in the Orientalist imagination that's already being woven—Jane Digby's later fate, like a prophet or a seer: "Her desire goes like a whirlwind in the desert, the desert whose ardent immensity appears to her, the desert full of azure, with its inalterable sky, with its cool starry nights," he writes about Lady Dudley before a long comparison of the West and the East, Lady Dudley like the Orient "exuding her soul, enveloping her devotees in a luminous atmosphere," and at Grandmother's house, in that squat armchair with the embroidered antimacassar, near the window whose white lace curtains let the light through, already filtered by the thin oaks at the forest's edge, I pictured myself on horseback with that British huntress Diana while still wishing (I was at the edge of childhood) that Félix would end up marrying the gloomy Henriette, hesitating as I too was between the transports of the soul and the pleasures of the flesh.

Balzac and Hanska, Majnun and Layla, Jane Digby and Sheikh Medjuel, there's some good material for a book, a book, why not, I could write a book, I can already picture the cover:

On the Divers Forms of Lunacie in the Orient
Volume the First
Orientalists in Love

There would be some good material there, with all sorts of people gone mad from love, happy or unhappy, mystical or pornographic, women and men, if only I were good for anything besides harping over old stories, sitting in my bed, if I had the energy of Balzac or Liszt, and especially the health—I don't know what will happen to me over the next few days, I'll have to give myself up to medicine, that is, to the worst, I can't picture myself at all in the hospital, what will I do with my nights of insomnia?

Victor Hugo the Oriental relates the dying agony of Balzac in *Things Seen*: M. de Balzac was in his bed, he says, his head resting on a pile of pillows to which they had added red Damascus cushions borrowed from the bedroom sofa. His face was purple, almost black, leaning to the right, beard unshaven, hair gray and cut short, eyes open and staring. An unbearable odor emanated from the bed. Hugo lifted the blanket and took Balzac's hand. It was covered in sweat. He squeezed it. Balzac did not respond to the pressure. An old woman—standing guard—and a male servant stood on either side of the bed. A candle was burning on a table behind the head of the bed, another on a commode near the door. A silver vase was placed on the bedside table. The man and the woman remained silent with a kind of terror, listening to the dying man groaning noisily, Mme Hanska had gone back to her room, no doubt because she couldn't bear her husband's death rattle, his agony: Hugo relates all sorts of horrors about the abscess on Balzac's leg, which had been lanced a few days before.

What a curse the body is, why didn't they give Balzac opium or morphine as they did to Heinrich Heine, poor Heine's body, he too, Heine, convinced he was dying slowly of syphilis whereas doctors today are more inclined to diagnose it as multiple sclerosis, in any case a long degenerative disease that confined him to bed *for years*, good Lord, a scientific article itemizes the doses of morphine that Heine took, helped by a kind pharmacist who had made this recent innovation available to him, morphine, the essence of the sap of the divine poppy—at least in the twenty-first century they don't refuse a dying man this medication, they just try to withhold it from the living. I forget which French writer reproached us for being alive while Beethoven is dead, which had irritated me no end, the title was *When I Think That Beethoven Is Dead While So Many Imbeciles Are Alive*, or something similar, it divided humanity into two categories, the idiots, and the Beethovens, and it was pretty clear that this author certainly counted himself among the Beethovens, whose immortal glory would redeem present defects, and he wished us all dead, to avenge the death of the maestro from Bonn: in that Parisian bookstore, Sarah, who sometimes lacks discernment, found this title funny — she must have reproached me once again for my seriousness, my intransigence, as if she weren't — intransigent, that is. The bookstore was on the Place de Clichy, at the end of our expedition to the home of Sadegh Hedayat on rue Championnet and to the Montmartre cemetery where we had seen the graves of Heine and Berlioz, before a dinner in a pleasant brasserie with a German name, I think. Probably my anger against that book (whose author also seems to me to have a German patronymic, another coincidence) was a desire on my part to draw attention to myself, to make myself noticed at the expense of that writer, to shine for my knowledge of Beethoven — Sarah was in the midst of writing her thesis, she had eyes only for Sadegh Hedayat or Annemarie Schwarzenbach. She had lost a lot of weight, was working fourteen or even sixteen hours a day, rarely went out, was thrashing about in her research, eating almost nothing; and despite it all she looked happy. After the incident in Aleppo, in the Baron Hotel room, I hadn't seen her for months, suffocated as I was by shame. It was very selfish on my part to bother her mid-thesis with my jealousy, what a pretentious idiot: I was acting jealous when I should have been taking care of her, looking after her, and above all not getting on my Beethovenian high horse, which I've noticed, with time, never makes me very popular with women. Maybe, at bottom, what annoyed me so much about the title, *When I Think That Beethoven Is Dead While So Many Imbeciles Are Alive*, is that its author had found a way to make himself funny and sympathetic in talking about Beethoven, something that generations of musicologists, mine included, have sought to do in vain.

Joseph von Hammer-Purgstall the Orientalist, him again, relates that he visited Beethoven in Vienna through Dr. Glossé. What a world these capitals were in the early nineteenth century, where Orientalists visited princes, Balzacs, and musicians of genius. His memoirs even contain a terrifying anecdote, from 1815: Hammer is attending a concert of Beethoven's, in one of those extraordinary Viennese salons; you can easily picture the cabriole chairs, the footmen, the hundreds of candles, the crystal chandeliers; it's cold, it's winter, the winter of the Congress of Vienna, and the home of Countess Thérèse Apponyi, the hostess, has been heated as much as possible—she is barely thirty, she does not know that a few years later she will have *le Tout-Paris* under her charm; Antoine and Thérèse Apponyi will be the hosts, at their Embassy in the faubourg Saint-Germain, of all the writers, artists, and important musicians there are in the French capital. The noble Austrian couple will be friends with Chopin, Liszt, the scandalous George Sand; they will play host to Balzac, Hugo, Lamartine and all the troublemakers of 1830. But that winter evening, it's Beethoven who is her guest; Beethoven, who hasn't gone out in society for months—like the big cats it's no doubt hunger that draws him out of his sad lair, he needs money, love and money. So he gives a concert for Countess Apponyi and her immense circle of friends, including Hammer. The diplomat Orientalist is indeed in the court during the Congress of Vienna, where he became close to Metternich; he associated with Talleyrand, about whom no one can decide whether he's a perverse ferret or a haughty falcon—a beast of prey, in any case. Europe is celebrating peace, rediscovering equilibrium in the game of power, and especially the end of

Napoleon, who is stamping his feet on the island of Elba; the Hundred Days will pass like a shiver of fear in the spine of an Englishman. Napoleon Bonaparte is the inventor of Orientalism, he's the one who drags science behind his army into Egypt and makes Europe penetrate the Orient beyond the Balkans for the first time. Knowledge rushes behind the soldiers and the merchants, into Egypt, India, China; texts translated from Arabic and Persian begin to invade Europe, Goethe the great oak started the race; long before Hugo's *Les Orientales*, at the very time Chateaubriand was inventing travel literature with his *Itinerary: From Paris to Jerusalem*, as Beethoven is playing that night for the little Italian countess married to a Hungarian surrounded by the finest costumes in Vienna, the immense Goethe is putting the final touches on his *West-östlicher Divan*, directly inspired by the translation of Hafez that Hammer-Purgstall published (Hammer-Purgstall is there of course, they take his coat, he bends forward to pretend to brush his lips against the glove of Teresa Apponyi, smiling, for he knows her very well, her husband is also a diplomat in the Metternich circle) in 1812, while that dragon Napoleon, that horrible Mediterranean, was thinking he could confront the Russians and their terrifying winter, three thousand leagues from France. That evening, as Napoleon is tapping his foot waiting for the boats in Elba, there is Beethoven, and there is the old Hafez, and Goethe, and thus Schubert, who will set to music some poems from the *West-östlicher Divan*, and Mendelssohn, and Schumann, and Strauss, and Schönberg, they too will use these poems by Goethe the immense, and next to Countess Apponyi is the impetuous Chopin, who will dedicate two Nocturnes to her; near Hammer sit Rückert and Mowlana Jalal ad-Din Rumi — and Ludwig van Beethoven, the master of all these fine people, sits down to the piano.

We can picture Talleyrand, warmed all of a sudden by the

faience stoves, dozing off even before the composer's fingers touch the keyboard; Talleyrand that lame devil who has played all night, but cards, not music: a little game of faro with wine, lots of wine, and his eyes are drooping. He's the most elegant of defrocked bishops, and the most original as well; he has served God, Louis XVI, the Convention, the Directory, Napoleon, and Louis XVIII, he will serve Louis-Philippe and become the statesman the French will look up to above all others, the French who sincerely believe that functionaries should be like Talleyrand, like permanent buildings and churches that resist all storms and embody the famous *continuity of State*, that is, the spinelessness of those who subordinate their convictions to power, whatever it may be — Talleyrand will pay homage to Bonaparte's expedition to Egypt and to all the knowledge that Denon and his scholars brought back about ancient Egypt, instructing his own body to be embalmed *à l'égyptienne*, mummified, going along with the fashion for pharaohs that invaded Paris, putting a little of the Orient into his coffin, Talleyrand the prince who had always dreamed of transforming his boudoir into a harem.

Joseph Hammer doesn't fall asleep, he's a music lover; he appreciates fine society, good company, splendid gatherings — he's a little over forty, and from years of experience of the Levant, he speaks six languages perfectly, has spent time with the Turks, the English and the French, and appreciates, though for different reasons, these three nations whose qualities he has been able to admire. He is an Austrian, son of a provincial civil servant, and all he lacks is a castle and a title to fulfill the Destiny he feels is his — he'll have to wait for both twenty more years and a stroke of luck to inherit Hainfeld and the barony that accompanies it, to become *von* Hammer-Purgstall.

Beethoven greets the audience. These years are much harder for him, he has just lost his brother Carl and has begun lengthy

proceedings to gain custody of his nephew; the onset of his deafness is isolating him more and more. He's forced to use those
enormous, strangely shaped copper ear trumpets that you can
see in Bonn, in a glass case in the Beethovenhaus, and that make
him look like a centaur. He is in love, but with a love that he
senses, either because of his illness or the young woman's high
birth, will produce nothing but music; like Harriet for Berlioz,
the object of that love is there, in the room; Beethoven starts to
play his twenty-seventh sonata, composed a few months earlier,
with vivacity, feeling, and expression.

The audience trembles a little; there's a murmur that Beethoven can't hear: Hammer relates that the piano, perhaps because
of the heating, hasn't kept its tune and sounds terribly off-key—
Beethoven's fingers play perfectly, and he can hear, internally,
his music as it should sound; for the audience, it's a sonorous
catastrophe, and although Beethoven can see his beloved from
time to time, he must perceive, little by little, that the faces are
overcome by embarrassment—shame, even, at witnessing the
great man's humiliation in this way. Fortunately Countess Apponyi is a lady of tact, she applauds loudly, discreetly motions
to shorten the recital, and we can picture Beethoven's sadness,
when he understands what a horrible farce he's been victim
of—this will be his last concert, Hammer tells us. I like to imagine that when Beethoven composes, a few weeks later, the lieder
cycle *An die ferne Geliebte*, to the distant beloved, it's that distance
of deafness he's thinking about, which is distancing him from
the world more surely than exile, and even though we still don't
know, despite the passionate research of the specialists, who
this young woman was, we can guess, in the final *Nimm sie hin
denn, diese Lieder*, all the sadness of the artist who can no longer
sing or play the melodies he writes for the woman he loves.

For years, I collected all possible performances of the Beethoven piano sonatas, good and bad, predictable and surprising, dozens of records, CDs, tapes, and every time I hear the second movement of the twenty-seventh, although very *cantabile*, I can't help but think of the shame and embarrassment, the shame and embarrassment of all declarations of love that fall flat, and I'll blush with shame sitting in my bed with the light on if I think of that again, we play our sonata all alone without realizing the piano is out of tune, overcome by our emotions: others hear how off-key we sound, and at best feel sincere pity, at worst a terrible annoyance at being confronted with our humiliation that sullies them when they themselves had, usually, asked for nothing— Sarah had asked for nothing, that night in the Baron Hotel, or else she did, maybe, I don't have a clue, I confess I've forgotten, today, after all this time, after Tehran, the years, tonight, as I'm plunging into illness like Beethoven and as, despite this morning's mysterious article, Sarah is more distant than ever, *ferne Geliebte*, fortunately I don't write poems, and I stopped writing music a long time ago.

My last visit to the Beethovenhaus in Bonn for that lecture on "*The Ruins of Athens* and the Orient" was a few years back, and that too was marked by shame and humiliation, the humiliation of poor Bilger's madness—I can see him again standing in the front row, saliva on his lips, beginning by ranting on about Kotzebue (the author of the libretto for *The Ruins of Athens* who'd asked nothing of anyone either and whose sole claim to fame is probably getting stabbed to death), and then Bilger went on to jumble everything together, archaeology and anti-Muslim racism, since the "Chorus of Dervishes" I had just spoken about mentions the Prophet and the Kaaba and that's why it's never performed these days, Bilger shouted, we respect al-Qaida too much, our world is in danger, no one is interested in Greek or Roman archaeology anymore, only al-Qaida, and Beethoven had realized you have to bring both sides together in music, the East and the West, to drive away the end of the world that's approaching and you, Franz (this is when the lady from the Beethovenhaus turned to me with a concerned look which I answered with a cowardly, dubious look signifying "I have absolutely no idea who this crackpot is") you know this but you don't say it, you know that art is threatened, that it's a symptom of the end of the world, all these people turning to Islam, to Hinduism and Buddhism, you just have to read Hermann Hesse to know this, archaeology is a science of the earth and everyone's forgetting it, just as we forget that Beethoven is the only German prophet— I was overcome with a sudden and terrifying need to urinate, suddenly I stopped hearing what Bilger was jabbering on about, standing in the middle of the audience, I could listen to nothing but my body and my bladder, it felt as if it were about to explode, I said to myself "I drank tea, I drank too much tea," I'm not going to make it, I have a formidable desire to piss, I'll wet my pants and my socks, it's terrible, in front of everyone, I won't be able to hold it in much longer, I must have turned visibly paler and as Bilger was still stammering his inaudible curses against me I got up and ran, squirming, hand on my crotch, to take refuge in the toilet, while behind me a thunder of applause greeted my departure, interpreted as my repudiation of the mad orator. When I returned, Bilger was gone; he had left, the brave lady from the Beethovenhaus told me, soon after my disappearance, not without first calling me a coward and a traitor, for which, I have to admit, he was not wrong.

This incident had saddened me profoundly; although I was delighted to see in detail the objects in the Bodmer collection, I spent scarcely ten minutes in the museum rooms; the curator accompanying me noticed my low spirits and tried to reassure me, you know, madmen, they're everywhere, she said, and even though her intention was laudable, the idea that there could be insane people like Bilger *everywhere* only compounded my depression. Had his excessive stays in the Orient made a pre-existent crack in his soul widen, had he contracted a spiritual disease over there, or might Turkey and Syria have nothing to do with any of it, might he have become just as mad without ever leaving Bonn, no one knows—a client for your neighbor, Sarah would have said, referring to Freud, and I confess I have absolutely no idea if the kind of paranoid delirium Bilger had might be *beyond* the help of psychoanalysis, more likely treatable by trepanation, despite all the sympathy good Dr. Sigmund and his acolytes aroused in me. "You are resisting," Sarah would have said; she had explained to me the extraordinary concept of *resistance* in psychoanalysis, I forget why, and I had been outraged by the simplicity of the argument, anything that goes against psychoanalytic theory falls into the realm of *resistance*, referring to sick people who refuse to get better, refuse to see light in the words of the good doctor. That's certainly my case, now that I think about it, I resist, I've resisted for years, I have never even entered the apartment of the cocaine-addicted specialist in the sexual lives of infants, I didn't even go with Sarah when she went, whatever you like, I said, I have no problem going to see women cut open in an anatomy museum but I won't visit that charlatan's apartment, in any case nothing has changed, you know, the fraud continues: they'll make you pay a fortune to see a completely empty apartment, since his possessions, his couch, his rug, his crystal ball, and his paintings of nude women are all in London. That was obviously bad faith, another way of trying to show off, I have nothing against Freud, of course, and she had guessed that, as usual. Maybe Freud could manage to make me fall asleep with his hypnotizer's pendulum, it's been an hour now that I've been sitting in my bed with the light on, glasses on my nose, article in hand, staring stupidly at the shelves of my bookcase—"The times are so bad that I've decided to talk to myself," said that Spanish essayist, Gómez de la Serna, and I understand him.

I too am managing to talk to myself.

To sing, even, sometimes.

Everything is quiet at Gruber's place. He must be sleeping, he'll get up around four a.m. for his needs, his bladder doesn't leave him alone, a little like mine in Bonn, how shameful, when I think about it, everyone thought I left the hall outraged by Bilger's statements, I should have shouted to him "Remember Damascus! Remember the Palmyra desert!" and maybe he'd have started awake, like a patient of Freud's who suddenly discovers, mid-session, that he has confused the "wee-wee maker" of his father with that of a horse and all of a sudden finds himself immensely relieved by this—that story of Little Hans is incredible all the same, I forget his real name but I know that afterward this man became an opera director, and that he agitated all his life for opera to be a popular spectacle, what became of his phobia of horses, did the good Dr. Freud cure him of it, I have no idea, one would hope he stopped using the expression "wee-wee maker" at least. Why opera? Probably because you come across a lot fewer "wee-wee makers" there than in, say, the cinema— and hardly any horses. I had refused to go with Sarah to Freud's place, I had stood my ground (or resisted, according to the terminology). She'd returned delighted, overflowing with energy, her cheeks red from the cold (a fine freezing wind was blowing over Vienna that day), I was waiting for her in the Maximilian café at the corner of the Votivkirche square, reading the paper, well-hidden in a corner behind the *Standard*, which is barely big enough to hide you from the students and colleagues who frequent this establishment, but which had at the time brought out a series of DVDs of a hundred Austrian films and deserved to be rewarded for this interesting initiative, this celebration of Austrian cinema; obviously, one of the first of the series was *The Piano Teacher*, a terrifying movie adapted from the novel by the no less terrifying Elfriede Jelinek, and I was thinking about these slightly sad things sheltering behind my *Standard* when Sarah returned all bright and cheerful from Mr. Freud's place: I immediately mixed up in my head little Hans with Jelinek's agoraphobia and her desire to cut off all "wee-wee makers"—men's as well as horses'.

Sarah had made a discovery, she couldn't get over it; she pushed back the newspaper and caught my hand, her fingers were freezing.

SARAH (*agitated, childlike*). You know what? It's incredible, can you guess what the name of Dr. Freud's upstairs neighbor is?

FRANZ (*confused*). What? What neighbor of Freud?

SARAH (*slightly irritated*). On the mailbox. Freud's apartment is on the first floor. And there are people who live in the building.

FRANZ (*Viennese humor*). They must have to put up with the shouts of hysterical people—that must be even more annoying than my neighbor's dog.

SARAH (*patient smile*). No no, seriously, do you know what the name is of the lady who lives in the apartment above Freud's?

FRANZ (*detached, slightly haughty*). No idea.

SARAH (*victoriously*). Well her name is Hannah Kafka.

FRANZ (*blasé*). Kafka?

SARAH (*ecstatic smile*). I swear. It's a wonderful coincidence. Karmic. Everything is connected.

FRANZ (*shameless exaggeration*). That's a typical French reaction. There are lots of Kafkas in Vienna, it's a very common family name. My plumber's name is Kafka.

SARAH (*outraged by my failure to react, vexed*). But you have to admit it's still extraordinary!

FRANZ (*cowardly*). I'm pulling your leg. Of course it's extraordinary. It could be Franz's distant cousin, who knows.

SARAH (*beaming, radiating beauty*). Right? It's ... a *fantastic* discovery.

Kafka was one of her passions, one of her favorite "characters," and the fact that she could come across him in this way above Freud's apartment in Vienna delighted her. She loves reading the world as a series of coincidences, fortuitous encounters that give meaning to the whole, that outline *samsara*, the wool skein of interdependent phenomena; she had obviously pointed out to me that my name was Franz, like Kafka: I'd had to explain to her that it was the first name of my paternal grandfather, whose name was Franz Josef, because he was born on the day the emperor of the same name died, on November 21, 1916; my parents had been good enough not to inflict the *Josef* on me, which had given her a good laugh—Can you believe it, you should be called François-Joseph! (She later called me François-Joseph many times in letters or phone messages. Fortunately Mother never realized she was making fun of her patronymic choices, she'd have been very grieved to know it.) By chance, my brother is named not Maximilian but Peter, I'm not sure why. Mother always felt, ever since she arrived in Vienna in 1963, as if she were a French princess whom a young Hapsburg nobleman had brought from the countryside to show her the glamour of his brilliant capital—she had kept a very strong French accent, as if from a film of that period, I was terribly ashamed of her intonation when I was little, her way of accenting every phrase and every word in every phrase on the last syllable, sprinkling it all with a few nasal vowels; of course the Austrians find this accent *charmant, sehr charmant*. For that matter, the Syrians outside the big cities were so surprised a foreigner could speak even a few words of Arabic that they would open their eyes wide and redouble their efforts to try to penetrate the mysteries of the exotic articulation of the Franks; Sarah speaks Arabic or Persian much better than German, it must be said, and it's always been difficult for me to hear her speak our idiom, perhaps— what a horrible thought—because her pronunciation reminds me of my mother's. We won't venture out onto that slippery terrain, let's leave that field to the good doctor, the downstairs neighbor of Mme Kafka. Sarah told me that in Prague, Kafka is a hero like Mozart, Beethoven, or Schubert in Vienna; he has his museum, his statues, his square; the tourist office organizes Kafka Tours and you can buy magnets with the writer's portrait on them to stick on your huge fridge in Oklahoma City when you go home—no one knows why young Americans have become infatuated with Prague and Kafka; they hang out there in groups, lots of them, spend months in the Czech capital, years even, especially budding writers just out of universities where they majored in creative writing; they flock to Prague the way they used to gravitate to Paris, for inspiration; they keep blogs and fill notebooks or blacken virtual pages in cafés, drink liters and liters of Czech beer, and I'm sure you can still find some of them in the same spot ten years later, still putting the finishing touches on the first novel or short story collection that will propel them to fame—in Vienna fortunately we have mostly *old* Americans, couples of a respectable age who enjoy the excessive number of luxury hotels, wait in line to visit the Hofburg, eat *Sachertorte*, go to a concert where musicians play Mozart in wigs and costumes, and then walk home in the evening back to their hotel, arm in arm, with the sensation of traveling through the entire eighteenth and nineteenth centuries, pleasantly exhilarated by the fear that a cutthroat might emerge from one of the deserted, silent, baroque alleyways and rob them, they stay for two, three, four days and then go to Paris, Venice, Rome, or London before returning to their suburban houses in Dallas and showing their awestruck friends their photos and souvenirs. Ever since Chateaubriand people have been traveling to tell stories; they take pictures, the medium for memory and sharing; they tell how in Europe "the bedrooms are tiny," how in Paris "the entire hotel room was smaller than our bathroom," which provokes shivers among the audience — and also a glint of envy in their eyes, "Venice is magnificently decadent, the French are incredibly rude, in Europe there's wine in all the grocery stores and supermarkets, everywhere," and everyone is happy, and one dies having *seen the world*. Poor Stendhal, he didn't know what he was doing when he published his *Memoirs of a Tourist*, he invented much more than a word, "thank Heaven," he said, "the present voyage has no aspiration to statistics or science," without realizing he was pushing generations of travelers toward futility, with the help of heaven, what's more. Amusing that Stendhal is associated not only with the word "tourist," but also with the traveler's medical syndrome that bears his name; apparently the hospital in Florence has a separate psychiatric ward for foreigners swooning in front of the Uffizi or the Ponte Vecchio, a hundred of them every year, and I forget now who told me that in Jerusalem there was a special asylum for mystical madmen, that merely the *sight* of Jerusalem could provoke fevers, dizziness, appearances of the Virgin, Christ, and every prophet possible, in the midst of intifadas and Orthodox Jews who attack miniskirts and plunging necklines just as their Arabic peers attack the soldiers, with stones, in the old style, the *qadim jiddan* way, in the midst of all the planet holds in the way of secular scholars and religious men bent over venerable texts, Torahs, scriptures, and even Korans in all the ancient languages and all the European ones, depending on the schools, German,

Dutch, British and American Protestants, French, Spanish, and Italian Papists, including Austrians, Croats, Czechs, not to mention the pack of autocephalous churches, Greek, Armenian, Russian, Ethiopian, Egyptian, Syriac, all with their Uniate versions, added to the infinity of possible variants of Judaism, reformed or not, rabbinical or not, and Muslim schisms, Muslims for whom Jerusalem is indeed less important than Mecca, yet remains a very holy place, even if only because they don't want to abandon it to the other faiths: all these scholars, all these authorities were grouped into so many schools, scholarly journals, exegeses; Jerusalem was partitioned among translators, pilgrims, hermeneuts, and visionaries, in the midst of the whole caboodle of the mercantile circus, sellers of shawls, icons, oils (holy and culinary), olivewood crosses, jewelry more or less sacred, pious or profane images, and the song that rose to the ever-pure sky was an atrocious cacophony mixing polyphonies with cantilenas, pious monodies with the pagan lyres of soldiers. You had to see in Jerusalem the feet of this crowd and the diversity of its shoes: Christ-like sandals, with or without socks, *caligae*, leather boots, flip-flops, thong sandals, moccasins with the heels worn through; pilgrims, soldiers, or strolling merchants could recognize each other without lifting their eyes from the filthy ground of the old city of Jerusalem, where you also saw bare feet, blackened feet that had walked at least from the Ben Gurion airport, but sometimes farther, swollen, bandaged, bleeding, hairy or smooth, masculine or feminine extremities — you could spend days in Jerusalem just observing the feet of the multitude, head lowered, eyes down in a sign of fascinated humility.

Stendhal would look like a beginner with his Florentine swoon compared to the mystic drunkenness of the tourists in Jerusalem. I wonder what Dr. Freud would make of these distresses; I should ask Sarah, specialist in oceanic feeling and loss of self in all its forms — how to interpret my own spiritual emotions, this force, for instance, that pushes me to tears when I go to a concert, at certain times, moments that are so strong and so brief, when I feel as if my soul were touching the ineffable in art and then missing, afterward, in sadness, that foretaste of paradise it had just experienced? What to think of my absences in certain places charged with spirituality, like Süleymaniye or the little monastery of dervishes in Damascus? So many mysteries for the next life, as Sarah would say — I want to go find her terrifying article on Sarawak, to reread it, check if it contains subtle allusions to our story, to God, transcendence, beyond the horror. To Love. To that relationship between the Lover and the Beloved. Perhaps the most mystical text by Sarah is this simple and edifying article, "Orientalism is a Humanism," devoted to Ignác Goldziher and Gershom Scholem, which happens to be published in a journal of the University of Jerusalem; I must have it somewhere, should I get up, getting up would mean giving up on sleep until dawn, I know myself.

I could attempt to go back to sleep, I'll put down my glasses and the Balzac offprint, look, my fingers have left traces on the yellowing cover, one forgets that sweat is acidic and leaves marks on paper; maybe it's fever that's making me sweat from my fingers, I do in fact have clammy hands, but the heat is off and I don't feel hot, there are a few drops of sweat on my forehead too, like blood — hunters call their quarry's blood *sweat*, in the hunt in Austria there is no blood but *sweat*, the only time I accompanied my hunter uncle I saw a deer hit in the breast, the dogs yapped in front of the animal without going near it, the deer shivered and dug into the dirt with its hooves, one of the hunters stuck a knife into its chest, as in a Grimm fairy tale, but it wasn't a Grimm fairy tale it was a fat gruff guy with a cap, I whispered to my uncle "We could have treated the poor thing," a strange naïve reflex that got me a good clout on the back of the head. The dogs were licking the dead leaves. "They're lapping up the blood," I noted, nauseated; my uncle gave me a black look and grumbled "It's not blood. There's no blood. It's *sweat.*" The dogs were too well trained to go near the dying deer; they contented themselves, sneakily, with the fallen drops, those traces they had followed so well, the *sweat* the beast had lost running to its death. I thought I was going to vomit, but I didn't; the dead deer's head rolled right and left as they carried it to the car, I looked at the ground the whole time, eyes on the twigs, chestnuts and dried acorns, to avoid walking in that *sweat* that I pictured dropping from the animal's pierced heart, and the other day, at the lab, when the nurse tied her elastic tourniquet around my biceps, I averted my eyes saying out loud "It's not blood. There's no blood. It's *sweat,*" the young woman must have taken me for a madman, that's for sure, and my phone began ringing at that precise instant, the moment she was about to stick her instrument into my vein, my phone was in my jacket near the desk, "*Avec la garde montante, comme de petits soldats*" resounded with its horrible digital twang throughout the doctor's office; the device that absolutely never rings chose precisely that instant to blare a chorus from *Carmen* at full volume, while that lady was getting ready to *sweat* me. The phone was five meters away, I was attached by a tourniquet, ready to be stuck by a needle, I've never been so embarrassed in my life—the nurse hesitated, syringe in the air; the music kept mounting guard like little soldiers, Bizet was becoming an accomplice in my humiliation, the extravasating functionary asked if I wanted to answer, I shook my head, she stuck me before I could look elsewhere; I saw the metal plunging into the prominent blue vein, felt the tourniquet snap, the blood looked to me as if it were boiling in the container, "Avec la garde montante," how many times can a phone ring, my *sweat* was black as the ink of those transparent red pens I use to correct student papers, "comme de petits soldats," none of that would ever end, sometimes life is long, says T. S. Eliot, life is very long, "Avec la garde montante," the nurse took out her plastic tube, the phone finally fell silent and she pitilessly put a second tube in place of the first, letting the abandoned cannula dangle for a few seconds on my arm.

It's not blood, there's no blood, it's *sweat*.

Fortunately I'm not bleeding but it's worrisome all the same, these nighttime sweats, this fever.

Kafka spat blood, which must have been far more unpleasant, those red spots on his handkerchief, how horrible; in 1900 one Viennese out of four died of tuberculosis, apparently, was it that disease that made Kafka so popular, was it that disease that was at the origin of the "misunderstanding" about his personality, perhaps it was. In one of his last, terrifying letters, Kafka wrote to Max Brod from the Kierling sanatorium, in Klosterneuburg near the Danube: "Tonight I cried many times for no reason, my neighbor died tonight," and two days later Franz Kafka died in turn.

Chopin, Kafka, a filthy disease to which we do owe *The Magic Mountain*, let's not forget—there is no chance, the great Thomas Mann was Bruno Walter's neighbor in Munich, their children played together, writes his son Klaus Mann in his memoirs, what a family great men make. Sarah had obviously noted down all the little links that united her "characters": Kafka appears in her thesis with two of his stories, "In the Penal Colony" and "Jackals and Arabs"; for Sarah, Kafkaesque *displacement* is closely linked to his border-identity, to his critique of an Austrian Empire that is coming to an end and, beyond that, to the necessity of accepting alterity as an integral part of oneself, as a fertile contradiction. On the other hand colonial injustice (and here lies all the originality of her thesis) is maintained with "Orientalist" knowledge, the same type of relationship the jackals have with the Arabs in Kafka's story; they may be inseparable, but the violence of one party can in no case be blamed on the other. For Sarah, regarding Kafka as a sickly, dreary Romantic lost in a Stalinist administration is an absolute aberration—that would mean forgetting the *laughter*, the mockery, and the jubilation that are born from the womb of his lucidity. Transformed into a product for tourists, poor Franz is nothing more than a mask for the triumph of capitalism, and this truth saddened her so much that, just when Kafka had turned up in conversation in the Café Maximilian at the corner of the Votivkirche square thanks to Dr. Freud's neighbor, she had refused to go to Klosterneuburg to see what remained of the sanatorium where the man from Prague had died in 1924. The idea of taking the S-Bahn didn't really appeal to me, so I didn't insist, even if, to make her happy, I'd have been ready to freeze my balls off in the wind of that noble suburb, which I suspected was perfectly glacial.

It's not blood, there is no blood, it's *sweat*.

Maybe I should have insisted, because the alternative turned out to be just as painful; I knew Sarah's passion for monstrosities, even if at the time this interest in death and the bodies of the dead didn't manifest as acutely as it does today. I'd already had to put up with the sinister exhibit of anatomical models and now she was taking me to the other side of the canal, to Leopoldstadt, to a museum "that Magris mentioned in *Danube*" and that had always intrigued her—the Museum of Crime, no less, which I'd heard of but had never set foot in: the official museum of the Vienna Police, more horror and more monsters, if it's bashed-in skulls and photos of mutilated corpses you want you can have your fill here, I wonder why she's interested in the entrails of my city when I could show her so many beautiful things, Mozart's apartment, the Belvedere and the paintings of Leopold Carl Müller nicknamed the Egyptian or *Orient-Müller*, with Rudolf Ernst and Johann Viktor Krämer one of the best Austrian Orientalist painters, and so many things having to do with me, the neighborhood where I grew up, my school, my grandfather's watch shop, etc. What could Balzac have visited in Vienna, aside from the battlefields and bookstores to find engravings of German uniforms, we know he took his footman to Hammer to accompany him on his walks, but we know nothing or almost nothing about his impressions; someday I'll have to read his *Letters to Madame Hanska* in their entirety, finally a love story that ends well, over fifteen years of patience, fifteen years of patience.

Lying on my back in the dark I'll need some of that, patience, let's breathe calmly, lying on my back in the profound silence of midnight. Let's not think about the threshold to that room in the Baron Hotel in Aleppo, let's not think about Syria, about the intimacy of travelers, about Sarah's body lying on the other side of the wall in her room in the Baron Hotel in Aleppo, an immense room on the second floor with a balcony overlooking Baron Street, ex-Général-Gouraud Street, the noisy artery a stone's throw from Bab el-Faraj and the old city by alleyways stained with waste oil and lamb's blood, peopled with mechanics, restaurant owners, strolling merchants, and fruit juice sellers; the clamor of Aleppo filtering through the shutters at dawn; it was accompanied by the effluvia of charcoal, diesel, and animals. For someone arriving from Damascus, Aleppo was exotic; more cosmopolitan perhaps, closer to Istanbul; Arabic, Turkish, Armenian, Kurdish, not far from Antioch, homeland of saints and crusaders, between the Orontes and Euphrates rivers. Aleppo was a city of stone, with endless labyrinths of covered souks leading to the glacis of an impregnable fortress, and a modern city, with parks and gardens, built around the train station, the southern branch of the Baghdad Bahn, which put Aleppo a week away from Vienna via Istanbul and Konya as early as January 1913; all the passengers who arrived by train stayed at the Baron Hotel, the Aleppo equivalent of the Pera Palace in Istanbul — the Armenian who owned the hotel when we stayed there for the first time in 1996 was the grandson of the founder, he hadn't known the illustrious guests who made the establishment famous: Lawrence of Arabia, Agatha Christie, and King Faisal had all slept in this building with its Ottoman ogival windows and its monumental staircase, with its old, worn-out rugs and shabby rooms where there were still useless bakelite telephones and metal clawfoot bathtubs whose pipes sounded like a heavy machine gun whenever you turned on the faucet, in the midst of faded wallpaper and rust-stained bedspreads. The charm of decadence, said Sarah; she was happy to find the shade of Annemarie Schwarzenbach there, her wandering Swiss woman, who had vented her melancholy there during the winter of 1933–1934 — the last vestiges of the Weimar Republic had collapsed, *ein Volk, ein Reich, ein Führer* was resounding throughout all Germany and the young Annemarie was traveling madly to escape the European sadness that was invading even Zurich. On December 6, 1933, Annemarie arrived at Aleppo, at the Baron Hotel; Sarah was beside herself with joy when she discovered, on a dusty yellowing page, the delicate, cramped handwriting of the traveler, who had filled out the registration form in French — she was waving the register around in the hotel lobby to the amused looks of the manager and the employees, who were as used to the famous names their establishment's archives spat out as a locomotive was to smoke; the manager hadn't had the good fortune to know the dead Swiss woman who'd earned him such a demonstration of affection (no one was ever insensitive to Sarah's charms) but he seemed sincerely happy for the discovery responsible for these transports of joy, so much so that he joined us to celebrate the findings at the hotel bar: to the left of the reception desk there was a little room cluttered with old club chairs and dark wood furniture, a bar with a brass rail and leather-covered stools, in a neo-British style equal in ugliness to the Orientalist salons of the Second Empire; behind the bar, a large ogival niche with dark shelves overflowed with promotional kitsch advertising liquor brands from the 1950s and 1960s, ceramic Johnnie Walkers, cats made of the same material, old bottles of Jägermeister, and on each side of this gloomy, dusty museum there hung, for no apparent reason, two empty cartridge belts, as if they had just been used to hunt the imaginary pheasants and porcelain dwarves they listlessly framed. In the evening, as the day faded, this bar filled up not only with hotel clients, but also with tourists staying elsewhere coming to soak in the nostalgia drinking a beer or an arak whose smell of anise, mixed with that of peanuts and cigarettes, was the only Oriental touch in the décor. The round tables overflowed with tourist guidebooks and cameras and you could just catch, in passing, in the conversations of the clients, the names T. E. Lawrence, Agatha Christie, and Charles de Gaulle — I can see Sarah again at the bar, black-stockinged legs crossed, on a stool, staring into the distance, and I know she's thinking of Annemarie, the Swiss journalist and archaeologist: she's picturing her in the same spot sixty years earlier, sipping an arak, after a good bath to rid herself of the dust from the road; she was arriving from a dig between Antioch and Alexandretta. Late at night, she writes a letter to Klaus Mann, which I had helped Sarah translate; a letter with the letterhead of this Baron Hotel that still reeked of nostalgia and decadence, just as today it reeks of bombs and death — I picture the closed shutters, riddled with shrapnel; the street with soldiers rushing down it, the civilians hiding, as well as they can, from the snipers and torturers; Bab el-Faraj in ruins, the square littered with debris; the souks burned down, their beautiful khans blackened and collapsing in places; the mosque of the Omayyads without its minaret, its stones lying scattered in the courtyard with the broken marble, and the stench — the stench of stupidity and sadness, everywhere. Impossible at the time, at the bar of the Baron Hotel, to foresee that civil war was about to seize hold of Syria, even if the violence of dictatorship was omnipresent, so present you'd rather forget it, for there was a certain comfort that foreigners found in police regimes, a muffled, silent peace from Deraa to Qamishli, from Kassab to Quneytra, a peace humming with suppressed hatred and fates bending under a yoke which all the foreign scholars willingly accommodated, the archaeologists, the linguists, the historians, the geographers, the political scientists, they all enjoyed the leaden calm of Damascus or Aleppo, and we did too, Sarah and I, reading the letters from Annemarie Schwarzenbach the inconsolable angel in the bar of the Baron Hotel, eating white-coated pumpkin seeds and long, narrow pistachios with light-brown shells, we were enjoying the calm of the Syria of Hafez el-Assad, the father of the Nation — how long had we been in Damascus? I must have arrived in early autumn; Sarah had already been there a few weeks, she welcomed me warmly and even put me up for two nights in her little apartment in Sha'alan when I arrived. The Damascus airport was an inhospitable place with sinister guys with mustaches and pleated trousers hiked up to their navels who we quickly learned were the henchmen of the regime, the famous *mukhabarat*, countless informers and secret police: these men in wing-collared shirts drove Peugeot 504 estate cars or Range Rovers decorated with portraits of President Assad and his whole family — one joke tells how, at the time, the best Syrian spy in Tel-Aviv had finally, after years, fallen into the hands of the Israelis because he had stuck a photo of Netanyahu and his children on his rear window—this story made us all die laughing, we Orientalists in Damascus, representing all disciplines, history, linguistics, ethnology, political sciences, art history, archaeology, and even musicology. You found all kinds in Syria, from Swedish specialists in female Arabic writers to Catalan exegetes of Avicenna, most were connected in some way to one of the Western research centers housed in Damascus. Sarah had received a scholarship for a few months of research at the French Institute of Arabic Studies, a huge institution gathering together dozens of Europeans, French of course, but also Spaniards, Italians, Brits, Germans, and this little world, when it wasn't engaged in doctoral or post-doctoral research, devoted itself to studying the language. All were trained together, in the purest Orientalist tradition: future scholars, diplomats, and spies sat side by side and immersed themselves together in the joys of Arabic grammar and rhetoric. There was even a young Roman Catholic priest who had left his parish behind to devote himself to study, a modern version of the missionaries from long ago—in all, fifty or so students and about twenty researchers made the most of the facilities of this institution and especially its huge library, founded at the time of the French mandate in Syria, over which the colonial shades of Robert Montagne and Henri Laoust still floated. Sarah was very happy to find herself among all these Orientalists, to observe them; sometimes she sounded as if she were describing a zoo, a caged world, where many people gave in to paranoia and lost all common sense, nurturing magnificent hatreds toward each other, madnesses, pathologies of all kinds, diseases of the skin, mystical deliriums, obsessions, "scholar's block" that drove them to work, work, to polish their desks with their elbows for hours on end without producing a thing, not a thing, aside from the brain-steam that escaped through the windows of the venerable institution to dissolve into the Damascus air. Some of them haunted the library at night; they would walk up and down between the shelves for hours, hoping the printed matter would seep out and impregnate them with science, and they would end up in the early hours of the day, despairing of everything, collapsed in a corner until the librarians scolded them at opening time. Others were more subversive; Sarah told me how a young Romanian researcher hid some perishable item (a lemon usually, but also sometimes an *entire* watermelon) behind a particularly inaccessible or forgotten shelf of books to see if, from the smell, the personnel could manage to locate the rotting object, which ended up provoking an energetic reaction from the authorities: they posted signs forbidding "the introduction of any organic matter into the building under penalty of permanent exclusion."

The librarian, a warm, pleasant man with an adventurer's tanned face, was a specialist in the poems that Arabic sailors used to use to jog their memory for navigation, and he often dreamed of sailing expeditions between Yemen and Zanzibar on board a dhow loaded with khat and incense, beneath the stars of the Indian Ocean, dreams he liked to share with all the readers who visited his institution, regardless of whether or not they knew the basics of sailing: he would talk about storms he had faced and shipwrecks from which he had escaped, in Damascus (where traditionally people were much more concerned with caravan camels and the entirely earth-bound piracy of Bedouins in the desert) all this was magnificently exotic.

The directors were university professors, usually unprepared to find themselves at the helm of such an imposing structure; often they would make do with barricading the doors to their offices and waiting, immersed in the complete works of Jahiz or Ibn Taymiyya, for time to pass, leaving the bother of organizing production in this factory of knowledge to their underlings.

The Syrians looked with an amused eye at these budding

scholars drifting around in their capital and, unlike in Iran where the Islamic Republic was very fussy about research activities, the regime of Hafez el-Assad let a royal peace reign over these scientists, archaeologists included. The Germans had their archaeology institute in Damascus, where Bilger, my landlord, officiated (Sarah's apartment, to my great sadness, was too small for me to stay there), and in Beirut the famous Orient Institut of the venerable Deutsche Morgenländische Gesellschaft led by the Koranic and no less venerable Angelika Neuwirth. Bilger had found a comrade from Bonn in Damascus, a specialist in Ottoman art and urbanism, Stefan Weber, whom I haven't seen in a very long time; I wonder if he still heads the department of Islamic art in the Pergamon Museum in Berlin — Weber was renting a beautiful Arabic house in the heart of the old city, on a little street in the Christian quarter, in Bab Tuma; this traditional Damascus home, with its big courtyard, black and white stone fountain, its *iwan*, and its covered passageway on the upper floor, aroused the jealousy of the entire Orientalist community. Sarah — like everyone else — adored Stefan Weber, who spoke Arabic perfectly, whose knowledge of Ottoman architecture was dazzling, two qualities that earned him the envy and repressed hostility of Bilger — when it came to competence and brilliance he could bear none but his own. Bilger's apartment was like him: flashy and huge. He lived in Jisr el-Abyad, "the white bridge": this luxurious neighborhood on the edge of the slopes of Mount Qasioun, close to the presidential palace and the homes of the important figures of the regime, owed its name to a bridge over a branch of the Barada River which was usually used more to get rid of household trash than for boating, but whose narrow banks were planted with trees, which could have made for a pleasant stroll if it had been provided with sidewalks worthy of the name. The "Bilger Residence" was entirely decorated in the Saudi or Kuwaiti style: everything, from the doorknobs to the taps, was covered in gold leaf; the ceilings were weighed down with neo-rococo moldings; the sofas were upholstered in black and gold. The bedrooms were equipped with pious alarm clocks: these models of the Mosque of the Prophet in Medina shouted the call to prayer at dawn in a nasal twang if you forgot to turn them off. There were two living rooms, a dining room with a table (also black and gold, with shiny palmetto feet) for twenty guests, and five bedrooms. At night, if by chance you used the wrong switch, dozens of neon wall lamps bathed the apartment in a pale green light and filled the walls with the ninety-nine names of Allah, a perfectly terrifying miracle to me but one that delighted Bilger: "There's nothing more beautiful than seeing technology in the service of kitsch." The two terraces offered a magnificent panorama of the city and the oasis of Damascus, to breakfast or dine there in the cool air was a delight. Aside from the apartment and the car, Bilger's household consisted of a cook and an odd-job man; the cook came at least three times a week to prepare the gala dinners and receptions that King Bilger offered his guests; the odd-job man (twenty years old, amusing, lively and pleasant, a Kurd from Qamishli, where Bilger had hired him for a dig) was named Hassan, slept in a little room behind the kitchen, and took care of household tasks, shopping, cleaning, washing, which, given the fact that his master (it's hard for me to think of him as "his employer") was often absent, left him with a lot of time off; he studied German at the Goethe Institut and archaeology at the University of Damascus and had explained to me that Bilger, whom he venerated like a demi-god, offered him this situation to allow him to pursue his studies in the capital. In the summer, during the big archaeological digs, this agreeable student factotum would resume his job as an excavator and accompany his mentor on the digs in Jazirah, where he was assigned to the shovel, of course, but also to sorting through and sketching pottery, a mission that delighted him and at which he excelled: at first glance he could recognize sigillates, coarse ceramics or Islamic glazes, working just from tiny shards. For prospecting work on untouched tells, Bilger always brought him along, and this closeness caused tongues to wag, of course—I remember suggestive winks whenever the pair was mentioned, expressions like "Bilger and *his* student" or, worse, "the great Fritz and his boy-toy," no doubt because Hassan was objectively young and very handsome, and because Orientalism has a certain relationship not only with homosexuality, but more generally with the sexual domination of the powerful over the weak, the rich over the poor. It seems to me today that for Bilger, unlike others, it was not the pleasure of Hassan's body that interested him, but the image of the nabob, the all-powerful benefactor that his own generosity reflected back to him—over the course of the three months I spent at his place in Damascus, never did I witness any sort of physical familiarity between them, quite the contrary; so whenever I had the opportunity I would refute the rumors running around about them. Bilger wanted to resemble the archaeologists of long ago, the Schliemanns, the Oppenheims, the Dieulafoys; no one saw, no one could see, how these dreams were becoming a form of madness, still mild, compared to the way he is today, that's for sure, Bilger the prince of archaeologists was mildly nutty and now he's a raging lunatic; on second thought everything was already obvious in Damascus, in his generosity and excessiveness: I know that despite his stupendous salary he returned to Bonn riddled with debts, of which he was proud, proud of having blown everything, he said, squandered everything in luxurious receptions, salaries for his acolytes, fabulous slippers, Oriental rugs, and even contraband antiques, especially Hellenistic and Byzantine coins, which he bought in antique shops in Aleppo mainly. This was the icing on the cake, for an archaeologist; like Schliemann, he would show his treasures to his guests, but he didn't steal them on the sites he excavated—he was content, he said, to *recover* objects that were on the market *to keep them from disappearing*. He would do the honors of his *numismata* to his guests, explain the lives of the emperors who had minted them, Phocas, the Comneni, give the likely provenance of these coins, usually from the Dead Cities of the North; the young Hassan was in charge of looking after these gleaming wonders; he would polish them, arrange them harmoniously on black felt display cases, not realizing the extraordinary danger they could represent: Bilger might risk only scandal, or expulsion and confiscation of his costly playthings, but Hassan could bid farewell, if he was caught, to his studies, and even to an eye, a few fingers and his innocence.

There was something obscene about Bilger's grand speeches: he was like an ecology activist draped in a golden fox or ermine cloak explaining why and how animal lives must be saved, gesturing grandly like an ancient soothsayer. It was during one particularly alcohol-heavy and embarrassing evening, when all present (young researchers, small-time diplomats) felt a terrifying shame, in the midst of the black sofas and green neon lights, when Bilger, his elocution slowed down by alcohol, standing in the center of the half circle of his guests, began to declaim his ten commandments of archaeology, the absolutely objective reasons why he was the most competent of all the foreign scholars present in Syria and how, thanks to him, science was going to *leap toward the future*—the young Hassan, sitting on the floor next to him, kept looking at him admiringly; the empty glass of whisky in Bilger's hand, shaken by his clumsy gestures, at times poured a few drops of melted ice onto the Syrian's brown hair, a horrible pagan baptism the young man, lost in contemplating his master's face, concentrating to understand an English so refined it bordered on pedantry, did not seem to notice. I related this biblical scene to Sarah, who hadn't been there, and she didn't believe me; as always she thought I was exaggerating, and I had all the difficulty in the world convincing her this episode did indeed take place.

Still, we owed to Bilger some magnificent expeditions into the desert, especially one night in a Bedouin tent between Palmyra and Rusafa, a night when the sky was so pure and the stars so numerous that they came down all the way to the ground, lower than you could see, a night such as only, I imagine, sailors can see, in the summer, when the sea is as calm and dark as the Syrian *badiya*. Sarah was delighted to be able to experience, more or less identically, the adventures of Annemarie Schwarzenbach or Marga d'Andurain sixty years earlier in the Levant under French mandate; that's what she was there for; Sarah felt, she confided in me in that bar in the Baron Hotel in Aleppo, what Annemarie wrote in the same place on December 6, 1933, to Klaus Mann:

Often, in the course of this strange journey, because of fatigue, or when I've drunk a lot, everything becomes vague: nothing is left of yesterday; there isn't a single face there. It's a great fright and, also, a sadness.

Annemarie then mentions the *inflexible face* of Erika Mann, which remains in the midst of this desolation, she imagines Erika's brother knows the role Erika plays in this sorrow — she has no other choice than to continue her journey, where would she go in Europe? The Mann family will also have to begin its exile, which will lead it to the United States in 1941 and probably, if she had been able to make up her mind to flee Swiss illusion and her mother's grip for once and for all, Annemarie Schwarzenbach would never have had that stupid bicycle accident that cost her life in 1942 and froze her forever in youth, at the age of thirty-four — she was twenty-five during that first trip to the Middle East, like Sarah more or less. That first evening in Aleppo, after we had settled into the Baron and celebrated the discovery of Annemarie's entry in the hotel register, we went out to dinner in Jdayde, a Christian neighborhood in the old city, where traditional homes were little by little being restored to be transformed into luxury hotels and restaurants — the oldest and most famous of them, at the beginning of a narrow alleyway overlooking a little square, was named Sissi House, which had cracked Sarah up, she said to me "poor thing, you're pursued by Vienna and Franz Josef, there's no escape" and had insisted that we eat there: I have to admit that, even though I am not what could be called a hedonist or a gourmet, the setting, the food, and the excellent Lebanese wine they served there (and especially the company of Sarah, whose beauty was brought out by the Ottoman *cortile*, the jewels, the cloth, the wooden *mashrabiyas*) have fixed that evening in my memory; we were princes, princes from the West that the Orient was welcoming and treating as such, with refinement, obsequiousness, suave languor, and all of this, conforming to the image our youth had constructed of the Oriental myth, gave us the impression of finally living in the lost lands of the *Thousand and One Nights*, which had reappeared for us alone: no foreigner, in that early spring, to spoil its exclusivity; our fellow diners were a rich family from Aleppo celebrating a patriarch's birthday, whose women, bejeweled, wearing white lace blouses with strict black wool vests, kept smiling at Sarah.

The hummus, the *mutabbal*, and the grilled meat seemed better to us than in Damascus, transcendent, sublime; the *sujuk* was spicier, the *basturma* more fragrant, and the Nectar de Kefraya more intoxicating than usual.

We went back to the hotel the long way round, in the half shadow of alleyways and closed bazaars — today all these places are prey to war, burning or burned, the metal shutters of shops deformed by the heat of fire, the little square of the Maronite Diocese invaded by collapsed buildings, its surprising Latin church with its twin red-tiled bell towers devastated by explosions: will Aleppo ever regain its splendor, maybe, you never know, but that evening our stay was a dream twice over, at once lost in time and recaptured by destruction. A dream with Annemarie Schwarzenbach, T. E. Lawrence, and all the clients of the Baron Hotel, the famous and forgotten dead, whom we were joining at the bar, on the round leather-upholstered stools, next to brand-name ashtrays and the two bizarre hunter's cartridge belts; a dream of Aleppo music, song, lute, zither — better think about something else, turn over, fall asleep to erase things, erase the Baron, Aleppo, the bombs, the war, and Sarah, let's try rather, with a movement of the pillow, to find her again in mysterious Sarawak, wedged between the Borneo jungle and the pirates on the China Seas.

God knows what association led me to have this melody in my head now; even with my eyes closed as I try to breathe deeply the brain still has to keep whirring, my own private music box starts playing at the most inopportune time, is this a sign of madness, I don't know, I'm not hearing voices, I'm hearing orchestras, lutes, songs; they're cluttering up my ears and my memory, they start up all by themselves as if, when one agitation goes away, another, pressed down beneath the first, overflows the consciousness — I know it's a phrase from *Le Désert* by Félicien David, or I think so, I seem to recognize old Félicien, the foremost Orientalist musician, forgotten like all those who have devoted themselves body and soul to the ties between East and West, without lingering over the fights between Ministers of War or Colonial

Secretaries, his music rarely played today, hardly ever recorded, and yet adored by the composers of his time as *having broken new ground*, as having given birth to *a new roar, a new sonority*, Félicien David, native of the South of France, from the Vaucluse or Roussillon, died (this I'm sure of, it's idiotic enough to remember) in Saint-Germain-en-Laye, a frightful district outside of Paris organized around a château filled up to its mullioned windows with carved flint and very Gaulish stones, Félicien David also died of tuberculosis in 1876, a holy man, because all Saint-Simonians were holy men, madmen, madmen and saints, like Ismaÿl Urbain the first Algerian Frenchman, or the first Algerian from France, it's about time the French remembered him, the first man, the first Orientalist to have worked for an *Algeria for Algerians* in the 1860s, against the Maltese, the Sicilians, the Spaniards, and the Marseillais who made up the embryonic colonists crawling through the ruts gouged by soldiers' boots: Ismaÿl Urbain had the ear of Napoleon III and with only a little urging, the fate of the Arab world could have been changed, but French and English politicians are crafty cowards who gaze mostly at their *wee-wee makers* in the mirror, and Ismaÿl Urbain friend of Abd el-Kader died, and there was nothing else to do, the politics of France and Great Britain were seized by stupidity, bogged down in injustice, violence, and spinelessness.

In the meantime, there had been Félicien David, Delacroix, Nerval, all those who visited the façade of the Orient, from Algeciras to Istanbul, or its backyard, from India to Cochin China; in the meantime, this Orient had revolutionized art, literature, and music, especially music: after Félicien David, nothing would be the same. This way of thinking is perhaps a pious wish, you're exaggerating, Sarah would say, but good Lord, I've demonstrated all that, I've written all that, I've shown that the revolution in music in the nineteenth and twentieth centuries owed everything to the Orient, that it was not a matter of "exotic procedures," as was thought before, this exoticism had a meaning, that it made external elements, alterity, enter, it was a large movement, and gathered together, among others, Mozart, Beethoven, Schubert, Liszt, Berlioz, Bizet, Rimsky-Korsakov, Debussy, Bartók, Hindemith, Schönberg, Szymanowski, hundreds of composers throughout all of Europe, over all of Europe the wind of alterity blows, all these great men use what comes to them from the Other to modify the Self, to bastardize it, for genius wants bastardy, the use of external procedures to undermine the dictatorship of church chant and harmony, why am I getting worked up all alone on my pillow now, probably because I'm a poor unsuccessful academic with a revolutionary thesis no one cares about. Today no one is interested anymore in Félicien David who became extraordinarily famous on December 8, 1844 after the premiere of *Le Désert* at the Paris Conservatoire, an ode-symphony in three parts for narrator, solo tenor, male chorus, and orchestra, based on the composer's memories of his journey to the Orient, between Cairo and Beirut; in the hall there is Berlioz, Théophile Gautier, and all the Saint-Simonians, including Enfantin, the great master of the new religion, who left for Egypt to find a wife to bear a child for him, a female messiah, and thus to reconcile Orient and Occident, join them in flesh, Barthélemy Enfantin would plan the Suez Canal and the railways of Lyon, he would try to interest Austria and an aging Metternich in his Oriental projects without success, the statesman refused to see him, after a Catholic cabal and despite the advice of Hammer-Purgstall who had seen them as a superb way to make the Empire enter the Orient. Barthélemy Enfantin great mystical fornicator, first modern guru and brilliant entrepreneur, is seated in the hall next to Berlioz who doesn't conceal his sympathies for the social aspect of the Saint-Simonian doctrine.

The desert invades Paris — "by unanimous opinion, it was the most beautiful storm music had ever produced, no maestro had ever gone so far," Théophile Gautier writes in *La Presse*, describing the storm assailing the caravan in the desert; it's also the premiere of the "Danse des almées," the Dance of the Almahs, an erotic motif whose subsequent fortune we know, and surprise of surprises, the first "Chant du muezzin," the first Muslim call to prayer that ever sounded in Paris: "It's at that morning hour we hear the voice of the muezzin," Berlioz writes in *Le Journal des débats* on December 15, "David limited himself here, not to the role of imitator, but to that of simple arranger; he erased himself completely to introduce to us, in its strange nudity and even in the Arabic language, the bizarre chant of the muezzin. That last line of this kind of melodic cry ends with a scale composed of intervals smaller than half steps, which M. Béfort executed very adroitly, but which caused great surprise in the audience. A contralto, a real feminine contralto (M. Béfort, father of three children) whose strange voice slightly disoriented, or rather oriented the audience by awakening in them ideas of the harem, etc. After the muezzin's prayer, the caravan resumes its march, moves away and disappears. The desert remains alone." The desert always remains alone, and the symphonic ode is such a success that David performs it throughout all of Europe, mostly in Germany and Austria, where the Saint-Simonians are trying, still in vain, to extend their influence; Félicien David will meet Mendelssohn the next year, will conduct in Frankfurt, in Potsdam in front of the Prussian court, in Munich and Vienna, in December, four Viennese concerts, an immense success which will be witnessed of course by Hammer-Purgstall, who will feel a little nostalgic, he relates, for that Orient now so remote from him.

Of course, we could reproach David for his difficulties in retranscribing Arabic rhythms in his score, but that would mean forgetting that Ottoman composers themselves find it difficult to transpose their own rhythms into "Western" notation; they tend to simplify them, as David does, and we had to wait for Béla Bartók and his journey to Turkey for this notation to be improved, even though, in the meantime, the great Francisco Salvador-Daniel, student of Félicien David, violin teacher in Algiers, first great ethnomusicologist before the term was even invented, left us a magnificent *Album of Arabic, Moorish and Kabyle Songs*: Rimsky-Korsakov would use these melodies (presented by Borodin) in several symphonic works. Francisco Salvador-Daniel, friend of Gustave Courbet and Jules Vallès, socialist and Communard, director of the Conservatoire during the Commune, Francisco Salvador-Daniel would end up being executed by the loyalists, caught weapons in hand on a barricade, having replaced his violin with a rifle — no burial place on this earth for Francisco Salvador-Daniel, dead at the age of forty and absolutely forgotten since then, in France, in Spain, and in Algeria, no burial place aside from the traces of his melodies in the works of Massenet, Delibes, Rimsky, works that are no doubt more accomplished, but that would be nothing without the material provided by Francisco Salvador-Daniel. I wonder when these people will be pulled from oblivion, when will we do justice to them, all those who have worked, out of love of music, for the knowledge of Arabic instruments, rhythms and repertories, Turkish or Persian. My thesis and my articles, a tomb for Félicien David, a tomb for Francisco Salvador-Daniel, a very somber tomb, where no one is disturbed in his eternal sleep.

12:55 A.M.

I'd rather be in my bed, eyes in the dark, lying on my back, head resting on a soft pillow, than in the desert, even in the company of Félicien David, even in the company of Sarah, the desert is an extraordinarily uncomfortable place, I'm not even talking about the sand desert, where you swallow silica all day long, all night long, it gets into all your orifices, your ears, your nostrils and even your navel, I'm talking about the Syrian-style desert of stones, pebbles, boulders, rocky mountains, heaps, cairns, hills with, here and there, oases where it's a mystery how the red earth shows through, and then the *badiya* is covered with fields, winter wheat or date palms. In Syria it should be said that "desert" is a misnomer, there were people even in the most remote regions, nomads or soldiers, and it was enough for a woman to stop to pee behind a mound by the side of the road for a Bedouin to immediately pop up and nonchalantly observe the milky hindquarters of the stunned Westerner, Sarah in this case, whom we saw running toward the car, disheveled, holding her pants up with one hand, as if she'd just seen a ghoul: Bilger and I thought at first that a jackal, or even a snake or a scorpion, had lashed out at her buttocks but, having overcome her fright, she explained to us, laughing uproariously, that a red and white keffieh had appeared behind a rock, and that beneath the keffieh there was a tanned nomad, standing, arms crossed, face impassive, observing in silence what for him too must have been a strange apparition, a foreign woman squatting in his desert. A real cartoon character, Sarah said giggling, buttoning up her trousers in the back seat, what a fright I had, and Bilger added with panache, "This region has been inhabited since the third millennium BC, you have just seen the proof."

Around us, though, there was nothing but kilometers of dull dust beneath the milky sky—we were between Palmyra and Deir ez-Zor, on the endless road that links the most famous ancient city in Syria to the Euphrates with its impenetrable reeds, in mid-expedition on the traces of Annemarie Schwarzenbach and Marga d'Andurain, the provocative queen of Palmyra who had owned, during the French mandate over Syria, the Zenobia Hotel, situated at the edge of the ruins of the caravan city, on the border of fields of broken columns and temples whose soft stone became tinged with ochre with the evening sun. Palmyra, overlooked by a rocky mountain crowned by an old Arab fortress from the sixteenth century, Qalat Fakhr ed-Din Ibn Maan: the view from up there over the site, the palm grove and the funeral towers, is so astounding that we decided, along with a group of budding Orientalists from Damascus, to set up camp there. Like soldiers, colonialists, or archaeologists from long ago, unconcerned with the regulations, or with comfort, we had made up our minds (encouraged by Sarah and Bilger: both of them, for very different reasons, were utterly enthusiastic at the idea of this expedition) to spend the night in the old citadel or on its parvis, regardless of what its guardians might think. This castle, closed in around itself, a compact block of dark Legos with no opening aside from its loopholes, invisible from a distance, seems to be teetering at the summit of the rocky slope; from the bottom of the archaeological site, it looks as if it's leaning over the edge and, as soon as a more powerful storm than usual comes along, it would threaten to slide on the gravel all the way to town, like a child on a sled—but the closer you got, and the more the road unwound itself onto the back of the mountain, the more the building took on, in the eyes of travelers, its real mass, its real size: that of a sheer donjon keep well-protected to the east by a deep fosse, a solid building with deadly projections, which didn't in the slightest make you want to be a soldier attacking it. The Druze prince of Lebanon, Fakhr ed-Din, who had ordered it built, knew a thing or two about military architecture—the thing seemed impregnable except by hunger or thirst: one could picture its besieged guards despairing of God, on their heaps of stones, contemplating from afar the coolness of the oasis, whose palm trees outlined a deep green lake beyond the ruins of the ancient city.

The view there was magical—at sunrise and sunset, the slanting light set ablaze by turns the temple of Baal, the camp of Diocletian, the agora, the tetrapylon, and the walls of the theater, and one could easily imagine the wonder of those Englishmen in the eighteenth century who discovered the oasis and brought back the first views of Palmyra, the Bride of the Desert: these drawings, engraved immediately in London, would be distributed throughout the whole of Europe. Bilger told how these reproductions were even at the origin of many neoclassical façades and colonnades in European architecture: our cities owed much to Palmyran capitals, a little of the Syrian desert lived secretly in London, Paris, and Vienna. I imagine today the pillagers are having a tremendous time dismantling the bas-reliefs of tombs, the inscriptions, the statues, to resell them to unscrupulous amateurs, and Bilger himself, if not for his madness, would no doubt have offered to buy these fragments torn from the desert—in the Syrian disaster bombs and excavators have replaced archaeologists' brushes; they say that mosaics are taken apart with pneumatic drills, that the Dead Cities or the sites on the Euphrates are excavated with bulldozers and the interesting pieces resold in Turkey or Lebanon, the vestiges are an underground fortune, a natural resource, like oil they've been exploited forever. In Iran on a mountain near Shiraz a slightly lost young man offered to sell us a mummy, a mummy from Luristan complete with its bronze jewels, its pectorals, its weapons — it took us some time to understand what he was offering us, so absolutely incongruous did the word "mummy" seem in this mountain village, what do you expect us to do with a mummy, I replied. "Well it's pretty, it's useful, and you can resell it if you need money." The boy (he couldn't have been over twenty) offered to deliver the mummy in question to us in Turkey, and since the conversation was going on forever it was Sarah who found a very intelligent way to rid us of this nuisance: We think Iranian antiquities should stay in Iran, Iran is a great country that needs all its antiquities, we don't want to do anything that could harm Iran, and that nationalist dousing seemed to cool the ardor of the amateur archaeologist, forcing him to agree even though, internally, he was not very convinced by the sudden nationalist fervor of these two foreigners. Watching the young man leave the little park where he had approached us, I imagined for an instant the mummy, this venerable corpse, crossing the Zagros and the mountains of Kurdistan on the back of a donkey to reach Turkey, then Europe or the United States, an illegal immigrant two thousand years old taking the same dangerous route as Alexander's armies or the Iranians who were fleeing the regime.

The pillagers of the Syrian tombs are not offering mummies, so far as I know, but bronze animals, cylinder-seals, Byzantine oil lamps, crosses, coins, statues, bas-reliefs, and even entablatures or sculpted capitals — in Palmyra the old stones were so numerous they comprised all the garden furniture in the Zenobia Hotel: capitals of columns used as tables, the columns themselves for benches, rubble for the flowerbeds, the terrace borrowed widely from the ruins it abutted. The hotel, bungalow-style, had been built by a great forgotten architect, Fernando de Aranda, son of Fernando de Aranda, the musician to the court of Abdulhamid in Istanbul, successor to Giuseppe Donizetti as conductor of the orchestra and of imperial military fanfares: in Palmyra, then, I was somewhat at home, the desert resounded with the distant accents of the music of the Ottoman capital. Fernando de Aranda Junior had carried out his entire career in Syria, where he died in the 1960s; he had constructed many important buildings in Damascus, in a style that could have been described as Orientalist Art Nouveau, including the Hejaz train station, the university, a number of grand houses, and the Zenobia Hotel in Palmyra, which was not yet called the Zenobia, but the Kattaneh, after the investment company that had commissioned it from the rising star of modern Syrian architecture, foreseeing the opening of the region to visitors—the building was abandoned even before it was finished, left to the care of the French garrison of Palmyra (mounted soldiers, pilots, low-grade officers with no future) who looked after Bedouin affairs and the immense desert territory all the way to Iraq and Jordan, where the British were running the show. Fernando de Aranda's hotel, of modest proportions to begin with, had one wing amputated, which made its front look lopsided: the pediment above the front door, with its two pilasters and its palmettos, no longer presided over a noble symmetry, but the beginning of a recess where the hotel terrace was, and this disequilibrium gave the whole a limping air, apt to provoke, depending on what feelings the disabled aroused in you, either tenderness or scorn. Tenderness or scorn were encouraged, too, by the interior of the building, with its strange old wicker chairs in the lobby and its tiny, stifling bedrooms, renovated today, but which, at the time, housed yellowing images of the Syrian Ministry of Tourism and dusty imitation-Bedouin furniture. Sarah and I inclined more toward tenderness, she because of Annemarie Schwarzenbach and Marga d'Andurain, and I happy to see the unsuspected fruits that the master of Ottoman music had, via his son, offered the Syrian desert.

The location of the Zenobia Hotel was extraordinary: on the side of the ancient city, you had before your eyes, scarcely a few dozen meters away, the Temple of Baal, and if you were lucky enough to get one of the rooms that overlooked the façade, you slept so to speak in the midst of the ruins, your head in the stars and ancient dreams, lulled by the conversations of Baalshamin, god of the sun and dew, with Ishtar, the goddess with the lion. Here reigned Tammuz, the Adonis of the Greeks, of whom Badr Shakir Sayyab the Iraqi sang in his poems; you expected to see the oasis covered in red anemones, born from the blood of that mortal whose only crime was to be too beloved of goddesses.

That day there was no question of a hotel, since we'd had the strange idea of sleeping in the citadel of Fakhr ed-Din to make the most of the beauty of the city at both sunset and sunrise. Of course we had no actual camping supplies; Bilger and I had piled six blankets into his SUV that could stand in for mattresses and sleeping bags, some pillows, plates, silverware, glasses, bottles of Lebanese wine and arak, and even the little metal barbecue from his terrace. As for who was taking part in this expedition aside from Sarah, I can see again a smiling French historian, a brunette with long hair, and her companion, just as dark-haired and smiling — I think today he's a journalist and travels the Middle East for a number of French media outlets: at the time he was dreaming of a prestigious post in an American university,

I think Sarah stayed in contact with that engaging couple who combined beauty with intelligence. It's strange, all the same, that I haven't kept any friends from Damascus aside from Sarah and Bilger the Mad, neither Syrians nor Orientalists, I realize now how unbearable I must have been with my demands and my pretentiousness, fortunately I've made a lot of progress since then, without that translating, in terms of new friendships, into an abundant social life, I have to admit. If Bilger hadn't gone insane, if Sarah hadn't been so unattainable, they would probably constitute the link with this past that knocks on my door at night, what were the names of that couple of French historians, Jeanne maybe, no, Julie and he was François-Marie, I can see his thin face, his dark beard and—mystery of a face's harmony— his humor and mischievous look that compensated for the harshness of the whole, memory is the only thing I don't lack, the only thing that doesn't tremble like the rest of my body—in the late morning we had bought some meat at a butcher's in the modern city of Palmyra: the blood of a freshly killed lamb stained the sidewalk in front of the shop window where there hung, from an iron hook, the animal's lungs, trachea and heart; in Syria no one could forget that the tender meat of kebabs came from a mammal whose throat was slit, a woolly, bleating mammal whose viscera adorned the shop fronts.

God is the great enemy of sheep; one wonders for what horrible reason He chose to replace, at the instant of sacrifice, Abraham's son with a ram instead of with an ant or a rose, thereby condemning poor ovines to slaughter for centuries to come. It was of course Sarah (amusing Biblical coincidence) who was in charge of the purchase, not just because the sight of the blood and the warm offal didn't bother her, but especially because her knowledge of the dialect and her great beauty always ensured the quality of the merchandise and a price that was more than reasonable, when they let her pay: it wasn't rare for shopkeepers hypnotized by the brilliance of this auburn angel with the crimson smile to try to keep her as long as possible in their shop, especially by refusing to take any money for their foodstuffs. The modern city of Palmyra, north of the oasis, was a well-ordered quadrilateral of low houses made of cheap concrete, bordered to the north and northeast by an airport and a sinister prison, the most famous in all of Syria, a black and blood-red prison, colors premonitory of the Syrian flag that the Assad dynasty had persisted in unfolding over the entire territory: in his jails, the most atrocious kinds of torment were a daily thing, medieval tortures systematic, a routine with no other aim than general terror, the spreading of fear over the whole country, like manure.

What interested Sarah especially about Palmyra, beyond the dazzling beauty of the ruins and the monstrosities of the Assad regime, were the traces of Annemarie Schwarzenbach and her strange landlady Marga d'Andurain, the owner of the Zenobia Hotel in the early 1930s — around the fire, in front of the citadel of Fakhr ed-Din, we spent a large part of the night taking turns telling stories, a real *Assembly*, a *Maqāma*, a noble genre of Arabic literature in which the characters speak one at a time to explore, each in turn, a given subject: that night, we wrote the *Maqāma Tadmoriyya*, the Assembly of Palmyra.

The guardian of the fort was a dry old man in a keffieh armed with a hunting rifle; his mission consisted of closing, with an impressive chain and padlock, the iron gate to the castle — our delegation took him entirely by surprise. We had left the Arabic speakers to negotiate with him and were observing the progress of the discussion — Bilger, François-Marie, and I — at some remove: the peasant guard was inflexible, the gate had to be closed at sunset and opened at dawn, that was his mission and he meant to carry it out, even if that didn't suit tourists;

our project was falling to pieces and we wondered how we had imagined for a second it could be otherwise, out of colonialist pretentiousness no doubt. Sarah didn't give up; she kept arguing with the Palmyran who was toying mechanically with the strap of his weapon while periodically directing anxious glances at us: he must have been wondering why we were letting him do battle with this young woman while we three men stood there, two meters away, placidly observing the confab. Julie came over to update us on the progress of the negotiations; the guardian was determined to carry out his duty, at opening and closing. On the other hand we could stay inside the citadel, locked in till dawn, that would not detract from his mission at all. Sarah had agreed to these conditions, as a starting point—she was trying, in addition, to obtain the key to the padlock, which would allow us to leave the noble donjon in case of emergency without having to wait for the deliverance of dawn as in a fairy tale. It should be acknowledged that the prospect of being locked inside an impregnable fortress, a few kilometers away from the most sinister prison in Syria, made me tremble a little—the building was just a pile of stones, without any conveniences, empty rooms around a short *cortile* piled with fallen rocks, staircases without any railings leading up to more or less crenellated terraces where bats wheeled. Fortunately, the guardian was fed up; after inviting us to go in one last time, and since we were still hesitant about being locked in voluntarily (did we really have everything we needed? Matches, newspaper, water?), he abruptly closed the gate, in a hurry to go home; Sarah asked him one last question, to which he seemed to reply in the affirmative, before turning his back on us to descend toward the valley of the tombs, straight down the slope.

"He has officially given us permission to set up here."

"Here" meant the small rocky parvis between the ancient

drawbridge and the gate's arch. The sun had disappeared behind our hill; its last rays spattered the colonnades with gold, turned the palm trees iridescent; the light breeze carried a smell of warm stones mingled, at times, with rubber and burnt household trash; down below, a tiny man was leading a camel on the oval track of the big stadium of dust where the dromedary races took place that attracted nomads from all over the country, those Bedouins Marga d'Andurain loved so.

Our camp was much more Spartan than those of the explorers of old: they say that Lady Hester Stanhope, first queen of Tadmor, proud English adventuress with an iron will, whose wealth and health the Orient sucked away until her death in 1839 in a village in the Lebanese mountains, needed seven camels to carry her equipment, and that the tent where she received the emirs of the land was by far the most sumptuous in all of Syria; legend has it that, along with her chamber pot (the only indispensable accessory in the desert, she said), the niece of William Pitt transported a gala dinner to Palmyra, a royal dinner where the most refined china and place settings were taken out of the trunks, to the great surprise of the guests; all the sheikhs and emirs in the land were dazzled by Lady Hester Stanhope, they say. Our own meal was comprised exclusively of grilled lamb, forget about *sauce anglaise* and ortolans, just a few skewers, the first ones burned, the second raw, at the mercy of our capricious fire in Bilger's *manqal*. Meat that we rolled up in delicious unleavened bread, that round of wheat cooked on a metal dome, which in the Middle East serves as starch, dish, and fork all at once. Our flames must have been visible for kilometers all around, like a lighthouse, and we expected the Syrian police to come kick us out, but Eshmun was watching over the Orientalists, and nothing disturbed us before dawn, aside from the freezing north wind: it was bone-numbingly cold.

Clustered around the little barbecue whose warmth was as illusory as that of the millions of stars around us, wrapped up in Bilger's sky-blue wool blankets, glasses in hand, we listened to Sarah tell stories; the little rocky cavity echoed slightly and gave resonance to her voice, depth to her timbre—even Bilger, who didn't understand French well, gave up his perorations to listen to her recount the adventures of Lady Hester, who had preceded us on this rock, a woman with an exceptional fate, she said, and I can understand her passion for this lady whose motivations were as mysterious as the desert itself: what motivated the rich and powerful Lady Hester Stanhope, niece of one of the most brilliant politicians of the time, to leave everything behind and settle in the Ottoman Levant, where she never stopped governing, reigning over the little domain she had carved out for herself, in the Chouf, between the Druzes and the Christians, like a farm in Surrey? Sarah told an anecdote about the way she administered her villagers: "Her people had a singular respect for her," Sarah said, "despite the fact that her Oriental justice was sometimes wrong. She knew the importance the Arabs attach to the respect for women, and pitilessly punished any infraction of the severe restraint she demanded of her servants. Her translator and secretary, son of an Englishman and a Syrian woman, whom she liked very much, came to tell her one day that another person she employed, named Michel Toutounji, had seduced a Syrian girl from the village, and that he had seen them both sitting under a cedar of Lebanon. Toutounji denied it. Lady Hester called the whole village together on the lawn in front of the castle; she sat on some cushions, with her governor to her right and Toutounji to her left, wrapped in their cloaks like us in our blankets, in a respectful attitude. The peasants formed a circle; 'Toutounji,' she said, taking from her lips the long amber stem of that pipe she's always shown smoking in the engravings, 'you are accused of a criminal liaison with Fattoum Aisha, Syrian girl, who is here before me. You deny it. You others,' she went on, addressing the peasants, 'if you know anything about this, speak up. I want justice to be done. Speak.' The villagers replied that they had no knowledge of this fact. So she turned to her secretary, who, with his hands crossed over his chest, was waiting for the sentence. 'You impute to this young man who is entering into the world, and whose sole wealth is his reputation, abominable things. Call your witnesses: where are they?' 'I don't have any,' he replied humbly, 'but I saw him.' 'Your word is without value before the testimony of all the people in the village and the good renown of the young man'; then, taking the severe tone of a judge, she turned to the accused Michel Toutounji: 'If your eyes and lips have committed the crime, if you have looked at this woman, if you have seduced and kissed her, then your eyes and lips will bear the punishment. Seize and hold him! You, barber, shave off the young man's left eyebrow and right mustache.' What was said was done: '*sam'an wa tâ'atan*, I hear and I obey,' as in the fairy tales. Four years later, Lady Hester, who was pleased with a justice that did so little harm to the condemned man, received a letter in which Toutounji amusedly told her that the story of the seduction was indeed true, and that his mustache and eyebrow were doing well."

This Orientalist parody of judgment à la Harun al-Rashid fascinated Sarah; whether or not it was true (and, given Lady Hester's habits, it probably was) didn't matter as much as showing to what extent the Englishwoman had integrated the supposed customs of these Lebanese Druzes and Christians of the mountain where she lived and how her legend had spread these attitudes; Sarah passionately described the engraving where we see Lady Hester, already older, seated in a noble, hieratic posture, that of a prophet or a judge, her long pipe in hand, far, very far

from the languid images of women in harems; she told us about
her refusal to wear the veil and her decision to dress in the Turkish fashion, but as a man. She told us about the passion Lady
Hester inspired in Lamartine, the orator-poet, friend of Liszt
and Hammer-Purgstall, with whom he shared a passion for the
history of the Ottoman Empire: for the French a poet without
equal, but also a prose-writer of genius — like Nerval, but to a
lesser degree, Lamartine revealed himself in his journey to the
Orient, freed himself of his Parisian bonds, evolved in his writing style; faced with the beauty of the unknown, the politician
threw off his dramatic gestures and his babbling lyricism. Perhaps — and this is sad to think — the loss of his daughter Julia,
who died of tuberculosis in Beirut, was necessary, so that the Levant could crystallize pain and death in him; like the Revelation
for others, it took the worst wound, the ultimate suffering for his
eyes, without the nepenthe of Helen of Troy encumbered with
tears, to draw the magnificent portrait, full of somber beauty,
of an original Levant: a magic fountain that almost as soon as
it was discovered began to spit out death. Lamartine came to
the Orient to see the choir of a church that turned out to be
walled up, to visit the cella of a temple that had been sealed off;
he stood straight ahead facing the altar, without noticing the
rays of the setting sun flooding the transept behind him. Lady
Hester fascinated him, since she was beyond his interrogations;
she was in the stars, said Sarah; she read the fate of men in the
stars — scarcely had Lamartine arrived than she offered to reveal
his future to him; the woman he called "the Circe of the deserts"
then explained to him, in between flavored pipes, his Messianic
syncretism. Lady Hester revealed to him that the Orient was
his true country, the country of his fathers, and that he would
return to it — she could divine it from his feet: "See," she said,
"your instep is very high, there's enough space between your

heel and toes, when your foot is on the ground, for water to pass under it without getting you wet—it's the foot of an Arab; it's the foot of the Orient; you are a son of these climates and we are approaching the day when everyone will return to the land of their fathers. We will see each other again."

This podiatrist anecdote had cracked us up; François-Marie couldn't help but take off his shoes to check if he was destined to return to the Orient or not—to his great despair he had, he said, a "Bordeaux foot," and he would return, at the end of days, not to the desert, but to a farmhouse in the Entre-Deux-Mers region, near Montaigne's home, which, all things considered, was just as desirable.

Now that I think about it, Sarah's feet have a perfect arch, under which a small river could easily flow; she spoke through the night and she was our desert magician, her tales enchanted the gleaming metal of the stones and stars—the adventurers of the Orient had not all known the mystical evolution of Mrs. Stanhope, the English recluse of Mount Lebanon, her journey toward the shedding of her things, her progressive abandonment of her western rags, the gradual construction of her own monastery, a monastery of pride or humility; not every woman traveler had received the tragic illumination of Lady Hester or Isabelle Eberhardt in the desert, far from it—it was François-Marie who took the stand next, despite an interruption from Bilger not just to serve drinks but to try to tell a story too, to recount part of the adventures of Alois Musil, called Lawrence of Moravia or Alois of Arabia, Orientalist and spy of the Hapsburgs unknown to the French—it was mostly Bilger's attempt to become the center of attention again: a disastrous attempt, which would have precipitated many guests into sleep, so incomprehensible was his French; out of self-importance or presumptuousness, he refused to speak English. Fortunately, and as I was beginning to feel ashamed for him and for Alois Musil, he was skillfully interrupted by François-Marie. This specialist in the history of the French mandate in the Levant used Lady Hester and Lawrence of Moravia to steer the conversation diplomatically back to Palmyra. The fate of Marguerite d'Andurain, known as Marga, represented for him the antithesis of Stanhope's, Eberhardt's, or Schwarzenbach's: their dark, shadowy twin. We were warming up again thanks to François-Marie's accent and especially to the Lebanese wine that Bilger had opened; my neighbor's long russet curls were turning redder from the last coals that shaped her face with chiaroscuro. The life of Marga d'Andurain was for François-Marie the story of a tragic failure—the beautiful adventuress was born at the very end of the nineteenth century to a good family in Bayonne (this detail was obviously emphasized by the Gascon historian; he had put his shoes back on to protect his toes from the cold), then married young to her cousin, a minor Basque nobleman who promised a great future but turned out to be rather feeble, indecisive, and obsessed almost exclusively with horses. Marga, on the contrary, was endowed with exceptional force, vitality, and resourcefulness. After a brief attempt at raising horses in prewar Argentina, the couple arrived in Alexandria in November 1925 and settled in Cairo, opposite the Groppi tea house on the Soliman Pasha Square, the center of the "European" city. Marga planned to open a beauty salon there and a trade in artificial pearls. Very soon she was frequenting Cairo high society, notably the British aristocrats from the Gezira Sporting Club on the island of Zamalek. That was when the title of "Countess" was added to her family name: she became ennobled, so to speak, by contagion. Two years later, she decided to accompany a friend, an Englishwoman, on a trip to Palestine and Syria, a journey whose guide would be Major Sinclair, head of military intelligence in Haifa. It was in his company that Marga first visited Palmyra, after an exhausting journey from Damascus, where, tired and jealous, her British friend preferred to wait for them. The tense relations between France and Great Britain in the Levant, the recent Syrian rebellion and its bloody repression, caused the French soldiers to be more than a little suspicious about the activities of foreigners in the territory of their mandate — the garrison in Palmyra would take a close interest in the couple that was settling into the hotel built by Fernando de Aranda. It was very likely that Sinclair and Marga became lovers there; their liaison fed the reports of idle French officers, reports that reached Colonel Catroux, who was then in charge of intelligence in Beirut.

The Palmyran adventure of the elegant Comtesse d'Andurain began with an accusation of espionage that was already poisoning her relations with the French authorities in the Levant — this reputation of spy would keep coming up throughout her life, whenever the press or the administration became interested in her.

A few months later, Sinclair died, having killed himself out of love, according to rumor. In the meantime, Marga d'Andurain had settled in Palmyra with her husband. She had fallen in love — not with a British major now, but with the region, the Bedouins, and the desert; she had acquired some land and was thinking of devoting herself (as in Argentina) to horse breeding. She writes in her memoirs about her gazelle hunts in the company of nomads, her nights spent under a tent, the filial tenderness she feels for the sheikh who leads this tribe. Soon, the couple gives up agriculture and is entrusted by the authorities with managing the hotel (the only one in the city at the time) in Palmyra, the ownership of which had reverted to the state, a hotel that they would eventually be allowed to purchase (or so it seems, added François-Marie; there is often, as with any testimony, a slight difference between what Marga relates and all the rest of the sources): she decides to call the establishment the Hotel Zenobia, in homage to the third century CE queen vanquished by Aurelian. All the tourists of the time pass through the d'Andurains's place; Marga looks after the hotel while her husband amuses himself however he can, horseback riding or visiting the officers at the Palmyran garrison who watch over the airfield and command a small troop of mounted soldiers, remnants of the Second Army of the Orient, decimated by the world war and the Syrian revolt.

Five years later, Marga d'Andurain grows bored. Her children have grown up; the queen of Palmyra realizes that her kingdom is nothing but a pile of stones and dust, romantic indeed, but lacking adventure or glory. That's when she thinks up a crazy plan, inspired by the female characters who people her imagination, Lady Hester, Jane Digby the lover, Lady Anne Blunt the granddaughter of Byron, or Gertrude Bell, who died a few years earlier and whose incredible story she learned from Sinclair and his British friends. She dreams of going farther than all these archetypes and of being the first European woman to make a pilgrimage to Mecca, then crossing the Hejaz and the Nejd to reach the Persian Gulf and fishing for (or simply buying) pearls. In the beginning of 1933, Marga finds a way to embark on this journey: she contracts a marriage of convenience with Suleyman Dikmari, a mounted soldier in Palmyra from Oneiza in the Nejd, from the tribe of the Mutayrs, who wants to go home but doesn't have the financial means. He's a simple, illiterate man; he has never left the desert. He agrees, in return for a steep sum, to accompany the so-called countess into Arabia, Mecca, and Medina, then onto the coast to Bahrain, and to bring her back to Syria. Before leaving she of course makes him swear in front of witnesses that he will not try to consummate the marriage and that he will obey her in everything. At the time (and now I have the feeling that François-Marie, in top form, gives us these details only for the pleasure of showing off his historical knowledge) the Nejd and the Hejaz had just been unified by Prince Ibn Saud, who defeated the Hashemites and chased them out his territory — all that's left to the descendants of the sharifs of Mecca are Iraq and Jordan, where they are supported by the British. Saudi Arabia is born just at the time when Marga d'Andurain decides to undertake her pilgrimage. The country is distinguished by its Bedouin identity and by its Wahhabite, puritanical, fundamentalist majority. The kingdom is forbidden to non-Muslims; obviously, Ibn Saud is mistrustful of any possible British or French interventions in his newly unified country. All legations are confined to Jeddah, port to Mecca, on the Red Sea, a hole between two rocks, without any fresh water, infested with sharks and cockroaches, where you had a choice between dying of thirst, sunstroke, or boredom — except during pilgrimage: the point of arrival in the peninsula for Muslims from the Indian Ocean and Africa, the little town sees dozens of boats carrying thousands of pilgrims pass through, with all the risks (police, health, morals) that come with it. It's in this setting that Marga d'Andurain and her "passport-husband," as she calls him, arrive at the beginning of the pilgrimage, after an official conversion to Islam and a (complicated) marriage in Palestine. Now her name is Zeynab (in homage, still, to Zenobia, queen of Palmyra). Unfortunately for her, things very quickly turn bad: the doctor in charge of immigration tells her that the law of the Hejaz requires a two-year waiting period between conversion and admission to the pilgrimage. Suleyman the Bedouin is thus sent to Mecca to solicit an exceptional permit from King Abdulaziz. Marga-Zeynab cannot accompany him, but, out of decency, she can't stay alone at the hotel either — so she is entrusted to the guard of the harem of the governor of

Jeddah, where she will remain shut up for some days, clearing away all humiliations, but managing to ingratiate herself with the wives and daughters of the governor. She hands down to us, said François-Marie, an interesting account about life in a provincial harem, one of the few we have for that region and period. Finally, Suleyman returns from Mecca without having obtained the exceptional permit for his wife; he must take her to his family, near Oneiza. In the meantime, Zeynab has become Marga again: she socializes with Jacques-Roger Maigret, a French consul (he will represent France in Jeddah for seventeen years, seventeen long years, without complaining too much, until 1945; I hope, said François-Marie, they at least made him a *chevalier* or a commander of some Republican order for that interminable reign), and especially his son, to whom she offers his first erotic excitement: for the very young man, the arrival of the beautiful Marga in the kingdom of Wahhabite puritanism is a ray of sunshine — despite the age difference, he takes her to swim secretly outside of the city; he parades Zeynab, in her long black veil, through the little streets of Jeddah. Marga pushes provocation to the point of secretly smuggling her young lover into the hotel room that the consul's power (despite the fact she is no longer legally French) managed to find for her to get her out of the harem. Suleyman insists on continuing on a journey that the countess no longer wants to complete: she fears being held prisoner, far away in the desert, where Maigret's influence would have no sway.

One night she hears knocking on her door: the royal police. She hides her lover under the bed, as in a bedroom farce, thinking it has to do with morality laws — but it's more serious than that: her passport-husband has expired. Suleyman is dead, poisoned, and has accused his wife Zeynab of giving him the deadly dose to get rid of him. Marga d'Andurain is thrown in prison, into a horrible dungeon which concentrates all the horrors of Jeddah: heat, humidity, flying cockroaches, fleas, filth, excrement.

She will spend two months there.

She runs the risk of the death penalty for murder and adultery.

Her fate is in the hands of the qadi of Mecca.

Consul Maigret makes no effort to save her.

On May 30, *L'Orient-Le Jour*, a daily paper in Beirut, announces her death by hanging.

François-Marie pauses—I can't help but glance over at the Zenobia Hotel, whose dark mass you can make out far below, then at Sarah's face, who's smiling at the effect produced by the storyteller. Marga d'Andurain did not in fact die hanged in the Hejaz, but twenty years later, she was killed in the most sordid fashion on her sailboat in Tangiers as she was getting ready to start a gold smuggling operation in the international zone. Suleyman Dikmari is only the second corpse strewing her way marked by violent death. The last will be her own, abandoned at the bottom of the sea, ballasted by concrete, in the Bay of Malabata.

François-Marie continues his tale; he explains that Marga was seen giving to her husband, on the morning of his death, at their last interview, a white packet. She claims it's a packet of Kalmine, a harmless remedy she uses constantly: some ten boxes of this medication are found in her luggage, containing mainly quinine and codeine. A sample is sent to Cairo for analysis. In the meantime, unbeknownst to her, the Oriental press relates her adventures. They describe the French-British spy, the Mata Hari of the desert, prisoner of the jails of Abdulaziz; she is executed at one point, only to be revived the next day; a conspiracy is imagined according to which the security services of Ibn Saud had liquidated the poor Bedouin husband to force Marga d'Andurain to go back home.

Finally, since no autopsy was carried out, in conformity with the strict religious law of the kingdom, and since the analysis of Kalmine carried out in Cairo demonstrated that the powder in the packets is harmless, she is acquitted for lack of proof after two months of detention.

François-Marie was looking at his audience with a little ironic smile; we sensed he had something to add. I thought about Kalmine, whose name struck me; I remembered those blue metal boxes that decorated my grandmother's bathroom in Saint-Benoît-la-Forêt, on which was written "malaise, fatigue, fever, insomnia, cramps"; I remembered it was the Métadier laboratories that made this panacea and that Paul Métadier, the first Balzacian of Touraine, had transformed the Saché château into a Balzac museum. Everything is connected. Balzac, after the Jane Digby–Lady Ell' affair, had one more link with Palmyra. Marga d'Andurain was certainly unaware, when she received a gift in the mail, after the publication of her version of the facts in *L'Intransigeant*, of a hundred packets of Kalmine sent directly by the laboratory to thank her for this free publicity, that the Kalmine fortune to which she had contributed would allow homage to be made, in this château he had liked, to the great man of letters. Paul Métadier would certainly not have sent these promotional remedies if he had suspected that it was indeed a packet stamped "Laboratoires Métadier—Tours" that had poisoned Suleyman Dikmari the warrior from the tribe of Mutayrs; François-Marie had this information from the unpublished memoirs of Jacques d'Andurain, the youngest son of the countess. Jacques d'Andurain told how, in Beirut, the time when his mother left for Mecca, she had confided to him her doubts about Suleyman, who according to her was the only real "weak link" in her journey; Suleyman, the desire of Suleyman, the virility of Suleyman, were the most uncontrollable obstacles in this venture. She would be at his mercy, in Mecca, in the Nejd; her "passport-husband" would have power (or so she thought) of life and death over her: it was logical that she too should have the ability to kill him. So she asked her son to acquire some poison for her, in Beirut, under the pretext of killing a dog, a large dog, a very large dog, quickly and painlessly. She kept this substance in a Kalmine packet, having thrown away its original contents.

We know no more than that.

François-Marie looked at us, happy with the effect he had produced. Sarah resumed speaking; she had gotten up to warm her hands at the dying coals.

"There is an amusing coincidence, Annemarie Schwarzenbach went through Palmyra during her second journey to the Levant, from Beirut to Tehran, in the company of her husband Claude Clarac, secretary at the embassy in Iran. She relates her stay at the Zenobia and her meeting with Marga d'Andurain in a short story called 'Beni Zainab.' She thinks it's very likely she did in fact poison her husband . . . Or at least, she thinks she had the character for it. Not of a poisoner, but of a woman so determined that she's ready to sweep aside all obstacles between her and the goal she has determined."

Julie and François-Marie seemed to agree.

"It's an existence marked entirely by violence, a metaphor for colonial violence, a parable. Soon after her return to Palmyra, once her administrative troubles were more or less over, her husband Pierre d'Andurain is savagely stabbed to death. People thought it was revenge by Suleyman's family, even though Marga and her son suspect (and denounce) a conspiracy of French officers pulling the strings. She goes back to France before the war and spends the Occupation between Paris and Nice, living on various kinds of trafficking: jewelry, opium; in 1945 her eldest son kills himself. In December 1946 she is arrested and placed in custody for poisoning her godson, Raymond Clérisse, an intelligence agent for the Resistance: that's when the press runs wild. She is credited with no fewer than fifteen murders, espionage affairs, a collaboration with the Bonny and Lafont gang, Parisian Gestapo crooks, and God knows how many other crimes. All these articles say a lot about French fantasies at the Liberation—between colonial stories, wartime spymania, memories of Mata Hari and the crimes of Dr. Petiot, the doctor with sixty-three corpses to his name, who has just been guillotined. Marga is finally released for lack of proof a few days later. Then too, she confesses her responsibility in the affair in veiled terms to her son, not long before her own death—that's more or less all we know about the somber fate of the queen of Palmyra."

Sarah pointed out how successful the association of sexuality, the Orient, and violence was in public opinion, even today; one sensationalist French novel, though not itself sensational, took up the adventures of the Countess d'Andurain, and was called *Marga, comtesse de Palmyre*. According to Sarah, this book, without respecting the facts or bothering with verisimilitude, laid great weight on the more "Oriental" aspects of the affair: lust, drugs, espionage, cruelty. For Sarah, what made the character of Marga so interesting was her passion for freedom—a freedom so extreme that it extended beyond even the lives of others. Marga d'Andurain had loved the Bedouins, the desert, and the Levant for this freedom, perhaps entirely mythical, surely exaggerated, in which she thought she could flourish; it had not measured up to her dreams, or rather it had, she'd persisted in it, to such a point that this beautiful freedom had been corrupted into a criminal pride, which ended up being fatal to her. The miracle of her life, moreover, was that she didn't encounter the executioner's axe or the dagger of revenge sooner, running through life thumbing her nose at Fate and at the law for all those years.

Bilger had gotten up in turn to warm himself a little — the keen air was getting to be freezing; beneath our hill, the lights of the city were going out one by one, it must have been around midnight. The Zenobia Hotel was still illuminated, I wondered if the present personnel of the establishment remembered the fake countess (and real murderess) and that husband of hers who died in the middle of this steel-gray desert that was not at all, in this cold night, a pleasant place, or even (I'd have been angry with myself if I had confessed this thought to my companions) a place endowed with the irresistible beauty that some people attributed to it.

Sarah's indulgence toward female criminals, traitors, and poisoners is still a mystery; this penchant for the lower depths of the soul reminds me of Faugier's passion for the lower depths of cities — so far as I know Sarah has never been a spy or killed anyone, thank God, but she has always had an interest in horror, monsters, crime, and gore: when I had abandoned, here in Vienna, my *Standard* whose masthead color of a monkey's backside suits the complexion of its readers so well, in the Maximilian café near the Votivkirche, after declining the expedition to Kafka's home, she forced me (grumbling as much as I could, what an idiot, a strange way to make yourself amiable, sometimes I do — we do — exactly the opposite of what the heart would command) to visit the Museum of Crime: on the ground floor and basement of a pretty eighteenth-century house in Leopoldstadt, we visited the museum of the Vienna Police, an official, typically Viennese museum, the museum of murderers and their victims, with skulls smashed in or pierced with bullets, weapons, evidence cases, photographs, atrocious photographs of mutilated bodies, of corpses cut up to be hidden in wicker baskets and thrown out in the trash. Sarah observed these horrors

with a calm interest, the same, I imagined, as that of Sherlock
Holmes or Hercule Poirot, the Agatha Christie hero you encountered everywhere in the Orient, from Istanbul to Aleppo to
Palmyra—Christie's husband was an archaeologist, and archaeologists were the first parasites to jump on the Oriental band-
wagon, ever since Vivant Denon and the expedition to Egypt:
the conjunction of romantic interest in ruins and of a renewal of
the historical sciences pushed dozens of archaeologists toward
the East, the origin of civilization and religion and, secondarily,
the source of objects that could be converted into prestige or
hard cash; the fashion for all things Egyptian—then Nabatean,
Assyrian, Babylonian, Persian—cluttered up museums and antique shops with all sorts of debris, the way Roman antiquities
were all the rage during the Renaissance. Bilger's ancestors
crisscrossed the Ottoman Empire from Bithynia to Elam, often
taking their wives with them, wives who became, like Jeanne
Dieulafoy or Agatha Christie, writers, when they didn't devote
themselves, like Gertrude Bell or Annemarie Schwarzenbach,
to the joys of archaeology. Archaeology was, along with mysticism, one of the most fertile ways of exploring the Near and
Middle East and Bilger agreed about this, that night in Palmyra
when, warmed by the Lebanese wine, he deigned to take part,
in English this time, in our Assembly, our *Maqāma Tadmoriyya*,
with all the British eloquence he had brought back from his
stay in Oxford, whence so many distinguished Orientalists
had emerged—he had remained standing; his round face was
wholly in shadow and you could only make out the blond edge
of his short hair, like a halo. Bottle in hand, as was his habit,
he made his contribution to the desert, as he put it, telling us
about the archaeologists and botanists who had contributed to
the exploration of mysterious Arabia: Bilger, so urban in most
ways, had also dreamed of the desert, and not only by following
the adventures of Kara Ben Nemsi on TV; before he became a

specialist of the Hellenistic period, he had tried without success to "make his niche" in the archaeology of pre-Islamic Arabia — the actions of the explorers of the peninsula held no secrets for him. He began by sweeping aside the appeal of characters like this Marga d'Andurain whom he had just discovered. In terms of violence, madness, and eccentricities, the travelers to the Nejd, the Hejaz, or the Jabal Shammar offered much more extraordinary tales — even, he added grandiloquently, real literary masterpieces. He then launched into a complicated story about the exploration of Arabia of which I don't remember much, aside from the names of the Swiss Burckhardt, of the Englishmen Doughty and Palgrave, the Frenchman Huber, and the German Euting — not to mention the figureheads of the desert, Richard Burton the man with the thousand lives, and the Blunt couple, incorrigible horse lovers who crisscrossed the sands in search of the finest horses whose lineage — the noble Arab thoroughbred — they then cultivated at their stud farm in Sussex. Anne Blunt was the most sympathetic to me of this whole bunch of explorers, since she was a violinist and had nothing less than a Stradivarius as her instrument. A Stradivarius in the desert.

There might perhaps be an apostil to add to my book, a coda, or even a codicil,

On the Divers Forms of Lunacie in the Orient
Addendum
Caravan of Cross-Dressers

which would testify to the passion of my colleagues from long ago for disguise and local costumes — many of these political or scientific explorers thought they had to disguise themselves, as much for comfort as to go unnoticed: Burton as a pilgrim in the caravan to Mecca; the amiable Hungarian Orientalist Armin Vambery, friend of the Comte de Gobineau, as a religious vag-

abond (shaved skull, Bukhara robe) to explore Transoxiana
from Tehran; Arthur Conolly, first player in the Great Game,
who would end up unmasked and beheaded in Bukhara, as a
Persian merchant; Julius Euting as a Bedouin, T. E.
Lawrence (who knew his Kipling) as a Howeitat warrior — they all tell
of the slightly childlike pleasure there is (if you love danger)
in passing yourself off as something you're not, with first place
awarded to the explorers of the Southern Sahara and the Sa-
hel, René Caillié the conqueror of Timbuktu disguised as an
Egyptian, and especially Michel Vieuchange, young lover of the
desert about whom we know nothing or almost nothing, who
disguised himself first as a woman and then as a sack of salt to
glimpse the city of Smara for a quarter of an hour, a mythical city
indeed, but ruined and abandoned long ago by its inhabitants,
he saw it before returning to his big jute sack, sick, tossed about
by the camels' footsteps for days, without light in an oven-like
heat: he finally expired of exhaustion and dysentery in Agadir,
at only twenty-six years of age. Sarah prefers the simplicity of a
few more forthright or less crazy souls, some with a fate just as
unfortunately tragic, like Isabelle Eberhardt, in love with Algeria and Muslim mysticism — Isabelle did indeed dress up as an
Arab horseman and call herself Si Mahmoud, but her passion for
Islam and her faith were so much deeper than that; she ended
up tragically drowned by a sudden flood, in Ain Sefra, down in
the south of Oran, an area that she loved so much. Sarah often
recalled, about Isabelle, that she had even conquered General
Lyautey, usually so little interested in eccentricities, to such a
point that he spent days, despairing, looking first for her body
and then for her diaries — he finally found them, those notebooks, in the ruins of Isabelle's hut, and the whole manuscript
of *The South of Oran* was lifted from the mud by soldiers with the
patience of stamp collectors ungluing stamps.

The real question in Palmyra for Bilger, who didn't care much about mystics or disguises, aside from amusing anecdotes about the inveterate tellers of tall tales of all kinds who peopled these lands (the funniest obviously concerned the adventures of the Frenchman Charles Huber and the German Julius Euting, veritable Laurel and Hardy of Arabia), was that of the relationship between archaeology and espionage, between military science and science pure and simple. How can we reassure Syrians today about our activities, Bilger moaned, if our more well-known predecessors played a political role, secret or public, in the Middle East? He was driven to despair by this observation: famous archaeologists had all, at one time or another, dabbled in affairs of State. He had to be reassured: fortunately or unfortunately, archaeologists had not been the only ones to serve the military, quite the contrary; pretty much every branch of science (linguists, specialists in religious studies, historians, geographers, writers, ethnologists) had all had relationships with their native governments during wartime. Of course not all of them had necessarily borne arms like T. E. Lawrence or my compatriot Alois Musil, the Lawrence of Moravia, but many (women included, like Gertrude Bell, Sarah added) had, at one time or another, placed their knowledge at the service of the European nation to which they belonged. Some out of nationalist conviction, others for the financial or academic gain they could win from it; others finally in spite of themselves — it was their work, their books, the stories of their explorations, which were used by the military. Everyone knows that maps serve only to wage war, said François-Marie, well, the same is true for travel narratives. Ever since Bonaparte in Egypt in 1798 had gotten scholars involved to write his proclamation to the Egyptians and try to pass as their liberator, scientists and artists had found themselves taking part, willingly or unwillingly, in the political and economic issues of the time. It was nevertheless not possible,

Sarah argued, to condemn all these people en masse; might as well blame chemistry for gunpowder and physics for ballistics: things had to be brought back to the individual and you had to abstain from fabricating a general discourse that became in turn an ideological construct, a subject with no other import than its own justification.

The debate became stormy; Sarah had mentioned the Great Name, the wolf had appeared in the midst of the flock, in the freezing desert: Edward Said. It was like invoking the Devil in a Carmelite convent; Bilger, horrified at the idea that he could be associated with any kind of *Orientalism*, immediately began an embarrassed auto-criticism, renouncing everything; François-Marie and Julie were more nuanced on the question, while still acknowledging that Said had asked a burning but pertinent question: the relationship between knowledge and power in the Orient—I had no opinion, and I still don't, I think; Edward Said was an excellent pianist, he wrote about music and created with Daniel Barenboim the West-Östlicher Divan Orchestra, managed by a foundation based in Andalusia, where the beauty of sharing and diversity is stressed.

The voices began to be conquered by the wine, the cold, and fatigue; we had set up our makeshift beds on the rock of the parvis. Julie and François-Marie on one side, Sarah and I on the other—Bilger (probably cleverer than us) had preferred to take refuge with his bottle in the car, parked a few meters below; we found Bilger again in the early morning, seated in the driver's seat, face crushed against the mud-covered window, with the empty bottle wedged in the steering wheel, pointing its accusing neck at the face of the sleeping archaeologist.

Two blankets underneath, two on top, that was our Palmyran bed; Sarah had rolled up into a ball against me, her back against my stomach. She had kindly asked if that bothered me: I had tried not to let my enthusiasm show through, of course not, not at all, and I blessed nomadic life—her hair smelled of amber and wood fire; I didn't dare move, from fear of disturbing her breathing, whose rhythm overwhelmed me; I tried to breathe like her, *adagio* at first, then *largo*; next to my chest I had the long curve of her back, barred by her bra, whose hooks I could feel against my folded arm; her legs were cold and she had entwined them slightly in my own—the nylon was at once soft and electric against my calves. My knees in the hollows of hers, I had to try not to think too much about this proximity, which was of course impossible: an immense desire, which I managed to stifle, consumed me despite everything, in silence. The intimacy of this position was at once chaste and erotic, like the Orient itself, and before burying my eyelids in her curls for some hours, I directed one last glance, beyond the blue wool, at the sky over Palmyra, to thank it for being so inhospitable.

Waking up was comical; the voices of the first tourists jarred us just before dawn—they were from Swabia and their sing-song dialect sounded completely out of place in Palmyra. Before pushing back the blanket we were shivering beneath, intertwined like lost souls, I was dreaming that I was waking up in an inn near Stuttgart: totally disoriented, I opened my eyes onto a group of hiking boots, thick socks, legs, some hairy, others not, topped off with sand-colored shorts. I suppose these good people must have been just as embarrassed as we; they had wanted to enjoy the sunrise over the ruins and fell into a camp of Orientalists. I was overcome with a terrible shame; I immediately pulled the blanket over our heads in an idiotic reflex that was even more ridiculous. Sarah had awakened as well and was tittering; stop it, she whispered, they'll think we're naked underneath—the Germans must have made out our bodies under the blankets and heard our whispering; no way am I getting out of here, I muttered. "Getting out" was an entirely relative expression, since we were outside, but just as children hide in an imaginary cave at the bottom of their sheets, it was out of the question that I would rejoin the outside world until these invaders had left. Sarah joined willingly in the game, laughing; she had arranged for a current of air that would allow us not to suffocate completely; from a fold she spied on the position of the enemy warriors around us, who seemed not to want to leave the parvis. I inhaled her breath, the smell of her body upon awakening. She was right up against me, lying on her stomach — I dared slip my arm around her shoulders, in a gesture I hoped could seem brotherly. She turned her face and smiled at me; I prayed to Aphrodite or Ishtar to transform our shelter into rocks, make us invisible and leave us there for eternity, in this corner of happiness that I had made without meaning to, thanks to these Swabian crusaders sent by an inspired god: she was looking at me, motionless and smiling, her lips a few centimeters from mine. My mouth was dry, I looked away, muttered some absurdity, and at about the same instant we heard the voice of François-Marie resounding: "*Good morning, ladies and gentlemen, welcome to Fakhr ed-Din's Castle*"; we risked a glance outside of our improvised tent and burst out laughing, together, when we saw that the Frenchman had emerged from his sleeping bag, his hair standing on end, dressed solely in a pair of boxer shorts as black as the hair that covered his chest, to greet the dawn visitors — this djinn succeeded almost immediately at putting them to flight, but I didn't make a move to lift the veil that was covering us, and Sarah didn't either: she stayed there, so close to me. The growing light spattered the inside of our cavern with glints of sunlight. I turned over, not knowing why; I curled up in a ball, I was cold, and she pressed against me, I could feel her breath on my neck, her breasts on my back, her heart beating with mine, and I pretended to fall back asleep, my hand in hers, as the sun of Baal slowly warmed me — as if I weren't hot enough.

Our first night in the same bed (she would say later that we couldn't reasonably call it the same *bed*) left me with an enduring memory, sore bones, and a rather glorious catarrh: I ended our expedition with my nose full of mucus, blushing from these otherwise harmless secretions, as if my nostrils revealed to the outer world, symbolically, what my unconscious had secretly distilled through the whole night.

The tourists finally dislodged us, or at least forced us to get up and surrender, the battle was lost in advance — patiently, burning some twigs, we managed to boil some water to prepare Turkish coffee; I can see myself again sitting on the rock, contemplating the palm grove far beyond the temples, with my cup in hand. I understood the verse that till then had been enigmatic by Badr Shakir Sayyab, "Your eyes are a forest of palm trees at dawn / or a balcony, with the moon far beyond" which opens his *Rain Song*; Sarah was happy that I mentioned this poor poet from Basra, lost in melancholy and illness. That night, that morning, this blanket had created an intimacy between us, our bodies had tamed each other, and they didn't want to leave each other anymore — they continued to press against each other, to lean against each other in a familiarity that the cold no longer justified.

Was that when I had the idea to set that poem to music, probably; was it the freezing sweetness of that night in the desert, Sarah's eyes, the Palmyra morning, the myths floating over the ruins that brought this project to birth, at least that's what I like to imagine — perhaps there was also a game of fate, now it's my turn to be alone, ill and melancholy in sleeping Vienna, like Sayyab the Iraqi, Sayyab whose fate so moved me in Damascus. I can't think of the terrifying future the medical books predict for me, like the Pythia, to whom could I confide my fears, to whom could I reveal that I'm afraid of degenerating, rotting like Sayyab, afraid my muscles and brain little by little will be liquefied, afraid of losing everything, of ridding myself of everything, my body and my mind, piece by piece, bit by bit, squama by squama, until I'm no longer able to remember, speak, or move, has this trajectory already begun, that's the most terrible thing, am I already at this moment less than I was yesterday, incapable of perceiving my failing — of course I take stock of myself in my muscles, in my folded hands, in the cramps, pains, crises of extreme fatigue that can pin me to the bed, or on the contrary the insomnia, hyperactivity, impossibility to stop thinking or speaking alone. I don't want to plunge into the names of disease, doctors or astronomers like to give their own names to their discoveries, botanists prefer to give them the names of their wives — if pressed, you could understand why they might want to lend their names to asteroids, but why did those great doctors leave their patronymics to terrifying and above all incurable diseases, their names are synonymous today with failure, failure and impotence, the Charcots, Creutzfeldts, Picks, Huntingtons, so many doctors who have (in a strange metonymic movement, the curer for the incurable) become the disease itself and if the name of mine is soon confirmed (the doctor is obsessed with the diagnosis; scattered symptoms must be gathered together and take on *meaning* in a whole: the good Dr. Kraus will be relieved to know I am mortally affected, finally a known syndrome, named as if by Adam himself) that will be after months of exams, wandering from department to department, from hospital to hospital — two years ago, Kraus sent me to consult an Aesculapian who specialized in infectious and tropical diseases, convinced I had brought back a parasite from one of my trips, and it was pointless for me to explain to him that

Iran is not overflowing with aggressive bacilli or exotic infusoria (and above all that it had been years since I left Europe), as a good Viennese, for whom the vast world begins on the other side of the Danube, Kraus took on his knowing and clever air, typical of scholars when they want to hide their ignorance, to gratify me with a "you never know," a phrase in which his proud Dr. Diafoirus attitude meant to convey "Me, I know, I have my own ideas." So I found myself face-to-face with a specialist in exotic infections, with my shabby symptoms (ophthalmic migraines, insomnia, cramps, debilitating pain in my left arm), all the more annoyed at having to wait in a hospital corridor since (obviously) Sarah was in Vienna at the time, and we had urgent and awful tourist visits on the burner. I had had to explain my appointment at the hospital to her, but I didn't tell her why: I was too afraid she'd think I was contagious, worry about her own health and put me in quarantine — it might be time for me to tell her about my difficulties, I haven't yet dared, but if tomorrow the disease transforms me into a priapic, slobbering animal, or a chrysalis dried out on its commode then I won't be able to tell her anything, it'll be too late. (Whatever the case, lost as she is apparently in Sarawak, how can I explain to her, what letter could I write, especially why write to her, what does she represent to me, or rather, even more of a mystery, what do I represent to her?) I don't have the courage either to tell Mother about it, how to announce to a mother that she will find herself, at almost seventy-five, wiping her son's ass, spoonfeeding him until he passes away, shriveled up enough to be able to return to her womb, it's an atrocity I can't commit, God save us, I'd rather die alone with Kraus. He's not a bad fellow, Kraus, I hate him but he's my only ally, unlike the doctors in the hospital who are apes, cunning and unpredictable. The specialist in tropical diseases wore an open white smock over a pair of blue canvas pants; he was a little chubby, with a big round face and a Berlin accent. How comical it is, I thought, obviously a specialist in exotic infections has to be German, our own empire has always been European, no Togo or Samoan Islands to study pestilential fevers in. Sarah asked me, That appointment, did it go well? I answered: Everything's fine, the specialist looked like Gottfried Benn, which immediately made her burst out laughing, you must be kidding, Gottfried Benn, but Benn looked like Mr. Everybody—exactly, Gottfried Benn doesn't look like anyone in particular, so this doctor is his spitting image. During the entire consultation I pictured myself in a lazaretto on the Belgian front in 1914 or in a horrible clinic for venereal diseases in the Weimar Republic; Gottfried Benn examined my skin in search of traces of parasitosis or "God knows what else," convinced that humanity was always *infected* by Evil. I never followed up on the absurd exam requests from Dr. Benn, defecating into a plastic container being absolutely beyond me, which I obviously didn't confess to Sarah—it should be said, in my defense, that being auscultated by the author of *Morgue* and *Flesh* doesn't inspire a whole lot of confidence in you. To muddy the issue with Sarah, I launched into a clumsy comparison of Benn and Georg Trakl, who should be both likened to and contrasted with him; Trakl the subtle, secret man whose poetry obscured reality in order to enchant it, Trakl the sensitive man from Salzburg whose lyricism dissimulates, hides the *self* in a complex symbolic forest, Trakl the *poète maudit*, drug addict, madly in love with his sister and with the sap of the poppy, whose work is shot through with moon and blood, sacrificial blood, menstrual blood, blood of deflowering, the underground river flowing to the scenes of carnage of the Battle of Grodek in 1914 and to the men dying in the first combats in Galicia—Trakl saved, maybe, by his so-premature death from the horrible political choices of Benn, it's Sarah who presented me with this atrocious verdict, dying young sometimes saves you from the terrifying mistakes of old age; imagine if Gottfried Benn had died in 1931, she said, would you judge him in the same way if he hadn't written *Der Neue Staat und die Intellektuellen*, The New State and the Intellectuals, and made such horrible statements against anti-fascist writers?

This argument was specious, I maintained; many people who hadn't died in 1931 still didn't exalt "the victory of new authoritarian States" like Benn; with Benn the body is not the shrine of the soul, it's nothing but a miserable instrument that must be improved by genetics to obtain a better, more efficient race. That scientists were later horrified by the consequences of their own theories does not absolve them. That Benn finally distanced himself from the Nazis shortly after their rise to power does not absolve him. The Benns took part in the Nazi illusion. Their subsequent terror when confronted by their Golem in no way excuses them.

Now the tachycardia and the suffocating sensation are coming back. The images of death, the smashed bones in Trakl's melancholy, the moon, the shadow of the ash tree in autumn, where the spirits of the massacred sigh; sleep and death, sinister eagles — "Sister with the melancholy of storm, look, a boat is rushing forth under the stars, toward the silent face of night" — the wild moan of broken mouths. I'd like to go back to the desert, or to the poems of Sayyab, the Iraqi with such an unfortunate face, huge ears that stuck out, who died in poverty, solitude, and suffering in Kuwait, where he shouted to the Persian Gulf: "O Gulf, you who offer pearls, shells, and death," with no other response than the echo, carried by the breeze of the Orient, "you who offer pearls, shells, and death," and now here's the agony, the noisy silence where only my own words resound, I'm drowning in my own breath, in panic, I'm a fish out of water.

Lift my head from the pillow quickly, this profound swamp of anguish, turn on the lamp, breathe in the light.

I'm still breathing in the light.

My books are all facing me, looking at me, calm horizon, prison wall. The lute from Aleppo is an animal with a round belly and a thin short leg, a lame gazelle, like the ones hunted by the Omayyad princes or Marga d'Andurain in the Syrian desert. The engraving by Ferdinand-Max Bredt looks like her; *The Two Gazelles*, the girl with the black eyes, in harem trousers, feeding the beautiful animal from her hand.

I'm thirsty. How much time do I have left to live? What did I do wrong, to find myself alone and awake in the night, heart beating, muscles trembling, eyes burning, I could get up, put my headphones on and listen to music, seek consolation in music, in Nadim's oud, for example, or in a Beethoven quartet, one of the late ones—what time is it in Sarawak, if I had dared to kiss Sarah that morning in Palmyra instead of turning over like a coward everything might have been different; sometimes a kiss changes an entire life, fate changes course, bends, makes a detour. Already when I returned to Tübingen after the Hainfeld conference, when I went back to my lover of the time (Sigrid, has she become the brilliant translator she dreamed of being, I have no idea), I realized how insipid our otherwise profound, daily connection seemed compared to what I had glimpsed with Sarah: I spent the following months thinking about her and writing to her, more or less regularly but always secretly, as if I was sure that in these nonetheless innocent letters such a powerful force was at work that it placed my relationship with Sigrid in danger. If my emotional life (let's look things squarely in the face) is such a failure, it's no doubt because I have always, consciously or not, kept a place for Sarah in it, and this waiting has prevented me, till now, from committing myself wholly to a love affair. Everything is her fault, the swish of a petticoat sweeps a man away more surely than a typhoon, that's common knowledge; if she hadn't carefully maintained the ambiguity, if she had been clear, we wouldn't be here, sitting in the middle of the night staring at the bookcase, hand still on the bakelite button (pleasant object, notwithstanding) of the bedside lamp switch. A day will come when I won't even be able to carry out this simple gesture, work the switch, my fingers will be so numb, so stiff that I'll have trouble shedding light on my night.

I should get up and drink something but if I leave my bed I won't get back in before dawn, one should always have a bottle of water within arm's reach, a goatskin bottle, like in the desert, a container that gives liquids its characteristic smell of goat and tar: kerosene and animal, that's the taste of Arabia — Leopold Weiss, who spent months on camel-back between Medina and Riyadh or between Ta'ef and Ha'il in the 1930s, would have agreed, Leopold Weiss or Muhammad Asad by his Muslim name, the most brilliant correspondent in the Middle East of his time, for the *Frankfurter Zeitung* and most of the major newspapers of the Weimar Republic, Leopold Weiss, a Jew from Galicia educated in Vienna not far from here: he's the man or rather the book responsible for my departure to Damascus after my stay in Istanbul. I can see myself again, in my last weeks in Tübingen, as Sigrid was taking a path that was leading her, as the days passed, inexorably away from mine, a distance that my trip to Turkey had accentuated even more, I can see myself again, between letters to that distant star that was Sarah, discovering, filled with wonder, the spiritual memoirs of Muhammad Asad, that extraordinary *Road to Mecca* that I read as if it were the Koran itself, sitting on a bench facing the Neckar, under a willow, thinking "if God needs intermediaries then Leopold Weiss is a saint," so much did his testimonial manage to give voice to the anxiety that had gripped me since my experience in Istanbul—I remember precisely the phrases that had taken my breath away and brought tears to my eyes: "This sonorous, solemn mingling and parting of voices is unlike any other chant of man. And as my heart pounds up to my throat in excited love for this city and its sounds, I begin to feel that all my wanderings have always had but one meaning: to grasp the meaning of this call . . ." The meaning of the call to prayer, of the *Allah akhbar* ululated at the top of all the minarets in the world since the age of the Prophet, the meaning of this unique melody that had overwhelmed me as well when I heard it for the first time in Istanbul, the city where nevertheless this *adhan* is among the most discreet, drowned in the racket of modernity. Sitting on my bench in Tübingen, in a setting quite remote from Arabia, I couldn't lift my eyes from these words, *to grasp the meaning of this call*, as if I were face-to-face with the Revelation, while this muezzin's voice was re-sounding in my ears, clearer than ever, that voice, that chant that had fascinated Félicien David or Leopold Weiss my compatriot to the point of transforming their lives—I too wanted to try to grasp the meaning of this cry, follow it, still wholly filled with the memory of the Süleyman Mosque; I had to leave, I had to discover what was behind this veil, the *origin* of this chant. You could say that my spiritual life has been the same disaster as my sentimental life. I find myself today as lost as before, without the consolation of faith—I am without a doubt not one of the elect; perhaps I lack the will of the ascetic or the creative imag-ination of the mystic; perhaps music, in the end, was my only true passion. The desert turned out to be (and this is putting it mildly) a heap of pebbles; the mosques remained for me as empty as the churches; the lives of saints and poets, their texts, in which I could catch glimpases of beauty, shone like prisms without their light, their Avicennan light, their essence, ever reaching me—I am condemned to the utopian materialism of Ernst Bloch, which in my case is a resignation, the "Tübingen paradox." In Tübingen, I could see three possible paths: religion, as of Leopold Weiss *alias* Muhammad Asad; utopia, as in Bloch's *The Spirit of Utopia* or *The Principle of Hope*; the madness and seclusion of Hölderlin, whose tower projected an unsettling shadow, between the weeping willows and the wooden boats of the Neckar, over the entire city. Why the hell had I chosen to take advantage of the European community's relative generosity toward students by going to Tübingen, and not to Paris, Rome, or Barcelona like all my comrades; probably the prospect of joining Hölderlin's poetry, Enno Littmann's Orientalism, and Ernst Bloch's musical philosophy together seemed a good program to me. I had devoured thousands of pages of Littmann's translation of the *Thousand and One Nights* and had begun to learn Arabic from his successors. It was strange to imagine that a hundred years before, Tübingen and even Strasbourg (where Theodor Nöldeke and Euting officiated, among others) had been, until the First World War turned the world of scholars upside-down, the most Oriental cities in the German Empire. In this great Orientalist network, Enno Littmann was one of the most important German connections; it was he who published, for example, the travel journals of that famous Euting whose adventures in Arabia, related by Bilger, had made us laugh so much in Palmyra; epigrapher, specialist in Semitic languages, Littmann traveled all around southern Syria as early as 1900 in search of Nabatean inscriptions; he describes, in a letter to Eduard Meyer, specialist in the ancient Orient, a dig in the Hauran in winter—battling with the cold, the wind, and the snowstorms, he relates his encounter with a Bedouin who calls himself Kelb Allah, "the dog of God": this humble nickname is a revelation to him. As it was for Leopold Weiss, the humility of nomadic life was one of the strongest images in Islam, the great renunciation, the stripping-away of worldly trappings in the nakedness of the desert—that purity, that solitude drew me in as well. I wanted to meet this God who was so present, so natural that His humble creatures, in complete destitution, call themselves *the dogs of God*. Two visions contrasted vaguely with each other in my mind: on one hand, the world of the *Thousand and One Nights*, urbane, wonderful, abundant, erotic; and on the other, the *Road to Mecca*, its emptiness and transcendence; Istanbul had signified my discovery of a contemporary version of the first form—I had hoped that Syria would allow me to discover, in the alleyways of Damascus and Aleppo with their enchanting names, the reverie and sensual sweetness of the *Arabian Nights*, but also let me glimpse, in the desert this time, the Avicennan light of the All. As with Muhammad Asad, my avid readings in Ernst Bloch, his *Traces* and his little text on Avicenna had (to the great despair of Sigrid, poor thing, to whom I read out loud endless extracts from his works) planted in my mind a fertile disorder, where the utopian materialist took the Muslim mystic by the hand, reconciled Hegel with Ibn Arabi, and everything in music; for hours on end, sitting cross-legged in the deep, battered armchair that stood in as a cell for me, opposite our bed, headphones in my ears, without letting myself be distracted by the comings and goings of Sigrid (white legs, muscular stomach, breasts high and hard) I would visit the thinkers: René Guénon, who became Sheikh Abd al-Wahid Yahya in Cairo, and who spent thirty years following the infallible compass of Tradition, from China to Islam, passing through Hinduism, Buddhism, and Christianity, without ever leaving Egypt—his works on initiation and the transmission of Truth fascinated me. I was not the only one; a number of my comrades, especially the French ones, had read Guénon's books, and these readings had launched the quest for the mystic spark for many, some among Sunni or Shiite Muslims, others among Orthodox Christians and the Eastern Churches, still others, like Sarah, among the Buddhists. In my case, I have to admit that the works of Guénon only added to my confusion.

Fortunately, reality puts your ideas back into place; a sterile formalism seemed to me to reign over all faiths in Syria, and my spiritual impetus soon shattered against the simpering airs of my co-disciples who went to roll on the ground, foaming at the mouth, in *zikr* sessions twice a week the way you go to the gym, a gym where the trances seemed to come a little too quickly to be genuine: repeating ad infinitum *"la ilaha illa Allah*, there is no god but Allah" while shaking your head in a monastery of dervishes no doubt by its very nature placed you in odd states, but that stemmed more from psychological illusion than the miracle of faith, at least as my compatriot Leopold Weiss described it in his beautiful sobriety. Sharing my doubts with Sigrid was no easy thing: my thoughts were so confused that she didn't understand anything, which was not surprising; her own world, Slavic languages, was very far from my own. We came together around Russian or Polish music, around Rimsky, Borodine, Szymanowski, of course, but for me it was Rimsky-Korsakov's *Scheherazade* or Szymanowski's *Songs of an Infatuated Muezzin*, the Orient in them, and not the banks of the Volga or the Vistula that I was passionate about — the discovery of Karol Szymanowski's *Songs of an Infatuated Muezzin*, his *"Allah akhbar"* right in the middle of Polish verses, this insane love ("If I didn't love you, would I be the madman who sings? And my hot prayers that fly up to Allah, aren't they to tell you that I love you?") diffused by melismata and coloratura seemed to me a beautiful European variation on an Oriental theme: Szymanowski had been very impressed by his trip to Algeria and

Tunisia in 1914, by the celebrations on the nights of Ramadan, *impassioned* even, and it was this passion that showed through in these *Songs of an Infatuated Muezzin*, songs that were nonetheless not very Arab: Szymanowski was content to use augmented seconds and the minor keys typical of *imitations* of Arab music, without concerning himself with the quarter tones introduced by Félicien David—but that wasn't his aim; Szymanowski didn't need, in this evocation, to rid himself of harmony or break with tonality. But he had heard these quarter tones; he would use them in his *Myths*, and I'm convinced that Arab music is at the origin of these pieces that radically transformed the violin repertoire of the twentieth century. An assimilated Arabic music, this time, not an exogenous element put into play to obtain an exotic effect, but a real possibility for renewal: a force of evolution, not a revolution, as he so justly stated himself. I forget if in Tübingen I was already familiar with the poems of Hafez or with Szymanowski's masterpiece, *The Song of the Night*, on the verses of Rumi—I don't think so.

It was hard for me to share my new passions with Sigrid; Karol Szymanowski to her was a part of the Polish soul, and meant nothing Oriental; she preferred the *Mazurkas* to the *Muezzin*, the dances of the Tatra Mountains to those of the Atlas. Her vision of his work was also entirely justified.

Perhaps freed from the correspondences of the soul, our bodies gave themselves to each other with abandon: I left my dogmatic armchair only to leap onto the bed and join the torso, legs, and lips I found there. The images of Sigrid's nakedness still excite me today, they've lost nothing of their power, her thin whiteness, lying on her stomach, legs slightly apart, when only a pink line, surrounded by crimson and blondness, emerged from the white sheets, I can see again with perfect clarity her firm buttocks, two low hills that came to meet her hips, and again the bones of her spine as it rose gently just before the furrow where the pages come together of that half-open book, her thighs, thighs whose skin, never exposed to daylight, were like rich cream slipping beneath the tongue when my hand lingeringly stroked the downy slope of her calf before I got to play in the parallel hollows of her knees — it makes me want to turn the light off again, to bring these visions into focus under my duvet, to find again in my imagination the clouds of Tübingen, so favoring the exploration of femininity, over twenty years ago: today the prospect of having to get used to the presence of another body, of someone else getting used to mine, exhausts me in advance — I feel an immense laziness, a lethargy close to despair; I should try to be seductive, forget the shame of my entirely disgraceful physique, so thin, marked by anguish and illness, forget the humiliation of being exposed, forget shame and age, making you slow and stiff, it seems impossible to me, this forgetting, except with Sarah, of course, whose name invites itself always into the depths of my most secret thoughts, her name, her face, her mouth, her breasts, her hands, and with that charge of eroticism go back to sleep now, in these feminine whirlwinds above me, angels, angels of lust and beauty — it's been what, two weeks since that dinner with Katharina Fuchs, obviously I haven't called her back, or seen her at the university, she'll think I'm avoiding her, and it's true, I am avoiding her, despite the undeniable charm of her conversation, her undeniable charm, I'm not going to call her back, let's be honest, the closer the dinner got to ending the more frightened I was of what could happen next, God knows though that I tried to be handsome, I had knotted over my white shirt that little wine-red silk scarf that makes me look so artistic and chic, I had combed my hair, spritzed myself with eau de cologne, so I was hoping for something from that tête-à-tête dinner, of course, I was hoping to go to bed with Katharina Fuchs, but I couldn't stop myself from watching the candle melt in its pewter holder like the announcement of a catastrophe, Katharina Fuchs is an excellent colleague, a precious colleague, it's definitely better to have dinner with her than to fondle female students like others do. Katharina Fuchs is a woman of my age and my status, a funny, cultivated Viennese woman who eats properly and doesn't cause any scandals in public. Katharina Fuchs is a specialist in the relationship between music and cinema, she can speak for hours about Friedrich Feher's *The Robber Symphony* and the films of Robert Wiene; Katharina Fuchs has a pleasant face, red cheeks, light-colored eyes, very discreet glasses, chestnut hair, and long hands with well-manicured nails; Katharina Fuchs wears two diamond rings—what came over me to arrange that dinner with her, to dream of sleeping with her, solitude and melancholy, no doubt, how pitiful. In that elegant Italian restaurant Katharina Fuchs asked me questions about Syria, Iran, she took an interest in my work, the candle consumed itself, casting an orange shadow on the white tablecloth, little balls of wax hung from the edge of the gray candlestick: I hadn't seen *The Robber Symphony*—you should, she said, I'm sure you'd love that film, I imagined myself undressing in front of Katharina Fuchs, oh I'm sure it's a masterpiece, and her stripping naked in front of me, that red lace lingerie—I had caught a glimpse of her bra strap—I can lend it to you if you like, I have it on DVD, she had interesting breasts of respectable size, the tiramisu is excellent here, and me, what underwear was I wearing? The plaid pink one that keeps falling down because of its broken elastic? Poor us, poor us, how wretched the body is, it's out of the question that I would get undressed in front of anyone today, not with that horrible rag on my hips, oh yes, a tiramisu, it's a little — how should I say — soft, yes, that's the word, tiramisu is often too soft for me, no thanks.

Did she get a dessert in the end? I had to flee my inability to find the courage of intimacy, flee and forget, what a humiliation I made Katharina Fuchs undergo, she must hate me today, what's more I must have prevented her from enjoying her soft tiramisu without meaning to — you have to be Italian to have the idea of *softening* ladyfingers in coffee, everyone knows it's impossible to soak them in anything, they seem hard but as soon as you soak them they begin to droop lamentably, droop and fall into the cup. What a bizarre idea to fabricate softness. Katharina Fuchs is angry at me that's for sure, she had no desire to sleep with me, she's angry at me for having left her standing there at the restaurant's doorway as if I were in a hurry to leave her, as if her company had bored me terribly, good night good night, there's a taxi, I'll take it good night, what an insult, I imagine that Sarah would find this story very funny, I'll never dare tell her this story, the guy who slips away because he's afraid of having put on his pink-and-white boxers with the loose elastic that morning.

Sarah has always found me funny. It was a little annoying in the beginning that she would laugh as soon as I confided my innermost thoughts to her. If I had dared to kiss her under that improvised Palmyran tent instead of turning over scared stiff everything would have been different, everything would have been different, or not, in any case we would not have avoided the Baron Hotel catastrophe or the Tehran catastrophe, the Orient of passions makes me do strange things, today we're an old couple, Sarah and I. The dream from just before is still floating in the air, Sarah languid in that mysterious crypt. Sarawak, Sarawak. She's the one I should take an interest in, selfish old man that I am, an old coward, she's suffering too. That article I received this morning is like a bottle from the sea, a terrifying sign of anguish. I've just realized that the name "Sarah" is in Sarawak. Another coincidence. A sign of fate, karma, she would say. I'm probably the one becoming delirious. Her obsession with death and perversion, crime, torture, suicide, cannibalism, taboos—all of that is nothing but a scientific interest. Like Faugier's interest in prostitution and the lower depths. Like my interest in Iranian music and Orientalist operas. What malady of despair have we come down with? Sarah despite her years of Buddhism, meditation, wisdom, and travel. Kraus was probably right in the end to send me to a specialist in exotic diseases, God knows what rot of the soul I could have caught in those distant lands. The way the crusaders, the first Orientalists, returned to their somber villages in the West loaded with gold, bacilli, and sorrow, aware of having, in the name of Christ, destroyed the greatest wonders they had ever seen, pillaging the churches of Constantinople, burning Antioch and Jerusalem. What truth has burned us, Sarah and me, what beauty have we glimpsed before it eludes us, what suffering, like Lamartine in Lebanon, has secretly ravaged us, suffering of the vision of the Origin or the End I have no idea, the answer was not in the desert, not for me in any case, my *Road to Mecca* was of another kind—unlike Muhammad Asad alias Leopold Weiss, the Syrian *badiya* was more erotic for me than spiritual: after our Palmyran night, having emerged from our blanket, we separated from Julie and François-Marie to continue our expedition with Bilger the Mad, toward the northeast and the Euphrates, via an old Omayyad castle lost in time among the rocks and a phantom Byzantine city, Resafa with the high walls, where the new Commander of the Faithful might have his headquarters today, Shadow of God on Earth, caliph of cutthroats and pillagers of the Islamic State in Iraq and Syria, may God protect him, it must not be easy to be a caliph these days, especially caliph of a band of brutes worthy of the lansquenets of Charles sacking Rome. Maybe someday they'll ransack Mecca and Medina, who knows, with their black flags worthy of the flags of the Abbasid revolution in the eighth century, that would be a change in the geopolitical equilibrium of the region, the kingdom of Ibn Saud the friend of Leopold Weiss might collapse under the saber blows of the bearded ones, great slitters of infidels' throats. If I had the strength, I'd like to write a long article on Julien Jalaleddin Weiss homonymous with Leopold, another convert, who has just died of cancer, a cancer that coincides so much with the destruction of Aleppo and Syria that one could wonder if the two events are linked — Weiss lived between worlds; he had become the greatest *qanun* player in the East and West, and an immense scholar as well. The Al-Kindi ensemble he founded accompanied the greatest singers in the Arab world, Sabri Mudallal, Hamzi Shakkur, Lotfi Buchnaq. Sarah had introduced him to me in Aleppo, she had met him thanks to Nadim, who sometimes played with him — he was living in a Mameluke palace lost in the labyrinth of the old city, a stone's throw away from the mounds of soap and sheep's heads of the souks, an austere stone façade behind which an enchanting courtyard opened up; the winter rooms were overflowing with musical instruments, lutes, zithers, reed flutes, percussion. I took an immediate dislike to that handsome blond man — I didn't like his pretentiousness, or his knowledge, or his grand Oriental sultan airs, or, above all, the childlike admiration Nadim and Sarah had for him, and this jealous mistrustfulness kept me for a long time ignorant of the beauty of his work, marked as it is by encounter, exchange, and a questioning of *tradition*, by the transmission of scholarly, mainly religious music. Perhaps my stay in Iran and my work with Jean During were both necessary for this questioning to take on all its meaning in me. I should write about the homage that Weiss and Al-Kindi made to Usama Ibn Munqidh, prince of Shaizar, the fortress town on the edge of the Orontes in Syria, a knight, hunter, and man of letters, witness and participant, over the course of his very long life that coincided almost entirely with our twelfth century, in the crusades and the establishment of Frankish kingdoms in the Levant. I imagine that prince, lover of spears and falcons, bows and horses, poems and singers, facing the heavy Frankish weapons, and the violent sobriety of those enemies from so far away that it took a lot of time and many battles to domesticate them, to sand down a thin layer of the barbarism on their armor — the Franks ended up learning Arabic, tasting apricots and jasmine, and nourishing a certain respect for these lands they had just delivered from the infidels; the prince of Shaizar, after a life of battles and lion-hunting, experienced exile — it was in this exile, in the fortress of Hosn Kayfa, on the edge of the Tigris, far from battles, aged almost eighty, that he composed treatises as diverse and magnificent as a *Praise of Women*; an *Epistle on Wands* devoted to miraculous staffs, from Moses's staff to the cane that Prince Usama himself used in his old days and that took, he said, by bending beneath his weight, the shape of the powerful bow of his bold youth; a *Treatise on Sleep and Dreams*; and that extraordinary autobiography, *The Book of Instruction by Example*, which is at once a history manual, a treatise on hunting, and a florilegium of literature. Usama Ibn Munqidh also found the time to gather together his poetic *oeuvre*, some extracts of which the Al-Kindi ensemble set to music.

Today the caravanserai of Jalaleddin Weiss in Aleppo has burned down, and he himself is dead, dead perhaps from seeing what he had built (a world of shared ecstasy, of a possibility for change, of participation in alterity) thrown to the flames of war;

he has joined Usama on the banks of another river, that great combatant who said of war:

Valor is indeed a sword more solid than any armor
But it protects the lion from the arrow no more
Than it consoles the conquered from shame and ruin.

I wonder what Usama Ibn Munqidh the brave would think of these hilarious photographs of the jihad fighters of today burning musical instruments, since they're *un-Islamic*: instruments that come no doubt from old Libyan military fanfares, drums, drums and trumpets sprinkled with gas and set on fire in front of a respectful troop of bearded men, as happy as if they were burning Satan himself. The same drums and trumpets, pretty much, that the Franks copied from the Ottoman military music centuries earlier, the same drums and trumpets that the Europeans described with terror, for they signified the approach of invincible Turkish Janissaries, accompanied by *mehters*, and no image better represents the terrifying battle that the jihadists are actually waging against the history of Islam than those poor guys in camo, in their slice of desert, attacking sad martial instruments of whose origin they are ignorant.

There wasn't a single medieval warrior or tattered cutthroat on the nice paved track between Palmyra and Resafa, just a sentry box planted by the side of the deserted road where a few Syrian conscripts were snoozing, shaded by some feeble sheet metal, in their dark-brown winter uniforms despite the heat, in charge of opening a chain that was barring the way and that Bilger only saw at the last moment, forcing him to slam on the brakes and causing the SUV's tires to screech on the overheated asphalt: who expects an unmarked roadblock in the middle of the desert? The two conscripts, sweating, skulls shaved almost bare, poorly cut, loose-fitting jackets the color of camel shit covered in dust, opened their eyes wide, caught hold of their weapons, walked over to the white Range Rover, observed the three foreigners inside, hesitated, seemed to want to ask a question but finally didn't dare; one of them lowered the chain, the other made a sweeping gesture with his arm, and Bilger started up again.

Sarah sighed, Bilger had held his tongue. For a few seconds at least.

DRIVER (*bragging*): I almost took that fucking chain at 120 kilometers per hour.

MALE PASSENGER (*in front, respectfully frightened*): You might try to drive a little slower and be more attentive.

FEMALE PASSENGER (*in back, in French with a touch of anxiety*): You think their rifles were loaded?

DRIVER (*incredulous*): A fucking roadblock in the middle of the desert, that's not normal.

FEMALE PASSENGER (*still in French, anxiety mingled with scientific curiosity*): Franz, there was a sign, but I didn't have the time to read it.

MALE PASSENGER (*in the same language*): I wasn't paying attention, sorry.

DRIVER (*sure of himself and in German*): There must be a military base near here.

MALE PASSENGER (*nonchalant*): Yes, I saw an army tank over there on the right.

FEMALE PASSENGER (*in English, addressing the driver, worried*): There are two guys with machine guns in the ditch, slow down, slow down!

DRIVER (*vulgarly, suddenly on edge*): What are those fucking assholes doing in my way?

MALE PASSENGER (*phlegmatic*): I think it's an infantry battalion on maneuvers.

FEMALE PASSENGER (*increasingly worried and again in French*): But look, good God, look, there are cannons on the hill, over there! And more machine guns on the left! Turn around, turn around!

DRIVER (*very Germanically sure of himself, addressing the passenger*): If they let us pass, it's because we have the right to pass. I'll just slow down a little.

MALE PASSENGER (*less sure of himself, in French*): Um, sure. We should just be careful.

FEMALE PASSENGER (*annoyed*): It's crazy though, look at all those soldiers running over there on the right. And those clouds of dust, is that wind, you think?

MALE PASSENGER (*suddenly anxious*): I think they're vehicles rushing through the desert. Tanks, probably.

SAME (*to the driver*): You're sure we're on the right road? According to your compass we're going more northwest than north. Toward Homs.

DRIVER (*annoyed*): I've taken this road hundreds of times. Unless they've paved a second road recently, it's the right one.

MALE PASSENGER (*matter-of-factly*): This road does look brand-new.

FEMALE PASSENGER (*driving in the nail*): This asphalt is too smooth to be trusted.

DRIVER (*openly angry*): OK, you cowards, I'll make a U-turn. What a bunch of scaredy-cats!

Bilger finally backtracked, doubly enraged, at having chosen the wrong road first of all, and secondly at having been stopped by an army on maneuvers—back at the checkpoint the two dusty sentries lowered the heavy chain with the same phlegm as on our way in; we'd had time to decipher, with Sarah's help, the poorly written wooden sign that said "Military terrain — Danger — No Entrance." It's strange to think that those tanks and machine guns we saw maneuvering are being used today to fight against the rebellion, to crush entire cities and massacre their inhabitants. We made fun so often of the ragged Syrian soldiers sitting in the shade of their ex-Soviet Jeeps broken down by the side of the road, hood open, waiting for an unlikely tow truck. As if that army had no power of destruction, no force of combat; the Assad regime and his tanks seemed to us like cardboard toys, marionettes, effigies empty of meaning on the walls of cities and villages; we did not see, beyond the apparent dilapidation of the army and the leaders, the reality of fear, death, and torture appearing behind the posters, the possibility of destruction and extreme violence behind the omnipresence of soldiers, badly dressed as they were.

Bilger shone, that day: mad as a hornet at his own mistake, he'd sulked for most of the day, once we had gotten back almost to our starting point, a few kilometers from Palmyra, where in fact the road forked, and the other road was in much worse shape (which explained why we had missed it) heading straight north through the hills of stones, he had insisted, to redeem himself, on showing us a magical place, the famous Qasr el-Heyr, an old Omayyad palace dating back to the end of the seventh century, a palace of pleasures, a gathering place for hunting, where the caliphs from Damascus came to hunt gazelles, listen to music, and drink, drink with their companions the wine that was so thick, so spicy, and so strong that it had to be diluted with water — the poets of the time described this mixture, Sarah said; the meeting of the nectar with water was explosive, sparks rose up; in the cup, the mixture was red as the eye of a rooster. There were in Qasr el-Heyr, Bilger explained, some magnificent frescoes of hunting and drinking scenes — hunting and drinking, but also music: in one of the most famous, you see a musician with a lute accompanying a singer, and even though, obviously, these frescoes had been removed, the idea of seeing this famous castle excited us immensely. Of course I didn't know that it was Alois Musil who had discovered and described this castle for the first time during his second expedition. To reach it, he'd had to follow the small paved road straight north for about twenty kilometers, then veer to the east on the labyrinth of paths that head out into the desert; our map was very sketchy, but Bilger had a point to prove in finding the castle in question, which he had already visited and which, he said, could be seen from very far away, like a fortress.

The afternoon sun shone white on the stones; here and there, in the midst of the monotony, a mangy thorn bush grew, God knows how; far in the distance you could glimpse a little group of black tents. This part of the *badiya* wasn't flat, far from it, but since the hills had no particular vegetation, or any shade, it was extremely difficult to make them out: a tent seen a second earlier would disappear suddenly behind an invisible prominence, as if by magic, which made orientation even more complicated; sometimes we would go down into deep depressions, cirques where an entire regiment of mounted soldiers could easily hide. The SUV jolted over the pebbles and was beginning to make some spectacular leaps whenever Bilger went over thirty kilometers per hour; he had to reach sixty, flying so to speak over the stones, for the machine to vibrate much less and for the passengers not to be shaken as in some sort of infernal massage chair—but that speed demanded great concentration: a sudden hump, a hole or a big stone sent the car flying; then the skulls of the occupants would crash violently against the roof and the engine would make a horrible grinding noise. So Bilger was clinging with both hands to the steering wheel, teeth clenched, eyes fixed on the road; the muscles of his forearm were prominent, the tendons on his wrist apparent—he reminded me of a war movie from my childhood, where a soldier in the Afrikakorps was driving a Jeep at breakneck speed somewhere in Libya, not on sand as usual, but on sharp, cutting stones, and the soldier was sweating, fingers white from the pressure on the steering wheel, like Bilger. Sarah didn't seem to realize how strenuous this was; she was reading us the story by Annemarie Schwarzenbach, "Beni Zainab," in a loud voice, in French, about the meeting in Palmyra with Marga d'Andurain we had talked about so much last night: we kept asking her if reading under such circumstances made her carsick, but no, unfortunately, aside from the book leaping in front of her eyes with every jolt, nothing seemed to bother her. Bilger didn't stop himself from making ironic remarks, in German of course: "You did well to bring an audio book, it's pleasant during long journeys. It allows me to improve my French." I'd so have liked to be next to her in the back seat; I hoped without believing it too much that the following night we'd again share the same blanket and this time I'd find the courage to leap into the water, or rather onto her mouth—Bilger said we'd probably be forced to camp in Qasr el-Heyr: impossible to drive in the desert at night, which would suit me nicely.

My wishes were about to be fulfilled, not exactly in the sense of my aspirations, but fulfilled nonetheless: we would be sleeping in the desert. Three hours later, we were driving more or less eastward at a speed wavering between five and sixty kilometers per hour. As none of us had thought to look at the odometer when we left, we didn't really know the distance we had traveled; the map was no help: it only indicated one east–west road in the sector whereas, on the ground, dozens of roads crossed and recrossed endlessly; only the little compass on Bilger's dashboard indicated that we were headed more or less northward.

Bilger was beginning to get annoyed. He swore as much as he could, tapped on the steering wheel; he said it was impossible, we should already have passed the Palmyra–Deir ez-Zor highway, look at the map, he shouted, it's impossible, it's completely impossible, it's ABSOLUTELY IMPOSSIBLE, but we had to face facts: we were lost. At least, not lost, but disoriented. I think I remember that it was Sarah who had introduced this nuance to assuage Bilger's pride, a nuance I had every difficulty in the world rendering into German: it consoled Bilger only a little, he kept cursing under his breath like a child whose toy isn't working. We had made a long stop to climb a rocky mound, hoping the panoramic view might offer us a reference point—the Deir ez-Zor highway or the famous Omayyad castle itself. But what seemed to us to be like a promontory turned out to be more or less at the same level as the environs, there was nothing to see, just our car which was a little lower than the general level of the desert. That green spot toward the north (was it really north?) was a field of spring wheat or a square of grass, those black points groups of tents. We weren't risking much, except not seeing Qasr el-Heyr today. The afternoon was well-advanced—the sun was beginning to set behind us, to Bilger's great despair; I thought of Alois Musil, great discoverer of Omayyad castles, and his exploration missions: in 1898, after studying all the Western documents on the region of Maan and the travelers' accounts at the library of the Jesuit Saint Joseph University in Beirut, he had set off, on camel-back, in the company of a few Ottoman gendarmes "loaned" by the *kaimmakam* of Akaba, into the desert to find the famous pleasure castle of Qasr Tuba, which no one had heard of for centuries, except the Bedouins. What courage, what faith, or what madness animated the little Catholic priest from Bohemia for him to burrow into the void like that, weapon on his shoulder, in the midst of tribes of nomads who were all more or less hostile to Ottoman power and who regularly engaged in pillaging or war? Had he too felt the terror of the desert, that solitary anguish that clenches your chest in the immensity, the great violence of the immensity that one imagines hides many dangers and pains — pains and perils of the soul and body together, thirst, hunger, of course, but also solitude, abandon, despair; it was amusing to think, from the top of this little pile of pebbles of no importance, that the Musil cousins, Alois and Robert, had, each in a very different way, experienced loneliness and abandonment: Robert in the debris of Imperial Vienna, Alois thousands of kilometers away, among the nomads; both had traveled through ruins. I remembered the beginning of *The Man Without Qualities* (is it really the beginning?), when Ulrich meets prowlers armed with lead-filled truncheons who leave him for dead on the Viennese sidewalk; he is helped by a very beautiful young woman who takes him into her car and he holds forth ironically, during the trip, on the similarities between the experience of violence and that of mysticism: for cousin Alois, the desert was — I thought while watching Sarah toil over the gravel on the slope of the little mound just as Ulrich had encountered his Bona Dea under the truncheon's blows — the place of illumination and of abandonment, where God also showed himself by his absence, by his contours, a contradiction that Ulrich, in Robert Musil's novel, pointed out: "Brutality and love are no farther apart than one wing of a big, colorful, silent bird is from the other. He had put the emphasis on the wings and on that bright, mute bird — a notion that did not make much sense but was charged with some of that vast sensuality with which life simultaneously satisfies all the rival contradictions in its measureless body. He now noticed that his neighbor had no idea what he was talking about, and that the soft snowfall she was diffusing inside the cab had grown thicker." Sarah is that snowfall over the desert, I thought as she had almost joined me on top of this observation post from which there was nothing to observe.

I think I'm dozing off, slowly falling asleep, my face caressed by a desert breeze, in the 9th district of this New Vienna that neither of the two Musils knew, on my pillow under my duvet—my indoor nomad tent, as deep and spacious as the one that welcomed us that night, in the desert: like Alois Musil's guides, a heavy, swaying truck had suddenly stopped near us, thinking we were in distress; its occupants (tanned, wrinkled faces wrapped in red keffiehs, stiff mustaches cutting their faces in half) had explained to us that the castle we were looking for was even farther toward the northeast, three good hours on the road, and that we'd never reach it before nightfall: they had invited us to sleep under their black tent, in true Bedouin tradition. We weren't the only ones invited: already sitting in the "salon" was a strange peddler, a strolling merchant of the desert who sold, from immense gray nylon bags, like huge wineskins, hundreds of objects made of plastic—cups, sieves, buckets, flip-flops, children's toys, or tin—teapots, coffeepots, dishes, cutlery; his huge sacks in front of the tent looked like two fat, shapeless larvae or the degenerate pods of some hellish plant. This peddler was from northern Syria and had no vehicle: he traveled the *badiya* at the mercy of the trucks and tractors of the nomads, going from tent to tent until he had sold everything, and then returning to Aleppo to stock up again in the labyrinth of souks. He would take up his travels as soon as his stock was complete, go down the Euphrates by bus, then crisscross the entire territory between the river, Palmyra and the Iraqi border, taking advantage (abusing, a Westerner would think) of the hospitality of the nomads, who were his customers as well as his hosts. This T. E. Lawrence of cutlery must no doubt have been something of a spy and informed the authorities about the deeds and movements of these tribes who maintained such close ties with Iraq, Jordan, Saudi Arabia, and even Kuwait: I was very surprised to learn that I was in a house (which is what a tent is called, in Arabic) of the clan of the Mutayrs, the famous warrior tribe that allied with Ibn Saud in the early 1920s and permitted his rise to power, before rebelling against him. The tribe of the passport-husband of Marga. Muhammad Asad the Jew from Arabia tells how he himself took part in an espionage operation in Kuwait for Ibn Saud, against the Mutayrs of Faysal Dawish. These great warriors seemed (at least in their Syrian version) to be the most peaceful variety: they were breeders of sheep and goats, and had a truck and some chickens. Out of modesty, Sarah had tied back her hair as well as she could in the car as we followed the Bedouins' truck to their tent: the setting sun, when she got out of the car, set her hair on fire just before she penetrated the shade cast by the black canvas; no more second night under the stars next to Sarah, what bad luck, I thought, what damn bad luck that we hadn't managed to reach that lost castle. The inside of the animal-skin house was dark and welcoming; a wall of reeds interwoven with red and green cloth divided the tent in half, one side for the men, the other for the women. The head of this home, the patriarch, was a very old man with a smile lit up by gold teeth, talkative as a magpie: he spoke three words of French, which he had learned in the army of the Levant in which he had served during the French mandate over Syria: *"Debout! Couché! Marchez!"* ["Stand up! Lie down! March!"], orders that he shouted two by two with intense joy, *"deboutcouché! couchémarchez!"* happy not just from the simple pleasure of the reminiscence, but also from the presence of a French-speaking audience that could appreciate these martial orders — our Arabic was too basic (especially Bilger's, which was limited to "dig, shovel, pickax," another version of "*deboutcouchémarchez*") to understand the many stories of that octogenarian clan chief, but Sarah managed, as much out of empathy as linguistic savvy, to follow the old man's tales and, more or less, to translate the general meaning when it escaped us. Of course, Sarah's first question to the local Methuselah was about Marga d'Andurain, countess of Palmyra — had he known her? The sheikh rubbed his beard and shook his head, no, he had heard of her, of that Palmyran *comta*, but no more — no contact with the legend, Sarah must have been disappointed. We drank a decoction of cinnamon bark, sweet and fragrant, sitting cross-legged on the wool rugs that were placed on the bare ground; a black dog had barked when we approached, the guard of the flock who protected the animals from jackals and even hyenas: the stories of hyenas that the grandfather, his sons and the peddler told us made our hair stand on end. Sarah was in seventh heaven, immediately recovering from her disappointment at not having met one of the last witnesses of the reign of Marga d'Andurain the desert poisoner; she turned often toward me with a complicit smile, and I knew she was finding in these magical stories the tales of ghouls and other fantastic animals she had studied: the hyena, which had almost disappeared from these lands, gathered the most extraordinary legends around it. The old sheikh was a first-rate storyteller, a great actor; with a brief sweep of his hand, he silenced his sons or the peddler to have the pleasure of telling a story he knew himself — the hyena, he said, hypnotizes men who have the misfortune of meeting its gaze; they are then forced to follow it through the desert up to its cave, where it torments and finally devours them. It pursues those who manage to escape it in their dreams; its contact makes horrible pustules appear — not surprising that these poor beasts have been extravagantly slaughtered, I thought. As for the jackal, it was contemptible but inoffensive; its long cry pierced the night — I found these groans particularly sinister, but they didn't come close, the Bedouins argued, to the atrocious call of the hyena, which had the ability to fix you to the spot and freeze you with terror: whoever heard this raucous growl remembered it for the rest of their lives.

After these considerations of supernatural zoology we tried, Sarah and I (like Alois Musil, I imagined, with his own nomads), to get information about the archaeological sites in the environs, the temples, the castles, the forgotten cities that only the Bedouins could know — this tactic vexed King Bilger, convinced that generations of Orientalists had "exhausted the desert"; the Grabars, Ettinghausens, and Hillenbrands had spent years describing the Islamic ruins so that their colleagues, specialists in Antiquity, could reveal Roman or Byzantine forts and villages: there's nothing left to discover, he thought — in fact, our hosts spoke to us about Qasr el-Heyr and Resafa, adding stories of hidden treasures that Bilger found moderately amusing, while he was still slightly upset by his mistake in direction. He explained to me, in German, that the natives observed the archaeologists' excavations and dug themselves as soon as the archaeologists had gone: these crows of archaeology were an affliction well-known at archaeological sites, whose surroundings, Bilger exaggerated, ended up full of holes and piles of earth, as if ravaged by giant moles.

The women, in their long dark embroidered dresses, brought us dinner; round unleavened bread, honey, wild thyme mixed with sumac and sesame, cheese, milk, yogurt — if not for its terrible burnt taste, the cheese could easily have been mistaken for soap, dry and salty. All the milk products had that same burnt taste for that matter, which has remained for me the taste of the desert, the land of milk, honey, and campfire. The old man didn't eat much, but kept urging us to take seconds of this or that; Sarah had engaged one of the women in conversation, one of the younger ones, I thought — out of a perhaps exaggerated modesty, I tried to avoid looking at them too much. We were still talking about mysteries and discoveries. The peddler got up and went out, probably to satisfy a natural need (I realized that unlike the camp sites in the Salzkammergut, this tent had no facilities nearby: Mother would not have appreciated this at all; she'd also have warned me against the food, even though the powerful burnt aroma seemed to indicate that the milk had been boiled), and the sheikh took advantage of the man's absence (which confirmed that the peddler was suspected of being an informer) to confide in us, in a whisper, that there were in fact forgotten, mysterious ruins, far to the southwest, at the border between the desert and the basalt mountain that separates the *badiya* from the Hauran plain, an entire city, said the old man, covered in bones; I had the greatest difficulty understanding this word, *bones, remains,* and I had to ask Sarah, what does *'adhm* mean? According to the sheikh, it was the ruins of one of the cities destroyed by the wrath of God, as was written in the Koran — he spoke of it with fear, said the place was cursed and that the Bedouins would never camp near there, not in a million years: they were content to contemplate the mountains of bones and rubble, meditate on them, and continue on their way. Bilger lifted his eyes to the sky in an exasperated way that was extremely discourteous to our host: it's easy to find, this city, he sneered, according to the Bible you just have to turn right at the crossroads of the woman turned into a pillar of salt. I tried to find out more, were they animal bones? A camel cemetery, perhaps? A volcanic eruption? My questions made the old man laugh, no, dromedaries don't hide themselves to die in a secret place, they die wherever they're standing, lie down and die like everyone else. Bilger assured me that volcanoes had been extinct in Syria for tens of thousands of years, which made the eruption theory not very likely; he seemed to consider all of it as so much nonsense from the superstitious imagination of natives. I pictured, on the slopes of a crater of lunar basalt, the remains of an ancient fortress and a vanished city, covered with the bones of their inhabitants, who had died in God knows what catastrophe — a nightmare vision, black, moon-mad. The peddler came back in, and I went out in turn; it was dark outside; the cold seemed to be rising from the stones straight into the sky, frozen with stars. I walked away from the tent to urinate, the dog accompanied me for a bit before abandoning me to sniff around further off in the darkness. Above me, high in the sky, indicating the west, was something we hadn't seen the night before: Palestine and the Mediterranean shone, a sudden revelation, a comet with a long tail of glowing dust.

2:20 A.M.

Sarah is lying down naked next to me; her long tresses form a stream, slowed down by the rocks of the vertebrae. I am tormented by remorse; I observe her and am full of remorse. The boat is taking us to Beirut: last port of call on the Austrian Lloyd line, Trieste–Alexandria–Jaffa–Beirut. I sense confusedly that Sarah is not going to wake up before we arrive tomorrow in Beirut, where Nadim is waiting for us for the wedding. All the better. I scrutinize her svelte, muscular, almost skinny body; she doesn't react when I play for a minute with her sex, she's sleeping so deeply. I know I shouldn't be there. Guilt is suffocating me. From the porthole, I can see the sea unfold its greenish, wintery infinity, covered in whitecaps; I leave the cabin, the long corridors are carpeted in red velvet, lit by bronze wall lamps, I wander in the damp heat of the ship, it's unsettling to get lost like this in stifling corridors when I'm late; on the cabin doors, oval plaques indicate the names of the occupants, their birth and death dates — I consider knocking on Kathleen Ferrier's door, then on Lou Andreas-Salomé's, but I don't dare disturb them, I'm too ashamed of getting lost, ashamed of having been forced to urinate in the corridor, into a magnificent umbrella stand, before the hostess (transparent evening gown, I gaze for a long time at her lingerie) takes me by the arm, "Franz, they're waiting for you upstairs, come, we'll go through the wings. Stefan Zweig is furious, he wants to disgrace you, challenge you to a duel; he knows you won't have the courage to face him and you'll be excluded from the *Burschenschaft*."

I try to kiss her on the mouth, she lets me, her tongue is soft and warm, I slip one hand under her dress, a hand she withdraws affectionately, murmuring "*nein, nein, nein, Liebchen*," I'm annoyed but I understand. There's a large crowd in the big foyer, Dr. Kraus is leading a standing ovation, we applaud the end of Schumann's *Geistervariationen* thunderously. I try to take advantage of the diversion to lift the hostess' dress again, again she pushes me away just as tenderly. I'm eager for us to get down to business. The Colonel is deep in conversation with Dr. Kraus; he explains to me that Kraus can't stand that his wife plays the piano better than he, and I agree, Lili Kraus is a wonderful pianist, in a different league than you, dear Doctor. I knock my glass of milk onto the Colonel's grand uniform, all the eagles are spattered with it, fortunately, milk doesn't stain uniforms, unlike evening gowns, which the hostess is forced to take off: she rolls it into a ball and hides it in a cupboard.

"What's going to become of us? This country is so small and so old, Colonel, there's no point in defending it. It would be better to change countries."

"That in fact is the solution to the Syrian problem," he says.

Outside the war is still raging on; we can't go out, we're going to have to stay locked up under this staircase.

"Isn't this where you hid your wedding dress? The one I stained by accident?"

Let's stay calm, calm. We're closely intertwined in the dark, but the hostess is not interested in me, I know she has eyes only for Sarah. I have to do something, but what? The Irish Sea is wild, you certainly won't get there for two or three days yet. Two or three days! Mr. Ritter, Kraus says gently, I think we can change your disease, now. It's time, you're right. It's time. Franz, look how that young woman is caressing herself! Put your face between her legs, you'll find it refreshing.

Kraus continues spouting his absurdities, I'm cold, I must at all costs find my cabin again and the sleeping Sarah, I reluctantly abandon the hostess to her masturbation. Soon it will be your turn, Mr. Ritter. Soon it will be your turn. The sea is very stormy, today. Play us something then, to pass the time! This lute isn't mine, but I should be able to improvise something. What mode do you prefer? *Nahawand? Hejazi? Hejazi!* That suits every circumstance. Go on, dear Franz, play us your waltz, you remember? Oh yes, the *Waltz of Death*, of course I remember, F, F-A, F-A#-B, B, B. My hands run over the neck of the oud with the sound of a violin. The bar on this boat, the opera foyer, opens onto the sea and the sea spray spatters the musicians and their instruments. Impossible to play in these conditions, dear audience. What a disappointment! We who so wanted to hear *The Waltz of Death! Der Todeswalzer!* We're headed straight for shipwreck, rejoice. I am rejoicing, dear audience, dear friends. Dear friends, Dr. Zweig has a speech to make (again that old Zweig with the long face, what a bore). I leave the stage with my lute to make way for him, there's a big puddle of water under the chair. Zweig scolds me, runs his hand through my hair and tells me to sit down. Ladies and gentlemen, he cries, this is war! Montjoie! Saint-Denis! It's war! Rejoice!

Everyone applauds, the soldiers, the sailors, the women, the Kraus couple and even Sarah, I'm surprised she's there, I rush over to her, you woke up? You woke up? I hide the lute behind my back, so she won't see that I stole it from Nadim — I stole it? I know the police are looking for me for this terrible crime I committed long ago. Are we arriving soon? It's war, I say. They're all rejoicing at dying in combat. Vienna is going to become the new capital of Syria. We'll all speak Arabic on the Graben.

Sarah mustn't hear about the murder and the body. Dr. Kraus!

Dr. Kraus! Your irises have grown on our corpses again! What a horrible Spring, with this endless rain, you wouldn't think you were in the Orient. Everything is rotting. Everything is growing moldy. The bones keep decomposing. We'll have a fine grape harvest this year, the wine of the dead will be abundant. Shhh, murmurs Sarah, don't mention the wine of the dead, it's a secret. A potion? Perhaps. Of love or death? You'll see.

A sailor sings, in the distance, "Toward the east heads the ship, cool breathes the wind toward our homeland, my Irish child, toward where is your life heading?"

Which gives Sarah a good laugh. She looks like Molly Bloom, I think, the one who wheels her barrow through narrow streets to sell cockles and mussels. God how vast the sea is!

How many children will we have, Dr. Kraus?

How many?

It would be unthinkable for me to indulge in these sorts of predictions, I am a serious doctor, Mr. Ritter. Do not share that syringe, you'll contaminate each other.

Franz, you have beautiful veins, you know that?

Mr. Ritter, I have warned you.

Franz, you have very beautiful veins, Sarah repeats.

Sweat, sweat, sweat.

Awful. How awful, my God. The light is still on, I'm still holding the switch. That image of Sarah holding a syringe, fortunately I awoke before the damage was done, Sarah injecting me with a repulsive liquid, her *wine of the dead*, under the depraved gaze of Dr. Kraus, what an atrocity, to think that some people find dreaming pleasant. Breathe, breathe. It's so tiresome, this sensation of lacking air as if I'm drowning in my sleep. Fortunately I don't remember my dreams aside from the last seconds, they're almost immediately erased from my memory, fortunately. I escape the guilt of the unconscious, the brutality of desire. That strange emotion often grips me in dream. As if I actually committed an atrocious crime that is about to be discovered. The wine of the dead. Sarah's article is haunting me, what an idea to send me this text from Sarawak, sick and fragile as I am now. I realize how much I miss her. How much she has missed me. How sick and fragile she might be too, in her lush jungle, with her ex-headhunters, great harvesters of corpses. What a trip. There's some work here for the charlatan on the Berggasse, Mrs. Kafka's neighbor. In the end it always amounts to the same thing. I think I remember that Jung, the first unconscious Orientalist, discovered that one of his patients was dreaming of the Tibetan Book of the Dead, which she had never heard of, and which put a germ in the disciple's mind and launched him on the path of the collective unconscious and archetypes. Me, I am not dreaming of the Tibetan or Egyptian Book of the Dead but of the far recesses of Sarah's brain. Tristan and Iseult. Potions of love and death. Dik el-Jinn the Mad. The old poet from Homs so mad with jealousy that he killed the woman he loved. But that's nothing, said Sarah, Dik el-Jinn was so passionate, torn apart from the suffering of having destroyed the object of his passion, that with the ashes of his beloved's corpse mixed with clay he modeled a cup, a deadly cup, magical and deadly, from which he drank wine, the first wine of Death, which inspired him to compose sublime love poems. He drank in the body of his beloved, he drank the body of his love, and this Dionysian madness became Apollonian by the play of the verses, of the regulated, codified meter where the energy of his necrophagic passion for the woman he had killed out of jealousy, giving in to rumors and hatred, became ordered: "I have returned you to the most complete nudity," he sang, "I have mixed your face with earth and even, if I could have borne watching you rot, I would have left your dead face to the great sun."

We know he drank heavily, this poet from Homs who lived for

almost seventy years, did he still get drunk from his mortal cup in the twilight of his life, it's possible, it's likely. Why is Sarah interested in these atrocities, necrophagy, black magic, devouring passions? I can see her at the Crime Museum in Vienna, strolling with a smile on her lips through that cave on Leopoldstadt, in the midst of skulls pierced with bullets and truncheons by all kinds of killers, political, dissolute, in love, all the way to the high point of the exhibit, an old dusty wicker basket in which was found, at the beginning of the twentieth century, a woman's body, arms and legs cut off, a woman-trunk, photographs of which were abundant at the time, naked and mutilated, pubis as black as the shoulders and thighs where the absent members had bled. A little further on there was also a disemboweled woman, raped before or after her evisceration. "You're funny, you Austrians," Sarah said, "you show images of women tortured to death, but you censor the only representation of pleasure in this whole museum." She was referring to a painting, in the part of the exhibit devoted to Viennese brothels, showing, in an Orientalist décor, an odalisque caressing herself, legs spread; a contemporary censor had placed a big black square over her hand and private parts. The caption said soberly, "Decorative painting from a bordello." Obviously I was embarrassed to find myself commenting on such an image with Sarah; I looked elsewhere, blushing, which she took for an avowal: a recognition of Viennese perversion — tortured women in the basement, censored eroticism and the most prudish chastity outside.

I wonder why I'm thinking about all that now, a hallucinatory trail perhaps, a comet's tail, a sensual afterglow contaminating the memory of the power of desire, I should accept that the night is dead, get up and go on to something else, correct that paper on Gluck or reread my article on *Marouf, the Cairo Cobbler*, the opera adapted from Charles Mardrus's translation of *The*

Thousand and One Nights; I'd like to send it to Sarah, that would be my answer to her opus on the wine of the dead in mysterious Sarawak. I could send her an email, but I know that if I write to her I'll spend the next few days glued to the computer like an idiot, waiting for her answer. Come to think of it, it wasn't so bad at the Crime Museum, at least she was there, I'd even have gone to the Funeral Museum or to the Narrenturm to look one more time, in the old Tower of Fools, at horrible genetic anomalies and terrifying pathologies, if she had wanted to go there.

Not much is missing from that article on *Marouf, the Cairo Cobbler*, just a touch of *je-ne-sais-quoi*, aha I could *ask Sarah for advice* right away, not just send it to her, that would be an entirely intelligent maneuver to make contact with her, instead of confessing to her straight out "I miss you" or subtly reminding her of the naked woman in the Crime Museum (do you remember, dear Sarah, the emotion that gripped me when we contemplated a pornographic image together in a bloody basement?), she too has studied the work of Dr. Mardrus and especially that of his wife Lucie, the first character in her collection of Orientalist women, along with Lou Andreas-Salomé and Jane Dieulafoy. Joseph Charles Mardrus the Caucasian of literature, whose grandfather had fought the Russians in the ranks of the imam Shamyl, there's a man I'd have liked to meet, Mardrus, in that high-society Paris of the 1890s; he was friends with Mallarmé, then with Apollinaire; as soon as he disembarked from the Messageries Maritimes liner where he officiated as ship's doctor he became, thanks to his charm and erudition, the heartthrob of the Parisian salons—that's what I need to write my great work, a few years' stay in a ship's cabin, between Marseille and Saigon. Mardrus translated the entirety of *The Thousand and One Nights* at sea; he grew up in Cairo, studied medicine in Beirut, Arabic was so to speak his native language, that's the big advantage he has over us Western-born Orientalists, all that time spent learning the language that he saved. The discovery of the *Nights* in Mardrus's translation provoked a wave of adaptations, imitations, continuations of the masterpiece, just as Victor Hugo's *Les Orientales*, Rückert's poems, or Goethe's *West-Eastern Divan* had done fifty years earlier. This time people thought it was the Orient itself that breathed its force, its eroticism, its exotic power directly into turn-of-the-century art; they loved the sensuality, the violence, the pleasure, the adventures, the monsters and djinns, they copied them, commented on them, multiplied them; they thought they could finally see, without any intermediary, the true face of the eternal and mysterious Orient: but in fact the Orient of Mardrus, still a reflection, another Third-Orient; it's the Orient, when all is said and done, of Mallarmé and of *La Revue blanche*, the eroticism of Pierre Louÿs, a representation, an interpretation. As in Joseph Roth's *Tale of the 1002nd Night* or Hofmannsthal's *Scheherazade*, the motifs in the *Nights* are used to suggest, to create a tension in a European context; the shah's desire, in Roth's novel, to sleep with Countess W. sets off an entirely Viennese intrigue, the way Rimsky-Korsakov's ballets in *Scheherazade* or Mata Hari's dances serve to arouse the Parisian bourgeoisie: in the end, any relationship they had with a so-called *real* Orient matters little. We ourselves, in the desert, under the Bedouins' tent, although faced with the most tangible reality of nomad life, were coming up against our own representations, which, by our preconceptions, interfered with the possibility of experiencing this life that was not our own; the poverty of these women and men seemed to us to be full of the poetry of the ancients, their destitution reminded us of that of the hermits and the mystics, their superstitions made us travel through time, the exoticism of their condition prevented us from understanding their vision of existence, just as they saw us — with our bareheaded woman, our SUV, and our rudimentary Arabic — as eccentric idiots, possibly whose money and even car they envied, but certainly not our knowledge or intelligence, not even our technology: the old sheikh had told us that the last Westerners he had welcomed, European without a doubt, had come in a camper van and that the terrible roar of their generator (for the fridge, probably) had kept them from sleeping all night. Only the peddler, I thought while I urinated under Halley's comet, scrutinizing the darkness to make sure the dog wasn't about to eat my balls, actually shared the life of this tribe, since he participated in it; eight months a year, he gave up everything to flog his trinkets. We remained travelers, enclosed in the self, capable, possibly, of transforming ourselves in contact with alterity, but certainly not of experiencing it profoundly. We are spies, we make the rapid, furtive contact of spies. When Chateaubriand invented travel literature with his *Itinerary from Paris to Jerusalem* in 1811, long before Stendhal and his *Memoirs of an Egotist*, more or less at the same time as the publication of Goethe's *Italian Journey*, Chateaubriand was spying for the sake of art; he was certainly no longer the explorer who spied for science or for the army: he spied mainly for literature. Art has its spies, just as history or the natural sciences have theirs. Archaeology is a form of espionage, botany, poetry as well; ethnomusicologists are spies of music. Spies are travelers, travelers are spies. "Don't trust the stories of travelers," says Saadi in the *The Gulistan*. They see nothing. They think they see, but they observe only reflections. We are prisoners of images, of representations, Sarah would say, and only those who, like her or like the peddler, choose to rid themselves of their lives (if such a thing is actually possible) can reach the other. I remember the sound of my urine falling on the stones in the intoxicating silence of the desert; I remember my little thoughts, very futile in light of the infinity of beings; I had no awareness of the ants and spiders I was drowning in the urine. We are condemned, as Montaigne says in his last *Essay*, to think the way we piss — on the fly, quickly and furtively, like spies. Only love, I thought as I went back to the tent, shivering from cold and desire at the memory of the previous night, opens us up to the other; love as renunciation, as fusion — nothing surprising in these two absolutes, the desert and love, encountering each other to produce one of the most important monuments in universal literature, the madness of Majnun who shouted his passion for Layla to the stones and horned vipers, Layla whom he loved, around the year 750, in a very similar tent. The goatskin wall was closed; the light from the gas lamp filtered through a little door, you had to stoop down to enter. Bilger was half lying on a wool mattress, a glass of cinnamon tea in his hand; Sarah had disappeared. She had been invited to go over to the women's side, in the tent's other room, while Bilger and I stayed with the men. They unrolled a bed covered with a quilt that smelled wonderfully of wood-fire and animal. The old man was lying down, the peddler had rolled himself up in a big black cloak, a prophet's posture. I am in the desert, like Layla's Qays the Mad, so in love that he gave up his being to live with the gazelles in the midst of the steppe. Me too, they've taken Sarah away from me, depriving me of my second night lying against her, chaste night of pure love, and I could have shouted some despairing verses to the moon or the comet, singing of the beauty of my beloved, which social conventions had just torn from my care. I thought of the long flights of Qays Majnun into the desert, to cry his despair onto the traces of Layla's family's camp, scratching myself furiously, convinced the wool or cotton of my mattress was overflowing with fleas and other rabid creatures ready to devour my legs.

I could hear Bilger snoring softly; outside a flagpole or a hal-

yard jangled in the breeze, it was like being in a moored sailboat—finally I fell asleep. It was a round moon, at ground level,
just before dawn, that woke me, as they were opening the tent
onto the gently blue-tinted immensity: the shadow of a woman
lifted the section of cloth and the smell of the desert (dry earth,
ash, animals) whirled around me, in the still-muted cackling
of the hens that were pecking at the ground, horrible furtive
monsters in the half-light, gathering up the breadcrumbs from
our dinner or the nighttime insects our heat had attracted—
then the dawn slipped its rosy fingers through the mist, jostling
the moon, and everything seemed to come to life at once: the
rooster crowed, the old sheikh chased away the overly adventurous chickens with a flip of his blanket, the peddler got up,
slipped the cloak he had rolled himself up in at night around
his shoulders and went out—only Bilger was still sleeping; I
glanced at my watch, it was five a.m. I got up in turn; the women
were busy in front of the tent, they motioned me over. The peddler was performing his ablutions sparingly, with a blue plastic
pitcher—one of the objects he sold, I imagined. Aside from
the slight reddishness in the sky to the east, it was still freezing
and very dark out; the dog was still sleeping, curled up against
the outer wall. I wondered if I would see Sarah come out too,
maybe she was sleeping, like the dog, like Bilger. I stayed there,
watching the sky open up, with Félicien David's oratorio in my
head, the first to have rendered the terrifying simplicity of the
desert in music.

If it was five o'clock already I could get up now, exhausted
as I am every morning, vanquished by the night; impossible to
escape these memories of Sarah, I wonder if it's better to chase
them away or abandon myself completely to desire and reminiscence. I am paralyzed, sitting up in bed, how long have I been
staring at the bookshelves, motionless, my head elsewhere, my

hand still clinging to the switch, a kid clutching his rattle? What time is it? Waking up is the crutch of the insomniac, I should buy myself a mosque-alarm clock like Bilger in Damascus, the mosque of Medina or Jerusalem, in gilded plastic, with a little compass built in to indicate the direction of prayer — that's the superiority of the Muslim over the Christian: in Germany they impose the Scriptures on you in the back of the bedside table drawer, in Muslim hotels they stick a little compass for you into the wood of the bed, or they draw a wind rose marking the direction of Mecca on the desk, compass and wind rose that can indeed serve to locate the Arabic peninsula, but also, if you're so inclined, Rome, Vienna, or Moscow: you're never lost in these lands. I even saw some prayer rugs with a little compass woven into them, carpets you immediately wanted to set flying, since they were so prepared for aerial navigation: a garden in the clouds with, like Solomon's carpet in Jewish legend, a canopy of doves to protect you from the sun — there would be a lot to write about flying carpets, about those fine illustrations, so propitious to daydreaming, of princes and princesses sitting cross-legged, in sumptuous outfits, right in the middle of a mythical sky, reddening to the west, carpets that owe no doubt more to the tales of Wilhelm Hauff than to the *Thousand and One Nights* themselves, more to the customs and sets of the *Scheherazade* of Russian ballets than to the texts of Arabic or Persian authors — once again, a linked construction, a complex work of time where imagination is superimposed atop imagination, creation over creation, between Europe and Dar el-Islam. The Turks and Persians are familiar with the translated versions of the *Nights* by Antoine Galland and Richard Burton, and only rarely bother to translate them from the Arabic; they imagine, in turn, what others before them have translated: the Scheherazade who finds Iran in the twentieth century has traveled far, she has weighed herself down with the France of Louis XIV, Victorian England, Tsarist Russia; her very face stems from a mingling of Safavid miniatures, Paul Poiret's costumes, Georges Lepape's fashionable women, and the Iranian women of today. "On the Cosmopolitan Fate of Magical Objects," there's a title for Sarah: it would include a discussion of genie lamps, flying carpets, and fabulous slippers; she could show how these objects are the result of successive shared efforts, and how what we regard as purely "Oriental" is in fact, very often, the repetition of a "Western" element that itself modifies another previous "Oriental" element, and so on; she could conclude that *Orient* and *Occident* never appear separately, that they are always intermingled, present in each other, and that these words — Orient, Occident — have no more heuristic value than the unreachable directions they designate. I imagine she'd finish it all up with a political projection on cosmopolitanism as the only point of view possible on the question. Me too, if I were more — more what? More brilliant, healthier, more decisive, I could develop this laughable article on *Marouf, the Cairo Cobbler,* Henri Rabaud and Charles Mardrus, and construct a real synthesis of that famous Third-Orient in French music, around the students of Massenet maybe, Rabaud himself, but also Florent Schmitt, Reynaldo Hahn, Ernest Chausson, and especially Georges Enesco, there's an interesting case, an "Oriental" who returns to the "Orient" after a stopover in France. All of Massenet's students composed Orientalist desert or caravan melodies, settings of Gautier's "La Caravane" ("The human caravan in the Sahara of the world . . .") to Jules Lemaître's "Petites Orientales" — I've always wondered who this Jules Lemaître was — no doubt very different from the caravan of "Through the Desert," the aria in the second act of *Marouf,* when Marouf, to trick the merchants and the sultan, invents a rich caravan of thousands of camels and mules that should be arriving any day and describes in detail its precious cargo, with a great deal of *Orientalism*, which is rather vertiginous: there is a *dream of the Orient* in Arabic tales themselves, dream of jewels, silks, beauty, love, and this dream that, for us, is an Oriental dream is in fact a Biblical and Koranic reverie; it resembles the descriptions of Paradise in the Koran, where we will be presented with golden vases and cups full of anything we might desire, and everything will charm our eyes, where we will have fruits in abundance, in gardens and springs, where we will wear clothing of fine silk and brocade, where we will have houris with beautiful eyes, where we will be served drinks of nectar scented with musk. The caravan of Marouf— that of the *Thousand and One Nights*—uses these elements *ironically*: of course, his description is exaggerated, outrageous; it's a lie, a lie made to charm the audience, a wonderful catalog, a catalog *of dream*. You could find in the *Nights* many examples of this exaggerated Orientalism in the Orient. Henri Rabaud's caravan aria adds a movement to this construction: Mardrus's translation of *The Tale of the Honey Cake* is adapted for *Marouf, the Cobbler of Cairo* by a librettist, Lucien Népoty, then set to music by Rabaud, with brilliant orchestration: here again, Massenet is in the shadows, hidden behind a dune in that imaginary desert through which wander (in G minor of course, with trills from the strings and glissandos from the woodwinds) the camels and mules of this extraordinary caravan of cloth, rubies, and sapphires guarded by a thousand Mamelukes, "handsome as moons." Very ironically, the music exaggerates, forces the issue: you can hear the mule drivers' sticks hitting the donkeys at each measure, a figuralism that would be pretty ridiculous, I must say, if it weren't actually funny, exaggerated, made to dupe the merchants and the sultan: they have to hear the caravan for them to believe in it! And, miracle of music as much as speech, they believe it!

I suppose Reynaldo Hahn, like his friend Marcel Proust, read the *Nights* in Mardrus's new translation; both were at the premiere of *Marouf* in 1914, in any case. Hahn praised the score of his former Conservatoire classmate in a major specialist journal; he noted the quality of the music, whose daring never alters its purity; he cited the finesse, the imagination, the intelligence, and especially the absence of vulgarity in the "accuracy of the Oriental feeling." In fact he greeted the appearance of a "French-style" Orientalism closer to Debussy than to the debauchery of violence and sensuality in the Russians — so many different musical cultures, so many Orients, so many exoticisms.

I wonder if I should extend the article, with all these superimposed Orients, and add one more layer, that of Roberto Alagna in Morocco. After all, that would give a slightly "current-events" side to a contribution that I must say is rather serious, and also it would make Sarah laugh, the image of the sprightly European tenor in the Orient of the twenty-first century — this video is truly priceless. In a festival in Fez, an Arab version, with oud and qanun, of "À travers le désert," Rabaud's caravan aria: one can imagine the good intentions of the organizers, the parody defused, the caravan finding the *real* desert of the authentic, of authentic instruments and settings — and, since the road to hell is, as we know, paved with good intentions, everything falls flat. The oud serves no purpose, the qanun, hardly at ease in Rabaud's harmonic progression, just inserts suitable commas into the silences of the voice; Alagna, in a white djellaba, sings as if on the Opéra-Comique stage, but with a microphone in hand; the percussions (clashing cymbals, jostling keys) try to fill by any means possible the great, immense void uncovered by this masquerade; the qanun player seems to be suffering martyrdom, hearing music that's so bad: only Alagna the Magnificent doesn't seem to notice anything, given over as he is to his grand gestures and his camel drivers, what a laugh, my God, if Rabaud heard that he'd die a second time. Maybe that's Rabaud's punishment, come to think of it—fate is punishing him for his behavior during the Second World War, his philo-Nazism, his haste to denounce the Jewish professors at the Conservatory of which he was director. Fortunately his successor, in 1943, would be more enlightened, more courageous, and would try to save his students rather than hand them over to the occupier. Henri Rabaud joins the long list of Orientalists (artists or scientists) who collaborated directly or indirectly with the Nazi regime—will I have to stress this moment of his life, an episode much later than the composition of *Marouf* in 1914, I have no idea. Still, the composer would himself conduct, at the Opéra, the hundredth performance of *Marouf, the Cairo Cobbler* on April 4, 1943 (the day of a terrifying bombing that destroyed the Renault factories and caused hundreds of deaths in western Paris) before an audience of German uniforms and well-known Vichyists. In the spring of 1943, when they were still fighting in Tunisia but when they knew that the Afrikakorps and Rommel were beaten, when the Nazi hopes of conquering Egypt were very remote, did *Marouf, the Cairo Cobbler* take on a special meaning, a nose-thumbing at the German occupier? Probably not. Just a moment of *good humor* that everyone agreed to find in the work, *good humor* to forget the war, *good humor* about which I wonder whether, in such circumstances, there was something criminal: they sang, "Through the desert, a thousand camels loaded with cloth march under the goads of my caravaners," while six days earlier, a few kilometers away, a convoy (the fifty-third) left carrying a thousand French Jews from the Drancy camp to Poland

and their extermination. That interested the Parisians and their German guests much less than the defeats of Rommel in Africa, much less than the adventures of Marouf the Cobbler, his wife Fattouma the Calamitous, and the imaginary caravan. And no doubt old Henri Rabaud, at the podium thirty years after the premiere of *Marouf*, didn't give a damn about those atrocious convoys. I don't know if Charles Mardrus was in the audience — it's possible but, at the age of seventy-five, he'd been living since the start of the hostilities secluded in Saint-Germain-des-Prés, went out very little, let the war pass by the way others do the rain. They say he left his apartment only to go to the Deux Magots or to an Iranian restaurant — you have to wonder how, in the midst of the occupation, that restaurant managed to find rice, saffron, and lamb. I know on the other hand that Lucie Delarue-Mardrus was not at the hundredth performance of *Marouf*; she was at her home in Normandy, where she was gathering her memories of the Orient — she was in the process of writing what would be her last book, *El Arab, l'Orient que j'ai connu*, in which she recounts her travels between 1904 and 1914 with her husband Mardrus. She would die not long after the publication of her last memoirs, in 1945: that book and its author fascinated Sarah; no doubt that's why I could solicit her help for the article — once again, our interests intersect; Mardrus and the musical adaptations of his translation by Rabaud or Honegger for me, Lucie Delarue, prolific, mysterious poetess and novelist, who in the 1920s had a passionate affair with Natalie Barney, for whom she wrote her most famous poems, *Nos secrètes amours*, as at ease in homosexual erotic poetry as in her Norman odes and poems for children. Her memories of her travels with J. C. Mardrus are astounding, Sarah quotes them in her book on women and the Orient. It's to Lucie Delarue-Mardrus that we owe this extraordinary phrase: "Easterners have no sense of the Orient.

It's we Westerners, we *Roumis*, as the Muslims call us, Christians, who have a sense of the Orient. (I mean the *Roumis*, still quite numerous, who are not boors.)" For Sarah, this passage all by itself summarizes Orientalism—Orientalism as reverie, Orientalism as lament, as a forever disappointing exploration. In fact, the *Roumis* appropriated this landscape of dream, it's they who now, long after the classical Arabic storytellers, exploit it and travel through it, so that all their journeys are a confrontation with this dream. There's even a fertile current that is built *on* this dream, without needing to travel, whose most famous representative is surely Marcel Proust and his *In Search of Lost Time*, the symbolic heart of the European novel: Proust makes the *Thousand and One Nights* one of his models—the book of night, the book of the struggle against death. Just as Scheherazade fights every evening against the sentence that hangs over her by telling a story to the Sultan Shahryar, Marcel Proust takes up the pen every night, for many nights, he says "maybe a hundred, maybe a thousand," to fight against time. Over two hundred times in the course of his *Search*, Proust alludes to the Orient and to the *Nights*, which he knows in the translations of Galland (that of chastity and childhood, of Combray) and of Mardrus (that, more confused, more erotic, of adulthood)—he weaves the golden thread of the wonderful book throughout his immense novel; Swann hears a violin like a genie outside of a lamp, a symphony reveals "all the jewels of *The Thousand and One Nights*." Without the Orient (that dream in Arabic, Persian, and Turkish, stateless, which we call the Orient) no Proust, no *In Search of Lost Time*.

With my flying carpet and its built-in compass, where would I go? The Viennese dawn in December will be worlds away from the desert dawn: dawn with fingers of soot staining the sleet, that's Homer's epithet for the Danube. Weather like this is not fit to put an Orientalist outside in. I am decidedly an armchair scholar, nothing like Bilger, Faugier, or Sarah who were only happy at the wheels of their SUVs, in the lower depths that were the most—how to say it—*exalting* or simply "on site," as ethnologists say—I'm still a spy, a bad spy, I probably would've produced the same knowledge if I had never left Vienna for those distant, inhospitable lands where they welcome you with hanged men and scorpions, I'd have had the same mediocre career if I had never traveled—my most-cited article is called "The First Oriental Orientalist Opera: *Layla and Majnun* by Uzeyir Hajibeyov," and it's quite obvious that I've never set foot in Azerbaijan, where they're wallowing, it seems to me, in oil and nationalism; in Tehran, we weren't far from Baku, and during our excursions by the Caspian Sea, we would dip our feet in the same water as the Azeri shores a few dozen kilometers to the north—in short, it's kind of depressing to think that academia will remember me for my analysis of the relationship between Rossini, Verdi, and Hajibeyov. This computerized tallying of quotations and cross-referencing is leading the university to its ruin, no one today will undertake difficult, costly, lengthy studies, better to publish well-chosen, brief articles than vast works of erudition—I don't delude myself as to the actual quality of my Hajibeyov article, it is cited in every publication dealing with the composer, mechanically, as one of the rare European contributions to studies on Hajibeyov the Azeri, and all the appeal I saw in this work—the emergence of an *Oriental* Orientalism—obviously goes by the wayside. No need to go to Baku for that. I should be fair, though: if I hadn't gone to Syria, if I hadn't had a tiny, almost chance experience of the desert (and a disappointment in love, let's admit it) I'd never have developed a passion for Layla's Majnun the Mad that led me to order (a complicated thing at the time) a score of

Hajibeyov's *Layla and Majnun*; I'd never have even known that the lover who shouted his passion to the gazelles and rocks had inspired a ton of novels in verse, in Persian or Turkish, including the one by Fuzuli that Hajibeyov adapted—me, I shouted my passion to Sarah, not my passion for her, but for Majnun, all the *Majnuns*, all the mad lovers, and my enthusiasm seemed to her nothing but high comedy: I can see us again in the leather armchairs at the French Institute for Research in Iran where, without meaning any harm by it (without meaning any harm?), she asked me for news of my "collection," as she called it, when she saw me returning from the bookshop with a package under my arm, so, she asked, still mad about Layla? And I had to agree, a madman for Layla, or for *Khosrow and Shirin*, or for *Vis and Ramin*—in brief a classic love story, a thwarted passion that resolves itself in death. Wickedly, she challenged me with "And where's the music, in all that?" with a false air of reproach, and I had found a reply: I am preparing the *definitive and universal* text on love in music, from the troubadours to Hajibeyov, including Schubert and Wagner, and I said that looking her straight in the eyes, and she burst out laughing, a monstrous laugh, the laugh of a djinn or fairy, a peri, a guilty laugh, look, I'm back to Sarah again, there's nothing to be done. What potion had we drunk, was it the Styrian wine in Hainfeld, the Lebanese wine of Palmyra, the arak of the Baron Hotel in Aleppo, or the wine of the dead, strange potion, which *a priori* works only one way—no, at the Baron Hotel in Aleppo the harm had already been done, what shame, my God what shame, I had managed to get rid of Bilger who stayed on the Euphrates, in the horrible Raqqa with the sinister clock, and brought Sarah (still vibrating from the night in Palmyra) to the delights of Aleppo, where she found, full of emotion, Annemarie Schwarzenbach, her letters to Klaus Mann, and all the melancholy of the androgynous Swiss woman. The description that Ella Maillart gives of Annemarie in *The Cruel Way* is not one that would arouse passion, though: a whining drug addict, never happy, unhealthily skinny in split skirts or harem pants, clinging to the steering wheel of her Ford, searching in travel, in the suffering of the long journey between Zurich and Kabul, for a good excuse for her suffering: a sad portrait. It was hard to see, beyond the description of that wreck with an angel's face, the committed anti-fascist, the combatant, the cultivated, charming writer with whom Erika Mann and Carson McCullers fell in love—perhaps because the sober Ella Maillart, the gyrovague nun, was not at all the right person to describe her; perhaps because in 1939, Annemarie was like Europe, panting, frightened, in flight. We spoke of her in that restaurant hidden in the depths of a little stone-paved street, that Sissi House with the waiters in black outfits with white shirts; Sarah told me about the brief and tragic life of the Swiss woman, the recent discovery of her texts, dispersed, scattered, and about her personality, also broken up between morphine, writing, and a probable homosexuality that was hard to live with in the conservative milieu by the lake in Zurich.

Time closed in around us; the restaurant with its wicker chairs, the delicious and timeless food—Ottoman, Armenian— in those little glazed ceramic dishes, our recent memory of the Bedouins and the desolate shores of the Euphrates with ruined fortresses, all that sheltered us in a strange intimacy, as welcoming, enveloping, and solitary as the narrow, dark streets lined with the high palace walls. I looked at Sarah with her copper hair and brilliant gaze, her illuminated face, her coral and mother-of-pearl smile, and that perfect happiness, barely dented by the discussion of melancholy in the guise of Annemarie, belonged as much to the 1930s as to the 1990s, as much to the sixteenth Ottoman century as to the heterogeneous world—without place or time — of *The Thousand and One Nights*. Everything around us took part in this décor, from the unusual lace doilies to the old objects (Biedermeier candlesticks, metal Arabic pitchers) placed on the ogive window sills looking out onto the covered patio and at the angle of the steep steps of the stairway, with beautiful wrought iron balustrades, leading to the *mashrabiyas* framed in black and white stones; I listened to Sarah speak Syrian with the headwaiter and with the Aleppo ladies at the table next to us, and I was lucky, it seemed to me, to have entered this bubble, this magic circle of her presence which would become my daily life since it was absolutely clear to me, after the night in Tadmor and the battle against the Swabian knights, that we had become — what? A couple? Lovers?

My poor Franz, you're still deluding yourself, Mother would have said in her so-gentle French, you've always been like that, a dreamer, my poor little boy. But you have read *Tristan and Iseult, Vis and Ramin, Layla and Majnun,* there are forces to be conquered, and life is very long, sometimes, life is very long, as long as the shadow over Aleppo, the shadow of destruction. Time has reasserted its power over the Sissi House; the Baron Hotel is still standing, its shutters closed in a deep sleep, waiting for the throat-slitters of the Islamic State to make it their headquarters, transform it into a prison, a fortress, or else blow it up: they'll blow up my shame and its ever-burning memory, along with the memory of so many travelers, dust will settle again over Annemarie, over T. E. Lawrence, over Agatha Christie, over Sarah's room, over the wide hallway (geometrically patterned tiles, walls painted in high-gloss cream); the high ceilings will collapse onto the landing where two great cedar chests rested, coffins of nostalgia with their funereal plaques, "London–Baghdad in 8 Days by Simplon Orient Express and Taurus Express," the debris will swallow up the pompous staircase I climbed on a sudden impulse fifteen minutes after Sarah had decided to go to bed around midnight: I can see myself knocking on her door, a double wooden door with yellowing paint, my fingers right next to the three metal numbers, with anxiety, determination, hope, blindness, the tightness in the chest of one who is undertaking a great endeavor, who wants to find the being guessed at under a blanket in Palmyra in an actual bed and pursue, hang on, bury himself in oblivion, in the saturation of the senses, so that tenderness will chase away melancholy and greedy exploration of the other opens the ramparts of the self.

None of the words come back to me, no speech, everything has fortunately been erased; only her slightly serious face remains and the upwelling of pain, the sensation of suddenly becoming an object in time, crushed by the fist of shame and thrust toward disappearance.

2:50 A.M.

I'm angry at myself for being so cowardly, cowardly and ashamed, fine I'll get up, I'm thirsty. Wagner read Schopenhauer's *The World as Will and Representation* in September 1854, just when he was starting to imagine *Tristan and Isolde*. There is a chapter on love in *The World ais Will and Representation*. Schopenhauer never loved anyone as much as his dog Atma, a Sanskritish dog with the name of the soul. They say that Schopenhauer named his dog as sole heir, I wonder if that's true. Gruber might do the same. That would be amusing. Gruber and his mutt must be sleeping, I can't hear anything upstairs. What a curse insomnia is. What time is it? I don't much remember Schopenhauer's theories on love anymore. I think he separates love as illusion linked to sexual desire on one hand and universal love, compassion, on the other. I wonder what Wagner made of it. There must be hundreds of pages written on Schopenhauer and Wagner and I haven't read any. Sometimes life is hopeless.

Love Potion, Death Potion, *Mort d'amour*, dead of love.

Maybe I'll make myself a little herbal tea.

Goodbye sleep.

Someday I'll compose an opera that will be called *Schopenhauer's Dog*—it will be about love and compassion, Vedic India, Buddhism, and vegetarianism. The dog in question will be a music-loving Labrador its master takes to the opera, a Wagnerian dog. What will the dog's name be? Atma? Günter. That's a nice name, Günter. The dog will be a witness to the end of Europe, to the ruin of culture and the return of barbarism; in the last act Schopenhauer's ghost will rise from the flames to save the dog (but only the dog) from destruction. The second part will be called *Günter, the German Dog* and will recount the dog's journey to Ibiza and its emotions upon discovering the Mediterranean. The dog will talk about Chopin, George Sand, and Walter Benjamin, about all the exiles who found love or peace in the Balearics; Günter will end his life happy, under an olive tree, in the company of a poet whom he will inspire to write beautiful sonnets about nature and friendship.

So that's what it is, I'm going crazy. I'm going completely crazy. Go make yourself a herbal tea, a muslin sachet that will remind you of the dried flowers of Damascus and Aleppo, the roses of Iran. Obviously the rejection that night in the Baron Hotel still burns after several years, despite how tactful she was, despite everything that occurred afterward, despite Tehran, and all the journeys; of course I had to confront her gaze the next morning, her embarrassment, my embarrassment: you were thunderstruck, you fell from the clouds, she had uttered the name Nadim, and the veil was torn apart. Selfishly, I cold-shouldered him during the following months and even years — jealous, jealous, it's sad to say, wounded pride, what a stupid reaction. Despite my veneration for Nadim, despite entire evenings spent listening to him play, listening to him improvise, learning to recognize, with great difficulty, one by one, the modes, the rhythms and typical phrases of traditional music, despite all the friendship that seemed to develop between us, despite Nadim's generosity I closed myself around my wounded pride, I retreated into my shell, like Balzac. I followed the road to Damascus on my own and now here I am on my feet looking for my trousers—I look for my trousers while whistling *Weinen, Klagen, Sorgen, Zagen,* feet on the bedside rug, that prayer rug (without a compass) from Khorassan bought at the Tehran bazaar that belonged to Sarah and that she never reclaimed. I seize my bathrobe, get tangled in the overly wide sleeves of this Bedouin emir's cloak embroidered with gold that always sparks sarcastic or suspicious comments from the postman and the people from the gas company, find my slippers under the bed, tell myself I'm very stupid for getting so upset for so little cause, walk over to the bookcase, drawn by the spines of the books like a moth by the candle, caress (for lack of a body, of skin to caress) the poetic works of Fernando Pessoa on its stand, open at random for the pleasure of feeling the Oxford India paper glide under my fingers, obviously I land (because of the bookmark) on "Opiary" by Álvaro de Campos: "It's before I take opium that my soul is sick. / To feel life is to wilt like a convalescent, / And so I seek in opium's consolation / An East to the east of the East." One of the great odes of de Campos, that creature of Pessoa's—a traveler, "Suez Canal, on board ship, March 1914": they think that signature is antedated, Pessoa cheated, he wanted to create with Álvaro de Campos a "French-style" poet, an Apollinaire, lover of the Orient and ocean liners, a modern man. "Opiary" is a magnificent imitation, which becomes more authentic than an original: Campos needed to have a "childhood," poems of youth, spleen, opium, and travels. One thinks of Henry Jean-Marie Levet, poet of spleen, opium, and ocean liners, one looks through one's bookshelf (not very far away, on the "forgotten French poets" shelf, next to Louis Brauquier, maritime poet, employee at the Messageries, another one of Sarah's "stars") and finds his *Cartes postales,* a tiny book: the complete works of Levet can be held in the palm of your hand, you can count his texts on your fingers. He died of tuberculosis at the age of thirty-two in 1906, a budding diplomat, sent on assignment to India and Indochina, consul at Las Palmas and whose poems we sang, in Tehran: I remember having written a few songs to his verses, frightful jazz tunes to amuse one's comrades, regretting that no real composer ever turned his attention to these texts, not even Gabriel Fabre, friend of the poets, a musician even more forgotten than Henry Levet himself—the two men were neighbors on the rue Lepic in Paris, and Levet dedicated his Port Said *Carte postale* to him:

> *We watch the fires of Port Said gleam,*
> *As the Jews gazed at the Promised Land:*
> *For we cannot disembark; it's forbidden*
> *—Apparently—by the Venice Convention*
>
> *To those in the yellow quarantine pavilion.*
> *We will not go to land to calm our anxious senses*
> *Or stock up on obscene photos*
> *Or that excellent tobacco from Latakia . . .*
>
> *Poet, we'd have liked, during the short stopover*
> *To tread for an hour or two the ground of the Pharaohs*
> *Instead of listening to Miss Florence Marshall*
> *Sing "The Belle of New York," in the salon.*

It would be nice to discover someday, in a forgotten trunk, a score by Fabre set to the verses of Levet—poor Gabriel Fabre, who sank into madness; he spent his last ten years in an asylum, abandoned by everyone. He had set to music Mallarmé, Maeterlinck, Laforgue, and even some Chinese poems, very old Chinese poems—one likes to imagine it was Henry Levet his neighbor who had offered to translate them for him. Musical settings without any genius, unfortunately, pale melodies—

that should please the poets: the *words* were more important than the song. (We can very easily imagine that this generous modesty cost Gabriel Fabre his share of posthumous fortune, too concerned as he was to ensure the fame of others.)

For Sarah, the *Cartes postales* was a treasure as precious as the works of Pessoa — what's more, she claims that the young Álvaro de Campos took his inspiration from Henry Levet, whom he had read in the Fargue and Larbaud edition. The figure of Henry, a dandy and traveler who died so young in the arms of his mother, moves her — one can understand why. In Tehran, in the deep Havana brown leather armchairs at the French Institute for Research in Iran, she told how as a teenager in Paris she loved ocean liners, the reverie of ocean liners, the Messageries Maritimes and all the colonial lines. Faugier would tease her by saying this was a boy's passion, that boats, as well as trains, had always been the playthings of boys, and that he didn't know a girl *worthy of that name* who was passionate about such things, steamships, heliographs, wind socks, buoys, the fat gold balls of compasses, embroidered caps, and the proud lines of a ship's bow. Sarah admitted that the technical aspects were of only moderate interest to her (even though she was capable, she stated, of remembering the specifications of each ship, its size, tonnage, draught, speed), she loved above all the names of the liners, and especially their routes: Marseille–Port Said–Suez–Aden–Colombo–Singapore–Saigon–Hong Kong–Shanghai–Kobe–Yokohama in thirty-five days, twice a month on Sunday, on board the *Tonkin*, the *Tourane* or the *Cao-Bang*, 6,700 tons at the time of its shipwreck in foggy weather in front of the island of Poulo Condore, where it was headed to relieve the wardens of an atrocious penal colony off the coast of Saigon. She dreamed of those slow maritime itineraries, of discovering the ports and the stopovers; the luxury dining rooms with their mahogany woodwork; the smoking rooms, the powder rooms, the spacious cabins, the gala menus, which became more and more exotic with each port of call, and the sea, the sea, the original liquid moved without qualms by the stars, the way a bartender shakes a silver shaker.

> *The Armand-Béhic (of the Messageries Maritimes)*
> *Sails at fourteen knots on the Indian Ocean . . .*
> *The sun sets in the pulp of crimes,*
> *In that sea flattened as if by a hand.*

For there is an East beyond the East, that was the dream of the travelers from long ago, the dream of colonial life, the cosmopolitan, bourgeois dream of wharves and steamers. I like to imagine Sarah as a girl, in an entirely earth-bound apartment in the 16th arrondissement of Paris, dreaming, lying down with book in hand, eyes on the ceiling, dreaming she's leaving for Saigon—what did she see in those illusory hours, in the room that one would've liked to enter like a vampire, to settle, like a seagull or kittiwake, on the bedframe, the rail of an ocean liner rocked by the evening, between Aden and Ceylon? Loti in Turkey, Rimbaud in Abyssinia, Segalen in China, those end-of-French-childhood readings, which call up the vocations of Orientalists or dreamers like Hesse's *Siddhartha* or Durrell's *Alexandria Quartet*—we always have the wrong reasons for doing things, our fates, in youth, are as easily swayed as the tip of a fishing float above its hook; Sarah loved reading, studying, dreaming and travel: what do we know of travel when we're seventeen, we appreciate the sound of it, the words, the maps and all our lives, afterward, we seek to rediscover, in reality, our childhood illusions. Segalen the Breton, Levet from Montbrison, or Hesse from Wurtemberg dreamed, in turn fabricating dreams the way Rimbaud had before them, Rimbaud that demon traveler about whom one senses that life, throughout, sought to wrap him in chains to prevent him from leaving, even amputating a leg to be sure he would no longer move—but even as a one-legged person he would buy himself an infernal Marseille–Ardennes round-trip, with a horrible stump that made him suffer terribly, on the jolts of those roads in France, so many divine ruts where he hid poems that exploded into memories at each turn of the wheels, at each grinding of metal against metal, at each steam-encased breath of mold. Terrifying summer of pain, from which the seer with a convict's face would die—he would be granted the aid of both morphine and religion; the first poet of France, the man of mad escapes, from the Northern hills to Java the mysterious, passed away on November 10, 1891, at the Conception Hospital in Marseille, at around two p.m., missing one leg and with an enormous tumor in his groin. Sarah pitied that thirty-six-year-old child (four years older than Levet, hundreds of poems, many kilometers, and ten years spent in the Orient older) who wrote to his sister, from his hospital bed: "Where are the races through mountains, the cavalcades, the promenades, the deserts, the rivers, and seas? Now the existence of Stumpy!"

I should add one more volume to our Great Work,

On the Divers Forms of Lunacie in the Orient
Volume the Second
Gangrene & Tuberculosis

and establish the catalog of the afflicted, consumptives, syphilitics, those who would end up developing an atrocious pathology, a chancre, rosacea, pestilential fungi, purulent bubos, bloody spittle, amputation, or asphyxia, like Rimbaud or Levet, those martyrs of the Orient—and despite my denial, I could devote a chapter to myself, or even two, "Mysterious Maladies" and "Imaginary Maladies," and grant myself a mention in the paragraph

on "Diarrhea and the Runs," which, more than any other affliction, are the true companions of the Orientalist: today, under Dr. Kraus's orders, I'm condemned to drinking yogurt and
eating greens, a mess of greens, from spinach to Iranian *sabzi*,
which is just as unpleasant, but less spectacular than an attack of
the runs: once on a bus between Tehran and the Caspian Sea, at
night, in the middle of a snowstorm, Faugier was forced to argue
vociferously with the driver who had refused to stop by the side
of a mountain road bordered with snowdrifts and who insisted
he wait for the rest stop, planned for a little later — Marc, pale
as a sheet, contorting his lower half, gripped the driver by the
collar, threatened to empty himself on his floor, and convinced
him to stop. I can clearly see Faugier running in the snow, then
disappearing (falling) behind a drift; a few seconds later, in the
snowflake-streaked light of the headlights, we had the surprise
of seeing a fine cloud of vapor rise up, like the smoke signals in
cartoons, which made the driver burst out laughing. A minute
later poor Faugier climbed back in with difficulty, shivering with
cold, pale, soaking wet, a faint relieved smile sketched on his
face. In fact, a few kilometers further on, the bus stopped to let
the passengers out at a crossroads in the middle of the mountains — behind us, the great shoulder of the Damavand massif
and its six thousand meters of rock darkened the winter a little
more; in front of us, forests of oak and hornbeam, dense and
steep, descended down to the coastal plain. The driver insisted
that Faugier drink a cup of tea from his thermos; tea cures everything, he said; two sympathetic women passengers offered the
sick man some preserved sour cherries, which he refused with a
holy terror; an old gentleman absolutely insisted on giving him
half a banana, supposed (at least that's how we understood the
Persian expression) to slow the stomach down — Faugier ran to
take refuge for a few minutes in the service station's bathroom,

before tackling the descent to Amol, a descent he bore bravely, completely rigid, sweat on his forehead, teeth clenched. Instead of tea, preserved fruit, or bananas, he treated his runs with opium, which ended up producing spectacular results: he joined me a few weeks later on the dark side of defecation, that of the chronically constipated.

Our Orientalist illnesses were of course only slight inconveniences compared to those of our illustrious predecessors, compared to the bilharzias, trachomas, and other eye diseases of the Egyptian army, compared to the malaria, plague, and cholera of ancient times — on the face of it, there was nothing exotic about Rimbaud's osteosarcoma, it could just as easily have afflicted him in Charleville, despite the fact that the poet attributed it to the fatigues of the climate and to long walks on foot and horseback. The sick Rimbaud's descent to Zeilah and the Gulf of Aden was quite a bit more difficult than Faugier's to the Caspian Sea, "sixteen black porters" for his stretcher, three hundred kilometers of desert from the mountains of Harar to the coast, with horrible suffering, in twelve days, twelve days of martyrdom that left him completely exhausted at his arrival in Aden, so exhausted that the doctor at the European Hospital decided to cut off his leg immediately, before reversing his decision and preferring that Arthur Rimbaud go get amputated elsewhere: Rimbaud the sailor, as his friend Germain Nouveau nicknamed him, caught a steamship headed for Marseille, the *Amazone*, on May 9, 1891. By the explorer of the Harar and of the Choa, that "man with soles of wind," Sarah would recite entire passages —

The storm blessed my sea-time awakenings.
Lighter than a cork I danced on the waves
Which they call eternal rollers of victims,
Ten nights, without missing the inane eye of lanterns!

And everyone would listen, in those deep Iranian arm-chairs where Henry Corbin himself had conversed with other authorities on Oriental enlightenment and Suhrawardi; we would watch Sarah transform herself into a Boat, a Rimbaudian Pythia —

And then, I bathed myself in the Poem
Of the Sea, infused with stars, and milky-white,
Devouring the green azures; where, pale, delighted
Float, a pensive drowned man sometimes descends

Her eyes shone, her smile became even more brilliant; she gleamed, she was resplendent with poetry, which slightly frightened the scientists present. Faugier would laugh, saying they should "muzzle the muse in her" and would gently warn her against those "assaults of Romanticism," which would in turn make her burst out laughing. Many, though, were the European Orientalists whose calling owed much to dreams of colonial life: punka fans with wooden blades, strong drinks, native passions and dalliances with servants. Those sweet illusions seemed more present among the French and English than the other Orientalists; the Germans, as a whole, had Biblical and archaeological dreams; the Spanish, Iberian fantasies, of Muslim Andalusia and celestial Gypsies; the Dutch, visions of spices, pepper plants, camphor trees and ships in storms off the Cape of Good Hope. Sarah and her adviser and director of the Institute, Gilbert de Morgan, were in this sense entirely French: they were passionate not just about Persian poets, but also about those whom the Orient in general had inspired, the Byrons, Nervals, Rimbauds, and those who had sought, like Pessoa through Álvaro de Campos, an "East to the east of the East."

An extreme Orient beyond the ardors of the average Orient, one begins to think that the Ottoman Empire used to be "the sick man of Europe": today Europe is its own sick man, aged, an abandoned body, hanged on its gallows, which watches itself rot thinking that *Paris will always be Paris*, in about thirty different languages, including Portuguese. "Europe is a recumbent figure leaning on its elbows," writes Fernando Pessoa in *Message*, those complete poetic works are an oracle, a somber oracle of melancholy. In Iran there are beggars in the streets armed with birds, they wait for a passerby to predict his future: for a little cash the bird (yellow or green parakeet, the cleverest of birds) points with its beak at a folded or rolled-up paper that is handed to you, a verse by Hafez is written on it, this practice is called *fal-e Hafez*, the oracle of Hafez: I'll try the oracle of Pessoa, see what the Portuguese world champion of anxiety is reserving for me.

A few pages after the "Opiary," I let my finger glide at random, closing my eyes, then opening them: "Great are the deserts and everything is desert," oh Lord, the desert again, by chance page 428, by chance still Álvaro de Campos, so one begins dreaming for a while that everything is in fact connected, that every word, every gesture is connected to all words and all gestures. All deserts are the desert, "I light a cigarette to put off the journey till later / To put off all journeys till later / To put off the entire universe till later."

The entire universe is in a bookcase, no need to go out: what's the point of leaving the Tower, said Hölderlin, the end of the world has already taken place, no reason to go experience it yourself; you linger, your fingernail between two pages (so soft, so creamy) where Álvaro de Campos, the engineer dandy, becomes more real than Pessoa, his flesh-and-blood double. Great are the deserts and everything is desert. There is a Portuguese Orient just as all European languages have an Orient, an Orient inside them and an Orient outside — one would like, the way in Iran on the last Wednesday of the year you jump over a campfire to bring yourself good luck, to leap over the flames of Palestine, Syria, and

Iraq, the flames of the Levant, to land feet together in the Gulf or in Iran. The Portuguese Orient begins in Socotra and Hormuz, stages on the road to the Indies, islands captured by Afonso de Albuquerque the Conqueror in the beginning of the sixteenth century. You are always in front of your bookcase, Pessoa in hand; you are standing at the prow of a thirsty ship — a ship of regrets, hungry for shipwrecks, once the Cape of Good Hope is passed nothing stops it anymore: the ships of Europe climb northward, Portugal in the lead. Arabia! The Gulf! The Persian Gulf is the trail of spittle of the Mesopotamian toad, warm, smooth sweat, barely disturbed on its edges by the clumps of oil, black and sticky, the dung from the tankers, those ruminants of the sea. You sway; you catch yourself with a thick book, a wooden post, your feet got caught in the rigging — no, in your bathrobe, old corsair's cape, tangled around the lectern. You contemplate your treasures on their shelves, forgotten treasures, buried under the dust, a wooden camel, a Syrian silver talisman engraved with ancient symbols (you think you recall that this illegible amulet was supposed to have calming properties, maybe even cure dangerous madmen, long ago), a miniature on wood, little diptych with brass hinges tarnished with verdigris, depicting a tree, a fawn, and two lovers, but you can't really remember to which romantic novel this pastoral scene belongs, bought at one of the antique shops on Manuchehri Avenue in Tehran. You imagine returning to Darakeh or Darband, high up in the mountains north of the city, a Friday excursion, by the edge of a stream apart from the crowd, out in the middle of nature, under a tree, with a young woman with a gray scarf and a blue coat, surrounded by poppies, flower of martyrdom, flower that likes these rocks, these ravines, and that every spring sows afresh its tiny seeds — the sound of the water, the wind, the smells of spices, charcoal, a group of young people nearby but out of sight, down below in the valley, from which only laughter and the smell of their meal reach us; we stay there, in the thorny shadow of a giant pomegranate tree, throwing pebbles into the water, eating cherries and candied plums hoping, hoping for what? A deer, an ibex, a lynx, none of those come; no one passes by aside from an old dervish with a strange hat, straight out of Rumi's *Masnavi*, who is climbing up to God knows what summit, who knows what refuge, his reed flute slung over his shoulder, stick in hand. You greet him, saying "*Ya Ali!*" slightly frightened by this omen, the invasion of the spiritual into a scene you'd much rather be extremely temporal, tender. "Listen to the flute, how it tells stories, complains about separation, when you cut it, in the reed bed; its cries sadden men and women." Is there a complete translation of Rumi's *Masnavi* in German? Or in French? Twenty-six thousand rhymes, thirteen thousand couplets. One of the monuments of literature. A summa of poetry and mystical wisdom, hundreds of anecdotes, stories, characters. Rückert unfortunately translated only a few ghazals, he didn't tackle the *Masnavi*. Rückert is in any case so poorly published these days. You find either cheap, slender contemporary anthologies, or else editions from the late nineteenth or early twentieth century, without any notes or commentaries, riddled with mistakes; the scholarly edition is underway, apparently, "the Schweinfurt edition" ("Good place, horrible name," said the poet), slowly, in ten or twelve volumes, impossible to find, exorbitantly priced — a luxury for academic libraries. Why is there no Pléiade collection in Germany or Austria? There's an invention that we could envy France for, those soft collections with the supple leather covers, so carefully edited, with introductions, appendices, commentary by scholars, where one finds all of French and foreign literature. A world away from the luxurious volumes of the Deutscher Klassiker Verlag, much less popular, I don't think many people get them for Christmas. If

Friedrich Rückert were French, he'd be in the Pléiade collection — there are three volumes of Gobineau after all, the racist Orientalist who specialized in Iran. The Pléiade is much more than a collection, it's a matter of State. The entrance of such-or-such author under the protection of the rhodoid dust jacket and the colored leather cover unleashes passions. The acme for a writer being of course to become part of the collection *during his lifetime* — to have the pleasant experience of posthumous glory before you're pushing up the daisies. The worst (but I don't think there's a proven case) would be, after entering la Pléiade, to be kicked out of it during one's lifetime. A banishment *ad vitam*. For one does leave it, this divine collection, and in Tehran, that gave rise to a scene worthy of Jahiz's *Epistle on the Wonders of Professors*: the director of the French Institute for Research in Iran, an eminent Orientalist, fumed in his office before leaving it, striding up and down the vestibule shouting "It's a scandal!" "A shame!" and causing immediate panic among his employees: the gentle secretary (greatly frightened by her employer's mood swings) hid behind her files, the tech guy dove under a table, screwdriver in hand, while the debonair general secretary found a cousin or an old aunt to call urgently, spewing out endless polite phrases, very loudly, on the telephone.

SARAH (*at the doorway to her office, worried*): But what's happening? Gilbert, is everything all right?

MORGAN (*fuming*): It's an incredible scandal, Sarah, you haven't heard yet? Brace yourself! What an affront for the society of scholars! What ruin for literature!

SARAH (*swaying, frightened, voice pinched*): Good God, I fear the worst.

MORGAN (*happy to be able to share his pain*): You won't believe it: they've just expelled Germain Nouveau from the Pléiade.

SARAH (*flabbergasted, incredulous*): No! How can that be? You can't expel someone from the Pléiade! Not Germain Nouveau! MORGAN (*appalled*): Yes. They just did. *Exit* Nouveau. Adieu. The second edition will only reprint Lautréamont, all alone, without Germain Nouveau. It's a debacle.

SARAH (*mechanically tugs at the pencil holding up her bun; her hair tumbles loose down to her shoulders; she looks like an ancient mourner*): We have to do something, get together a petition, mobilize the scholarly community . . .

MORGAN (*grave, resigned*): It's too late . . . The Lautréamont came out yesterday. And the editor says there will be no solo Germain Nouveau in the years to come.

SARAH (*indignant*): How horrible. Poor Nouveau! Poor Humilis!

FRANZ (*observing the scene from the door to the guest researchers' office*): Is something serious happening? Can I be of any help?

SARAH (*inflicting her bad mood on the poor intruder*): I do not see how Austria or even Germany could be of any help at all to us at this precise moment, thanks all the same.

MORGAN (idem, *without the slightest touch of irony*): You find us in the midst of national mourning, Franz.

FRANZ (*not a little annoyed, closing the office door*): You have my condolences, then.

I had absolutely no idea who this Germain Nouveau could be whose deposition was hurling scholarship into suffering and affliction: I found out quite quickly, through Sarah obviously, who gave me a complete seminar on the subject, a seminar and some reprimands, since obviously I had not read her article "Germain Nouveau in Lebanon and Algeria" published in *Lettres françaises*, the title of which, to my great shame, was however vaguely familiar. Half an hour after the national mourning she invited me over for funereal tea "upstairs," in the living room of the guest apartment, to rebuke me: Germain Nouveau was a travel companion of Rimbaud (whom he had followed to London) and Verlaine (whom he had followed into drunkenness and Catholicism), without the fame, admittedly, of either of his companions, but an excellent poet and someone who had also lived an extraordinary life, as unusual as the lives of the other two. A man from the South, he had arrived in the capital very young, very young but old enough to frequent the bars in the Latin Quarter and Montmartre. He wanted to become a poet.

This idea is entirely surprising today, that you could leave Marseille in 1872 and go to Paris hoping to become a poet, with two or three sonnets in your pocket, a few gold francs, and the names of the cafés where bohemians went: Tabourey, Polidor . . . Imagine a young man from Innsbruck or Klagenfurt setting out these days for Vienna with only a missive from his German teacher and his poems on his iPad, he'd have quite a bit of trouble finding comrades — Czech absinthe and drugs of all kinds to disturb his senses, definitely, but poetry, no way. It is (fortunately for poetry) likely that I don't know my city well at all, given that I don't frequent cafés at night, poets even less, who have always seemed suspicious seducers to me, especially in the beginning of the twenty-first century. Germain Nouveau was a real poet, he sought God in asceticism and prayer and went mad, attaining "melancholy delirium with mystic ideas" according to his doctors in Bicêtre where he was first committed, for six months. As Sarah noted in her article, Nouveau's first fit of madness corresponded exactly with Rimbaud's coming down from Harar, and lasted until Rimbaud's death; Nouveau left the asylum when Rimbaud died, in November 1891. Of course Germain Noveau was unaware of the sad fate of his former travel companion but after the failure of his move to Lebanon and after long wanderings in France, Germain tried an Oriental adventure again, in Algiers; from there he wrote a letter to Arthur Rimbaud, addressed to Aden, to confide his plan to him: he wanted to become a painter and decorator, in Alexandria or Aden, and asked Rimbaud, in the name of their old friendship, for "tips." "I haven't seen Verlompe in almost two years," he wrote. Sarah found this letter to a dead man very moving; Verlompe-Verlaine might have told him about Rimbaud's death, which took place precisely two years earlier. A whisper in the night. It's pleasant to think that even today, researchers try to demonstrate, making up for lack of proof with sheer stubbornness, that Germain Nouveau was the author of *Illuminations* and not Rimbaud the sailor — we'll likely never know.

Sarah had patiently retraced the adventures (or rather misadventures) of Germain Nouveau in Beirut and Algiers. He too had dreamed of the Orient, and had even tried to settle there as a teacher in a Greek Catholic high school in Beirut. Sarah had visited all the Greek Catholic institutions in Lebanon to try to find, in archives scattered by time and wars, the correspondence surrounding his appointment, and especially the reason for his dismissal, a few weeks after his arrival, from his post as teacher — without any success. Only a legend survives, according to which Germain had an affair with the mother of one of his students. But given his French professional records and the many appalled reports of his superiors in France ("This man is anything but a teacher," said one headmaster) Sarah thought it was rather his incompetence that got Germain Nouveau fired. He stayed in Beirut, penniless, jobless, until autumn, trying to claim his wages. They say he fell in love with a blind young woman he sent begging for two in Bab Idriss; it could be the woman (blind or not) he describes in one of his sonnets from Lebanon, which are so many Orientalist paintings:

Oh! To paint your hair with the blue of smoke,
Your golden skin with a tone that might almost make one see
A burnt rose! and your fragrant skin,
In great robes of an angel, as in a fresco.

He may finally have won his case and some compensation, or else was repatriated to Marseille by the French Consul, on the liner *Tigre* of the Messageries Maritimes, which stopped over in Jaffa — the very Christian Germain Nouveau couldn't resist the proximity of the Holy Sites and went on foot to Jerusalem, then to Alexandria, begging his way; he embarked again a few weeks later on *La Seyne* which landed in Marseille and he found Verlaine, absinthe, and Parisian cafés at the beginning of 1885.

I open this Pléiade that gathers together Nouveau and Lautréamont, Germain's Orient with Isidore's Uruguay, this Pléiade in which today Ducasse de Lautréamont reigns alone, rid of his accidental rival — that's the fate of Humilis, the name Nouveau chose for himself; the humble, the beggar poet, the fool for Christ never wanted to republish the little there was of his published work, and today (at least this is Sarah's conclusion) it shines, *Stella Maris*, like a star hidden behind the clouds of oblivion.

And it's mad that I will die,
And yes, Madame, I am sure,
But first . . . from your slightest gesture,
Mad . . . from your heavenly passing by
That leaves a fragrance of ripe fruit,

From your alert, open appearance,
Yes, mad from love, yes, mad from love,
Mad about your sacred . . . curve of hip,
Which drives into my heart white . . . fear,
More surely than the roll of a drum.

The poor man did in fact die mad, mad from love and mad from Christ, and Sarah thinks, perhaps rightly, that his months in Beirut and his pilgrimage to Jerusalem (as well as his "encounter" with Saint Benedict Labre, his and Verlaine's patron saint) were the beginnings of this melancholy disturbance that led to the crisis of 1891: he traced signs of the cross on the ground with his tongue, muttered incessant prayers, rid himself of his clothing. Prey to auditory hallucinations, he stopped answering external solicitations. He was committed to an asylum. And either because he took it upon himself to hide the signs of his holiness as well as he could, or because the effect of the absinthe passed, a few months later they let him go—then he picked up his bag and stick and went to Rome on foot, like Saint Benedict Labre in the eighteenth century:

> *It's God who led to Rome,*
> *Placing a staff in his hand,*
> *The saint who was just a poor man,*
> *Swallow on the great way,*
> *Who left his whole corner of Earth,*
> *His solitary cell,*
> *And the monastery soup,*
> *And his bench that's warming in the sun,*
> *Deaf to his century, to its oracles,*
> *Welcomed only by tabernacles,*
> *But clothed in the gift of miracles*
> *And coiffed with the vermilion halo.*

The practice of poverty: that's what Sarah calls the rule of St. Germain the New. Witnesses tell how during his last years in Paris, before leaving for the South, he lived in a garret, where he slept on a cardboard box; more than once he was seen, armed with a hook, looking for his food in bins. He begged his friends to burn his works, started proceedings against anyone who published them despite his wishes; he spent the last years of his existence in prayer, fasting more than is reasonable, content with the bread given to him by the hospice: he ended up dying of starvation, from a prolonged fast, just before Easter, on his pallet, with only the fleas and spiders as company. Sarah found it extraordinary that all anyone knows of his great work, *The Doctrine of Love*, is what an admirer and friend, the Comte de Larmandie, had learned by heart. No manuscript. Larmandie said: Like the explorers of dead cities, I have concealed and hidden in my heart, to restore them to the sun, the jewels of a vanished king. This transmission, with all the shadows of uncertainties it projected onto the work (didn't Nouveau write to Larmandie when he discovered "his" book pirated in such a way: "You make me say any old thing!"), brought Nouveau closer to the great old texts, to the mystics of the olden days and to the Oriental poets, whose verses were retained orally before being written down, often years later. Sarah explained to me, in those famous armchairs, over tea upstairs, the *love* she bore for Nouveau, probably because she had the presentiment that she herself, a little later, would in turn choose asceticism and contemplation, even though the tragedy that would be responsible for this choice had not yet occurred. She was already interested in Buddhism, followed the teachings, practiced meditation — all of which I had trouble taking seriously. Do I have Sarah's "Germain Nouveau in Lebanon and Algeria" somewhere, last night I got out most of the offprints of her articles — it's in the center of the bookcase, on the Sarah shelf. Set the Pessoa back on its stand, replace Nouveau next to Levet, Sarah's texts are placed in the middle of musical criticism, why, I don't remember anymore. Maybe so that her works can be behind the compass from Bonn, no that's idiotic, so that Sarah would be in the center of the bookcase as she is in the center of my life, that's equally idiotic, because of the size and the pretty colors of the spines of her books, that's much more likely. One looks in passing at the Portuguese Orient, the framed photo of the island of Hormuz, a much younger Franz Ritter sitting on the barrel of the old sand-covered cannon, near the fort; the compass in its box, just in front of *Les Orients féminins*, Sarah's first book, *Désorients*, the abridged version of her thesis, and *Dévorations*, her book on the eaten heart, the revelatory heart and all kinds of holy terrors of symbolic cannibalism. An almost Viennese book, which deserves to be translated into German. It's true that in French they talk about a *devouring* passion, which is the whole subject of the book—between passion and gluttonous ingestion. The mysterious article from Sarawak is moreover only a continuation of this little book, a little more advanced in atrocity. The wine of the dead. The juice of the corpse.

This photo of the island of Hormuz is really beautiful. Sarah has a gift for photography. These days it's a clichéd art, everyone photographs everyone, with mobile phones, computers, tablets—that makes for millions of painful images, disgraceful flashes that wipe out faces that are supposed to be foregrounded, unartistic blurriness, annoying backlighting. In the era of film photography people took more care, it seems to me. But maybe I'm still just mourning ruins. What an incurable nostalgic I am. I must say I look rather charming, in this photo. So much so that Mother framed an enlargement of it. Checked blue shirt, short hair, sunglasses, chin resting firmly on right fist, a pensive look facing the light blue of the Persian Gulf and the cyan of the sky. In the distant background, you can make out the coast and probably Bandar Abbas; to my right, the red and ochre of the collapsed walls of the Portuguese fortress. And the cannon. As I remember it there was another cannon that doesn't appear in the photo. It was winter, and we were happy to have left Tehran—it had snowed profusely for several days, and then a cold wave had gripped the city in ice. The *djoub*, those canals by the sidewalks, were invisible, covered in snow, and made excellent traps for pedestrians, and even for cars: here and there you'd see overturned Paykans, two wheels stuck in those little rivers around a bend. North of Vanak, on the Avenue Vali-Asr, the immense plane trees discharged their painful fruits of frozen snow onto passersby whenever the wind blew. In Shemiran a calm silence reigned, in the smell of wood fire and charcoal fire. On Tajrish Square, we took refuge in the little bazaar to escape the freezing blast that seemed to be streaming down from the mountains through the Darband Valley. Even Faugier had given up frequenting the parks; the whole northern half of Tehran, from the Avenue Enqelab, was numb from snow and ice. The travel agency was on that avenue, near Ferdowsi Square; Sarah had gotten the tickets, a nonstop flight straight to Bandar Abbas from a new company with the lilting name of Aria Air, in a magnificent thirty-year-old Ilyushin renovated by Aeroflot where everything was still written in Russian — I was mad at her, what was she thinking, cutting corners like that, you gain a few hundred rials in the price difference but you risk your skin, your penny-pinching, you'll copy it out for me, you'll copy out a hundred times "I will never travel again with preposterous companies using Soviet technology," she laughed, my cold sweats made her laugh, I was scared stiff at take-off, the engine shook everything as if it were about to fall apart on the spot. But it didn't. For the two hours of the flight I was very attentive to ambient noises. I broke out in a cold sweat again when that ancient heap of metal finally landed, as lightly as a hen on its straw. The steward announced it was 26 degrees Celsius at arrival. The sun was scorching, and Sarah soon began to curse her Islamic coat and black scarf — the Persian Gulf was a mass of whitish haze slightly bluish at the base; Bandar Abbas a flat city, which ran alongside a very long beach, where a wide concrete jetty, very high, penetrated far into the sea. We went to drop off our luggage at the hotel, a building that looked quite recent (brand-new elevator, fresh paint) but whose rooms were in complete ruin: old damaged armoires, threadbare rugs, bedspreads pockmarked with cigarette burns, rickety bedside tables with dented lamps. We heard the truth of the matter a little later: the hotel was indeed in a new building, but its contents (the construction must have consumed all its owner's money) had simply been moved from the previous establishment and, the receptionist informed us, the furniture had suffered somewhat from the move. Sarah immediately saw this as a magnificent metaphor for contemporary Iran: new buildings, same old things. I'd have liked a little more comfort, even beauty, that latter quality seeming to be completely absent from downtown Bandar Abbas: you needed a lot of imagination (a *lot*) to see the ancient harbor where Alexander the Great passed through on his way to the country of the Ichthyophagi, the former Porto Comorão of the Portuguese, their landing stage for merchandise from the Indies, the port city renovated with the help of the English, named Port Abbas in homage to Shah Abbas, the ruler who reconquered for Persia this port on the strait of Hormuz as well as the island of Hormuz, thus putting an end to the Portuguese-speaking presence in the Persian Gulf. The Portuguese had called Bandar Abbas "the Port of the Prawn," and once our luggage was deposited in our horrible rooms we went off in search of a restaurant to try the immense white prawns from the Indian Ocean that we had seen being unloaded, all shiny from the ice, at the fishmonger's in the Tajrish bazaar in Tehran. *Chelow meygu,* a chowder made from these swimming decapods, was indeed delicious — in the meantime Sarah had put on a lighter Islamic coat, made of cream-colored cotton, and had hidden her hair under a flowered scarf. The promenade by the water confirmed that there was nothing for us to see in Bandar Abbas aside from a row of more or less modern buildings; on the beach, we could see here and there women in traditional clothing, with the decorated leather mask that made them look slightly disturbing, monstrous characters from a morbid masked ball or a novel by Alexandre Dumas. The bazaar was laden with all sorts of dates, from Bam or Kerman, mountains of dates, dried or fresh, dark or light, which alternated with red, yellow, and brown pyramids of chilies, turmeric, and cumin. In the middle of the jetty was the passengers' port, a landing stage that advanced straight into the sea for a hundred meters or so — the sea floor was sandy and very gently sloping; the heavily loaded boats couldn't approach the shore. The curious thing was that there were no heavily loaded boats, just little ferries, rather slender motorboats, equipped with enormous outboard motors, the same kinds of vessels that the Guardians of the Revolution, I seemed to remember, used during the war to attack oil tankers and cargo ships. To board a boat, then, you had to climb down a metal ladder from the landing dock to the motorboat waiting below: the dock actually served no purpose except to gather potential passengers. At least for those who wanted (and there weren't many of them) to go to the island of Hormuz: the travelers going to Kish or Qeshm, the two large neighboring islands, took their seats on comfortable ferries, which made me insinuate timidly to Sarah, "Listen, why don't we go to Qeshm instead?": she didn't even bother to reply and began, helped by a sailor, her descent on the ladder to the tub swaying on the waves three meters below. To give me courage I thought of the Austrian Lloyd line, whose proud vessels left Trieste to crisscross the seas of the globe, and also of the daysailers I had skippered once or twice on Trauen Lake. The sole advantage of the excessive speed of our tub, where only the drive shaft and propeller of the motor touched the water, its prow pointing uselessly up to the sky, was to shorten the time of the crossing, which I spent clutching the gunwale, trying not to fall ridiculously backward, then forward, whenever a tiny wave threatened to transform us into a strange kind of hydroplane. Surely the captain and sole member of the crew had once piloted a suicide boat, and the failure of his mission (suicide) still haunted him twenty years after the end of the conflict. I have no memory of our landing in Hormuz, proof of my emotion; I can see again the Portuguese fort, the focal point of Sarah's gaze—a wide almost square tower, collapsed at the top, of red and black stone, two rather low walls, pointed archways and rusty old cannons, facing the strait. The island was a big dry rock, a rock that seemed deserted—but there was a little village, a few goats and some Guardians of the Revolution: contrary to what we feared, these Pasdaran in sand-colored clothes were not about to accuse us of espionage, on the contrary they were delighted to be able to exchange a few words with us, and to show us the path that led around the fort. Imagine, said Sarah, the Portuguese sailors from the sixteenth century who found themselves here, on this rock, guarding the strait. Or opposite, in Porto Comorão, where all the commodities necessary for soldiers and artisans came from, including water. It's probably here the word *nostalgia* was used for the first time. Weeks on the sea to find yourself on this little island, in the scorching, humid heat of the Gulf. What solitude . . .

She was picturing—much better than I could, I have to admit—the torments of those Portuguese adventurers who had braved the Cape of Storms and the giant Adamastor, "king of the deep" in Meyerbeer's opera *L'Africaine*, to colonize this round rock, the pearls of the Gulf, the spices and silks of India. Afonso de Albuquerque was, Sarah told me, the architect of the policies of the King of Portugal Dom Manuel, policies that were much more ambitious than these small-scale ruins, which led one to believe: by establishing themselves in the Gulf, by taking on the Mamelukes of Egypt whose fleet on the Red Sea they had already defeated from the rear, the Portuguese intended not only to establish a cluster of commercial ports from Malacca to Egypt but also, in one final crusade, to liberate Jerusalem from the infidels. This Portuguese dream was still half-Mediterranean; it corresponded to that shifting moment when the Mediterranean little by little stopped being the sole political and economic stake of the maritime powers. The Portuguese at the end of the fifteenth century dreamed *at the same time* of the Indies and the Levant, they were (at least Dom Manuel and his adventurer Albuquerque) between two bodies of water, between two dreams and two eras. In the beginning of the sixteenth century, Hormuz was impossible to keep without a foothold on the continent, whether it was on the Persian side like today, or on the Omani side as it was at the time of that sultanate of Hormuz to which Afonso de Albuquerque, governor of the Indies, put an end, with his cannons and his twenty-five ships.

As for me, I thought that the Portuguese word *saudade*—longing, melancholy—is, as its name indicates, a very Arabic and very Iranian sentiment, and that these young Pasdars on their island, unless they came from Shiraz or Tehran and went back home every night, must have recited poems around a campfire to stave off their sadness—not the poems of Luís de Camões, that's for sure, unlike Sarah perched on the rusty cannon. We sat down in the sand in the shade of an old wall, facing the sea, each in our own *saudade*: my *saudade* for Sarah, too close for me not to wish to bury myself in her arms, and her *saudade* for the melancholy shadow of Badr Shakir Sayyab which was reflected on the Gulf, far to the north, between Kuwait and Basra. The poet with the long face had gone to Iran in 1952, probably to Abadan and Ahvaz, to flee the repression in Iraq, while no one knew anything about the repression in Iraq, or about his Iranian travels. "I cry to the Gulf / O Gulf, you offer pearls, shells and death / and the echo comes back, like a sob / You offer pearls, shells and death," these lines that I too turn over in my mind, return to me like an echo, the "Song of the Rain" by the Iraqi chased from his childhood and the village of Jaykur by the death of his mother, launched into the world and into suffering, an infinite exile, like this island in the Persian Gulf strewn with dead shells. There were echoes in his work of T. S. Eliot, whom he had translated into Arabic; he had gone to England, where he had suffered terribly from solitude, according to his letters and texts — he had experienced the *Unreal City*, had become a shade among the shades on London Bridge. "Here, said she, is your card, the drowned Phoenician Sailor. (Those are pearls that were his eyes. Look!)" Birth, death, resurrection, the land lying fallow, as sterile as the oil plain of the Gulf. Sarah hummed my *lied* on the verses of the "Song of the Rain," slowly and gravely, as funereal as they were pretentious, whereas Sayyab had been modest to the end. It's a good thing I stopped composing songs, I lacked the humility of Gabriel Fabre, his compassion. His passion too, probably.

We recited the poems of Sayyab and Eliot in front of the old Portuguese fort until two goats came to draw us out of our contemplation, goats with brownish red coats, accompanied by a little girl whose eyes shone with curiosity; the goats were gentle, smelled very strong, they began nuzzling us, gently but firmly: this Homeric attack put an end to our intimacy, the child and her animals had obviously decided to spend the afternoon with us. They were obsequious enough to accompany us back (without saying a word, or answering any of our questions) to the landing dock where the boats left for Bandar Abbas: Sarah found this little girl comical — she didn't let anyone approach and, unlike the goats, fled as soon as you held out your hand to her, but returned to a distance of one or two meters a few seconds later; I however found her rather frightening, mostly because of her incomprehensible muteness.

The Pasdars at the dock didn't look the least bit bothered by this girl who stuck to us like glue with her goats. Sarah turned back to wave at the child without getting any reaction from her, not even a gesture. For a long time we discussed the reason for such wild behavior; I maintained that the girl (ten or twelve at most) must have been disturbed, or deaf, perhaps; Sarah just thought she was shy: that's probably the first time she's ever heard a foreign language, she said, which seemed unlikely to me. Whatever the case, this strange apparition, and those soldiers, were the only inhabitants we glimpsed on the island of Hormuz. The skipper on the way back wasn't the same as the one going out, but his motorboat and nautical technique were identical — with the one exception that he dropped us off at the beach, lifting his motor and beaching his boat on the sandy bottom, a few meters from shore. So we were lucky enough to be able to dip our feet in the water of the Persian Gulf and verify two things: first, the Iranians are less strict than one might think, and no policeman hidden under a pebble rushed at Sarah to order her to conceal her ankles (an entirely erotic part of the female body, according to the censors) and roll down her trousers; and second, sadly, is that if I had doubted for a single instant the presence of hydrocarbons in the region, I could be entirely reassured: the sole of my foot was stained with thick, sticky spots that despite all my strenuous efforts in the hotel shower left me for a long time with a brownish ring on my skin and toes: I keenly missed Mother's specialized detergents, the little bottles of Doktor something or other, whose efficacy I imagine, wrongly no doubt, is due to years of unmentionable

experiments to remove stains from Nazi uniforms — so hard to
clean, as Mother says about white tablecloths. While we're on the subject of goats and cloth, I absolutely
have to have this bathrobe shortened, I'll end up tripping and
and knocking myself out against a corner of the furniture, farewell Franz, farewell, finally the Middle East will have triumphed
over you, but not with some terrifying parasite, worms that devour your eyes from inside or poison you through the soles of
the feet, but just an overlong Bedouin cloak, the revenge of
the desert — one can imagine the announcement in the press,
"Killed by his terrible taste in clothing: the mad academic was
disguised as Omar Sharif in *Lawrence of Arabia*." As Omar Sharif
or rather Anthony Quinn, the Auda Abu Tayya of the film —
Auda the proud Bedouin of the Howeitats, a tribe of courageous
warriors who took Akaba from the Ottomans with Lawrence
in 1917, Auda the ferocious in the pleasures of war, obligatory
guide for all Orientalists in the desert: he accompanied Alois
Musil the Moravian as well as Lawrence the Englishman and
Father Antonin Jaussen the man from the Ardèche. This Dominican priest who was trained in Jerusalem also met the other
two, and they became the three musketeers of Orientalism, with
Auda Abu Tayya as d'Artagnan. Two priests, one adventurer, and
a Bedouin fighter, great decapitator of Turks — unfortunately
the whims of international politics willed it so that Musil fought
in the opposite camp to Jaussen and Lawrence's; as for Auda,
he began the Great War with one and ended allied to the other
two, when Faysal, son of the sharif Hussein of Mecca, managed
to convince him to place his valorous cavalrymen in the service
of the Arab Revolt.

It's quite certain, moreover, that if Jaussen's country had asked
his advice, he'd rather have gone over to the side of the Austrian
explorer-priest, with whom he'd have enjoyed conversing,

during the long expeditions on camel-back through the scree of Al-Sham, about theology and Arab antiquities, instead of on the side of the lanky Brits, whose strange mysticism gave off the frightful stench of paganism, and whose government had the musty smell of secret treachery. Antonin Jaussen and Alois Musil were forced by events (relatively forced: both, while they were protected from soldiers by their priest's clothes, volunteered for service) to fight against each other for domination of the Arabic Orient and more precisely for those warrior tribes between the Syrian *badiya* and the Hejaz, tribes that were familiar with raids and clan warfare. Auda *alias* Anthony Quinn was angry at neither; he was a pragmatic man who appreciated above all battles, weapons, and the bellicose poetry of ancient times. They say his body was covered in scars from his wounds, which excited the curiosity of the women in his region; according to legend he married a good twenty times, and had a large number of children.

Look, I've forgotten to turn off the radio. I still haven't bought myself one of those Bluetooth headsets that let you listen to music wirelessly. I could stroll into the kitchen with Reza Shajarian or Franz Schubert in my ears. When I switch on the electric kettle, the light bulb on the ceiling still flickers a little. Things are connected. The kettle is in communication with the ceiling light, even though, in theory, the two objects have nothing to do with each other. The laptop is yawning on the table, half-open, like a silver frog. Where did I put those teabags? I'd like to listen to a little Iranian music, some *tar*, *tar* and *zarb*. The radio, friend of insomniacs. Only insomniacs listen to *Die Öl Klassiknacht* in their kitchens. Schumann. I'd swear it was Schumann, string trio. Impossible to get that wrong.

Oh, here we are. Samsara Chai or Red Love — we're still stuck in it, that's for sure. What came over me to buy these things. Samsara Chai must be caffeinated. OK fine, a little cup of Red

Love. Rose petals, dried raspberries, hibiscus flowers, according to the box. Why don't I have any chamomile in my cupboards? Or verbena, or even lemon balm? The herbalist on the corner of the street closed five or six years ago, a very nice lady, she liked me a lot, I was her sole customer apparently; it should be said that the age of her shop was not venerable enough to inspire confidence, it was just a horrible store from the 1970s, with no charm in its disrepair or anything special on its Formica shelves. Since then I've had to buy Samsara Love or God knows what at the supermarket.

Ah yes, Schumann, I knew it. Good Lord it's three a.m. The news is still depressing, despite the generally reassuring (thanks to its smoothness) voice of the speaker. A hostage decapitated in Syria, in the desert, by a killer with a London accent. One imagines a whole scenario set up to frighten the Western spectator, the sacrificer masked in black, the hostage kneeling, head lowered—these atrocious videos of beheadings have been fashionable for a dozen years, ever since the death of Daniel Pearl in Karachi in 2002, and even before possibly, in Bosnia and Chechnya, how many since then have been executed in the same way, dozens, hundreds of people, in Iraq and elsewhere: one wonders why this method of execution, throat-slitting with a kitchen knife till the head comes off, maybe they're unaware of the power of the saber or the axe. At least the Saudis, who decapitate myriads of poor devils every year, do it with all the weight of tradition, so to speak—with a saber, which one pictures handled by a giant: the executioner comes down with a single blow of the weapon onto the condemned man's neck, immediately breaking his spine and (but in the end it's of secondary importance) separating the head from the shoulders, as in the time of the sultans. *The Thousand and One Nights* are full of decapitations, according to the same *modus operandi*, saber on neck; in the novels of chivalry too, one decapitates "with all one's strength," as the French say, with the sword or axe, head placed on a block like Milady, Athos's wife in *The Three Musketeers*, as I remember that was a privilege of the nobility, to be decapitated instead of being quartered, burned, or strangled — the French Revolution would sort that out, by inventing the guillotine; in Austria we had our gibbet, like the Spanish garrotte, strangling that was entirely manual. Of course there was an example of this gibbet in the Museum of Crime, Sarah had been able to discover how it functioned as well as the personality of the most famous executioner in the history of Austria, Josef Lang, thanks to that extraordinary photograph dating back to around 1910 where you see him, bowler hat on his head, mustache, bowtie, big smile on his face, perched on his stepladder behind the corpse of a tidily executed man, hanging there dead, well-strangled, and around him the assistants, all smiling as well. Sarah looked at this photo and sighed, "The smile of the worker in front of a job well done," showing she had understood perfectly the psychology of Josef Lang, a horrifically normal guy, a pathetic loser, good family man who boasted about making you die expertly, "with pleasant sensations." "What a passion for death, all the same, your fellow citizens have," Sarah said. For macabre memories. And even the heads of the dead — a few years ago all the Vienna papers were talking about the burial of a skull, the skull of Kara Mustafa, no less. The great vizier who had led the second siege of Vienna in 1683 and lost the battle had been strangled, by order of the sultan, in Belgrade where he had retreated — I can see myself telling the incredulous Sarah that after being strangled by the silk cord Kara Mustafa was decapitated postmortem, that the skin of his face was then removed to be sent to Istanbul as proof of his death, and his skull buried (with the rest of his bones, one supposes) in Belgrade. The Hapsburgs discovered him, in the corresponding grave, five years later, when they occupied the city. The skull of Kara Mustafa, Mustafa the Black, was given to some Viennese prelate, who donated it to the Arsenal, then to the Municipal Museum, where it was exhibited for years, until one scrupulous curator thought this morbid old thing no longer had a place among the illustrious collections of the history of Vienna, and decided to get rid of it. The skull of Kara Mustafa, whose tent was set up a stone's throw away from here, a few hundred meters from the glacis, near the Danube, couldn't go in the trash; they found a burial place for it in an anonymous niche. Did that Turkish relic have anything to do with the fashion for mustachioed Turks that adorn the pediments of our beautiful city? There's a question for Sarah, I'm sure she is unbeatable on the subject of decapitation, the Turks, their heads, hostages and even the executioner's dagger — over there in Sarawak she must hear the same headlines as we do, the same radio news, or maybe not, who knows. In Sarawak perhaps there's more talk about the latest decisions of the Sultan of Brunei and nothing about masked killers of Islam, the macabre farce with the black flag. It's such a European story, in the end. European victims, killers with London accents. A new and violent radical Islam, born in Europe and the United States, from Western bombs, and the only victims that count when it comes down to it are Europeans. Poor Syrians. Their fate interests our media much less, in reality. The terrifying nationalism of corpses. Auda Abu Tayya the proud warrior of Lawrence and Musil would probably fight today with the Islamic State, the new worldwide jihad following many others — who had the idea first, Napoleon in Egypt or Max von Oppenheim in 1914? Max von Oppenheim the archaeologist from Cologne was already old when the hostilities broke out, he had already discovered Tell Halaf; like many Orientalists and Arabic scholars of the time he joined the Nachrichtenstelle für den Orient, a Berlin office intended to gather information of military interest coming from the East. Oppenheim was an habitué of the corridors of power; he was the one who convinced Wilhelm II to carry out his official voyage to the Orient and the pilgrimage to Jerusalem; he believed in the power of pan-Islamism, which he discussed with Abdulhamid the Red Sultan himself. A hundred years later, German Orientalists were more *au fait* with Oriental realities than Bonaparte's Arabic specialists, who were the first to try, without much success, to make the little Corsican pass as the liberator of the Arabs from the Turkish yoke. The first European colonial expedition to the Near East was a fine military fiasco. Napoleon Bonaparte did not experience the success he expected as saviour of Islam and conceded a very bitter defeat to the perfidious British — decimated by plague, vermin, and English cannonballs, the last fragments of the glorious army of Valmy must have been abandoned on site, with the only sciences benefiting even a tiny bit from the adventure being, in order of importance, military medicine, Egyptology, and Semitic linguistics. Did the Germans and Austrians think of Napoleon when they launched their appeal for global jihad in 1914? The idea (submitted by Oppenheim the archaeologist) was to call for the disobedience of the Muslims of the world, Moroccan troops, Algerian and Senegalese infantry corps, Indian Muslims, Caucasians, and Turkmens whom the Triple Entente sent to fight on the European Front and to use riots or guerrilla tactics to create disorder in the English, French, and Russian Muslim colonies. The idea delighted the Austrians and the Ottomans, and the jihad was proclaimed in Arabic in the name of the sultan-caliph in Istanbul on November 14, 1914, in the mosque of Mehmet the Conqueror, probably to give all the symbolic weight possible to this rather complex fatwa, since it didn't call for holy war against all infidels, and excluded from the impious the Germans, the Austrians and the representatives of neutral countries. I can see the beginnings of a third volume to the work that will earn me glory:

On the Divers Forms of Lunacie in the Orient
Volume the Third
Portraits of Orientalists as Commanders of the Faithful

This summons was immediately followed by a solemn march to the German and Austrian embassies, then by the first bellicose action: after the speech, a Turkish policeman emptied his weapon point-blank into a noble English clock in the lobby of the Grand Hotel Tokatliyan, the starter pistol for the jihad, if we are to believe the memories of the German dragoman Schabinger, one of the artisans of this solemn proclamation that precipitated all Orientalist forces into battle. Alois Musil was dispatched to his dear Bedouin tribes and to Auda Abu Tayya the bellicose to ensure their support. The British and French were not to be outdone; they mobilized their scholars — the Lawrences, Jaussens, Massignons, and company — to launch a counter-jihad, with the success we know: the great cavalcade of Faysal and Auda Abu Tayya in the desert. The beginning of the legend of Lawrence of Arabia that, unfortunately for the Arabs, ended in French and English mandates on the Middle East. I have on my computer Sarah's article on the French colonial soldiers and the German jihad, with images of that model camp for Muslim prisoners of war near Berlin where all the ethnologists and Orientalists of the time passed through; an article "exposing the facts" for an illustrated journal, *History* or God knows what publication of that kind, here's something that will make a wonderful accompaniment to the herbal tea and the radio news:

We know these two men only from the archives preserved in the collections of the Ministry of Defense, which patiently digitalized some one million three hundred and thirty thousand files for the million three hundred and some thousand men who died for France between 1914 and 1918. These handwritten files, filled out in beautiful cursive script in black ink, are succinct; surnames, first names, date and place of birth of the deceased soldier are recorded, along with the rank, army corps to which he belonged, his serial number, and this terrifying line, which does not bother with the euphemisms of civilians: "Kind of death." The *kind of death* does not embarrass itself with poetry; the *kind of death* is nonetheless a silent, brutal poetry, where words unfold in terrifying images of "killed by the enemy," "wounds," "disease," "torpedoed and sank" in an infinity of variations and repetitions—and erasures, as well; the mention "wound" might be crossed out, written over with "disease": "disappeared" might be crossed out later, replaced by "killed by the enemy," which signifies that later on the body of this disappeared soldier who would not return was found; this non-reappearance while alive would earn him the mention "died for France" and the honors that ensued. Then, still on the same file, the place where the *kind of death* in question is inscribed, which means giving a definitive end to the soldier's journey on this Earth. We know, then, very little about the two combatants who interest us here. Even their civilian status is fragmentary, as is so often the case for colonial soldiers. Just the year of birth. First names and family names reversed. I suppose, though, that they were brothers. Brothers in arms, at least. They came from the same city of Niafunké by the Niger River, south of Timbuktu, in the French part of Sudan that today is called Mali. They were born two years apart, in 1890 and 1892. They were Bambaras, from the Tamboura clan. Their names were Baba and Moussa. They were assigned to different regiments. They were volunteers, or at

PARTIE À REMPLIR PAR LE CORPS.

Nom... *BABA*

Prénoms... *TAMBOURA*

Grade... *1er classe*

Corps... *77e Bon sénégalais*

N° Matricule. { *30.414* au Corps. — Cl. *1911*
                { *30.414* au Recrutement *Issa-Ber*

Mort pour la France le... *17 Février 1917*

à *bord de l'athos repris torpillé et coulé*

Genre de mort... *Torpillé et coulé*

Né le... *environ en 1890* *Soudan*

à *Sfia femaké gantoga* Département... *Soudan*

Arr¹ municipal (p¹ Paris et Lyon), à défaut rue et N°. *de Soubroagou Tamba*

est inscrit à Issa-Ber *C. d'Issa Ber*

{ Jugement rendu le... *18 Juin 1919*
{ par le Tribunal de... *Marseille*
{ acte ou jugement transcrit le... *7 Juillet 1919*
{ à... *Marseille*
{ N° du registre d'état civil...

534-708-1921. [26434.]

least that's how conscripted colonials were known: the governors of each region were required to provide their quota of soldiers; not much concern was given, in Bamako or Dakar, to the way in which they were obtained. We also do not know what Baba or Moussa left behind in Mali—a job, a mother, a wife, children. We can on the other hand guess their feelings, at the time of departure, their perhaps modest pride in the uniform; their fear of the unknown, probably, and especially that deeply felt, keen wrenching feeling that goes with leaving one's native country. Baba was lucky, Moussa less so. Baba was first assigned to an engineer's battalion, he barely escaped a departure for the butchery of the Dardanelles and would remain for several months billeted in Africa, in Somalia.

Having reached Marseille in France in the beginning of 1916, Moussa was trained to handle weapons in the camp of Fréjus, before joining the fray in the spring of 1916 at Verdun. One can imagine the power of discovering Europe for these Senegalese infantrymen. The unknown forests of trees, the calm rivers that streak the plains so green in the springtime, the surprising cows with black and white spots. And suddenly, after a detour by a camp in the rear and an endless march from Verdun, all hell breaks loose. Trenches, barbed wire, shells, so many shells that silence becomes a rare and unsettling thing. The colonial troops would discover death at the same time as the white soldiers dying at their side. Never had the expression "cannon fodder" been so justified. The men broke into pieces like mannequins under the effect of the explosives, they were torn apart like paper under the shrapnel, shouted, bled; the parapets disgorged human debris crushed by the pepper mill of the artillery. Seven hundred thousand men fell in Verdun, on both sides of the Meuse. Buried, burned alive, torn to pieces by machine guns or the millions of shells that furrowed the terrain. Moussa, like all of his comrades, experienced fear, first of all, then very great fear, then immense terror; he found courage in the heart of the horror, the courage to follow a corporal to mount an assault upon a position that was too well-defended; he'd have to give up conquering it, after seeing his brothers in arms fall around him, not really understanding for what strange reason he remained unharmed. The sector had a fitting name, *le Mort-Homme*, Dead-Man; it's hard to believe there could have been a village in this mass grave that the spring rains transformed into a swamp where, instead of aquatic plants, fingers and ears floated. Moussa Tamboura would finally be captured on May 24, 1916, with most of his squad in front of that hill 304 that ten thousand soldiers had just died defending in vain.

While Moussa, who had narrowly escaped death, was wondering whether his brother was still alive, Baba was setting up his tent in the environs of Djibouti. His battalion would be reformed, with other colonial elements. Soldiers arrived from Indochina to join them before going on to France. For Moussa captivity was a relief, why deny it; the Germans reserved special treatment for Muslim soldiers. Moussa Tamboura was sent to a prisoners' camp south of Berlin, a thousand kilometers away from the front. During the trip, he no doubt thought that German landscapes looked like what he had seen of the North of France. The camp where he was interned was called the "Camp of the Crescent," Halbmond-Lager, in Zossen near Wünsdorf; it was reserved for "Mahomedan" prisoners, or prisoners presumed to be so. There were Algerians, Moroccans, Senegalese, Malians, Somalis, Gurkhas from the Himalayas, Sikhs and Indian Muslims, Comorians, Malays, and, in a neighboring camp, Muslims from the Russian Empire, Tatars, Uzbeks, Tajiks, and Caucasians. The camp was conceived as a little village, with a pretty wooden mosque in the Ottoman style; it was the first mosque in the environs of Berlin. A mosque of war.

Moussa guessed that the battles were over for him, that the shells would never catch up to him so far away, in the depths of Prussia; he was hesitant about rejoicing in this. True, he no longer risked horrible wounds, worse than death; but the feelings of defeat, exile, and remoteness were other, more insidious pains—on the front, the constant tension, the daily fighting against the mines and machine guns occupied your mind. Here, between the barracks and the mosque, he was among survivors; people endlessly told each other stories from their countries, in Bambara, and the language sounded strange there, so far from the Niger, in the midst of all these languages and all these fates. Ramadan began on July 2 that year; fasting on those endless northern summer days was

a real torture—there were barely five hours of darkness at night. Moussa was no longer cannon fodder, but fodder for ethnologists, Orientalists, and propagandists: all the scholars of the German Empire visited the camp and conversed with the prisoners, to learn their customs, their habits; these men in white smocks photographed them, described them, measured their skulls, made them tell stories about their countries, which they recorded in order to later study their languages and dialects. From these Zossen camp recordings a number of linguistic studies would emerge—for example, those of Friedrich Carl Andreas, husband of Lou Andreas-Salomé, on the Iranian languages of the Caucasus.

The only image we possess of Moussa Tamboura was taken in this camp. It's from a propaganda film for the Muslim world,

Gefangenenlager Zossen · Mohammedaner (Kamelreiter)

which shows the festival of Eid al-Fitr at the end of Ramadan, on July 31, 1916. A Prussian nobleman was the guest of honor, along with the Turkish ambassador to Berlin. We see Moussa Tamboura in the company of three of his comrades, in the process of preparing a ritual fire. All the Muslim prisoners are seated; all the Germans are standing, with fine mustaches. The camera then lingers over the Gurkhas, the handsome Sikhs, the Moroccans, the Algerians; the ambassador from the Sublime Porte has a vacant look, and the prince looks full of curiosity about these ex-enemy soldiers of a new sort, whom they would very much encourage to desert *en masse* or rebel against colonial authorities: they tried to show that Germany was a friend of Islam, as it was an ally of Turkey. A year before, in Istanbul, all the Orientalists of the German Empire had written a text in classical Arabic calling on Muslims around the world to wage jihad against Russia, France, and Great Britain, in the hope of making the colonial troops rise up against their masters. Hence the camera, which Moussa Tamboura did not seem to notice, absorbed as he was in building the fire.

In this model Zossen camp, a journal, soberly titled *Jihad*, was written and printed in runs of fifteen thousand copies, "a journal for Mahometan prisoners of war" which was published simultaneously in Arabic, Tatar, and Russian; another journal, *The Caucasus*, for Georgians; and a third, *Hindustan*, in two editions, Urdu and Hindi. The translators and writers of these publications were prisoners, Orientalists, and "natives" experienced in German politics, most of them coming from the provinces of the Ottoman Empire. Max von Oppenheim, the famous archaeologist, was one of those responsible for the Arabic version of the publication. The Minister for Foreign Affairs and the War Minister hope to be able to "reuse" the colonial soldiers, after their hoped-for "reconversion" to the new holy war.

We don't know much about the actual repercussions of the German jihad in the territories concerned; they were probably almost nonexistent. We do not even know if the announcement reached Baba Tamboura in Djibouti, for example. Baba was unaware that his brother was taking part against his will in the German enterprise; he imagined him on the front, perhaps dead, rumors making their way through censorship, to

the borders of the Red Sea: heroism, glory, and sacrifice, that's how Baba imagined the war. He must have been sure his brother was a hero, over there, in France, that he was fighting bravely. He might have been less sure of his own feelings, a confused mixture of desire for action and apprehension. Finally, at the beginning of December 1916, as the freezing Berlin winter was starting for Moussa, Baba learned that his battalion would finally be sent, via Port Said and the Suez Canal, to the front in France. At the end of December, 850 infantrymen boarded the liner *Athos* of the Messageries Maritimes, a handsome almost-new ship 160 meters long and weighing thirteen thousand tons, coming from Hong Kong with a consignment of Chinese coolies who were already occupying the hold—in the end, the ship wouldn't depart until the beginning of February while, in Berlin, Moussa was ill, coughing and shivering from cold in the Prussian winter.

The *Athos* left Port Said on February 14, 1917, and, three days later, a few miles away from the island of Malta, just when the infantrymen were starting to get used to the wildness of the sea in the depths of their third-class hold, the *Athos* crossed the path of German U-Boat No. 65, which sent a torpedo right into its port side. The attack claimed the lives of 750 of its passengers, including Baba, who will have seen of the war only its sudden, ferocious end, a terrifying explosion followed by cries of pain and panic, cries and bodies soon drowned by the water flooding the holds, the bridges, the lungs. Moussa would never hear about his brother's death since, a few days later, he died of *disease in captivity in the Zossen camp hospital*, if we are to believe the *kind of death* in his "died for France" file, today the only trace of that suffering of exile in the Camp of the Crescent.

What madness that first truly worldwide war was. Drowning in the darkness of a hold, how horrible. I wonder if that jihadist mosque still exists, south of Berlin, in those sandy plains of the March of Brandenburg interrupted by lakes, interlaced with marshes. I should ask Sarah — one of the first mosques in northern Europe, the war has strange consequences indeed. That German jihad makes for the most incongruous bedmates — scholars like Oppenheim or Frobenius, soldiers, Turkish and German diplomats, Algerians in exile or pro-Ottoman Syrians like Shakib Arslan the Druze prince. The way holy war today is anything but spiritual.

They say that the Mongols made pyramids of cut-off heads to frighten the inhabitants of the lands they invaded — now the jihadists in Syria are using the same method, horror and fear, by applying to men an atrocious technique of sacrifice reserved till now for sheep, their throats slit, then the neck cut with difficulty till it separates, this in the name of holy war. Another horrible thing constructed by both East and West. Jihad, at first sight an idea that's as foreign, external, exogenous as possible, is a long and strange collective movement, the synthesis of an atrocious, cosmopolitan history — God save us from death and *Allah akbar*, Red Love, decapitation and Mendelssohn-Bartholdy, *Octet for Strings*.

Thank God the news is over, back to music, Mendelssohn and Meyerbeer, sworn enemies of Wagner, especially Meyerbeer, object of all Wagner's hatred, a terrifying hatred — I've always wondered if that was the cause or the effect of Wagner's anti-Semitism: maybe Wagner became anti-Semitic because he was terribly jealous of Meyerbeer's success and money. Wagner wasn't without his contradictions: in his *Judaism in Music*, he insults Meyerbeer, the same Meyerbeer he had buttered up for years, the same Meyerbeer he dreamed of imitating, the same Meyerbeer who helped him put on *Rienzi* and *The Flying Dutchman*. "People take revenge for the help others give them," said Thomas Bernhard, there's a phrase for Wagner. Richard Wagner did not measure up to his work; he was hypocritical, like all anti-Semites. Wagner took revenge for the help Meyerbeer gave him. In his observations, Wagner blames Meyerbeer and Mendelssohn for not having a native language and hence jabbering an idiom that, generations later, still reflects "Semitic pronunciation." This absence of personal language condemns them to an absence of their own style and to plagiarism. The horrible cosmopolitism of Mendelssohn and Meyerbeer prevents them from attaining art. What incredible stupidity. But Wagner is not stupid, hence he is operating with bad faith. He is aware that his statements are idiotic. It's his hatred speaking. He is blinded by his hatred, as he will be by his wife Cosima Liszt during the republication of his pamphlet, this time under his own name, twenty years later. Wagner is a criminal. A criminal full of hate. If Wagner knows Bach and that harmony he uses so magnificently to revolutionize music, it's to Mendelssohn he owes that knowledge. Mendelssohn who, in Leipzig, pulls Bach out of the relative oblivion into which he had fallen. I can see again that atrocious photo where a very self-satisfied German policeman, with a mustache and spiked helmet, poses in front of the statue of Mendelssohn chained to a crane, ready to be demolished, in the mid-1930s. That policeman is Wagner. Say what you like, but even Nietzsche was disgusted by Wagner's hypocritical nature. And it doesn't matter if it was also for personal reasons that he rejected the little policeman from Leipzig. He is right to be disgusted by Wagner the anti-cosmopolitan, lost in the illusion of the Nation. The only acceptable thing to come out of Wagner are Mahler and Schönberg. The only palatable work of Wagner's is *Tristan and Isolde*, since it's the only one that isn't atrociously German or Christian. A Celtic or Iranian legend, or else invented by an unknown medieval author, it doesn't matter. But Vis and Ramin are in Tristan and Iseult. There is the passion of Majnun the Mad for Layla, the passion of Khosrow for Shirin. A shepherd and a flute. *Desolate and empty, the sea.* The abstraction of the sea and of passion. No Rhine, no gold, no Rhine maidens swimming ridiculously on the stage. Ah Wagner's productions in Bayreuth, that must have been something else, in terms of bourgeois kitsch and pretentiousness. The spears, the winged helmets. What was the name of that mare Ludwig II the Mad offered for the production? A ridiculous name that I've forgotten. There must be images of that famous nag; the poor thing, they had to put cotton in its ears and blinders on its eyes so it wouldn't take fright or graze on the river maidens' nets. It's amusing to think that the first Wagnerian of the Orient was the Ottoman sultan Abdülaziz, who sent a large sum of money to Wagner for the theater at the Bayreuth festival—unfortunately he died before he could enjoy the spears, helmets, mare, and unparalleled acoustics of the place he had helped erect.

The Iranian Nazi at the Abguineh museum in Tehran may have been Wagnerian, who knows — what a surprise when that round, mustachioed guy in his thirties approached us as we were standing between two magnificent vases in that almost deserted room, arm raised, bellowing "Heil Hitler!" First I thought it was a joke in very bad taste, I thought the man mistook me for a German and that it was a kind of insult; then I realized that I was speaking French with Faugier. The fanatic watched us, smiling, still with his arm raised; I replied What's come over you, what's your problem? Faugier next to me had burst out laughing. Suddenly the man looked contrite, like a beaten dog, and sighed in despair, "Ah, you're not German, how sad." Sad *indeed*, we are neither German nor Nazi-lovers, unfortunately, Faugier joked. The fellow looked particularly disappointed, he launched into a long Hitlerian diatribe, with pathetic accents; he insisted on the fact that Hitler was "Handsome, very handsome, Hitler *qashang, kheyli qashang*," he bawled, gripping his fist over an invisible treasure, the treasure of the Aryans, no doubt. He explained at great length that Hitler had revealed to the world that the Germans and Iranians formed one single people, that this people was destined to preside over the fate of the planet, and according to him it was very sad, yes, very sad that these magnificent ideas have not yet been realized. There was something both terrifying and comical about this vision of Hitler as an Iranian hero, in the midst of the cups, rhytons, and decorated plates. Faugier tried to pursue the discussion, to find out what made the last Nazi of the Orient (or maybe not the last) "tick," what he actually knew of National Socialist theories and especially of their consequences, but soon abandoned the idea, since the young lunatic's answers were limited to wide gestures around him to signify no doubt "Look! Look! See the greatness of Iran!" as if these venerable glass trinkets were in themselves an emanation

of the superiority of the Aryan race. The man was very polite; despite his disappointment at not having fallen upon two
Nazi Germans, he wished us an excellent day, a magnificent
stay in Iran, insisted on asking if we needed anything at all; he
smoothed his Wilhelm II-style mustaches, clicked his heels and
walked off, leaving us stunned and speechless. This evocation of
old Adolf in the heart of the little neo-Seljuk palace of the Abguineh museum and its wonders was so incongruous that it left
us with a funny taste in our mouths—between bursts of laughter and consternation. A little later, after we returned to the
Institute, I related this encounter to Sarah. Like us, she began
by laughing at it; then she questioned herself on the meaning
of this laughter—Iran seemed to us so remote from European
questions that an Iranian Nazi was only a harmless, offbeat eccentric; whereas in Europe that man would have aroused anger
and indignation in us, here, we had trouble believing he grasped
the profound meaning of it. And the racial theories linked to
Aryan-ness seem to us today as absurd as those phrenologists
measuring the skull to determine the position of the bump for
languages. Pure illusion. But this encounter said a lot, Sarah
added, about the power of the Third Reich's propaganda in
Iran—as during the First World War, and often with the same
personnel (including the ever-present Max von Oppenheim),
Nazi Germany had sought to attract the favor of Muslims to
get them to attack the English and Russians from the rear, in
Central Soviet Asia, India, and the Middle East, and had again
called for jihad. Scholarly societies (universities including the
Deutsche Morgenländische Gesellschaft) had been so Nazified
since the 1930s that they'd entered into the spirit of the game:
Islamologist Orientalists were even consulted to find out if the
Koran somehow predicted the Führer's rise to power; despite
all their good will, the scholars were unable to give a positive

response. Still, they offered to write texts in Arabic hinting at it. There was even a plan to spread throughout the lands of Islam a delightful *Portrait of the Führer as Commander of the Faithful*, with turban and decorations inspired by the great Ottoman epoch, suitable for edifying the Muslim masses. Goebbels, shocked at this horrible image, put an end to the operation. Nazi hypocrisy was ready to use "sub-humans" for justified military ends, but not to the point of placing a turban or a tarboosh on the head of its supreme leader. SS Orientalism, spearheaded by *Obersturmbannführer* Viktor Christian, eminent director of its Viennese branch, had to content itself with trying to "de-Semitize" ancient history and demonstrate, at the cost of inventing a hoax, the historic superiority of Aryans over the Semites in Mesopotamia and opening a "school for mullahs" in Dresden, where the SS imams in charge of the education of Soviet Muslims were supposed to be trained: in their theoretical approximations, the Nazis had a hard time of it deciding if that institution would train imams or mullahs, and what name was suitable to give the strange enterprise.

Faugier joined the conversation; we had made tea; the samovar was shuddering gently. Sarah picked out a piece of rock candy, which she let melt in her mouth; she had taken off her shoes and tucked her calves under her thighs in the leather armchair. A *setar* recording was filling the silence — it was autumn, or winter, it was dark already. Faugier was going round in circles, as he did every day at sunset. He would manage to hold it together for another hour, then the anguish would become overbearing and he'd be forced to go smoke his pipe or joint of opium, before he surrendered and yielded himself to the night. I remembered his own expert advice, earlier in Istanbul — apparently he hadn't followed it. Eight years later, he had become an opium addict; he was terribly worried about the idea of going back to Europe, where his drug would be much harder to find. He knew what was going to happen; he'd end up taking heroin (which he already smoked a little, though rarely, in Tehran) and would experience the pain of addiction or the agony of detox. The idea of going back, aside from the material difficulties it entailed (end of research funding, absence of any immediate prospects of employment in that secret society that is the French University, that secular monastery where the novitiate can last an entire lifetime), was coupled with a terrifying lucidity about his state, his panicked fear of taking leave of opium — which he compensated for by excessive activity: he increased the number of walks he took (like that day to the Abguineh museum where he'd brought me), meetings, weird expeditions, sleepless nights, to try to stretch time out and forget in pleasure and drugs that his stay was reaching its end, thereby increasing his anxiety from day to day. Gilbert de Morgan, the director, was not unhappy about getting rid of him — it should be said that the aging Orientalist's old-fashioned solemnity didn't marry well with Faugier's liveliness, free-and-easy ways, and strange research topics. Morgan was convinced that it was "the contemporary" that caused all his trouble, not just with the Iranians, but also with the French embassy. Literature (classical, if possible), philosophy, and ancient history, that's what found favor in his eyes. Can you believe it, he would say, they're sending me another politician. (That's what he called students of contemporary history, geography, or sociology.) They're crazy in Paris. We're fighting to try to get visas for researchers, and we find ourselves presenting dossiers we know very well the Iranians won't like at all. So we have to lie. What madness.

Madness was in fact a key element of European research in Iran. Hatred, hiding one's feelings, jealousy, fear, manipulation were the only bonds the community of scholars managed to develop—in their relationships to institutions in any case. Collective madness, downward spiraling—Sarah had to be strong not to suffer too much from this ambiance. Morgan had found a simple name for his management policy: the knout. Old-style. Wasn't the Iranian administration thousands of years old? One had to go back to healthy principles of organization: silence and the whip. Of course this infallible method had the inconvenience of slowing down projects quite a bit (as with the pyramids, or the palace of Persepolis). It also increased the pressure on Morgan, who spent all his time complaining; he had no time to do anything else, he said, except supervise his administrative underlings. The researchers were spared a little. Sarah was spared. Faugier much less so. The foreigners passing through—the Pole, the Italian, and I—counted for nothing, or as the French say, *nous comptions pour du beurre.* Gilbert de Morgan respectfully scorned us, considerately ignored us, let us take advantage of all the facilities at his institute, especially the big apartment above the offices, where Sarah sipped her tea, where Faugier couldn't stand still, where we discussed our theories on the madman of the Abguineh museum (we finally decided he was mad)—we talked about Adolf Hitler posing with a tarboosh or a turban on his head and about the man from the previous century who had inspired him, the Comte de Gobineau, inventor of Aryan-ness: the author of *An Essay on the Inequality of Human Races,* he too was an Orientalist, first secretary to the French legation in Persia, then ambassador, who spent time in Iran twice in the middle of the nineteenth century—his works are given the privilege of three handsome volumes in the famous Pléiade collection that had so unfairly, according to Morgan and Sarah, ejected poor Germain Nouveau. The first racist in France, the inspirer of Houston Stewart Chamberlain, great theoretician of hate-filled German-ness who discovered him thanks to the advice of Cosima Liszt and Wagner, friends of Gobineau from November 1876: Gobineau was also a Wagnerian; he wrote about fifty letters to Wagner and Cosima. The legacy of the darkest part of his work couldn't have come at a better time, unfortunately; it was through the Bayreuth circle (mainly Chamberlain, who would marry Eva Wagner) that his Aryan theories on the evolution of the human races followed their horrible path. But as Sarah noted, Gobineau was not an anti-Semite; quite the contrary. He regarded the "Jewish race" as among the noblest, most knowledgeable and industrious, the least decadent, most preserved from the general decline. Anti-Semitism was Bayreuth, it was Wagner, Cosima, Houston Chamberlain, Eva Wagner who added it to his theories. The frightening list of the disciples of Bayreuth, the terrifying testimonials, Goebbels holding Chamberlain's hand while he died, Hitler at his funeral, Hitler, close friend of Winifred Wagner—what injustice when you think about it, an allied aircraft dropped two fire bombs on poor Mendelssohn's Gewandhaus in Leipzig and not a single one on the theater of the Bayreuth Festival. Even the Allies were complicit despite themselves in Aryan myths—the destruction of the Bayreuth theater would have been a great loss for music, true. But what does that matter, they'd have rebuilt an exact copy of it, but Winifred Wagner and her son would have experienced a little of that destruction they'd unleashed so furiously on the world, a little of that suffering of loss seeing the criminal legacy of their father-in-law and grandfather go up in flames. If bombs can atone for crime. It's infuriating to think that one of the links that unite Wagner to the Orient (beyond influences received through Schopenhauer, Nietzsche, or reading Burnouf's *Introduction to the History of Indian Buddhism*) is his admiration for the Comte de Gobineau's book, his *Essay on the Inequality of the Human Races*—who knows, Wagner might also have read *Three Years in Asia* or *The New Asiatics*. Cosima Wagner herself translated into German, for the *Bayreuther Blätter*, a paper by Gobineau, "What Is Happening in Asia?"; Gobineau often visited the Wagners. He accompanied them to Berlin for the triumphant premiere of the *Ring*, in 1881, five years after the creation of Bayreuth, two years before the maestro's death in Venice—he was still thinking, they say, at the end of his life, about writing a Buddhist opera, *The Victors*, whose title seems so un-Buddhist it made Sarah burst out laughing at least as much as at some of poor Gobineau's remarks: she had gone to look for his complete works "in the cave," in the Institute's library, and I can see us now, as the second movement of Mendelssohn's *Octet* is starting, reading out loud some fragments of *Three Years in Asia*. Even Faugier had stopped his anguished circling to pay attention to the poor Orientalist's prose.

There was something touching about Gobineau as a person—he was a terrible poet and a somewhat pedestrian novelist; only his travel narratives and the stories he drew from his memories seemed to present any real interest. He was also a sculptor, and had even exhibited a few busts, including a *Valkyrie*, a *Sonata Appassionata*, and a *Queen Mab* (Wagner, Beethoven, Berlioz: the fellow had taste), marble sculptures that were quite expressive and finely wrought, according to the critics. He had been rather famous in the circles of power; he had met Napoleon III and his wife, as well as his ministers; he had a long career as a diplomat, posted to Germany, then twice to Persia, to Greece, Brazil, Sweden, and Norway; he knew Tocqueville, Renan, Liszt, and many Orientalists of his time, August Friedrich Pott the German Sanskritist and Jules Mohl the French scholar of Iran, first translator of the *Shahnameh*. Julius Euting himself, the great Orientalist from German Strasbourg, bought Gobineau's entire legacy for the Reich after his death: sculptures, manuscripts, letters, rugs, all the trinkets an Orientalist leaves behind: chance and the First World War willed it so that this collection became French again in 1918 — it's strange to think that the millions of deaths from that idiotic war had no other objective, in the last analysis, than to deprive Austria of the Adriatic beaches and to recover the Gobineau inheritance bogarted by the Teutons. Unfortunately, all those people died for nothing: there are millions of Austrians on vacation in Istria and the Veneto, and the University of Strasbourg's little museum long ago gave up exhibiting the relics of Gobineau, victim of the theoretical racism of his century, which burned the fingers of the site's successive curators.

The Comte de Gobineau loathed democracy — "I have a deadly hatred of popular power," he said. He knew he harbored bitter resentment against the supposed stupidity of the times, a world populated by insects armed with instruments of ruin, "bent on crushing all that I have respected, all that I have loved; a world that burns cities, destroys cathedrals, wants no more books or music or paintings, and substitutes the potato, bloody beef, and unripe wine for everything," he writes in his novel *Les Pléiades*, which opens with this long diatribe against imbeciles — one somewhat reminiscent of the discourse of the intellectuals of the extreme Right today. The foundation of Gobineau's racist theories was lamentation: his sense of the long decadence of the West, his resentment of the vulgar. Where is the empire of Darius, where the grandeur of Rome? But unlike his later disciples, he did not regard "the Jewish element" as being responsible for the fall of the Aryan race. For him (and this obviously is an element that must not have been to the taste of Wagner or Chamberlain), the best example of the purity of the Aryan race is the French nobility — a rather comical notion. The work of his youth, *Essay on the Inequality of the Human Races*, owes as much to linguistic approximations as to the early stages of the human sciences—but Gobineau would see the reality of Iran, in Persia, during his two missions as representative of Imperial France; he would be convinced, discovering Persepolis and Ispahan, of having been right about the greatness of the Aryans. The narrative of his stay is brilliant, often funny, never *racist* in the modern sense of the word, at least where the Iranians are concerned. Sarah read passages to us that made even the anguished Faugier laugh. I remember this phrase: "I confess that, among the dangers that await a traveler in Asia, I count as foremost, without any doubt, and without concerning myself with wounding the feelings of tigers, snakes, and banditry, the British dinners one is forced to undergo." An absolutely delightful judgment. Gobineau waxed eloquent on the "downright Satanic" dishes served by the English at whose homes, he said, one leaves the table ill or starving, "martyred or dead of hunger." His impressions of Asia combine the most knowledgeable descriptions with the most comical observations.

This herbal tea has the acidic, artificial taste of candy, an English taste, Gobineau would have said. Far from the flowers of Egypt or Iran. I'll have to revise my opinion of Mendelssohn's *Octet*, it's even more interesting than I thought. *Öl Klassiknacht*, my life when it comes down to it is rather sinister, I could be reading instead of going over old Iranian memories in my head while listening to the radio. The madman of the Abguineh museum. God, how sad Tehran was. Eternal mourning, the grayness, the pollution. Tehran, or the capital of pain. This sadness was reinforced, framed, by the slightest sign of light; the bewildering parties of the golden youth in the northern part of the city, while they distracted us for a little while, hurled us afterward, by their stark contrast with the death of the public space, into that profound depression the French call spleen. Those magnificent young women who danced, in very erotic outfits and poses, drinking Turkish beer or vodka, to forbidden music from Los Angeles, and then put on their head scarves and coats and were lost in the mass of Islamic propriety. This so-Iranian difference between *biroun* and *andaroun,* inside and outside the house, private and public, which Gobineau already noticed, was pushed to its extreme by the Islamic Republic. You entered an apartment or a villa in northern Tehran and you suddenly found yourself in the midst of a group of youths in swimsuits having fun, drinks in hand, around a pool, speaking perfect English, French, or German, and they forgot, in the contraband alcohol and amusements, the grayness of the outside, the absence of future within Iranian society. There was something desperate about these parties; a despair you sensed could be transformed, for the more courageous or less well-off, into the violent energy required for revolutionaries. Raids by the morality police were, depending on the time and government, more or less frequent; you heard rumors saying so-and-so had been arrested, someone else beaten, some girl humiliated by a gynaecological exam to prove she hadn't had sexual relations outside of marriage. These stories, which always reminded me of the atrocious proctology probe undergone by Verlaine in Belgium after his quarrel with Rimbaud, formed part of the daily life of the city. Intellectuals and academics, for the most part, no longer had the energy of the young, so were divided into several categories: those who had managed, on average, to build a more or less comfortable existence for themselves "on the margins" of public life; those who redoubled their hypocrisy to take full advantage of the sinecures of the regime; and those — and there were many — who suffered from chronic depression, intense sadness that they treated more or less successfully by taking refuge in erudition, imaginary journeys, or artificial paradises. I wonder what's become of Parviz — the great poet with the white beard hasn't been in touch with me for ages, I should write to him, it's been so long since I did. What pretext could I use? I could translate one of his poems into German, but it's a terrifying experience to translate from a language you don't really know, you feel as if you're swimming in the dark — a calm lake seems like a raging sea, an ornamental water feature like a deep river. In Tehran it was simpler, he was there and could explain the meaning of his texts to me, almost word by word. Maybe he isn't even in Tehran anymore. Maybe he's living in Europe or the United States. But I doubt it. Parviz's sadness (like that of Sadegh Hedayat) came precisely from the double failure of his brief attempts at exile, in France and Holland: he missed Iran; he had returned after two months. Obviously, back in Tehran, it only took a few minutes for him to detest his fellow citizens all over again. With the women of the border police wearing *marnay* who take your passport in the Mehrabad airport, he said, you can recognize neither the killer, nor the victim; they wear the black hood of the medieval executioner; they do not smile at you; they're flanked by brutish soldiers in khaki parkas armed with G3 assault rifles *made in the Islamic Republic of Iran*, you don't know if they're there to protect the women from the foreigners getting off these impure planes or to shoot them in case they show them too much sympathy. We still don't know (and Parviz professed this with an ironic resignation, an entirely Iranian mixture of sadness and humor) if the women of the Iranian Revolution are the mistresses or hostages of power. The chador-wearing functionaries of the Foundation for the Poor are among the wealthiest and most powerful women in Iran. The phantoms are my country, he said, these shades, these crows of the people to whom their black veil is solidly attached when they're executed by hanging, to avoid any indecency, because it is not death that is indecent here, death is everywhere, but the bird, the flight, the color, especially the color of the flesh of women, so white, so white — it never sees the sun and could blind martyrs with its purity. In our country, the executioners in the black hood of mourning are also the victims that are hanged at leisure to punish them for their implacable beauty, and they hang, they hang, they whip, they fight to their heart's content against what we love and find beautiful, and beauty itself takes the whip, the rope, the axe, and gives birth to the poppy of the martyrs, flower without smell, pure color, red, red, red — all make-up is forbidden to our flowers of martyrdom, for they are pain itself and die naked, while they have the right to die red without being clothed in black, the flowers of martyrdom. Lips are always too red for the State that sees indecent competition in them — only saints and martyrs can blow the red sweetness of their blood over Iran, it's forbidden to women who must out of decency tint their lips black, black, and show discretion when we strangle them, look! Look! Our pretty dead bodies have no cause to be envious of anyone, they sway nobly on the top of cranes, decently executed, don't come blaming us for our lack of technology, we are a people of beauty. Our Christians, for example, are magnificent. They celebrate death on the Cross and remember their martyrs just like us. Our Zoroastrians are magnificent. They wear leather masks where the fire reflects the greatness of Iran, they give their bodies to rot and feed the birds with their dead flesh. Our butchers are magnificent. They slit animals' throats with the greatest respect as in the time of the prophets and the light of God. We are as great as Darius, greater, Anushirvan, greater, Cyrus, greater, the prophets preached revolutionary fervor and war, in war we breathed in blood as we did the gases of battle.

We were able to breathe in blood, fill our lungs with blood and enjoy death to the fullest extent. For centuries we transmuted death into beauty, blood into flowers, into fountains of blood, filled the museum cases with blood-stained uniforms and eyeglasses smashed in by martyrdom and we are proud of it, for each martyr is a poppy that is red, that is a little bit of beauty that is this world. We have produced a liquid, red people, it lives in death and is happy in Paradise. We have stretched a black canvas over Paradise to protect it from the sun. We have washed our corpses in the rivers of Paradise. Paradise is a Persian word. We give passersby the water of death, to drink from it under the black tents of mourning. Paradise is the name of our country, the cemeteries where we live, the name of sacrifice.

Parviz didn't know how to speak in prose; not in French, in any case. In Persian he saved his darkness and pessimism for his poems, he was much less serious, full of humor; those who, like Faugier or Sarah, knew the language well enough to appreciate it often burst out laughing—he would happily tell funny, salacious stories—anywhere else in the world, you'd be surprised a great poet knew those sorts of stories. Parviz also often spoke about his childhood in Qom in the 1950s. His father was a religious man, a scholar, whom he always calls "the man in black" in his texts, if I remember correctly. It was thanks to "the man in black" that he read the philosophers of Persian tradition, from Avicenna to Ali Shariati—and the mystical poets. Parviz knew by heart a number of extraordinary classical poems, by Rumi, Hafez, Khadjou, Nezami, Bidel, as well as modern ones, by Nima, Shamlou, Sepehri and Akhavan-Sales. A walking library—Rilke, Yesenin, Lorca, Char, he knew (in Persian and in the original version) thousands of poems by heart. The day we met, when he found out I was Viennese, he searched through his

memory, the way you leaf through an anthology, and returned
from that brief internal voyage with a poem by Lorca, in Spanish, "*En Viena hay diez muchachas, un hombro donde solloza la muerte
y un bosque de palomas disecadas,*" which I obviously didn't understand a word of, so he had to translate: "In Vienna there are ten
young girls, a shoulder on which death is sobbing, and a forest of
stuffed pigeons," then he looked at me very seriously and asked
me, "Is that true? I've never been."

It was Sarah who replied for me, "Oh it's true, yes, especially
about the stuffed pigeons."

"How interesting, a taxidermist city."

I wasn't sure the conversation was going in a direction that was
very favorable to me, so I looked reprovingly at Sarah, which immediately delighted her, Oh look the Austrian is upset, nothing
makes her happier than publicly exposing my faults—Parviz's
apartment was small but comfortable, full of books and rugs;
strangely, it was located on an avenue with a poet's name, Nezami or Attar, I can't remember. One so easily forgets important
things. I have to stop thinking out loud, if anyone ever recorded
me, how shameful that would be. I'm afraid of being taken for a
madman. Not a madman like the one at the Abguineh museum
or like my friend Bilger but a madman all the same. The guy who
talks to his radio and his laptop. Who has conversations with
Mendelssohn and his cup of acidic Red Love. Hmm, I could have
brought back a samovar from Iran too. I wonder what Sarah has
done with hers. Bringing back a samovar instead of CDs, musical instruments, and books by poets that I'll never understand.
Did I talk out loud to myself, before? Did I invent roles, voices,
characters? My old Mendelssohn, I have to confess to you that
when it comes down to it I don't know your oeuvre very well.
What can I say, you can't listen to everything, you're not angry I
hope. I know your house, though, in Leipzig. The little bust of

Goethe on your desk. Goethe your godfather, your first master. Goethe who heard two child prodigies, the little Mozart and you. I have seen your watercolors, your beautiful Swiss landscapes. Your living room. Your kitchen. I have seen the portrait of the woman you loved and the souvenirs from your trips to England. Your children. I pictured a visit from Clara and Robert Schumann, you would hurriedly emerge from your study to welcome them. Clara was radiant; she wore a little cap, her hair pinned back, a few ringlets fell onto her temples and framed her face. Robert had some scores under his arm and a little ink on his right sleeve, you laughed. You're all sitting in the living room. That same morning you had received a letter from Ignaz Moscheles from London agreeing to come teach in Leipzig in the brand-new conservatoire you've just founded. Moscheles your piano teacher. You tell this excellent news to Schumann. You're all going to work together, then. If Schumann accepts, of course. And he accepts. Then you have lunch. Then you all go out for a walk, and I've always pictured you great walkers, Schumann and you. You have four years left to live. In four years Moscheles and Schumann will be carrying your coffin.

Seven years later, it will be Schumann who will plunge into the Rhine and madness, in Düsseldorf.

I wonder, my old Mendel, which will take me first, death or madness.

"Dr. Kraus! Dr. Kraus! Please answer this question. Apparently, after the latest investigations by those physicians of the soul that are *post mortem* psychiatrists, Schumann was no more mad than you or I. He was simply sad, profoundly sad from the difficulties of his relationship with Clara, the end of his passion, a sadness he drowned in alcohol. Clara left him to die, abandoned him for two long years in the depths of his asylum, that's the truth, Dr. Kraus. The only person (along with Brahms, but you'll agree, Brahms doesn't count) who visited him, Bettina von Arnim, Brentano's sister, confirmed this. According to her, Schumann was unfairly locked up. He wasn't Hölderlin in his tower. What's more, the last great cycle for piano by Schumann, *Songs of Dawn*, composed barely six months before his internment, is inspired by Hölderlin and dedicated to Bettina Brentano von Arnim. Was Schumann thinking about Hölderlin's tower by the shores of the Neckar, was he afraid of that, Kraus, what do you think?"

"Love can devastate us, I am profoundly convinced of that, Dr. Ritter. But one can't swear to anything for sure. In any case I recommend you take this medicine to help you rest a little, my friend. You need calm and rest. And no, I will not prescribe opium to *slow down your metabolism*, as you say. One does not delay the instant of death by *slowing down one's metabolism*, by stretching out time, Dr. Ritter, that's an entirely childish idea."

"But really, dear Kraus, what did they give Schumann for two years in his asylum in Bonn? Chicken soup?"

"I do not know, Dr. Ritter, I have absolutely no idea. I just know that the doctors at the time diagnosed a *melancholia psychotica* that required his internment."

"Ah, doctors are terrible, you would never contradict a colleague! Charlatans, Kraus! Charlatans! Sell-outs! *Melancholia psychotica, my ass!* He was behaving like a charm, that's what Brentano says! He just had a little episode. A little episode, the Rhine woke him up, even revived him like a good German, the Rhine resuscitated him, the Rhine maidens caressed his privates and there you go! Just think, Kraus, that already before la Brentano's visit he was asking for music paper, an edition of Paganini's *Caprices*, and an atlas. An atlas, Kraus! Schumann wanted to see the world, leave Endenich and his torturer Dr. Richarz. See the world! There was no reason to bury him in that house of madmen. It's his wife who was responsible for his unhappiness. Clara who, despite all the reports she received from Endenich, never went to get him. Clara who followed *to the letter* Richarz's criminal recommendations. It was already Clara who was responsible for the attack that medicine transformed into one long burial. It was passion, the end of passion, the anguish of love that made him sick."

"What do you mean by that, Dr. Ritter, as you finish your horrible potion of artificial petals, do you think that you yourself, perhaps, are not so seriously afflicted? That you too just have 'a little episode' due to a matter of love and not a chronic and terrifying illness?"

"Dr. Kraus I'd so like for you to be right. I'd so like for me to be right about Schumann too. The *Songs of Dawn* are so . . . so unique. Outside of Schumann's time, outside of his writing. Schumann was *outside of himself* when he wrote the *Songs of Dawn*, a few weeks before the fatal night, just before the final *Ghost Variations*, which have always frightened me, composed around the time of (during) his dive into the Rhine. E-flat major. A theme born from an auditory hallucination, melodic tinnitus or divine revelation, poor Schumann. E-flat major, the key of Beethoven's sonata 'Les Adieux.' Phantoms and farewells. Dawn, farewells. Poor Eusebius. Poor Florestan, poor *Davidsbündler,* brotherhood of David. Poor us."

3:45 A.M.

Sometimes I wonder if I'm hallucinating. Just as I mention Beethoven's "Les Adieux," *Die Öl Klassiknacht* announces the Opus 111 sonata by that same Beethoven. Maybe they program music backward, late Schumann, then Mendelssohn, Beethoven; Schubert's missing—if I listen for long enough I'm sure they'll play a symphony by Schubert, chamber music first, piano next, the orchestra's all that's missing. No sooner do I think of "Les Adieux" than it's the 32nd Sonata, which Thomas Mann calls, in *Doctor Faustus,* "the farewell to the sonata." Is the world really conforming to my desires? Now it's that magician Mann who appears in my kitchen; when I talk about my youth to Sarah, I always lie, I tell her "my vocation as a musicologist comes from *Doctor Faustus,* it was when I read *Doctor Faustus* at the age of fourteen that I had the revelation of music," what a huge lie. My vocation as a musicologist does not exist. At best I am the learned Serenus Zeitblom, a creature of pure invention; at worst Franz Ritter, who dreamed, as a child, of becoming a clockmaker. An unmentionable vocation. How to explain to the world, dear Thomas Mann, dear Magician, that, as a child, my passion was for watches and grandfather clocks? They'll immediately take me for a constipated conservative (which I am, actually), they won't see the dreamer in me, the creator obsessed with time. From time to music it's just a small step, my dear

Mann. That's what I say to myself when I'm sad. True, you haven't progressed in the world of wonderful mechanisms, cuckoos, and clepsydras, but you have conquered time by music. Music is time domesticated, reproducible time, time shaped. And as for watches and clocks, you want time to be perfect, not to deviate by a microsecond, you see where I'm heading, Dr. Mann, dear Nobel Prize-winner, beacon for European literature. My calling as a clockmaker comes to me from my grandfather, who taught me, very tenderly, very gently, love for beautiful mechanisms, for gears calibrated under a loupe, for correct springs (the difficulty of the circular spring, he said, unlike the vertical weight, is that it uses more energy at the beginning than at the end of the movement; so you have to compensate for its expansion via subtle limitations, without overusing it). My watchmaking fervor predestined me to study music, where it's also a matter of springs and counterweights, archaic springs, beats, and clicks and so, here's the ultimate goal of this digression, I'm not lying to Sarah, not really, when I tell her that I had a calling for musicology, which is to music what watchmaking is to time, *mutatis mutandis.* Ah Dr. Mann I see you furrowing your brow, you've never been a poet. You wrote *the* novel of music, *Faustus,* everyone agrees about that, except poor Schoenberg who, they say, was very jealous about it. Ah, those musicians. Never content. Huge egos. You say that Schoenberg is Nietzsche plus Mahler, an inimitable genius, and he complains. He complains that you called him Adrian Leverkühn and not Arnold Schoenberg, probably. Maybe he'd have been very happy that you devoted six hundred pages of a novel to him, four years of your genius, calling him by his name, Schoenberg, even though when it comes down to it, it wasn't him, but a Nietzsche who reads Adorno, father of a dead child. A syphilitic Nietzsche, of

course, like Schubert, like Hugo Wolf. Dr. Mann, without meaning to upset you, that story of the brothel seems a tiny bit exaggerated to me. You see my point, you can catch entirely exotic
illnesses without being forced to fall in love with a low-class
prostitute because of an occupational disease. What a terrifying
story, that man who follows the object of his love beyond the
brothel and sleeps with her knowing all the while he's going to
contract her terrible spirochetes. Maybe that's why Schoenberg
was mad at you, incidentally, because you implied offhandedly
that he was syphilitic. Imagine his sex life after the publication
of *Doctor Faustus*, poor guy. His partners' doubts. Of course I'm
exaggerating and no one ever thought about that. For you the
disease contrasted with Nazi *health*. To be unapologetic about a
sick body and mind was to confront directly those who decided
to kill all mental patients in the first gas chambers. You're right.
You could possibly have chosen another disease, tuberculosis,
for example. Excuse me, sorry, obviously that was impossible.
And tuberculosis, even if you hadn't written *The Magic Mountain*, implies isolation from society, a gathering together of sick
people among themselves in glamourous sanatoriums, whereas
syphilis is a curse that you keep to yourself, one of those diseases
of solitude that eat away at you in private. Tuberculars and syphilitics, there's the history of art in Europe — the public, the social, tuberculosis, or the private, the shameful, syphilis. Instead
of Dionysian or Apollonian, I propose these two categorisations
for European art. Rimbaud: tubercular. Nerval: syphilitic. Van
Gogh? Syphilitic. Gauguin? Tubercular. Rückert? Syphilitic.
Goethe? A great tubercular, of course! Michelangelo? Terribly
tubercular. Brahms? Tubercular. Proust? Syphilitic. Picasso? Tubercular. Hesse? Became tubercular after syphilitic beginnings.
Roth? Syphilitic. The Austrians in general are syphilitic, except

Stefan Zweig, who is of course the model of the tubercular. Look at Bernhard: absolutely, terribly syphilitic, despite his diseased lungs. Musil: syphilitic. Beethoven? Ah, Beethoven. People have wondered if Beethoven's deafness was due to syphilis, poor Beethoven, they found all ills in him *a posteriori*. Hepatitis, alcoholism, cirrhosis of the liver, syphilis, medicine persecutes great men, that's for sure. Schumann, Beethoven. Do you know what killed him, Herr Mann? We know now, more or less definitively: it was lead. Lead poisoning. Yes sir. No more syphilis than butter in a branch, as they say in France. And where did this lead come from, you wonder? From doctors. It's the odious absurd treatments of those charlatans that killed Beethoven and that probably made him deaf as well. Terrifying, don't you think? I've been to Bonn twice. First when I was a student in Germany, and then again more recently to give a lecture on Beethoven's Orient and *The Ruins of Athens*, during which I found the ghost of my friend Bilger. But that's another story. Have you seen Beethoven's hearing aids at the Beethovenhaus in Bonn? There's nothing more terrifying. Heavy ear trumpets, cans fitted together, they look like you need both hands to hold them up. Ah here's Opus 111. In the beginning, we're still in the sonata. No adieu yet. The whole first movement is built on surprises and shifts: that majestic introduction, for example. You feel as if you're catching a train already underway, as if you've missed something; you enter a world that had already begun turning before you were born, a little disoriented by the diminished seventh — the columns of an ancient temple, those *forti*. The portico of a new universe, a portico of ten measures, under which we pass to C minor, power and fragility together. Courage, cheerfulness, grandiloquence. Are the manuscripts of the 32nd Sonata also in the Bodmer rooms in Bonn? Dr. Mann, I know you met the famous Hans Conrad Bodmer. The great Beethoven collector. He patiently gathered everything together, bought it all, between 1920 and 1950—scores, letters, furniture, the most diverse objects; he filled his Zurich villa with them, and showed these relics to the great performers passing through, Backhaus, Cortot, Casals. Drawing on his fortune, Bodmer reconstituted Beethoven as one reconstitutes a broken ancient vase. Glued back together what had been scattered for almost a hundred years. You know the one that moves me the most, among all the objects, Dr. Mann? Beethoven's desk? The one that Stefan Zweig owned, on which he wrote most of his books, and which he finally sold along with his manuscript collection to his friend Bodmer? No. His traveling writing case? His miniature hearing aids? Not those either. His compass. Beethoven owned a compass. A little metal compass, made of copper or brass, that you can see in a case next to his cane. A pocket compass, round, with a cover, very similar to today's models it seems to me. A beautiful colorful face with a magnificent wind rose. We know that Beethoven was a great walker. But he walked around Vienna, in town in the winter, and in the countryside in the summer. No need for a compass to leave Grinzing or find the Augarten—but did he carry this compass during his excursions in the Vienna woods, or when he crossed the vineyards to reach the Danube in Klosterneuburg? Was he planning a great journey? Italy, perhaps? Greece? Had Hammer-Purgstall convinced him to see the Orient? Hammer-Purgstall had suggested to Beethoven that he set to music some "Oriental" texts, his own, but also some translations. Apparently the master never agreed to this. There are no "Oriental" lieder by Beethoven aside from the *Ruins of Athens* by the horrible Kotzebue. There is just the compass. I own a replica of it—or at least a similar model. I don't have much occasion to use it. I think it has never left this apartment. So it always shows the same direction, ad infinitum, on its shelf, its cover closed. Pulled unremittingly by magnetism, on its drop of water, the double red and blue needle points east. I have always wondered where Sarah found this bizarre artifact. My Beethoven compass points east. Oh it's not just the face, no no, as soon as you try to orient yourself, you notice that this compass points to the east and not to the north. A joke compass. I've played with it for a long time, incredulous, I've made dozens of attempts, at the kitchen window, the living room window, the bedroom window — and it always indicates east. Sarah could hardly contain her laughter, seeing me turn this damn compass in every direction. She would say "So, have you found your bearings yet?" And it was absolutely impossible to orient yourself with this instrument. I would point toward the Votivkirche, the needle would quickly stabilize itself, become quite motionless, I'd turn the wheel to place the N under the needle, but then the azimuth would affirm that the Votivkirche was to the east instead of to the south. It is quite simply wrong, it doesn't work. Sarah would titter, very happy with her joke, you don't even know how to use a compass! I'm telling you it points east! And in fact, miraculously, if you placed the E under the needle instead of the N, then everything, as if by magic, found its right place again: north became north, south became south, the Votivkirche by the edge of the Ring. I didn't understand how that was possible, by what magic a compass could exist that points east and not north. The magnetism of the earth rises up against this heresy, this object possesses black magic! Sarah was laughing so hard at seeing me so disconcerted that she had tears in her eyes. She refused to explain the thing to me; I was terribly upset; I turned and turned again the damn compass in every direction. The witch responsible for the enchantment (or, at least, for its purchase: even the greatest magicians buy their tricks) finally took pity on my lack of imagination and confided to me that actually there were *two* needles separated by a card; the magnetized needle was below, invisible, and the second, subjected to the first, formed a ninety-degree angle with the magnet, thus always indicating an east-west axis. To what purpose? Aside from immediately having under your eyes the direction of Bratislava or Stalingrad without having to make any calculations, I didn't see the point.

"Franz, you lack poetry. You now own one of the rare compasses that point to the Orient, the compass of Illumination, the Suhrawardian artifact. A mystical diviner's wand."

You may be wondering, dear Herr Mann, what Suhrawardi, the great twelfth-century Persian philosopher decapitated in Aleppo by order of Saladin, has to do with Beethoven's compass (or at least the version of it tampered with by Sarah). Suhrawardi, native of Suhraward in northwestern Iran, discovered for Europe (and also for most Iranians) by Henry Corbin, the Heidegger specialist who switched to Islamic studies, and who devoted to Suhrawardi and his successors an entire volume of his great oeuvre, *En Islam iranien*. Henry Corbin is probably one of the most influential European thinkers in Iran, whose long labor of publishing and exegesis was instrumental in the revival, in tradition, of Shiite thought. Especially in the revival of the interpretation of Suhrawardi, the founder of "Oriental theosophy," of the wisdom of Illumination, heir to Plato, Plotinus, Avicenna, and Zoroaster. As Muslim metaphysics was dying out, in the darkness of the West, with the death of Averroes (and Latin Europe died with him), it continued to shine in the East in the mystical theosophy of the disciples of Suhrawardi. This is the way shown by my compass, according to Sarah, the path to Truth, in the rising sun. The first Orientalist in the strict sense of the word was that decapitated man in Aleppo, sheikh of Oriental illumination, of *Ishraq*, the Illumination from the East. My friend Parviz Baharlou the poet in Tehran, scholar with the joyful sadness, often spoke to us of Suhrawardi, of that knowledge of the *Ishraq* and its relationship with the Mazdan tradition of ancient Iran, the underground link that joined modern Shiite Iran with ancient Persia. For him, this current was much more interesting and subversive than Ali Shariati's rereading of Shiism as a revolutionary weapon of combat, which he called "the dry river," since tradition didn't flow into it, the spiritual flux was absent from it. According to Parviz, the Iranian mullahs in power unfortunately couldn't care less about either one or the other: not only were the revolutionary ideas of Shariati no longer current (already Khomeini, in the beginning of the Revolution, had condemned his thinking as blameworthy innovation) but also the theosophical, mystical aspect was erased from the religion of power and replaced by the dryness of *velayat-e faqih*, the "government of jurists": clerics are in charge of earthly administration, until the Parousia — or Return — of the Mahdi, the hidden imam who will bring justice to Earth; the clerics are the temporal, not spiritual, intermediaries of the Mahdi. This theory had, in its day, provoked the wrath of great ayatollahs like Ayatollah Shariatmadari who had trained Parviz's father in Qom. Parviz also added that the *velayat-e faqih* had had huge consequences for vocations — the number of aspiring mullahs had multiplied by a hundred, since a temporal magistery allowed you to fill your pockets much more easily (and God knows how deep they were, the pockets of mullahs) than a spiritual priesthood rich in rewards in the beyond but not very remunerative for this lowly world: so turbans flourished, in Iran, at least as much as functionaries did in the Austro-Hungarian Empire, which is saying something. So much so that certain religious men complain today that there are more clerics than the faithful in mosques, that you find too many shepherds and fewer and fewer sheep to be shorn, somewhat similar to how there were, at the end of Imperial Vienna, more civil servants than constituents. Parviz himself would say that as he lived in the Paradise of Islam on Earth, he didn't see why he should go to the mosque. The only religious gatherings where there were a lot of people, he said, were political rallies that gathered everyone together: a number of buses were chartered to pick up the inhabitants in the south of the city and they boarded cheerfully, happy with this free trip and the meal offered them at the end of common prayer.

Philosophical, mystical Iran was always there, though, and streamed like an underground river below the feet of indifferent mullahs; the holders of *erfan*, spiritual knowledge, pursued the tradition of practice and commentary. The great Persian poets took part in this prayer of the heart, inaudible perhaps in the racket of Tehran, but whose muted beating was one of the most intimate rhythms in the city, in the entire country. Spending time with intellectuals and musicians, you almost forgot the black mask of the regime, that funeral crepe stretched over all things within its reach; one was almost freed of the Zahir, the apparent, while one came closer to the Batin, the womb, the hidden, the powers of dawn. Almost, for Tehran also knew how to take you by surprise and wrench your soul from you and send you back to the most superficial sadness, where there was neither ecstasy nor music—that crazed would-be-Gobineau of the Abguineh museum, for example, with his Hitler salute and his mustache, or that mullah I met at the university, professor of something or other, who took us aside and explained that we Christians had three gods, advocated human sacrifices and drank blood: so we were not simple miscreants, but *stricto sensu* terrifying pagans. That was, when I think about it, the first time anyone ever labeled me a *Christian*: the first time the evidence of my baptism was used by someone else to single me out and (under the circumstances) look down on me, just as, in the Abguineh museum, it was the first time someone had imposed the label "German" on me to enroll me among the followers of Hitler. This violence of identity pinned on you by the other and uttered like a condemnation — Sarah felt it much more strongly than I did. The Name she could have borne had to remain a secret, in Iran: even though the Islamic Republic officially protected Iranian Jews, the little community present in Tehran for four millennia was prey to bullying and suspicion; the last remnants of Achaemenid Judaism were sometimes arrested, tortured, and hanged after resounding court trials that had more to do with medieval witchcraft than modern justice, accused as they were — among a thousand other crackpot charges — of adulterating medications and trying to poison the Muslims of Iran for the benefit, of course, of the State of Israel, mention of which, in Tehran, had the terrifying power of monsters and wolves in childhood fairy tales. And even if Sarah was, in reality, no more Jewish than Catholic, she had to be careful (given the ease with which the police fabricated spies) and hide the few links she might have with that Zionist entity that Iranian official discourse so ardently desired to annihilate.

It's strange to think that today in Europe one so easily places the label "Muslim" on anyone who has a last name that's Arabic or Turkish. The violence of imposed identities.

Oh, the second exposition of the theme. One should examine it under the microscope. Everything vanishes. Everything flees. We are advancing into new territory. Everything is *fugue*. It should be acknowledged that your pages on Beethoven's 32nd sonata are apt to provoke the jealousy of musicologists, dear Thomas Mann. That stammering speaker, Kretzschmar, who plays the piano while bellowing his commentaries to be heard over his own *fortissimi*. What a character. A stammerer to talk about a deaf man. Why is there no third movement to the Opus

111? I'd like to submit my own theory on this matter. That famous third movement is present *implicitly*. By its absence. It is
in the heavens, in silence, in the future. Since we expect it, that
third movement, it breaks the duality of the confrontation of the
first two parts. It would be a slow movement. Slow, so slow or
so fast that it lasts in an infinite tension. At bottom it's the same
question as that of the resolution of the Tristan chord. The dual,
the ambiguous, turmoil, the fleeing. The fugue. That false circle,
that impossible return is inscribed by Beethoven himself at the
very beginning of his score, in the *maestoso* that we've just heard.
That diminished seventh. The illusion of the expected key, the
vanity of human hopes, so easily deceived by fate. What we think
we hear, what we think we expect. The majestic hope for resurrection, love, consolation is followed only by silence. There is no
third movement. It's terrifying, isn't it? Art and joy, the pleasures
and sufferings of humans resound in the void. All those things
we cling to, the fugue, the sonata, all of it is fragile, dissolved by
time. Listen to the end of the first movement, the genius of that
coda that ends in the air, suspended, after that long harmonic
meandering — even the space between the two movements is
uncertain. From fugue to variation, from flight to evolution. The
little aria pursues, *adagio molto*, to one of the most surprising
rhythms, its march toward the simplicity of nothing. Another
illusion, Essence; we don't discover it in the variation any more
than we discern it in the fugue. We think we're touched by the
caress of love, and we find ourselves rushing head over heels
down a staircase. A paradoxical staircase that doesn't even lead
to its starting point — or to paradise, or to hell. The genius of
these variations, you'll no doubt agree, Herr Mann, resides also
in their transitions. That's where life lies, fragile life, in the link
between all things. The beauty is the passage, the transformation, all the schemes of the living. This sonata is alive, precisely
because it goes from fugue to variation and ends up at nothing.

"What is inside the almond? Nothing. There it stays and stays."
Of course you can't know those lines by Paul Celan, Herr Mann,
you were dead when they were published.

> *A Nothing*
> *we were, are now, and ever*
> *shall be, blooming:*
> *the Nothing-, the*
> *No-One's-Rose.*

Everything leads to that famous third movement, in silence
major, a rose of nothing, a rose of no one.

But I am preaching to the choir, dear Thomas Mann, I know
you agree with me. Would it bother you if I turned off the radio? In the end Beethoven makes me sad. Especially that endless
trill just before the final variation. Beethoven sends me back to
nothingness; to the compass of the Orient, to the past, to illness,
and to the future.

Here life ends on the tonic, simply, *pianissimo*, in C major, a
very monotone chord followed by a semiquaver rest. And then
nothing.

The important thing is not to lose east. Franz, don't lose east.
Turn off the radio, stop this conversation out loud with the
phantom of Mann the magician. Mann the friend of Bruno
Walter. Friend even in exile, friend of thirty-five years. Thomas
Mann, Bruno Walter, and the Wagner case. The Wagner aporia, always. Mahler's disciple, Bruno Walter, whom the Munich
bourgeoisie would end up dismissing from his post as conductor
since, as a Semite, he was soiling German music. He wasn't making the Wagnerian statue gleam brightly enough. In the United
States he would become one of the greatest conductors of all
time. Why am I so wound up against Wagner tonight? Maybe

it's the influence of Beethoven's compass, the one that points east. Wagner is the *zahir*, the apparent, the sinister dry West. He dams underground rivers. Wagner is a dam, with him the stream of European music overflows. Wagner closes everything. Destroys opera. Drowns it. The total artwork becomes totalitarian. What is there in his almond? Everything. The illusion of Everything. Song, music, poetry, theater, painting with our sets, bodies with our actors and even nature with our Rhine and our horses. Wagner is the Islamic Republic. Despite his interest in Buddhism, despite his passion for Schopenhauer, Wagner transforms everything into that Christian alterity in *self*. *The Victors*, Buddhist opera, becomes *Parsifal*, Christian opera. Nietzsche is the only one who was able to distance himself from that magnet. Who was able to perceive its danger. Wagner: tubercular. Nietzsche: syphilitic. Nietzsche the thinker, poet, musician. Nietzsche wanted to *Mediterraneanize* music. He loved the exotic exuberances of *Carmen*, the sound of Bizet's orchestra. He loved them. Nietzsche saw love in the sun reflecting on the sea in Rapallo, in the secret lights of the Italian coast, where the densest greens suffer the heat. Nietzsche had understood that Wagner's question was not so much the summits he'd been able to climb but the impossibility of his succession, the death of a tradition that was no longer invigorated (in its own self) by the other. Horrible Wagnerian modernity. *Belonging to Wagner will cost you dearly*. Wagner wanted to be an isolated rock, he hurled the boats of all his successors onto the reefs.

For Nietzsche, the Christianity rediscovered in *Parsifal* is unbearable. Percival's *Graal* sounds almost like a personal insult. Seclusion in the self, in Catholic illusion.

Wagner is a calamity for music, Nietzsche asserts. A disease, a neurosis. The remedy is *Carmen*, the Mediterranean and the Spanish Orient. The Gypsy. A myth of love much different from Tristan's. Music must be bastardized, Nietzsche claims as much. Nietzsche attended about twenty performances of *Carmen*. Blood, violence, death, bulls; love as a blow of fate, like the flower thrown to you that condemns you to suffering. The flower that withers with you in prison without losing its perfume. A pagan love. Tragic. For Bizet, the Orient is Italy—it was in Sicily that the young Georges Bizet, winner of the Prix de Rome, discovered the traces of the Moors, the skies burning with passion, the lemon trees, the mosques turned into churches, the women dressed in black in Prosper Mérimée's stories, that same Mérimée whom Nietzsche loved. In a letter (the letter called "from the flying fish," where he declares he's living "strangely on the crests of waves"), the mustachioed seer explains that the *tragic coherence* of Mérimée passes into Bizet's opera.

Bizet married a Jewish woman and invented a Gypsy lady. Bizet married the daughter of Halévy, the composer of *La Juive*, the most-performed opera at the Paris Opéra into the 1930s. They say that Bizet died while conducting *Carmen*, during the trio of the Tarots, at the very instant the three Gypsy card-readers uttered the word *death! death!* while turning over the fatal card. I wonder if that's true. There's a whole network of deadly Gypsies in literature and music, from Mignon, the androgyne in Goethe's *Wilhelm Meister*, to Carmen, including the sulfurous Esmeralda of Victor Hugo—as a teenager I was terribly frightened by *Isabella of Egypt*, the novella by Ludwig Achim von Arnim, husband of Bettina Brentano; I can still remember the ominous beginning of the text, when the old Gypsy woman shows the young Bella a dot on the hill, telling her it's a gibbet, near a stream; it's your father who is hanged up there. Don't cry, she tells her, tonight we'll go throw his body into the river, so he'll be brought back to Egypt; take this dish of meat and this glass of wine and go celebrate the funeral meal in his honor. And

I pictured, under the implacable moon, the little girl contemplating the gallows in the distance where the corpse of her father was swaying; I could see Bella, alone, eating that meat and drinking that wine while thinking about the Duke of the Gypsies, that father whose corpse she would have to take down from the gallows to consign it to the torrent, a torrent so powerful it could bring bodies back to the other side of the Mediterranean, to Egypt, homeland of the Dead and of Gypsies, and in my still-childlike imagination, all the terrifying episodes in Bella's adventures, the fabrication of the magic homunculus, the meeting with the young Charles V, all that was nothing compared to the horrible beginning, the remains of the Duke Michel creaking in the night on top of the gibbet, the child alone with her funeral meal. My own Gypsy is Bella, more than Carmen: the first time I was allowed to accompany my parents to the Vienna Opera, a rite of passage for every bourgeois son, it was for a performance of *Carmen* conducted by Carlos Kleiber—I had been fascinated by the orchestra, the sound of the orchestra, the number of musicians in it, by the singers' fancy gowns and the burning eroticism of the dances, but terribly shocked by the horrible French pronunciation of those goddesses: alas, instead of an exciting Spanish accent, Carmen was Russian, and Micaëla German, she said to the soldiers *"Non non, cheu refiendré"* — "No no, ah vill re-toorn"—which seemed to me (how old was I, twelve maybe) absolutely hysterical. I was expecting a French opera set in wild Spain, and I couldn't understand a word either of the spoken dialogue or the arias, uttered in a kind of Martian gobbledegook that I did not yet know was the lingua franca of today's opera, unfortunately. On stage, it was a huge leaping hubbub, of Gypsies, soldiers, donkeys, horses, straw, knives— you expected to see emerging from the wings a real bull that Escamillo (also Russian) would have killed in situ; Kleiber was leaping on his podium, trying to make the orchestra play more loudly, more loudly, always more loudly, with such exaggerated accents that even the donkeys, the horses, the thighs under the gowns, and the breasts in their décolletés seemed like a tame village parade — the triangles were struck so hard it seemed they would dislocate shoulders, the brass instruments blew so powerfully they made the violinists' hair and the cigar-making ladies' petticoats fly up, the strings covered the voices of the singers, who were forced to bellow like donkeys or mares to make themselves heard, losing all nuance; only the children's chorus, *Avec la garde montante*, etc., seemed to be amused by this overemphasis, shouting over each other while brandishing their wooden weapons. There were so many people on stage that one wondered how anyone could move without falling into the orchestra pit, hats, toques, bonnets, roses in their hair, parasols, rifles, a mass, a magma of life and music of a confusion that was constantly reinforced, as I remember it (but memory always exaggerates), by the diction of the actors, reducing the text to mumblings — fortunately my mother, patiently, had told me the sad love story of Don José for Carmen beforehand; I can remember my question perfectly, But why does he kill her? Why kill the object of his love? If he loves her, why stab her? And if he doesn't love her anymore, if he married Micaëla, then how can he still feel enough hatred to kill her? This story seemed highly unlikely to me. It seemed very strange to me that Micaëla, alone, would manage to discover the smugglers' hideout in the mountains, while the police didn't succeed. Nor did I understand why, at the end of the first act, Don José let Carmen escape from prison, when he barely knew her. She had slashed a poor young girl with a knife, after all. Didn't Don José have any sense of justice? Was he already a killer in the making? My mother sighed that I understood nothing of the force of love. Fortunately, Kleiber's exuberance allowed me to forget the story and concentrate on the bodies of the women dancing on the stage, concentrate on their clothes and suggestive poses, on the sensual seductiveness of their dances. Gypsies are all about passion. Beginning with *The Little Gypsy* by Cervantes, Gypsies have represented in Europe an alterity of desire and violence, a myth of freedom and travel — even in music: by the characters they furnish operas, but also by their melodies and rhythms. In his *On Gypsies and Their Music in Hungary*, Franz Liszt describes, after a sinister anti-Semitic ninety-page introduction devoted to Jews in art and music (always the absurd Wagnerian arguments: dissimulation, cosmopolitanism, absence of creation, of genius, replaced by imitation and talent: Bach and Beethoven, geniuses, against Meyerbeer and Mendelssohn, talented imitators), *freedom* as the first characteristic of "that strange" Gypsy race. Liszt's brain, eaten away by the concept of race and anti-Semitism, struggles to save the Gypsies — if they are the opposite of the Jews, he argues, it's because they don't hide anything, they have no Bible or Testament unique to them; they are thieves, Gypsies, indeed, for they do not bend to any norm, like the love in *Carmen*, "which has never known any law." The children of "Bohemia" run after "the electric glimmer of a sensation." They are ready to do anything to *feel*, at any price, in communion with nature. The Gypsy is never so happy as when he falls asleep in a birch wood, Liszt tells us, when he breathes in the emanations of nature through all his pores. Freedom, nature, dream, passion: Liszt's "Bohemians" are the romantic people *par excellence*. But where Liszt is most profound, most in love, probably, is when he forgets the limitations of race he has just placed on the Roma and turns his attention toward their contribution to Hungarian music, to the gypsy motifs that feed Hungarian music—the Bohemian *epic* feeds music, Liszt will make himself the rhapsodist of these musical adventures. The mixture with Tatar elements (according to the supposed origins, at that time, of the mysterious Hungarians) signals the birth of Hungarian music. Unlike Spain, where the Zingari produce nothing good (an old guitar with the sound of a saw in the laziness of a grotto in Sacromonte or the ruined palaces of the Alhambra cannot be regarded as music, he says), it's in the immense plains of Hungary that the gypsy fire will find its most beautiful expression, according to Liszt—I imagine Liszt in Spain, in the forgotten splendor of the Almohad remains, or in the mosque of Córdoba, looking passionately for Gypsies to hear their music; in Grenada, he read the *Tales of the Alhambra* by Washington Irving, he heard the heads of the Abencerrages falling under the executioners' sabers, in the basin of the lion fountain—Washington Irving the American, friend of Mary Shelley and Walter Scott, the first writer to make the deeds of the Spanish Muslims live again, the first to rewrite the chronicle of the conquest of Grenada and to live for a time in the Alhambra. It's strange Liszt didn't hear, in the songs around that evil guitar, as he called it, anything but banalities: he did acknowledge, however, that he was dogged by bad luck. The lucky one was Domenico Scarlatti, who, during his long stay in Andalusia, at the little court of Seville, no doubt listened to many traces of lost Moorish music, transported by the Gypsies in the emergent flamenco; that air invigorated Baroque music and, through Scarlatti's originality, contributed to the evolution of European music. Gypsy passion, at the edges of Europe, in Hungarian landscapes and Andalusian hillsides, transmitted its energy to so-called "Western" music—one more stone to add to Sarah's idea of "common construction." That, moreover, was Liszt's contradiction: by isolating the Gypsies' contribution in a

Gobineau-like "race," he distanced it, neutralized it; although he recognized that contribution, he could only conceive of it as an ancient stream, which flowed from "that people foreign as the Jews" into the earliest Hungarian music: Liszt's rhapsodies are entitled *Hungarian Rhapsodies,* not *Gypsy Rhapsodies* . . . That great movement of "national" exclusion, the historical construction of "German," "Italian," "Hungarian" music as the expression of each nation, in perfect balance with it, is immediately contradicted, in reality, by its own theoreticians. The modal augmentations of some sonatas by Scarlatti, the alterations of the Gypsy scale (Liszt speaks of "very bizarre glints of offensive brilliance") are so many knife-twists in classical harmony, the twist of Carmen's knife, when she slashes the face of one of the cigar-making girls with a Saint Andrew's cross. I could suggest to Sarah that she turn her attention to the Gypsies of the Orient, so little studied, the Turkish Çingane, the Syrian Nawar, the Iranian Lulis — nomads or sedentary people who could be found from India to Central Asia to the Maghreb since the Sassanid era and King Bahram Gūr. In classical Persian poetry, the Gypsies are free, joyful, music-loving; they are the beauty of the moon, they dance and seduce — they are objects of love and desire. I know nothing of their music, is it different from the music of Iran or, on the contrary, is it the substratum on which Iranian modes grow? Between India and the plains of Western Europe beats the free blood of their mysterious languages, of all they have carried with them in their movements — outlining another map, a secret map of an immense country that stretches from the Indus Valley to the Guadalquivir.

I circle around love. I stir my little teaspoon in the empty cup. Do I want another herbal tea? I'm not sleepy at all, that's for sure. What is Fate trying to tell me tonight? I could read the cards, if I had the slightest competence in the matter I'd throw

myself on the Tarots. "Madame Sosostris, famous clairvoyante
. . . is known to be the wisest woman in Europe, with a wicked
pack of cards." Here's my card, the Drowned Phoenician Sailor.
The Oriental aquatic hanged man, basically. *Fear death by drowning.* Or, in Bizet:

> *But if you must die,*
> *If the fearful word*
> *Is written by fate,*
> *Start over twenty times,*
> *The pitiless card*
> *Will repeat: Death!*
> *Again! Again!*
> *Always death!*
> *Again! Despair!*
> *Always death!*

To die by the hand of Carmen or Mme Sosostris, it all comes
down to the same thing, it's six of one and half a dozen of the
other, or *kif-kif bourricot* as the French say. The announcement
of imminent death, as in the beautiful soberness of the post-
script to one of the last letters of Nietzsche, the giant with the
mustaches of clay,

> *P.S. This winter, I'll stay in Nice. My summer address is: Sils-Maria,*
> *Haute-Engadine, Switzerland. I've stopped teaching at the university. I*
> *am three-quarters blind.*

which resounds like an epitaph. It's hard to imagine there is a
final night, that one could already be three-quarters blind. Sils
in the Engadine is among the most beautiful mountain landscapes in Europe, they say. Sils Lake and Silvaplana Lake which
Nietzsche was going to circumnavigate by foot. Nietzsche the

Persian, Nietzsche the reader of the Avesta, last or first Zo-
roastrian of Europe, blinded by the light of the fire of Ahura
Mazda the Great Brightness. Always these paths keep crossing
and recrossing; Niezsche in love with Lou Salomé, that same
Lou who would marry an Orientalist, Friedrich Carl Andreas,
specialist in Iranian languages, who almost stabbed himself to
death, since she refused him her body and made him mad with
desire; Nietzsche met Annemarie Schwarzenbach in Sils-Maria,
where the Schwarzenbachs owned a sumptuous chalet;
Annemarie Schwarzenbach met the ghost of Nietzsche in Tehran, where she stayed several times; Annemarie Schwarzenbach
met Thomas Mann and Bruno Walter through Erika and Klaus
Mann, to whom she sent those distraught letters from Syria
and Iran. Annemarie Schwarzenbach met Arthur de Gobineau
without realizing it in the Lahr Valley, a few dozen kilometers
north of Tehran. The compass is still pointing east. In Iran,
Sarah took me to visit these places, one after the other: the villa
in Farmaniyeh where Annemarie resided with her husband the
young French diplomat Claude Clarac, a beautiful house with
neo-Persian columns, with a magnificent garden, today the residence of the Italian ambassador, an affable man, delighted to
show us around his home and to learn that the melancholy Swiss
woman had lived there for a time — Sarah shone in the shadows
of the trees, her hair was like those golden fish shimmering in
brown water; her happiness at discovering that house was transformed into an endless smile; I myself was so happy with her
childlike pleasure that I felt full of a springtime-like jubilation,
powerful as the perfume of the countless roses in Tehran. The
villa was sumptuous — the Qajar faïences on the walls told the
stories of Persian heroes; the furniture, most of it antique, var-
ied between old Europe and immortal Iran. The building was
modified and enlarged in the 1940s, an inextricable mingling

of Italian neo-Gothic architecture and nineteenth-century Persian, harmonious for the most part. The city around us, usually so harsh, softened by the vision of Sarah kneeling on the edge of a fountain, her white hand distorted by the water in a basin covered in water lilies. I found her again in Iran a few months after Paris and her thesis defense, many months after her marriage and my jealousy, after Damascus, Aleppo and the closed door of her room at the Baron Hotel, slammed in my face — the pain is vanishing little by little, all pains vanish, shame is a feeling that imagines the other in the self, that takes responsibility for the vision of the other, a dividing in two, and now, dragging my old slippers toward the living room and my desk, bumping as usual against the porcelain umbrella stand invisible in the dark, I tell myself that I was very shabby to have cold-shouldered him like that, and at the same time to scheme in every possible and imaginable way to see her again in Iran, looking for research subjects, fellowships, invitations to get me to Tehran, completely blinded by that idée fixe, to the point of upsetting my cherished university plans; everyone asked me, in Vienna, Why Tehran, why Persia? Istanbul and Damascus, OK, but Iran? and I had to invent tortuous rationalizations, investigations into "the meaning of musical tradition," into classical Persian poetry and its echoes in European music, or else deliver myself of a very peremptory: "I have to go back to the sources," which had the advantage of immediately shutting up the curious, sure as they were I had been touched by grace or, more often, by the wind of madness.

Now look, I've unthinkingly awakened my computer, Franz, I know what you're going to do, you'll start searching through old stories, your Tehran notes, reread Sarah's emails and you know that's not a good idea, you'd be better off making another cup of tea and going back to bed. Or else revise, revise that infernal paper on the Orientalist operas of Gluck.

A puff of Iranian opium, a puff of memory, it's a kind of forgetfulness, a forgetfulness of the advancing night, of encroaching illness, of the blindness that's overtaking us. Maybe that's what Sadegh Hedayat lacked when he turned the gas up high in Paris in April 1951, a pipe of opium and memory, a companion: the greatest Iranian prose writer of the twentieth century, the darkest, the funniest, the nastiest ended up giving in to death out of exhaustion; he let himself go, stopped resisting, his life didn't seem worth pursuing, here or there — the prospect of going back to Tehran was as unbearable to him as that of staying in Paris, he was floating, floating in that studio he had so much trouble obtaining, on the rue Championnet in Paris, the City of Light, in which he saw so little. In Paris, he liked the brasseries, the cognac and hard-boiled eggs, since he'd been a vegetarian for a long time, ever since his travels in India; in Paris he liked the memory of the city he had known in the 1920s, and the tension between the Paris of his youth and the Paris of 1951 — between his youth and 1951 — was a daily source of suffering, in his walks through the Latin Quarter, in his long *flâneries* through the outskirts. He spent some time (that's an overstatement) with a few Iranians, exiles like him; those Iranians found him a bit haughty, a bit scornful, which was probably true. He no longer wrote much. "I write only for my shadow, projected by the lamp onto the wall; I have to make it know me." He would burn his final texts. No one loved and hated Iran as much as Hedayat, Sarah said. No one was as attentive to the language of the streets, to the characters in the streets, the zealots, the humble, the powerful. No one could construct as savage a critique or as immense a praise of Iran as Hedayat. He may have been a sad man, especially at the end of his life, both caustic and bitter, but he was not a bitter writer, far from it.

Like Hedayat, I have always been intimidated by Paris; the

strange violence you feel there, the lukewarm peanut-smell on the metro, the habit its inhabitants have of running instead of walking, eyes down, ready to knock over anything in their way to reach their destination; the filth, which seems to have been accumulating in the city unceasingly at least since Napoleon's time; the river, so noble and so constrained in its paved banks, scattered with haughty, disparate monuments; the whole of it, under the soft, milky eye of the Sacré-Coeur, always seems to me of a Baudelairean, monstrous beauty. Paris, capital of the nineteenth century and of France. I was never able to rid myself, in Paris, of my tourist's hesitations, and my French, despite the fact that I make it a point of honor for it to be polished, sober, perfect, is always in exile there — I feel as if I understand every other word, and even worse, the height of humiliation, they often make me repeat my sentences: ever since Villon and the end of the Middle Ages, in Paris they've been speaking nothing but slang. And I don't know if these characteristics make Vienna or Berlin seem gentle and provincial or if, on the contrary, it's Paris that remains stuck in its province, isolated in the heart of that Île-de-France whose name might be at the origin of the singularity of the city and its inhabitants. Sarah is a true Parisian, if that adjective really has any meaning: I have to admit that Sarah — even grown thin from overexertion, her eyes slightly lined, her hair shorter than usual, as if she had entered a monastery or prison, her hands pale and almost bony, her wedding band grown too big jiggling on her finger — remained the ideal of feminine beauty. What pretext had I found for that brief Parisian visit, I can't remember; I stayed at a little hotel right next to the Place Saint-Georges, one of those miraculously-proportioned squares transformed into a kind of hell by the invention of the automobile — what I didn't know was that "a stone's throw from the Place Saint-Georges" (according to the brochure of the hotel that I must have chosen, unconsciously, because of the friendly sound of the name of that saint, much more familiar than, for example, Notre-Dame-de-Lorette or Saint-Germain-l'Auxerrois) unfortunately also meant a stone's throw from the Place Pigalle, that gray monument raised to all sorts of visual atrocities where the hustlers for hostess bars grab you by the arm to tell you to come in for a drink and don't let go of you until they have showered copious insults on you, sure of the leap in virility their invectives would cause, insults like "queer" and "impotent." Curiously, the Place Pigalle (and the adjacent streets) lay between Sarah and me. Sarah and Nadim's apartment was a little higher up, on the Place des Abbesses, halfway up the hill that takes you (O Paris!) from the whores of Pigalle to the young monks of the Sacré-Coeur and, beyond the Butte where the Communards rolled their cannons, to the last residence of Sadegh Hedayat. Nadim was in Syria when I visited, which suited me fine. The higher I climbed to reach Sarah, in those alleyways that lead without warning from the sordid to the touristy, then from the touristy to the bourgeois, the more I realized I still had hope, a mad hope that refused to say its name, and then, as I descended the big staircase on the rue du Mont-Cenis, after getting a little lost and passing a surprising vineyard stuck between two houses whose old vine stocks reminded me of Vienna and Nussdorf, step after step toward the town hall of the 18th arrondissement, toward the poverty and simplicity of the faubourgs that follow the ostentation of Montmartre, that hope was diluted in the gray that seemed to make even the trees on the rue Custine sad, cramped in their iron railings, this so-Parisian limitation on vegetal exuberance (nothing represents the modern mind more than that strange idea, the tree fence. It's pointless to try to convince you that these imposing pieces of wrought iron are there to protect the chestnut or plane tree, for their own good, to prevent their roots from being harmed; there is, I think, no more terrible representation of the life and death struggle between the city and nature, and no more eloquent sign of the victory of the former over the latter) and when I finally reached, after more hesitations, a town hall, a church, and a loud traffic circle at the rue Championnet, Paris had vanquished my hope. The place could have been pleasant, charming even; some buildings were elegant, with their five floors and attic under zinc roofing, but most of the shops looked abandoned; the street was deserted, stiff, endless. Opposite the Hedayat residence was a curious ensemble, a low, old house, from the eighteenth century probably, side-by-side with a fat brick building marking the entrance to a parking lot for Parisian buses. As I waited for Sarah, I had plenty of time to observe the windows of 37 *bis* which, under the colorless, pale-gray sky, didn't exactly inspire cheerfulness. I thought about that forty-eight-year-old man plugging his kitchen door with dishrags before turning on the gas, lying down on the floor on a blanket and falling asleep forever. The Orientalist Roger Lescot had more or less finished his translation of *The Blind Owl*, but Grasset either didn't want to publish it anymore or no longer had the means. José Corti, bookseller and publisher of the Surrealists, would be fascinated by the text that would come out two years after the death of its author. *The Blind Owl* is a dream of death. A violent book, of a savage eroticism, where time is an abyss whose contents come gushing back in deadly vomit. A book of opium.

Sarah was coming. She was walking quickly, her satchel slung over her shoulder, head slightly bent; she hadn't noticed me. I recognized her, despite the distance, from the color of her hair, from the hope that insinuated itself again with an anguished pang into my heart. She's in front of me, long skirt, ankle boots, immense sienna-colored scarf. She holds out her hands to me, smiles, says she's very happy to see me again. Of course I should not have pointed out to her right away that she had lost a lot of weight, that she was pale, her eyes lined, that wasn't very clever; but I was so surprised by these physical transformations, so pushed to futility by anguish, that I couldn't help myself, and the day, that day I had brought about, worked on, waited for, imagined, started off on a lamentable footing. Sarah was annoyed—she tried not to show it, and once our tour of the Hedayat apartment was over (or rather just the staircase, the present renter of the studio having refused to open the door to us: he was, according to Sarah, who had spoken with him on the phone the day before, very superstitious and terrified by the idea that a mysterious stranger could have put an end to his days on his kitchen linoleum), as we were climbing back up the rue Championnet headed west, then the rue Damrémont toward the Montmartre Cemetery, before pausing for lunch in a Turkish restaurant, she kept a sticky silence, while I lurched into hysterical chatter—when you're drowning you struggle, wave your arms and legs; I was trying to cheer her up, or at least interest her in something; I told her the latest news from Vienna, as far as there was any news from Vienna, and talked about the Oriental lieder of Schubert—my passion at the time—then about Berlioz, whose grave we were going to visit, and my very personal reading of *Les Troyens*—until she stopped right in the middle of the pavement and looked at me with a half smile:

"Franz, you're getting on my nerves. It's incredible. You've been talking without interruption for two kilometers. Good Lord how talkative you can be!"

I was very proud of having intoxicated her with my fine words and wasn't about to stop while I was on a roll:

"You're right, I'm chattering, I'm chattering and I'm not letting you get a word in edgewise. So tell me, the thesis, how's it going? Will you finish it soon?"

This had an unexpected, if not unhoped-for, effect: Sarah let out a great sigh, there, on the sidewalk on the rue Damrémont, held her face in her hands, then shook her head, lifted her arms to the sky and let out a long cry: an exasperated shout, a call to the gods, a supplication full of rage that left me wordless, surprised, wounded, wide-eyed. Then she fell silent, turned to me and sighed again:

"Come on then, let's go have lunch."

There was a restaurant across the street; a restaurant with exotic décor, wall hangings, cushions, all sorts of bibelots, old things as dusty as the window, opaque from filth, with no customers aside from us, since it was just barely noon and Parisians, priding themselves no doubt on more southern influences, on a greater freedom than the rest of their fellow citizens, had lunch late. If by chance they ever lunched in this spot. It seemed to me that we were the only customers all week, maybe all month, so surprised the owner (hunched over a table, trying to beat his personal Tetris record) looked when we walked in. An owner whose pale complexion, accent, bad humor, and prices proved he was entirely Parisian: forget about Oriental gentleness, we had fallen upon the only Turkish restaurant run by a Parisian native, who deigned to abandon his computer to welcome us only with many sighs and after finishing his game.

It was my turn to fall silent, mortally wounded by Sarah's ridiculous shouting. Who did she take herself for, then? I take an interest in her and what do I get? The screeching of one possessed. After several minutes of vengeful silence, my sulking hidden behind the menu, she offered an apology.

"Franz, I'm sorry, forgive me, I don't know what came over me. But you don't exactly make things any easier."

(Mortally wounded, with pathetic accents) "It's nothing, let's drop it. Let's see instead what sort of edible thing there is to eat in this sumptuous inn you've brought us to."

"We can go somewhere else if you like."

(Definitively, with a hint of hypocrisy) "You can't leave a restaurant after you've sat down and read the menu. It isn't done. As you say in France: When the wine is opened, you have to drink it."

"I could pretend to be sick. If you don't change your attitude, I *will* be sick."

(Shiftily, still hidden behind the menu) "You are indisposed? That would explain your mood swings."

"Franz, you're going to make me lose it. If you go on like this, I'm leaving, I'll go back to work."

(Cowardly, frightened, confused, suddenly putting down the menu) "No, no, don't leave, I was just saying that to annoy you, I'm sure it's very good here. Delicious, even."

She began to laugh. I no longer remember what we ate, I only remember the little *ding* of the microwave oven that resounded throughout the deserted restaurant just before the dishes arrived. Sarah talked to me about her thesis, about Hedayat, Schwarzenbach, her beloved characters; about the mirrors between East and West that she wanted to break, she said, by making the promenade continue. Bring to light the rhizomes of that common construction of modernity. Show that "Orientals" were not excluded from it, but that, quite the contrary, they were often the inspiration behind it, the initiators, the active participants; to show that in the end Said's theories had become, despite themselves, one of the most subtle instruments of domination there are: the question was not whether or not Said was right or wrong, in his vision of Orientalism; the problem was the breach, the ontological fissure his readers had allowed between a dominating West and a dominated East, a breach that, by opening up well beyond colonial studies, contributed to the realization of the model it created, that completed *a posteriori* the scenario of domination which Said's thinking meant to oppose. Whereas history could be read in an entirely different way, she said, written in an entirely different way, in sharing and continuity. She spoke at length on the postcolonial holy trinity—Said, Bhabha, Spivak; on the question of imperialism, of difference, of the twenty-first century when, facing violence, we needed more than ever to rid ourselves of this absurd idea of the absolute otherness of Islam and to admit not only the terrifying violence of colonialism, but also all that Europe owed to the Orient—the impossibility of separating them from each other, the necessity of changing our perspective. We had to find, she said, beyond the stupid repentance of some or the colonial nostalgia of others, a new vision that includes the other in the self. On both sides.

The décor was fitting: the fake Anatolian cloth on the "Made in China" curios and the very Parisian customs of the manager seemed the best example to support her theory.

The Orient is an imaginal construction, an ensemble of representations from which everyone picks what they like, wherever they are. It is naïve to think, Sarah continued in a loud voice, that this repository full of Oriental images is specific to Europe today. No. These images, this treasure chest, are accessible to everyone and everyone adds to it, according to cultural productions, new sketches, new portraits, new music. Algerians, Syrians, Lebanese, Iranians, Indians, Chinese take turns drawing from this travel buffet, this imagination. I'll take a very current, striking example: the veiled princesses and flying carpets of the Disney studios can be seen as "Orientalist" or "Orientalizing"; actually they amount to the latest expression of this recent construction of an imaginal reality. It's not for nothing that these films are not only authorized in Saudi Arabia, but even omnipresent. All the didactic shorts copy them (to teach how to pray, to fast, to live like a good Muslim). Prudish contemporary Saudi society is like a film by Walt Disney. Wahhabism is like a Disney film. In doing this, the filmmakers who work for Saudi Arabia add images to the common pool. Another, shocking example: public decapitation, with the curved saber and the executioner dressed in white, or even more terrifying, throat-slitting till the head comes off. That's also the product of a common construction based on Muslim sources transformed by all the images of modernity. These atrocities take their place in this imaginal world; they continue the common construction. We Europeans see them with the horror of otherness; but this otherness is just as terrifying for an Iraqi or a Yemenite. Even what we reject, what we hate emerges in this common imaginal world. What we identify in these atrocious decapitations as "other," "different," "Oriental," is just as "other," "different," and "Oriental" for an Arab, a Turk, or an Iranian.

I was half listening to her, absorbed as I was in contemplating her: despite the lines and thinness, her face was powerful, determined, and tender at the same time. Her gaze burned from the fire of her ideas; her chest seemed smaller than a few months before; the V-neck of her black cashmere sweater revealed scalloped lace of the same color, the edge of a camisole — a thin line under the wool in the middle of her shoulder hinted at a shoulder strap. The freckles on her breastbone followed the edge of the lace and went up to her collarbone; I could glimpse the top of the bone above which her earrings dangled, two imaginary heraldic coins engraved with unknown blazons. Her hair was pulled up, held in by a little silver comb. Her pale hands with long bluish veins fanned the air as she spoke. She had scarcely touched the contents of her dish. I was thinking again of Palmyra, of the contact with her body, I'd have liked to huddle against her until I disappeared. She had gone on to another subject, her difficulties with Gilbert de Morgan, her thesis advisor whom I had, she reminded me, met in Damascus; she was worried about his mood swings, his fits of alcoholism and despair—and especially his unfortunate propensity to look for salvation in the smiles of first- and second-year students. He would rub up against them as if youth were contagious. And these women weren't all comfortable with being vampirized. This evocation elicited a lascivious sigh and a little snigger from me that earned me a fine scolding, Franz, it's not funny, you're as macho as he is. Women are not objects . . . and so on. Did she realize my own concealed desire, all disguised in consideration and respect? She changed the subject again. Her relationship with Nadim was becoming more and more complicated. They had gotten married, she confided, to make it easier for Nadim to come to Europe. After a few months in Paris, he missed Syria; in Damascus or Aleppo, he was a renowned soloist; in France, just another immigrant. Sarah was so absorbed in the work on her thesis that she unfortunately didn't have much time to devote to him; Nadim had taken a strong dislike to his adopted country, saw racists and Islamophobes everywhere; he dreamed of going back to Syria, which his recently secured permanent resident ID had finally made possible for him. They were more or less separated, she said. She felt guilty. She was obviously exhausted; tears suddenly shone in her eyes. She didn't realize the selfish hopes these revelations aroused in me. She apologized, I tried to reassure her clumsily, after the thesis everything will be better. After the thesis she'd find herself without a job, without money, without any projects, she said. I was dying to shout to her that I loved her passionately. The phrase transformed in my mouth, became a bizarre suggestion, you could move to Vienna for a while. Stunned at first, she began to smile, thank you, that's very kind. It's kind of you to be concerned about me. Very. And since magic is a rare and fleeting phenomenon, that instant was quickly interrupted by the owner: he flung us a bill we hadn't asked for in a frightful bamboo dish with a painted bird on it. *"Bolboli khun jegar khorad o goli hasel kard,* a suffering nightingale who was losing its blood gave birth to a rose," I thought. I just said "Poor Hafez," Sarah immediately understood what I was alluding to and laughed.

Then we started out for the Montmartre Cemetery and the reassuring company of the dead.

4:30 A.M.

S trange, the dialogues that start up in the random geography of cemeteries, I thought as I meditated in front of Heinrich Heine the Orientalist ("Where will the final rest of the weary walker be, under the palm trees of the South or the lindens of the Rhine?"—none of the above: under the chestnut trees of Montmartre), a lyre, some roses, a marble butterfly, a thin face bent forward, between a family named Marchand and a lady named Beucher, two black tombstones framing Heine's immaculate white, overlooking them like a sad guardian. An underground network joins the burial sites together, Heine with the musicians Hector Berlioz and Charles Valentin Alkan nearby or to Halévy the composer of *La Juive*, they're all there, they keep each other company, rub elbows down below. Théophile Gautier the friend of the *good Henri Heine* a little further on, Maxime Du Camp who accompanied Flaubert to Egypt and experienced pleasure with Kuchuk Hanim and with the very Christian Ernest Renan, there must be many secret debates between these souls, at night, animated conversations transmitted by the roots of the maples and the will o' the wisps, underground, silent concerts attended by the eager audience of the defunct. Berlioz shared his tomb with his *poor Ophelia*, Heine was apparently alone in his, and this thought, childlike as it was, made me feel a little sad.

Sarah was strolling at random, letting herself be guided by the names of the past, without consulting the map obtained at the welcome desk — her footsteps led us naturally to Marie du Plessis the Lady of the Camellias and to Louise Colet whom she introduced me to, so to speak. I was surprised by the number of cats found in Parisian cemeteries, companions of dead poets as they always were during their lifetimes: an enormous tomcat, bluish-gray, was lazing on a handsome nameless statue, whose noble drapery seemed to care neither about the affront of the pigeons nor the friendliness of the mammal.

Everyone lying down together, the cats, the bourgeois, the painters and pop stars — the mausoleum with the most flowers, visited by the most tourists, was that of the singer Dalida, the Italian from Alexandria, right next to the entrance: a full-length statue of the artiste, surrounded by round boxwood shrubs, advancing with one foot forward, in a transparent robe, toward the onlookers; behind her a brilliant sun projected its golden rays on a black marble plaque, in the center of a gray marbled monumental arch: one would be hard-pressed to guess what divinity the singer worshipped during her lifetime, aside perhaps from Isis in Philae or Cleopatra in Alexandria. This intrusion of the Oriental dream into the resurrection of the body no doubt pleased the many painters enjoying eternal rest in the Montmartre cemetery, including Horace Vernet (his sarcophagus was very sober, a simple stone cross that contrasted with the exuberant paintings of that martial Orientalist) or Théodore Chassériau, who combines the erotic precision of Ingres with the fury of Delacroix. I imagine him in an animated confab with Gautier, his friend, on the other side of the cemetery — talking about women, the bodies of women, and discussing the erotic merits of the Alexandrine singer's statue. Chassériau traveled to Algeria, lived for a time in Constantine, where he set down his easel and painted the chaste, mysterious beauty of Algerian women. I wonder if Halil Pasha owned a painting by Chassériau, probably: the Ottoman diplomat friend of Sainte-Beuve and Gautier, future Minister of Foreign Affairs in Istanbul, owned a magnificent collection of Orientalist paintings and erotic scenes: he bought *The Turkish Bath* by Ingres, and it's pleasant to think that this Turk originally from Egypt, descendent of a great family of servants of the State, collected by preference Orientalist canvases, the women of Algiers, nudes, harem scenes. There would be a fine novel to write about the life of Halil Pasha of Egypt, who joined the diplomatic corps of Istanbul instead of the one in his native country because, he explains in the letter he writes in French to the Grand Vizier, "there are ocular problems caused by the dust of Cairo." He began his brilliant career in Paris, as Egyptian commissar of the World's Fair of 1855, then the next year took part in the congress that put an end to the Crimean War. He could have met Faris al-Shidyaq the great Arab author dear to Sarah's heart, who was submitting his immense novel to be printed in Paris at the same time, at the printing house of the Pilloy brothers, located at 50 boulevard de Montmartre, a stone's throw from these tombs we were visiting so religiously. Halil Pasha is buried in Istanbul, I think; one day I'd like to go put flowers on the tomb of that Ottoman of the two shores — I have no idea whom he visited here in Vienna, between 1870 and 1872, while Paris was experiencing a war and then another revolution, the Commune that would force his friend Gustave Courbet into exile. Halil Pasha met Courbet during his second stay in Paris, and commissioned paintings from him — first the tender *Sleepers*, bought for twenty thousand francs, an evocation of lust and lesbian love, two sleeping women, nude, intertwined, a brunette and a blonde, whose hair and complexions contrast wonderfully with each other. I would give a lot to have a transcription of the conversation that gave rise to this commission, and even more to have been present at the next one, the conversation during the commission of *The Origin of the World*: the young Ottoman treats himself to a close-up of a woman's sex, painted by one of the artists most gifted at the realism of the flesh, an absolutely scandalous painting, direct and straightforward, which would remain hidden from the public for decades. One can imagine Halil Pasha's pleasure at owning such a secret jewel, a brown vulva and two breasts, which the small format makes easy to conceal, in his bathroom cabinet, behind a green cloth, if we are to believe Maxime Du Camp, who hated Courbet as much as the whims and wealth of the Ottoman. The identity of the owner of this deep brown pubic hair and these marmoreal breasts remains still to be determined; Sarah would very much like it to be the sex of Marie-Anne Detourbay *alias* Jeanne de Tourbey, who died as the Comtesse de Loynes, who aroused Gustave Flaubert's passions, and was the mistress — the muse — of a good part of the literary *Tout-Paris* of the 1860s, including possibly the dashing Halil Bey. The tomb of Jeanne de Tourbey was somewhere in that Montmartre cemetery, not far from the graves of Renan or Gautier whom she had received in her salon, at a time when she was given the terrifying name of *demimondaine*; we couldn't find that grave, either because vegetation was hiding it, or because the authorities, tired of sheltering such scandalous pelvic bones, had decided to remove the sarcophagus from the concupiscent gaze of passersby. Sarah liked to imagine, under the chestnut trees of the great avenue bordered by mausoleums, that for Halil Bey this slightly parted sex was the memory of a desired woman, whose face he had asked Courbet to hide out of discretion; he could thus contemplate her intimacy without risking compromising the lady.

Whatever the actual identity of the model, if they ever discover her, the fact remains that we owe one of the jewels of

European erotic painting to the Ottoman Empire and to one of its most eminent diplomats. The Turks themselves were not insensitive to the beauties of Orientalist mirages, far from it, said Sarah—just take Halil Bey the collector-diplomat, or the first Orientalist painter of the Orient, the archaeologist Osman Hamdi, to whom we owe the discovery of the sarcophagi of Saida and some magnificent paintings of Oriental "genre scenes."

This stroll through the wonderful world of memory had given Sarah a boost of energy; she forgot about writing her thesis while she traveled from one tomb to another, from one epoch to another, and when the dark shadow of the Caulaincourt bridge (the graves it overlooks are in eternal darkness) and its riveted metal pillars began to invade the necropolis, we regretfully had to leave the past and go back to the turmoil of the Place de Clichy: I had a bizarre mixture of gravestones and female private parts swimming around in my head, an entirely pagan *camposanto*, sketching in my imagination an *Origin of the World* as red as Sarah's hair descending to the big square cluttered with tourist buses.

Despite all my efforts this desk is as cluttered as the Montmartre cemetery, a frightful mess. I tidy, tidy, tidy, all in vain. The books and papers pile up with the force of a rising tide whose ebb I wait for to no avail. I move, arrange, stack up; the world persists in pouring its truckloads of shit onto my tiny workspace. To put down the computer I have to push aside the clutter every time, like sweeping away a pile of dead leaves. Ads, bills, statements that need to be sorted through, classified, archived. A fireplace, that's the solution. A fireplace or a paper shredder, the office worker's guillotine. In Tehran an old French diplomat told us that before, when the prudish Islamic Republic forbade the importing of alcohol even for embassies, the gloomy consular pen-pushers had transformed an old manual shredder into a press and made wine in their basement, in collaboration with the Italians across the way, to dispel their boredom; they would order crates of good grapes from Urmia, press them, make it into wine in laundry buckets and bottle it. They even printed pretty labels, with a little sketch, *Cuvée Neauphle-le-Château*, from the new name that revolutionary Iran had imposed on the former Avenue de France, Avenue Neauphle-le-Château. These worthy descendants of the monks of the Abbey of Thélème thus offered themselves some small consolation in their cloister, and they say that in the autumn the whole avenue smelled strongly of plonk, whose acid odor escaped through the basement windows and taunted the Iranian policemen on duty in front of the august edifices. The vintages were of course subject to circumstances arising not only from the quality of the grapes, but also from the manual labor: civil servants were often replaced, and a given oenologist (otherwise accountant, registry agent, or encrypter) was sometimes recalled to the mother country, causing despair in the community if that departure had to occur before the bottling.

I didn't give any credit to these stories until the diplomat exhumed in front of our astonished eyes one of these divine phials: despite the dust, the label was still legible; the level of liquid had lowered by a good quarter and the cork, covered in mildew, half out of the bottleneck, was a bulbous bubo, greenish and streaked with purple veins that didn't at all encourage you to tug it out. I wonder if the shredder in question is still in a basement in the French Embassy in Tehran. Probably. An instrument of that kind would work wonders in my office — no more papers, transformed into thin strips, into skeins easy to ball up and throw out. "Students in the lineage of the Imam" had patiently reconstituted, in Tehran, all the cables and reports of the American embassy, for days on end; boys and girls had tackled the huge puzzle in the Yankee baskets, carefully gluing back together the pages that had been fed through the shredder, thereby proving that it was much better, in Iran, to use these machines to press grapes than to destroy secret documents: all the confidential telegrams had been published by the "Students in the lineage of the Imam" who had stormed the embassy, that "nest of spies"; a dozen volumes had been published, and the black lines on the pages showed, as if that were necessary, the marvels of patience that had been evinced to place end-to-end these three-millimeter-wide strips of paper with the sole aim of embarrassing Uncle Sam by making his secrets public. I wonder if these days the destroyers of paper still function in the same way or if an American engineer has been ordered to improve them to prevent a cohort of Third-World students from deciphering, armed only with magnifying glasses, the best-kept secrets of the State Department. After all, WikiLeaks is only the postmodern version of the glue sticks of Iranian revolutionaries.

My computer is a faithful friend, its bluish light a moving painting in the night — I should change that image, that painting by Paul Klee has been there for so long I don't even see it anymore, covered by the desktop icons accumulating there like virtual pieces of paper. One has one's rituals, open the email, chuck out the undesirables, the spam, the newsletters, no actual message from the fifteen new ones in the inbox, just dregs, residue from the perpetual avalanche of shit that is the world today. I was hoping for an email from Sarah. OK, I'll have to take the initiative. New. To Sarah. Subject, From Vienna. Dearest, I received this morning — oops, no, yesterday morning — your offprint, I didn't know they were still printing those . . . Thank you very much, but how horrible, that wine of the dead! I'm worried, all of a sudden. Are you doing well? What are you doing in Sarawak? Here it's everything as usual. The Christmas market has just opened in the middle of the university. Atrocious odors of mulled wine and sausages. Do you plan on coming back through Europe soon? Send me news. Much love. Sent without thinking at 4:39. I hope she won't notice, it's a little pathetic to send messages at 4:39 a.m. She knows I go to bed early, usually. She might think I'm returning from a night out. I could click on her name and all her emails would appear at once, arranged in chronological order. That would be too sad. I still have a folder called Tehran, I don't delete anything. I'd make a good archivist. Why did I tell her about mulled wine and sausages, what an idiot. Much too relaxed to be honest, this email. You can't get a message back once it's thrown into the Great Mystery of electronic streams. That's too bad. Oh look, I had forgotten what I wrote after I got back from Tehran. Not its blood-curdling contents. I can see Gilbert de Morgan again in his garden in Zafaraniyeh. That strange confession, a few weeks before Sarah left Iran so hurriedly. There is no such thing as chance, she would say. Why did I insist on writing down the story of that afternoon? To rid myself of that sticky memory, to go over it again and again with Sarah, to embellish it with all my knowledge about the Iranian Revolution, or for the pleasure—so rare—of writing in French?

Gilbert de Morgan had been speaking in a slightly annoyed voice; the late afternoon was stifling; the ground was an oven tile that sent back all the heat accumulated during the day. Pollution slipped its pinkish veil over the mountains still inflamed by the last rays of the sun; even the dense arbor above our heads seemed to be emphasizing the dryness of the summer. The housekeeper, Nassim Kahnom, had served us some refreshments, a delicious iced bergamot water to which Morgan added generous dashes of Armenian vodka: the level of alcohol in the pretty carafe became steadily lower, and Sarah, who had already witnessed her advisor's cantankerous tendencies, was watching him, it seemed to me, in a slightly worried way—but perhaps it was just steady attentiveness. Sarah's hair was gleaming in the evening light. Nassim Khanom was bustling around, bringing us all sorts of sweets, pastries or saffron-scented candied fruit and, in the midst of the roses and petunias, we forgot the noise of the street, the horns and even the gas exhaust from the buses rushing past just on the other side of the garden wall, making the ground shake slightly and the ice cubes clink together in their glasses. Gilbert de Morgan continued his story, without paying any attention either to Nassim Khanom's movements or to the racket on the Avenue Vali-Asr; sweat stains were growing around his armpits and on his chest.

"I should tell you the story of Frédéric Lyautey," Morgan went on, "a young man from Lyon, also a researcher just starting out, a specialist in classical Persian poetry, who was visiting the University of Tehran when the first demonstrations against the Shah broke out. Despite our warnings, he took part in all the marches; he was passionate about politics, about the works of Ali Shariati, about clerics in exile, about activists of every kind. In the autumn of 1977, during the demonstrations that followed the death of Shariati in London (they were sure, at the time, that he had been assassinated), Lyautey was arrested a first time by the SAVAK, the Secret Police, then released almost immediately when they saw he was French; released after a mild beating all the same, as he said, which had frightened us all: we saw him reappear at the Institute covered in bruises, his eyes swollen, and especially, even more terrifying, with two fingernails missing from his right hand. He didn't seem overly affected by this ordeal; he almost laughed about it and this display of courage, instead of reassuring us, made us worry: even the strongest have been rattled by violence and torture, but Lyautey drew a swaggering energy from it, a feeling of superiority so bizarre that he made us suspect that his reason, at least as much as his body, had been affected by the torturers. He was scandalized by the reaction of the French Embassy which, he said, had made it clear to him that, all in all, he'd got his comeuppance, he shouldn't get mixed up in these demonstrations that had nothing to do with him and he should consider himself warned. Lyautey had laid siege to the office of the ambassador Raoul Delaye for days, with his arm still in a sling and his hand bandaged, to air his grievances, until he managed to accost him during a reception: we were all present — archaeologists, researchers, diplomats — and we saw Lyautey, his bandages filthy, his hair long and greasy, lost in a baggy pair of jeans, taking the polite Delaye, who had no idea whatsoever who he was, to task — it should be said in the ambassador's defense that unlike today there were many French researchers and students in Tehran. I remember perfectly Lyautey, red and spluttering, spitting out his rancor and his revolutionary messages in the face of Delaye, until two gendarmes threw themselves on the maniac, who began declaiming poems in Persian, shouting and gesticulating, very violent poems that I wasn't familiar with. A little concerned we saw how, in a corner of the embassy's gardens, Lyautey had to prove his status as a member of the Institute for the gendarmes to agree to let him go and not hand him over to the Iranian police.

"Of course, most of those present had recognized him and some kind souls hurried to inform the ambassador of the identity of the nuisance: pale with anger, Delaye promised to have this 'furious madman' expelled from Iran but, moved either by the tortures the young man had undergone or by his surname and the relationship he might have with the late Maréchal of the same name, he did nothing; nor did the Iranians, who might have had other fish to fry, instead of worrying about foreign revolutionaries — they didn't put him on the first plane to Paris, which they must later have regretted.

"The fact remains that after this reception, we found him calmly sitting on the sidewalk in front of the Italian Embassy, a few steps from the door of his residence, smoking; he seemed to be talking to himself, or still muttering those unknown poems, like a mystic or a beggar, and I'm a little ashamed to confess that if a colleague hadn't insisted we bring him back to his place, I'd have gone up the Avenue de France in the other direction, abandoning Lyautey to his fate.

"'The Lyautey Affair' was mentioned two days later by Charles-Henri de Fouchécour, then Director of our Institute, who must have been severely reprimanded by the Embassy; Fouchécour is a great scholar, so he was able to forget the incident almost immediately and plunge back into his beloved princely mirrors, and while we should have been worried about Lyautey's health, we all—friends, researchers, authorities—preferred not to get involved."

Gilbert de Morgan paused in his narrative to empty his glass, still full of ice cubes; Sarah again threw me a worried glance, even though nothing in the calm discourse of the scholar hinted at the slightest trace of intoxication—I couldn't help but think that he too, like Lyautey whose story he was telling, bore a famous surname, famous at least in Iran: Jacques de Morgan was the founder, after Dieulafoy, of French archaeology in Persia. Did Gilbert share any kinship with the official pillager of tombs of the French Third Republic, I have no idea. Night was falling over Zafariniyeh and the sun was finally beginning to disappear behind the foliage of the plane trees. The Avenue Vali-Asr must have been a huge traffic jam at that hour—so blocked that there was no point in blaring your horn, which brought a little calm to the garden of the tiny villa where Morgan, after pouring himself another glass, continued with his story:

"We didn't hear any more of Fred Lyautey for some weeks—he would appear from time to time at the Institute, have tea with us without saying anything special, and leave. His physical appearance had become normal again; he didn't take part in our discussions on the social and political agitation; he would just look at us and smile with a vaguely superior air, perhaps a tiny bit scornful, in any case it was extremely irritating, as if he was the only one who understood the events that were occurring. The Revolution was underway, even though, in early 1978, in the circles we frequented, no one could believe in the fall of the Shah—and yet, the Pahlavi dynasty had no more than a year left.

"Around the end of February (it was not long after the 'uprising' in Tabriz), I saw Lyautey again at the Café Naderi, by chance. He was in the company of a magnificent, not to say sublime, young woman, a student of French literature named Azra, whom I had already seen once or twice and, why prevaricate, noticed for her great beauty. I was flabbergasted to find her in the company of Lyautey. At the time, he spoke Persian so well that he could pass for an Iranian. Even his features had been slightly transformed, his complexion had gotten a little darker, it seemed to me, and I think he was dyeing his hair, which he wore shoulder-length, in the Iranian style. He called himself Farid Lahouti, since he thought it sounded like Fred Lyautey."

Sarah interrupted: "Lahouti, like the poet?"

"Yes, or like the rug merchant in the bazaar, go figure. Still, the waiters, all of whom he knew, greeted him with *Agha-ye Lahouti* here, *Agha-ye Lahouti* there, so much so that I wonder if he himself ended up believing that was his real family name. It was absolutely ridiculous and annoyed us no end, out of jealousy no doubt, since his Persian was really perfect: he had mastered all the registers, the spoken language as well as the meanderings of classical Persian. I found out later that he had even managed to obtain, God knows how, a student's card in the name of Farid Lahouti, a card with his photograph on it. I have to confess, I was shocked to discover him there, in the company of Azra, at the Café Naderi—which was our regular haunt. Why had he brought her precisely to that place? At the time there were many cafés and bars in Tehran, not at all like today. I imagined he wanted to be seen with her. Or perhaps it was a simple coincidence. Still, I sat down with them," Morgan sighed, "and an hour later I was no longer the same man."

He was looking into his glass, concentrating on the vodka, on his memories; perhaps he saw a face in the liquid, a phantom.

"I was bewitched by the beauty, the grace, the delicacy of Azra."

His voice had lowered a tone. He was talking to himself. Sarah threw me a glance as if to say "he is completely drunk." I wanted to find out more, to learn what had happened next, at the Café Naderi, in the middle of the revolution—I had been there, in that café where Sadegh Hedayat was a regular, Sarah had taken me there; like all the cafés in post-revolutionary Tehran, the place was a little depressing, not because you could no longer drink alcohol there, but because the young people who emptied their fake Pepsis while gazing into each other's eyes or the poets who read the paper there with a cigarette dangling from their lips all looked a little sad, defeated, crushed by the Islamic Republic; the Café Naderi was a vestige, a remnant from long ago, a memory of the center of the city from before, when it was open and cosmopolitan, and thus apt now to propel its customers into profound nostalgia.

Sarah was waiting for Gilbert de Morgan to either continue his story or collapse, conquered by the Armenian vodka, onto the well-cut grass of the little garden in front of the terrace; I was wondering if we'd do better to leave, go back down to the lower part of the city, but the prospect of finding ourselves in an immense traffic jam in this heat was not very encouraging. The Tehran metro was far enough from the little villa in Zafariniyeh that, on foot, you'd be sure to reach it soaked in sweat, especially Sarah, under her Islamic headscarf and her *roopoosh*. It was better to stay a little while longer in this typically Iranian garden, savoring the nougats from Ispahan offered by Nassim Khanom, even playing a little game of croquet in the tender grass, which had remained green thanks to the care of the tenant and the shadow of the tall trees, to stay until the temperature fell a little and the high mountains seemed to inhale the heat from the valleys around sunset.

Morgan paused for a long while, a somewhat embarrassing pause for those listening. He was no longer looking at us; he was gazing into his empty glass at the sun's reflections transforming the ice cubes into fragile diamonds. Finally he raised his head.

"I don't know why I'm telling you all this, forgive me."

Sarah turned to me, as if to seek my approbation — or to apologize for the hypocritical platitude of her next phrase:

"You're not boring us at all, on the contrary. The Revolution is a fascinating period."

The Revolution immediately snapped Morgan out of his reverie.

"It was a rumbling that grew louder, now muffled, now louder, every forty days. At the end of March, for the commemoration of those who died in Tabriz, there were demonstrations in several large cities in Iran. Then more on May 10, and so on. *Arbein*. The forty-days' mourning. The Shah had taken measures, though, to pacify the opposition — replacing the bloodiest leaders of the SAVAK, ending censorship and allowing freedom of the press, freeing a number of political prisoners. So much so that in May the CIA sent a famous memo to its government, in which its agents posted in Iran stated that 'the situation was returning to normal and Iran was not in a prerevolutionary, even less revolutionary, situation.' But the rumbling became even more amplified. Ordered to fight against inflation, the main complaint of the people, the Prime Minister, Jamshid Amouzegar, had applied a draconian measure: he had systematically put a damper on activity — cut off public investments, stopped the government's large building projects, and put in place systems of fines and humiliations against 'profiteers,' mainly the bazaar merchants who passed along price increases. This rigorous policy had been crowned with success: in two years, he had gotten the economic crisis under control, and had brilliantly succeeded at replacing inflation with a massive, urban unemployment rate, alienating not just the middle and working classes, but also the traditional merchant bourgeoisie. Which is to say that in fact, aside from his huge family who were conspicuously spending the billions from oil pretty much all over the world, and a few corrupt generals parading through the weapons exhibitions and the salons of the American Embassy, Reza Shah Pahlavi no longer had any real support in 1978. He was floating over everyone. Even those who had gotten rich thanks to him, those who had benefited from the free education, those who had learned to read thanks to his literacy campaigns — in short everyone he naively thought should have been grateful to him desired his departure. His only supporters were so by default.

"As for us, young French scholars, we were following the events from something of a distance, along with our Iranian colleagues; but no one, and I mean no one (aside possibly from our intelligence services at the embassy, but I doubt it) could imagine what lay in wait for us the following year. Except for Frédéric Lyautey, of course, who was not only *imagining* what could happen — the overthrow of the Shah, the Revolution — but *desired* it. He was a revolutionary. We saw less and less of him. I knew through Azra that he was active, like her, in an 'Islamist' (the word had another meaning at the time), progressive splinter group that wanted to apply the revolutionary ideas of Ali Shariati. I asked Azra if Lyautey had converted — she looked at me in an entirely surprised way, without understanding. For her, obviously, Lahouti was so Iranian that his Shiism *went without saying* and, if he'd had to convert, that had happened a long time ago. Of course, and I want to insist on this, Iranology and

Islamology have always attracted religious nutcases to a degree. Someday I'll tell you the story of the French colleague who during Khomeini's funeral in 1989 wept copiously, crying out 'Emam is dead! Emam is dead!' and almost died of sorrow in Behesht-e Zahra, in the middle of the crowd in the cemetery, sprinkled with rosewater by the helicopters. She had discovered Iran a few months earlier. That was not the case for Lyautey. He wasn't devout, I know that. He had neither the zeal of the converted nor that mystical force you sense in some people. It's incredible, but he was simply Shiite like any other Iranian, naturally and simply. Out of empathy. I'm not even sure he was a real believer. But Shariati's ideas on 'red Shiism,' the Shiism of martyrdom, revolutionary action, faced with the 'black Shiism' of mourning and passivity, inflamed him. The possibility that Islam could be a force for renewal, that Iran could draw the concepts of its own revolution from itself, filled him with enthusiasm. As well as Azra and thousands of other Iranians. What I found amusing (and I wasn't the only one) is that Shariati had been trained in France; he had attended the classes of Massignon and Berque; Lazard had directed his thesis. Ali Shariati, the most Iranian or at least the most Shiite of the thinkers of the Revolution, had constructed his thinking around French Orientalists. That should please you, Sarah. One more stone to add to your cosmopolitan concept of 'common construction,' Does Edward Said mention Shariati?"

"Um, yes, I think, in *Culture and Imperialism*. But I forget in what terms."

Sarah had bit her lip before replying; she hated being caught out. As soon as we got back, she'd hurry to the library—and complain if by chance Said's complete works weren't there. Morgan took advantage of this detour in the conversation to pour himself another little glass of vodka, without insisting, thank goodness, that we accompany him. Two birds were flitting around us, occasionally perching on the table to try to peck at some seeds. They had yellow breasts; their heads and tails were bluish. Morgan kept making wide, comical-looking gestures to try to scare them away, as if they were flies or hornets. He had changed a lot since Damascus and even since Paris and Sarah's thesis defense, when I had seen him before going to Tehran. Because of his beard, his hair plastered back in sections, and his clothes from a different era—his satchel with its blue-and-black imitation leather, a promotional gift from Iran Air in the 1970s; his cream-colored jacket, grimy at the elbows and along the zipper—because of all these fragile details that were accumulating on his body, and because of his breathing, which was becoming increasingly more labored, we thought he was falling, that he was in free fall. The slightly neglected aspect sometimes presented by some academics, scholarly and absent-minded by nature, was not the issue here. Sarah thought he had come down with one of those diseases of the soul that devour you in solitude; in Paris, she said, he treated this disorder with red wine, in his little two-room apartment, where bottles were lined up in front of the bookshelf, under the respectable *divans* of classical Persian poets. And here, in Tehran, with Armenian vodka. This great professor was full of bitterness, even though his career seemed to me brilliant, entirely enviable, even; he was respected worldwide; he was earning sums that were no doubt stupendous thanks to his new post abroad and yet he was falling. He was falling, and was trying to catch himself in his fall, catch hold of branches, women especially, young women, he sought to cling to their smiles, their gazes, which gnawed at his wounded soul, painful balms on an open wound. Sarah had known him for over ten years, and was afraid of finding herself alone with him, especially if he'd been drinking: not because the old scholar was a fearful tiger, but because she wanted to avoid humiliating him, avoid making him feel rejected, which would only have aggravated his melancholy, if she had been forced to turn him down. As for me, I thought the eminent professor, great specialist in Persian and European lyric poetry, who knew Hafez as well as Petrarch by heart, Nima Yooshij as well as Germain Nouveau, was just showing all the symptoms of the noonday devil, or rather the three-in-the-afternoon demon, considering his age; the climacteric is hard for an inveterate seducer, a man whose ruins showed he had once been handsome and charismatic, and it seemed likely to set off a definite moroseness, a moroseness interspersed with desperate manic phases, like the one we were witnessing, in the midst of the roses and birds, the bergamot and the nougat, in this heat that was weighing more heavily over Tehran than all the veils of Islam.

"After our meeting, we saw Lyautey regularly, with Azra, throughout 1978. She was officially Frédéric Lyautey's 'fiancée,' or rather Farid Lahouti's, with whom she spent her time agitating, demonstrating, discussing the future of Iran, the possibility and then the reality of the Revolution. The Shah was putting pressure on the neighboring Iraqi government, during the summer, for it to expel Khomeini from Nadjaf, thinking this would cut him off from the Iranian opposition. Khomeini was in the Parisian suburbs in Neauphle-le-Château, with all the power of the Western media in his hands. Much farther away from Tehran, indeed, but infinitely closer to the ears and hearts of his compatriots. Once again, the measures taken by the Shah were turning against him. Khomeini called for a general strike and paralyzed the country, all the administrations, and especially—much more serious for the regime—the oil industry. Farid and Azra took part in the occupation of the campus of the University of Tehran, then in the clashes with the Army which would lead to the riots of November 4, 1978: the violence was becoming general, Tehran was in flames. The British Embassy partly burned down; shops, bars, banks, post offices burned—

anything that represented the empire of the Shah or Western influence was attacked. The next morning, November 5, I was with Azra at my place. She had come by without warning around nine in the morning, more beautiful than ever, despite her air of sadness. She was absolutely irresistible. She was floating in the burning wind of freedom that was blowing over Iran. Her face was so harmonious, sculpted with shadows, delicate, her lips the color of pomegranate seeds, her complexion slightly dark; she gave off the scent of sandalwood and warm sugar. Her skin was a balsam talisman, which made anyone she came in contact with lose their reason. The sweetness of her voice was such that she could have consoled a dead man. Speaking, exchanging words with Azra was so hypnotic that very quickly you let yourself be lulled without replying, you became a faun put to sleep by the breath of an archangel. In that mid-autumn, the light was still splendid; I prepared some tea, the sun was pouring onto my tiny balcony, which overlooked a little *koucheh* parallel to the Avenue Hafez. She had come to my place only once, with a party of the little group from the Café Naderi, before the summer. Most of the time, we would see each other in cafés. I spent my life outside. I haunted those bistros in the hope of seeing her. And now she was turning up at my apartment, at nine in the morning, after crossing a city in chaos on foot! She had remembered the address. The day before, she told me, she had witnessed clashes between the students and the army on campus. The soldiers had fired real bullets, some young people had died, she was still trembling with emotion. The confusion was so great that it had taken her hours to get away from the university and reach her parents' house. They had formally forbidden her from returning—she had disobeyed. Tehran is at war, she said. The city smelled of fire; a mix of burning tires and burnt trash. Curfew had been declared. Curfews—that's the Shah's political strategy. That very afternoon he announced a military government, saying: 'People of Iran, you have risen up against oppression and corruption. As Shah of Iran and an Iranian, I can only salute this revolution of the Iranian Nation. I have heard the message of your revolution, people of Iran.' I too had seen, from my window, the smoke from the riots, heard the shouts and the noises of windows being broken on the Avenue Hafez, seen dozens of young men running down my dead-end street — were they looking for a bar or a restaurant with a Western name to attack? The orders from the embassy were clear, stay home. Wait for the storm to end.

"Azra was worried, she couldn't stand still. She was afraid for Lyautey. She had lost sight of him during a demonstration three days earlier. She hadn't heard any news of him. She had called him a thousand times, had gone to his place, had gone to the University of Tehran to find him despite her parents' interdiction. Without success. She was terribly anxious and the only person she knew among his 'French friends' was me."

The mention of Azra and the revolution gave Morgan a slightly alarming air. His passion had become cold; his face remained impassive, immersed in memory; while he spoke he was looking at his glass, clutching it with both hands, profane chalice of memory. Sarah was showing signs of embarrassment, boredom possibly, or both. She kept crossing and uncrossing her legs, tapping the arm of her wicker chair, playing absent-mindedly with a sweet before finally setting it down, uneaten, in the saucer her glass rested on.

"That was the first time we had spoken of Lyautey. Usually Azra avoided the subject out of modesty; me out of jealousy. I have to admit it: I had no wish whatsoever to inquire into the fate of that madman. He had stolen the object of my passion from me. He could go to the devil, it was all the same to me. Azra was at my place, that was enough for my happiness. I was counting on taking advantage of this for as long as possible. So

I told her it was very likely that Lyautey would call or come by my place without warning, as was his habit, which obviously was a lie.

"She stayed for most of the day. She reassured her parents on the phone, telling them she was safe at a girlfriend's. We watched TV and listened to the BBC at the same time. We heard the shouts, the sirens in the street. Sometimes we thought we heard gunfire. We could see smoke rising up over the city. Both of us sitting on the sofa. I can even remember the color of that couch. That moment has been following me for years. The violence of that moment. The pain of that moment, the smell of Azra on my hands."

Sarah dropped her cup; it bounced, rolled into the grass without breaking. She got up from her seat to pick it up. Morgan stared for a long time at her legs, then her hips, without attempting to hide it. Sarah didn't sit back down; she remained standing in the garden, looking at the strange, irregular façade of the villa. Morgan again chased away the blue birds with the back of his hand and poured himself another glass, this time without ice. He muttered something in Persian, some lines from a poem probably, I thought I caught a rhyme. Sarah started pacing up and down the little property; she looked at each rose bush, each pomegranate tree, each Japanese cherry tree. I could imagine her thoughts, her embarrassment, her pain even at hearing her adviser's confession. Morgan wasn't speaking to anyone. The vodka was having its effect, I imagined that quite soon he'd start crying a drunkard's tears, feeling sorry once and for all for his fate. I wasn't sure I wanted to hear him out to the end, but before Sarah could come back and give me a chance to get up in turn, Morgan resumed his story, in a voice that was even lower and more breathless:

"I admit that the temptation was too strong. Being there next to her, almost touching her . . . I remember her frosty surprise

when I revealed my passion to her. Unfortunately she was—
how should I put it—indisposed. Like in *Vis and Ramin*, the
novel of love. The memory of the ancient romance woke me
up. I became afraid. I ended up accompanying her back at the
end of the afternoon. We had to skirt round the ravaged center
of the city, occupied by the army. Azra walked with her eyes on
the ground. Then I went back home alone. I'll never forget that
evening. I felt both happy and sad.

"Lyautey ended up reappearing in a military hospital in the
northern part of the city. He had gotten hit badly in the head,
the authorities notified the Embassy which called the Institute.
I immediately jumped into a car to visit his sickbed. In front of
his door an officer from the army or the police was standing, his
chest covered in medals; he apologized, with all Iranian polite-
ness, for this mistake. But you know, he said, smiling ironically,
it's not easy to distinguish an Iranian from a Frenchman in the
middle of a violent demonstration. Especially a Frenchman
who's shouting slogans in Persian. Lyautey was covered in bandages. He looked exhausted. He began by telling me that the
Shah didn't have much time left, I agreed. I then explained to
him that Azra was looking for him, that she was worried to death;
he asked me to call her to reassure her—I offered to deliver a
letter to her in person that very evening if he liked. He thanked
me warmly for this solicitude. He wrote a brief note in Persian
while I watched. He had to stay under observation for three
more days. I then went to the Embassy; I spent the rest of the
day convincing our dear diplomats that, for his own good, they
should send Lyautey back to France. That he was crazy. That
he was calling himself Farid Lahouti, that he was assuming an
Iranian identity, that he was agitating, that he was dangerous to
himself. Then I went to Azra's to give her Fred's note. She didn't
let me in, didn't even favor me with a glance; she stayed behind
the half-open door, which she slammed as soon as the paper

was in her hands. Four days later, discharged from the clinic, officially repatriated for reasons of health, Fred Lyautey was on the plane to Paris. Actually, expelled by the Iranians through the Embassy's intervention, he was forbidden to return to Iran.

"So I had Azra all to myself. But I had to convince her to forgive my impulsiveness, which I bitterly regretted. She was very affected by the departure of Lyautey, who wrote to her from Paris, saying that he was the victim of a monarchist conspiracy and he would return 'at the same time as freedom did to Iran.' In these letters, he called me 'his only French friend, the only Frenchman he trusted in Tehran.' Because of the strikes that were paralyzing the mail, he wrote to me via the diplomatic pouch, asking me to pass them on. One or two letters a day, which I received in packets of eight or ten a week. I couldn't help but read them, these letters, and they made me mad with jealousy. Long erotic poems in Persian, of extraordinary beauty. Desperate songs of love, somber odes illuminated by the winter sun of love which I was to carry to the mailbox of the interested party. Carrying these letters myself to Azra tore apart my heart every time with impotent rage. It was a real torture—Lyautey's unconscious revenge. I acted as the postman only in the hope of meeting Azra on the ground floor of her building. Sometimes the pain was so strong that I burned some of those envelopes after opening them—when the poems were too beautiful, too erotic, too likely to reinforce Azra's love for Lahouti, when they made me suffer too much, I destroyed them.

"In December, the Revolution gained the upper hand, grew even stronger. The Shah was secluded in his Niavaran palace, you sensed he'd only emerge feet first. The military government was obviously incapable of reforming the country, and the administrations were still paralyzed by the strikes. Despite the curfew and the ban on demonstrations, the opposition continued to organize; the role of the clergy, in Iran as well as in exile, became more and more prominent. The religious calendar was no help: December was the month of *Muharram*. The celebration of the martyrdom of Imam Husayn promised to give rise to massive demonstrations. Once again, it was the Shah himself who precipitated his own fall; faced with the pressure from the clerics, he authorized the peaceful religious marches on 10 *Muharram, Ashura*. Millions of people marched throughout the country. Tehran was taken over by the crowd. Strangely, there was no major incident. It felt as if the opposition had reached such a mass, such a power, that violence was now pointless. The Avenue Reza-Shah was a great human river that flowed into Shahyad Square, which had become a trembling lake overlooked by the monument to royalty that seemed to be changing its meaning—it was becoming a monument to the Revolution, to freedom and to the power of the people. I think all the foreigners present in Tehran in those days remember the impression of extraordinary force that emanated from that crowd. In the name of Imam Husayn forsaken by his own people, in the name of justice faced with tyranny, Iran was rising. We all knew that day that the regime would fall. We all believed that day that the era of democracy was beginning.

"In France, Frédéric Lyautey, with his mad determination, had offered his services to Khomeini in Neauphle-le-Château as an interpreter: for a few weeks he was one of the imam's many secretaries; he answered the mail from French admirers on his behalf. The cleric's entourage mistrusted him, they thought he was a spy, which upset him terribly—he telephoned me often, in a very friendly tone, commented on the latest news of the Revolution, told me how lucky I was to be on the ground during those 'historic' moments. He apparently was unaware of the scheming that had been done to get him expelled and of my passion for Azra. She hadn't told him anything. In fact he was the one who urged her to come back to me. Azra's father was arrested at his home on December 12 and sent to a place that was kept secret, probably the Evin Prison. Almost no one was being arrested at that time; the Shah was trying to negotiate with the opposition to bring an end to the military government and, in one last desire for reform, to call for free elections afterward. The arrest of Azra's father, a simple secondary school teacher and a recent member of the Toudeh Party, was a mystery. The Revolution seemed inevitable, but the repressive machine kept working bizarrely in the shadows, in an absurd way—no one understood why this particular man had been jailed, when the day before or the day before that, millions of others were shouting 'death to the Shah' openly in the streets. On December 14, there was a counterdemonstration in favor of the regime; a few thousand henchmen and soldiers in mufti marched in turn, holding up portraits of the Pahlavis. We obviously couldn't foresee events, couldn't guess that a month later the Shah would be forced to leave the country. The anguish of Azra's family was all the stronger since the confusion and revolutionary energy were at its highest point. It was Lyautey who, by phone, convinced Azra of the necessity of contacting me. She called me not long before Christmas; I didn't want to go back to France for the holidays; believe it or not, I didn't want to go far away from her. Finally I would see her again. In that month and a half, my passion had only increased. I hated myself and desired Azra to the point of madness."

Sarah had come close to the garden table; she was still standing, her hands on the back of her chair, watching, impartial. She was listening with a distant, almost scornful air. I made a movement with my head toward her, a sign that for me meant "shall we go?" to which she did not respond. I was torn (as she was too, probably) between the desire to learn the end of the story and a certain shame mingled with propriety that made me want to run away from this scholar lost in his passionate, revolutionary memories. Morgan didn't seem aware of our hesitations; he seemed to find it entirely normal that Sarah was still standing; he would no doubt have continued his reminiscences all by himself if we had left. He interrupted himself only for a swig of vodka or a lustful gaze at Sarah's body. The housekeeper hadn't reappeared, she had taken refuge inside, no doubt she had other things to do besides watching her employer get drunk.

"Azra asked me to use my connections to get information about her father's detention. Her mother, she told me, was imagining the craziest possibilities — that her father had actually been leading a double life, that he was a Soviet agent, things like that. Lyautey had seen me, from his hospital bed, having a lively conversation with an officer covered in medals; his madness had concluded that I personally knew all the chiefs of the SAVAK. I didn't disabuse Azra. I asked her to come to my place to talk it over, which she refused. I suggested we meet at the Café Naderi, assuring her that in the meantime I'd have looked into her father's situation. She agreed. My joy was boundless. It was the first day of the month of *Dey*, the winter solstice; I went to a poetry reading: a young woman was reading *Let Us Believe in the Beginning of the Cold Season*, by Forugh Farrokhzad, especially 'I Feel Sorry for the Garden,' whose simple and profound sorrow froze my soul, I don't know why — I still know that poem half by heart, '*kasi be fekr-e golha nist, kasi be fekr-e mahiha nist*,' 'there is no one to think of the flowers, no one to think of the fish, no one wants to believe the garden is dying.' I suppose the prospect of seeing Azra again had made me extremely sensitive to all the sorrows of others. Forugh's poetry filled me with a snowy sadness; that abandoned garden with its empty basin and its weeds was the portrait of my own dereliction. After the reading, everyone gathered for drinks — unlike me, the company was quite cheerful, vibrant with revolutionary hope: all the talk was about the end of the military government and the possible nomination of Shahpur Bakhtiar, a moderate opponent, to the post of Prime Minister. Some even went so far as to predict the imminent abdication of the Shah. Many wondered about the army's reactions—would the generals attempt a coup d'état, supported by the Americans? This 'Chilean' hypothesis frightened everyone. The stinging memory of the overthrow of Mossadegh in 1957 was more present than ever. I paced in circles that evening. I was asked many times for news of Lahouti, I evaded the question and quickly moved on to someone else. Most of those present—students, young professors, budding writers—knew Azra. I learned from one of the guests that ever since Lyautey had left she had stopped going out.

"I asked a friend at the Embassy about Azra's father—he immediately sent me packing. If he's an Iranian, nothing can be done. Even for someone with dual citizenship, it's difficult. Plus everything's a mess now in the administration, we wouldn't even know who to ask. He was probably lying. So I myself was forced to lie. Azra sat opposite me at the Café Naderi; she was wearing a thick cabled wool jumper, over which her black hair shone; she didn't look me in the eyes, or shake my hand; she greeted me in a tiny voice. I began by apologizing at length for my mistakes of the month before, for my abruptness, then I spoke to her of love, my passion for her, with all the gentleness I could muster. Then I mentioned my investigation into her father's situation; I assured her I'd get results very soon, probably the next day. I told her that seeing her so worried and dejected made me very sad, and that I would do everything I could so long as she visited me again. I begged her. She kept looking elsewhere, at the waiters, the customers, the white tablecloth, the painted chairs. Her eyes shone. She remained silent. I was not ashamed. I'm still not ashamed. If you've never been overwhelmed by passion you can't understand."

As for us, we were ashamed—Morgan was slumping more and more over the table; I saw Sarah stunned, petrified by how the confession had developed; I had only one desire, to leave this burning garden—it was just seven o'clock. The birds were playing between the shadows and the setting sun. I stood up in turn.

I too had strolled a little in the garden. Morgan's villa in Zafariniyeh was a magical place, a doll house, probably built for the guardian of a grand estate which had since disappeared, which would explain its strange location, almost on the edge of Avenue Vali-Asr. Morgan had rented it from one of his Iranian friends. The first time I went there, at Morgan's invitation, in the winter, not long before our trip to Bandar Abbas, when the snow covered everything, the rose bushes shone with frost, there was a fire in the fireplace—an Oriental fireplace, whose rounded hood and pointed mantelpiece were reminiscent of the fireplaces in the Topkapi Palace in Istanbul. Everywhere, precious rugs with bright but subtle colors, purples, blues, oranges; on the walls, china from the Qajar dynasty and costly miniatures. The living room was small, with a low ceiling, suitable for winter; the professor would recite poems there by Hafez—for years he had been trying to learn all of the *Divan* by heart, like the scholars of long ago: he asserted that learning Hafez by heart was the only way to learn intimately what he called the *space* of the ghazal, the way the lines linked together, the structure of the poems, the reappearance of characters and themes; knowing Hafez was like having an intimate experience of love. "I'm afraid my tears will betray my sorrow and that this mystery will go round the world. Hafez, you who hold the musk of her hair in your hand, hold your breath, otherwise the zephyr will blow away your secret!" Penetrate the mystery, or mysteries—phonetic mysteries, metrical mysteries, mysteries of metaphors. Alas, the fourteenth-century poet rejected the old Orientalist:

despite all his efforts, remembering all of the 480 ghazals that make up the *Divan* turned out to be impossible. He would mix up the order of the lines, forget some of them; the aesthetic rules of the collection, especially the unity of each of the distichs, perfect as pearls threaded one by one on the line of meter and rhyme to produce the necklace of the ghazal, made them easy to forget. Out of the four thousand lines the work contains, Morgan lamented, I know maybe thirty-five hundred. I still lack five hundred. Still. They're never the same. Some appear, others go away. They compose a cloud of fragments that stands between Truth and me.

These mystical considerations by the fireside we had taken for the expression of a literary whim, the latest fad of a scholar — the revelations of that summer gave them an entirely different meaning. Secrecy, love, guilt, we could glimpse their source. And if I wrote this grave and solemn text when I got back to Vienna it's probably to record them in turn, as much as to rediscover, through prose, the presence of Sarah who had gone — plunged into mourning, overwhelmed — to confront her sadness in Paris. What a strange sensation, rereading yourself. An aging mirror. I am attracted and repulsed by this former self as by another. A first souvenir, inserted between memory and me. A diaphanous leaf of paper that light passes through to outline other images on it. A stained-glass window. *I* is in the night. Being exists always in this distance, somewhere between an unfathomable self and the other in oneself. In the sensation of time. In love, which is the impossibility of fusion between self and other. In art, the experience of otherness.

We couldn't manage to leave any more than Morgan could finish his story — he continued his confession, perhaps just as surprised by his ability to speak as by ours to listen. Despite all my signaling, Sarah, although revolted, remained clinging to her wrought iron garden chair.

"Azra finally agreed to come back to my place. Several times even. I told her lies about her father. On January 16, following the advice of his general staff, the Shah left Iran, supposedly 'on vacation,' and turned power over to a transitional government led by Shahpur Bakhtiar. Bakhtiar's first measures were the dissolution of the SAVAK and the liberation of all political prisoners. Azra's father did not reappear. I think no one ever found out what had become of him. The Revolution seemed over. An Air France Boeing brought Ayatollah Khomeini back to Tehran two weeks later, against the advice of the government. Hundreds of thousands of people welcomed him like the Mahdi. I had only one fear: that Lyautey was on the plane. But he wasn't. He would come very soon, he told Azra in those letters that I read. He assured her of his love; just a few more days, he said, and soon we'll be reunited, be brave. He did not understand the pain and shame she spoke to him about, he said, without giving him reasons for them.

"Azra was so sad, during our meetings, that little by little I ended up being disgusted with myself. I loved her passionately and wanted her to be happy, joyful, passionate as well. My caresses drew only cold tears from her. I might possess her beauty, but she escaped me. The winter was endless, freezing and dark. Around us, Iran was veering into chaos. For an instant we'd thought the Revolution was over, but it was only beginning. Khomeini's clerics and supporters fought against the moderate democrats. A few days after he returned to Iran, Khomeini had appointed his own parallel Prime Minister, Mehdi Bazargan. Bakhtiar had become an enemy of the people, the last representative of the Shah. We began hearing slogans shouted in favor of an 'Islamic Republic.' In every neighborhood, a revolutionary committee was organized. 'Organized' is a bit of an overstatement. Weapons abounded. Cudgels, truncheons, then, after a meeting with part of the army on February 11, assault rifles: Khomeini's supporters occupied all the administrative buildings and even the emperor's palace. Bazargan became the first government leader appointed not by the Shah, but by the Revolution—actually by Khomeini. You could sense danger, imminent catastrophe. The revolutionary forces were so disparate that it was impossible to guess what form the new regime might take. Communists from the Toudeh Party, Marxist-Muslims, the Mujahedeen of the People, Khomeinyite clerics who supported the *velayat-e faqih*, pro-Bakhtiar liberals, and even Kurdish autonomists struggled more or less directly for power. There was complete freedom of speech and publications appeared left and right—newspapers, pamphlets, poetry collections. The economy was in a catastrophic state; the country was so disorganized that basic products started to go missing. The opulence of Tehran seemed to have disappeared overnight. Despite everything, we found ourselves among friends; we ate tin after tin of smuggled caviar with big greenish grains, with *sangak* bread and Soviet vodka—we bought all that in dollars. Some people were beginning to fear a total collapse of the country and were looking for foreign currency.

"I had known for some time why Lyautey hadn't returned to Iran: he was hospitalized in a clinic in the Parisian suburbs. Serious depression, hallucinations, delirium. He spoke only Persian and was convinced his actual name was Farid Lahouti. The doctors thought it was linked to overexertion and shock connected with the Iranian Revolution. His letters to Azra became even more numerous; more numerous and darker every time. He didn't tell her about his hospitalization, only his torments of love, of exile, of his suffering. Images kept reoccurring, glowing embers that turned into charcoal, hard and friable, in absence; a tree with branches of ice killed by the winter sun; a foreigner faced with the mystery of a flower that never opens. Since he himself didn't mention it, I didn't reveal Lyautey's state of health to Azra. My blackmail and my lies weighed on me. I wanted Azra to be mine completely; possessing her body was only a foretaste of an even more complete pleasure. I tried to be attentive, to charm her, not to force her anymore. More than once I was about to reveal the truth to her, the whole truth — my ignorance about her father's situation, Lyautey's state in Paris, my scheming to get him expelled. My mystifications were actually proofs of love. I had only lied out of passion, and I hoped she would understand.

"Azra realized that her father would probably never come back. All the Shah's prisoners had already been freed, quickly replaced in the prisons by the supporters and soldiers of the old regime. Blood flowed — they hastily executed soldiers and high-ranking civil servants. Khomeini's Revolutionary Council now saw Mehdi Bazargan, its own Prime Minister, as an obstacle to the establishment of the Islamic Republic. These first confrontations, and later the transformation of the Committees into 'Guardians of the Revolution' and 'Volunteers for the Oppressed,' prepared the ground for the confiscation of power. Given over entirely to revolutionary exuberance, the middle classes and the most powerful political groups (the Toudeh Party, the Democratic Front, the Mujahedeen of the People) didn't seem to realize the rising danger. The itinerant revolutionary tribunal headed by Sadegh Khalkhali *aka* The Butcher, both judge and executioner, was already underway. Despite all that, at the end of March, after a referendum advocated among others by the Communists and the Mujahedeen, the Empire of Iran became the Islamic Republic of Iran, and launched into the redrafting of its Constitution.

"Azra had apparently abandoned the theories of Shariati and

had grown closer to the Communist Toudeh. She continued to agitate, took part in demonstrations and published feminist articles in the papers close to the Party. She had also gathered some of Farid Lahouti's poems, the most political ones, into a little collection that she had entrusted to no less than Ahmad Shamlou himself—already the most visible poet of the time, the most innovative, the most powerful—who had found it (even while he was not generous to the poetry of his contemporaries) magnificent: he was astounded to learn that this Lahouti was actually a French Orientalist, and had some of these texts published in influential journals. This success made me mad with jealousy. Even interned thousands of kilometers away, Lyautey managed to make my life impossible. I should have destroyed all those cursed letters instead of being content to throw just a few into the flames. In March, when Spring was returning, when the Iranian New Year was consecrating Year 1 of the Revolution, when the hope of an entire people was growing with the roses, a hope that would burn as surely as the roses, when I was making plans to marry the object of my passion, this stupid collection, because of the esteem of four intellectuals, was reinforcing the bond between Azra and Fred. She could talk of nothing but that. How much so-and-so had appreciated these poems. How such-or-such an actor would read these verses at a soirée organized by such-and-such a fashionable magazine. This triumph gave Azra the strength to despise me. I could feel her scorn in her gestures, in her gaze. Her guilt had transformed into a scornful hatred of me and all I represented—France, the University. I was in the process of scheming to get her a scholarship fund, so that, after my stay in Iran, we could move back to Paris together. I wanted to marry her. She contemptuously rejected all my ideas. Even worse: she refused herself to me. She just came to my apartment to taunt me, to talk to me about these poems and the Revolution, and pushed me away. Two months earlier I'd held her to me and now I was nothing but an abject wretch she rejected with horror."

Gilbert knocked over his glass while gesticulating too broadly at the birds who had gotten bold enough to peck at the candy crumbs on the table. He immediately poured himself another, and emptied his little goblet in one gulp. He had tears in his eyes, tears that didn't seem to come from the power of the alcohol. Sarah had sat back down. She was watching the two birds flitting to the shelter of the shrubbery. I knew she was wavering between compassion and anger; she looked away from him, but didn't leave. Morgan remained silent, as if the story were over. Nassim Khanom suddenly reappeared. She took away the glasses, the saucers, the dishes of candied fruit. She was wearing a dark-blue *roopoosh* knotted firmly under her chin and a gray blouse with a brown pattern; she didn't look once at her employer. Sarah smiled at her; she returned her smile, offering her tea or lemonade. Sarah thanked her kindly for her efforts, in the Iranian style. I realized I was dying of thirst, so I conquered my timidity and asked Nassim Khanom for a little more lemonade: my Persian pronunciation was so atrocious that she didn't understand me. Sarah came to my aid, as usual. I had the impression — oh how vexing — that she repeated exactly what I had just said, but this time, Nassim Khanom understood right away. I immediately imagined a conspiracy, by which this respectable lady ranked me on the side of men, on the side of her terrifying boss, who still remained silent, his eyes red with vodka and memory. Sarah noticed my vexed confusion and misinterpreted it; she stared at me for a bit, as if she were taking my hand to extract us from the lukewarm mud of this late afternoon, and her sudden tenderness pulled the bonds between us so taut that a child could play with them like rubber bands, in the middle of this sinister garden burned by summer.

Morgan had nothing more to add. He was revolving his glass

in his hand, over and over, eyes on the past. It was time to go. I pulled on those famous invisible strings and Sarah got up at the same time as me.

Thank you, Gilbert, for this wonderful afternoon. Thank you. Thank you.

I swallowed the glass of lemonade that Nassim Khanom had just brought. Gilbert didn't get up, muttered some Persian verses I couldn't hear a word of. Sarah was standing; she put her purple silk veil over her hair. I absentmindedly counted the freckles on her face. I thought about Azra, Sarah, almost the same sounds, the same letters. The same passion. Morgan too was looking at Sarah. Seated, his eyes were fixed on her hips hidden by the Islamic cloak that she had just put on despite the heat.

"What became of Azra?" I asked the question to shift his gaze from Sarah's body, stupidly, jealously, the way you remind a man of his wife's first name so her phonemes will whip him, along with the good Lord and moral Law.

Morgan turned to me, a look of suffering on his face:

"I don't know. They told me she had been executed by the regime. It's likely. Thousands of activists disappeared in the early 1980s. Men and women alike. The Homeland in danger. Iraqi aggression, instead of weakening the regime as planned, reinforced it, gave it an excuse to rid itself of all internal opposition. The young Iranians who'd lived between the Shah and the Islamic Republic, that middle class (a terrible expression) that had shouted, written, fought in favor of democracy, all ended up hanged in an obscure prison, killed on the front, or forced into exile. I left Iran soon after the start of the war; I returned eight years later, in 1989. It wasn't the same country anymore. The university was full of former combatants incapable of putting two words together, who had become students by the grace of the Basij militia. Students who would become teachers. Ignorant teachers who in turn trained students destined for mediocrity. All the poets, all the musicians, all the scholars were in internal exile, crushed by the dictatorship of mourning. All of them in the shadow of martyrs. With every bat of an eyelash, they were reminded of a martyr. Their streets, their alleys, their grocery stores bore the names of martyrs. The dead, the blood. The poetry of death, songs of the dead, flowers of death. Lyrical poetry turned into names of offensives: *Dawn I, Dawn II, Dawn III, Dawn IV, Dawn V, Kerbela I, Kerbela II, Kerbela III, Kerbela IV,* and so on until the Parousia of the Mahdi. I don't know where or when Azra died. In Evin Prison, probably. I died with her. Long before her. In 1979, Year 1 of the Revolution, solar Year 1357 of the Hegira. She didn't want to see me anymore. It was as simple as that. She dissolved into her shame. While Khomeini was fighting to consolidate his power, Azra, emboldened by her love of Lahouti's poems, left me once and for all. She had learned the truth, she said. A truth — how I had schemed to distance her lover, how I had lied about her father — but not *the* truth. The truth is my love for her, which she could see every instant we were together. That's the only truth. I've never been whole except those times when we were together. I never married. I've never made any promises to anyone. I've waited for her all my life.

"Fred Lyautey didn't have my patience. Lahouti hanged himself from an elm with a sheet, on the grounds of his clinic, in December 1980. Azra hadn't seen him for almost two years. A kind soul told her about his death. But Azra didn't come to the evening of homage we organized for Lyautey at the Institute. And none of those famous poets who supposedly respected his work came. It was a beautiful evening, meditative, fervent, intimate. He had designated me, with his usual grandiloquence, as his 'executor for his literary affairs.' I burned all his papers in a sink, along with mine. All the memories from that period. The photos contorted, yellow in the flames; the notebooks burned up, slow as logs."

We left. Gilbert de Morgan was still reciting mysterious poems. He made a little gesture with his hand at us when we passed through the gate in his garden wall. He remained alone with his housekeeper and that family of birds we call *Spechte* in German, often capped with red, that nest inside tree trunks.

In the taxi that brought us back to the center of Tehran, Sarah kept repeating "what a poor guy, good Lord, why tell us that, what nonsense," in an incredulous tone, as if, in the end, she couldn't bring herself to admit the truth of Gilbert de Morgan's story, couldn't convince herself that this man, whom she had known for over ten years, who had counted for so much in her professional life, was actually an other, a Faust who needed no Mephisto to sell his soul to Evil and possess Azra, a character all of whose knowledge was constructed on a moral imposture so great that it became unreal. Sarah couldn't grasp the truth of this story simply because he himself had told it. He couldn't be crazy enough to self-destruct, and so — at least this was Sarah's reasoning, Sarah's way of protecting herself — he was lying. He was inventing stories. He wanted us to blame him for God knows what obscure reason. Perhaps he was taking someone else's horrors on himself. If she was angry at him and called him a filthy pig, it was mostly because he had spattered us with these base acts, these betrayals. He couldn't confess so simply that he had raped and blackmailed that girl, he couldn't recount that so coldly, in his garden, drinking vodka, and I could sense her voice wavering. She was on the verge of tears, in that taxi that was rushing at top speed down the Modarres motorway, previously named, during the time of Azra and Farid, the motorway of the King of Kings. I was not convinced that Morgan was lying. On the contrary, the scene we had just witnessed, that settling of accounts with himself, seemed extraordinarily honest to me, even in its historical implications.

The twilight air was warm, dry, electric; it smelled of the burnt grass of flowerbeds and of all the lies of nature.

In the end I think I sympathized with him, this Gilbert de Morgan with the long face. Did he already know he was sick, on the afternoon of that confession? It's likely—two weeks later he left Iran once and for all for reasons of health. I don't remember showing this text to Sarah; I should send it to her, in a version with all the commentaries about her taken out. Would she be interested? She'd probably read these pages differently. Farid and Azra's love story would become a parable of imperialism and the Revolution. Sarah would contrast the characters of Lyautey and Morgan; she'd draw from it a meditation on the question of otherness: Fred Lyautey completely denied it and plunged into the other, thought he became the other, and almost succeeded, in madness; Morgan tried to possess it, that otherness, to dominate it, pull it toward him, appropriate it and take pleasure from it. It is extremely depressing to think that Sarah is incapable of reading a love story for what it is, a love story, that is, the abdication of reason in passion; it's *symptomatic*, the good doctor would say. She resists. For Sarah love is nothing but a bundle of contingencies, at best a universal potluck, at worst a game of domination in the mirror of desire. How sad. She's trying to protect herself from the pain of emotions, that's for sure. She wants to control whatever can affect her; she defends herself in advance from the blows that could hit her. She isolates herself.

All Orientalists, yesterday's as well as today's, ask themselves this question of difference, of self and other—not long after Morgan left, when my idol the musicologist Jean During had just arrived in Tehran, we received a visit from Gianroberto

Scarcia, eminent Italian specialist in Persian literature, student
of the brilliant Bausani, father of Italian Iranology. Scarcia was
an extraordinarily brilliant man, erudite, amusing; he was interested in, among other things, the Persian literature of Europe:
this expression, *Persian literature of Europe*, fascinated Sarah.
That classical poems could have been composed in Persian a
few kilometers away from Vienna up to the end of the nineteenth century delighted her just as much (even more, possibly) as the memory of the Arabic poets of Sicily, the Balearic
Islands or Valencia. Scarcia even argued that the last Persian
poet of the West, as he called him, was an Albanian who had
composed two novels in verse and written erotic ghazals until
the 1950s, between Tirana and Belgrade. The language of Hafez
had continued to irrigate the old continent after the Balkan War
and even the Second World War. What was fascinating, Scarcia
added with a childlike smile, is that these texts continued the
great tradition of classical poetry, but fed it with modernity—
just as Naim Frashëri, the bard of the Albanian nation, the last
Persian poet of the West, also composed in Albanian and even in
Turkish and Greek. But at a very different time: in the twentieth
century Albania was independent, and Turkish-Persian culture
was dying out in the Balkans. "What a strange position," Sarah
said, captivated, "that of a poet who writes in a language that no
one or almost no one, in his country, understands anymore, or
wants to understand!" And Scarcia, with a mischievous spark in
his clear eyes, added that a history of the Arab-Persian literature
of Europe should be written to rediscover this forgotten heritage. The other in the self. Scarcia seemed sad: "Unfortunately, a
large part of these treasures were destroyed with the libraries of
Bosnia in the early 1990s. These traces of a different Europe are
frowned upon. But books and manuscripts remain in Istanbul,
Bulgaria, Albania, and at Bratislava University. As you say, dear

Sarah, Orientalism should be a humanism." Sarah opened her eyes wide in astonishment—Scarcia must have read her article on Ignác Goldziher, Gershom Scholem, and Jewish Orientalism. Scarcia had read everything. From the height of his eighty years, he saw the world with a curiosity that was never disappointed.

The construction of a European identity as a friendly puzzle of nationalisms erased anything that didn't fit into ideological boxes. Goodbye difference, goodbye diversity.

A humanism based on what? What is universal? God, who makes Himself very discreet in the silence of the night? Between the throat-slitters, the starvers, the polluters—can the unity of the human condition still be based on anything? I have no idea. Knowledge, perhaps. Knowledge and the planet as a new horizon. Man as mammal. Complex residue of a carbon-based evolution. A plant rot. A bug. There's no more life in man than in a bug. Just as much. More matter, but just as much life. I complain about Dr. Kraus but my condition is enviable enough compared to that of an insect. The human species isn't doing its best these days. You want to take refuge in your books, your records and your memories of childhood. Turn off the radio. Or drown yourself in opium, like Faugier. He was there too during Gianroberto Scarcia's visit. He was returning from an expedition into the lower depths. That ever-joyful specialist in prostitution was concocting a lexicon of Persian slang, a dictionary of horrors—the technical terms for drugs, of course, but also the expressions of the male and female prostitutes he frequented. Faugier was AC/DC—or as the French say *"il marchait à voile et à vapeur,"* he used both sail and steam; he would tell us about his excursions, in his outspoken street-urchin way, like Victor Hugo's Gavroche, and often I wanted to block my ears. If you listened only to him, you could easily imagine that Tehran was a huge brothel for drug addicts—an exaggerated image but not entirely divorced from reality. One day while leaving Tajrish

Square in a taxi, the driver, very old—his steering wheel didn't seem to be affected by his violent trembling—had asked me the question very directly, almost point-blank: How much does a whore cost in Europe? He had had to repeat this phrase several times, so difficult did the word *jendeh* seem to me, both to pronounce and understand: I had never heard it in anyone's mouth. I'd had to justify my ignorance laboriously; the old man refused to believe I had never visited any prostitutes. Finally just to get some peace and quiet, I blurted out a number at random, which seemed to him incredible; he began laughing, and saying ah, now I understand why you don't go to whores! At that price, you might as well get married! He told me that as recently as yesterday, he had ridden a whore in his taxi. "After eight p.m.," he said, "women alone are usually whores. The one yesterday offered me her services."

He was zigzagging on the motorway at top speed, passing people on the right, blowing his horn, all the while shaking his steering wheel like a damned soul; he turned around to look at me and the old Paykan took advantage of his distraction to veer dangerously to the left.

"You are Muslim?"

"No, Christian."

"I'm a Muslim, but I like whores a lot. The one yesterday, she wanted twenty dollars."

"Oh."

"You think that's expensive too? Here, they're whores because they need money. It's sad. It's not like in Europe."

"In Europe it's not exactly a bed of roses either, you know."

"In Europe they take more pleasure from it. Here they don't."

I weakly left him to his certainties. The old man interrupted himself for a minute to illegally pass a bus and a huge Japanese 4x4. On the flowerbeds bordering the motorway, some gardeners were pruning the roses.

"'Twenty dollars is too much.' I said, 'Make me a deal! I'm old enough to be your grandfather!'"

"Oh."

"I know how to deal with whores."

When I got back to the Institute I told Sarah this extraordinary story, which didn't make her laugh at all, but Faugier found it hilarious. That was not long before he was attacked by the Bassijis; he had taken a few cudgel blows, without the motive for the quarrel being very clear — a political attack aimed at France or a "simple matter of morals," he never found out. Faugier dealt with his bruises with laughter and opium, and while he refused to go into the details of the confrontation, he repeated to anyone willing to listen that "sociology was really a combat sport." He reminded me of Lyautey in Morgan's story — he refused to take notice of the violence of which he was the object. We knew that Iran was a potentially dangerous country, where the henchmen of power, official or covert, didn't exactly worry themselves with kid-glove treatment, but we all thought we were protected by our nationalities and our status as academics — we were wrong. The internal upheavals in Iranian power could indeed reach us, without our really knowing why. The main person concerned here was not wrong, though: his research was his lifestyle, his lifestyle was part of his research, and danger was one of the reasons these subjects attracted him. He argued that you were more likely to get stabbed in a shady bar in Istanbul than in Tehran, and he was probably right. In any case his stay in Iran was coming to an end (to the great relief of the French Embassy); this thrashing, this hiding, he said, was like a sinister song of farewell, and his bruises were a gift, a souvenir of the Islamic Republic. Faugier's tastes, his passion for trouble, did not prevent him from being terribly lucid about his condition — he was his own object of study; he admitted that (like many Orientalists and diplomats who don't easily confess it) he had chosen the East — Turkey and Iran —

out of erotic desire for the Oriental body, an image of lascivious-
ness, permissiveness that had fascinated him since adolescence.
He dreamed of the muscles of oiled men in traditional gymnasi-
ums, of the veils of perfumed dancers, of eyes — both masculine
and feminine — lined in kohl, of the mist of hammams where all
fantasies became reality. He pictured himself as an explorer of
desire, and he had become one. This Orientalist image of the
almah and the ephebe, he had searched through reality for it,
and this reality had impassioned him so much that he substituted
himself for his initial dream; he loved his old dancer-prostitutes,
his hostesses in the sinister cabarets of Istanbul; he loved his out-
rageously made-up Iranian transvestites, his furtive encounters
in the back of a park in Tehran. Too bad if the Turkish baths were
sometimes sordid and filthy, too bad if the badly shaven cheeks
of ephebes scraped like currycombs, he'd always had a passion
for exploration — for pleasure and for exploration, added Sarah,
to whom he had shown his "field journal," as he called it: the idea
that Sarah could plunge into such a document was obviously
odious to me, I was terribly jealous of this strange relationship
forged through his diary. Even though I knew Sarah felt no at-
traction for Faugier, or Marc for her, imagining that Sarah could
glimpse his intimate life in this way, the details of his *scientific* life,
which in this precise case corresponded to those of his *sexual* life,
was unbearable to me. I saw Sarah in the place of Louise Colet
reading Flaubert's Egypt diary.

"Almahs — blue sky — the women are sitting in front of their
doors — on palm mats or standing — the madams are with
them — light-colored clothes, pieces layered over each other
which float in the hot wind."

Or else much worse.

"I go downstairs with Sophia Zoughaira — very corrupt, rest-
less, pleasure-taking, little tigress. I stain the sofa.

"Second fuck with Kuchuk — kissing her shoulder I could

feel her round neck under my teeth — her cunt polluted me like rolls of velvet — I felt ferocious."

And so on, all the perversions of which Orientalists are capable. Thinking of Sarah in the process of savoring the (revolting, needless to say) prose of that foppish erotomaniac, who I was sure was capable of writing some ghastly thing like *her cunt polluted me*, was pure torture. How Flaubert was able to inflict this agony on Louise Colet is incomprehensible; the Norman must have been very convinced of his genius. Or perhaps he thought, like Faugier when it came down to it, that these notes were *innocent*, that the obscenity portrayed there didn't belong to the realm of the real, but was of another order, science or travel, an investigation that distanced these pornographic considerations from his being, his own flesh; when Flaubert writes "fuck, refuck full of tenderness," or "her pussy warmer than her belly warmed me like a hot iron," when he says how, once Kuchuk has fallen asleep in his arms, he plays at crushing bedbugs on the wall, bedbugs whose smell mingles with the sandalwood of the young woman's perfume (the black blood of the insects draws pretty lines on the whitewashed wall), Flaubert is convinced these observations arouse interest, and not disgust: he is surprised that Louise Colet is horrified by this passage through the city of Esna. He tries to justify himself in a letter that's at least as atrocious: "Entering Jaffa," he says, "I breathed in the smell of lemon trees at the same time as that of corpses." For him, horror is everywhere; it is mixed with beauty; beauty and pleasure would be nothing without ugliness and pain, you have to feel them all together. (Louise Colet would be so struck by this manuscript that she would go to Egypt as well, eighteen years later, in 1869, for the inaugural ceremonies of the Suez Canal, when all of Europe was rushing to the shores of the Nile — she would see the almahs and their dances, which she would find vulgar; she would be shocked by two Germans so hypnotized by the bells on their necklaces that they would disappear, miss the boat, and reappear a few days later, "shamefully exhausted and smiling"; she too would stop at Esna, but to contemplate the ravages done by time on the body of that poor Kuchuk Hanim: she would have her revenge.)

Desire for the Orient is also a carnal desire, a physical domination, an erasing of the other in pleasure: we know nothing of Kuchuk Hanim, that dancer-prostitute of the Nile, aside from her erotic power and the name of the dance she performed, "The Bee"; aside from her clothes, her movements, the matter of her cunt, we know nothing about her, neither her words nor her feelings — she was probably the most famous of the almahs of Esna, or perhaps the only one. We do however possess a second testimonial about Kuchuk, by an American this time, who visited the city two years before Flaubert and published his *Nile Notes of a Howadji* in New York — here, George William Curtis devotes two chapters to Kuchuk — he calls her Kushuk Arnem; two poetic chapters, full of mythological references and voluptuous metaphors (*O Venus!*), the dancer's body writhing like the hose of a narghileh and the snake of original sin, a body that's "profound, oriental, intense, and terrible." Of Kuchuk we would know only her country of origin: Syria, Flaubert tells us, Palestine according to Curtis, and a single word, "*buono*" — according to Curtis, "one choice Italian word she knew." *Buono*, all the sordid pleasure stripped of the weight of Western propriety that Kuchuk could arouse, the pages of *Salammbô* and of *The Temptation of Saint Anthony* that she inspired, and nothing more.

Marc Faugier, in his "participatory observation," is interested in life stories, in the voices of the almahs and khawals of the twenty-first century; he examines their personal itineraries, their sufferings, their joys; in this sense, he joins the original Orientalist passions to the aspirations of today's social sciences, just as fascinated as Flaubert by the mixture of beauty and horror, by the blood of the crushed bug—and the sweetness of the body he is possessing.

Before you can comprehend beauty, you have to dive into the deepest horror, and travel completely through it, said Sarah— Tehran was feeling more and more like violence and death, between the attack on Faugier, Morgan's illness, the hangings, and the perpetual mourning for the Imam Husayn. Fortunately, there was Iranian music, tradition, the instrumentalists whom I met thanks to Jean During, worthy successor of the great Strasbourg Orientalist school—within strict and puritan Islam still shone the fires of music, literature, mysticism, humor, and life. For every hanged person, a thousand concerts, a thousand poems; for every head cut off, a thousand sessions of *zikr* and a thousand bursts of laughter. If only our journalists wanted to interest themselves in something besides pain and death—it's five thirty a.m., the silence of night; the screen is a world in itself, a world where there's neither time nor space. *Ishq, hawa, hub, mahabba,* the Arabic words for passion, for the love of humans and of God, which is the same. Sarah's heart, divine; Sarah's body, divine; Sarah's words, divine. Iseult, Tristan. Tristan, Iseult. Iseult, Tristan. Potions. Unity. Azra and Farid with the tragic luck, beings crushed under the Wheel of Destiny. Where is the light of Suhrawardi, what Orient will the compass show, what archangel dressed in purple will come open our hearts to love? *Eros, philia,* or *agapé,* what drunken Greek in sandals will come again, accompanied by a flute player, forehead encircled with violets, to remind us of the madness of love? Khomeini wrote love poems. Poems about wine, drunkenness, the Lover mourning the Beloved, roses, nightingales transmitting messages of love. For him martyrdom was a message of love. Suffering a gentle breeze. Death a poppy. This is how it is. I feel as if these days only Khomeini talks about love. Farewell compassion, long live death.

I was jealous of Faugier for no reason, I know he was suffering, that he was suffering martyrdom, that he was running away, that he had fled, that he had been fleeing from himself for a very long time, until he ended up in Tehran on a rug, curled up, knees under his chin, convulsing; his tattoos, said Sarah, mingled with the bruises to form mysterious drawings; he was half-naked, had difficulty breathing, she said, he kept his eyes open and staring, I lulled him like a child, added Sarah, terrified, I was forced to cradle him like a child, in the middle of the night in the garden of eternal spring whose red and blue flowers were becoming frightening in the twilight — Faugier was struggling between anguish and loss, anguish amplified the loss and the loss amplified the anguish, and these two monsters attacked him at night. Giants, fantastic creatures tortured him. Fear, distress in the absolute solitude of the body. Sarah consoled him. She said she stayed with him till dawn; at daybreak, he fell asleep, his hand in hers, still on the rug where the fit had thrown him. Faugier's dependence (on opium and then, later, as he himself had predicted, heroin) was coupled with another addiction, at least as strong, with that other oblivion which is sex, carnal pleasure, and Oriental dream; his path to the East stopped there, on that rug, in Tehran, in his own impasse, in that aporia, between self and other, which is identity.

"Sleep is good, death better," says Heinrich Heine in his poem "Morphine," "best never to have been born." I wonder if someone was holding Heine's hand in his long months of suffering, someone who wasn't brother Sleep with the poppy crown, the one who gently strokes the sick man's forehead and delivers his soul from all pain — and I, will I live my dying moments alone in my bedroom or at the hospital, don't think about that, turn away from illness and death, like Goethe, who always avoided dying people, corpses, and funerals: the traveler from Weimar makes sure each time to avoid the spectacle of death, to avoid the contagion of death; he thought of himself as a ginkgo, that tree from the Far East, immortal, ancestor of all trees, whose bilobed leaf so magnificently represents Union in love that he sent one, dried, to Marianne Willemer — "Don't you feel, in my songs, that I am One and double?" The pretty Viennese lady (round cheeks, ample figure) was thirty, Goethe sixty-five. For Goethe, the Orient is the opposite of death; looking to the East is turning your eyes away from the False. Fleeing. Into the poetry of Saadi and Hafez, into the Koran, into distant India; the *Wanderer* walks toward life. Toward the Orient, youth and Marianne, against old age and his wife Christiane. Goethe becomes Hatem, and Marianne Suleika. Christiane would die alone in Weimar, Goethe would not hold her hand, Goethe would not go to her funeral. Am I too turning away from the inevitable, in my obsession for Sarah, searching through the memory of this computer to find her letter from Weimar —

Dearest François-Joseph,

It's rather strange to find myself in Germany, in this language, so close to you, without you here. I don't know if you've ever traveled to Weimar; I suppose you have — I imagine Goethe, Liszt, and even Wagner must have drawn you. I remember you studied for a year in Tübingen — not very far from here it seems to me. I've been in Thuringia for two days: snow, snow, snow. And freezing cold. You wonder what I'm doing here — a conference, of course. A comparative conference on travel literature in the nineteenth century. Leading figures. Met Sarga Moussa, great specialist in visions of the Orient in the nineteenth century. Magnificent contribution on travel and memory. A little jealous of his knowledge, all the more so since he speaks German perfectly, like most of the attendees. I presented for the umpteenth time a paper on the travels of

Faris al-Shidyaq in Europe, in a different version, of course, but I still feel as if I'm rehashing things. The price of glory.

Of course we visited Goethe's house—you feel as if the master is about to get up from his armchair to greet you, so well-preserved the place seems. A collector's house—objects everywhere. Cabinets, filing cabinets for drawings, drawers for minerals, bird skeletons, Greek and Roman casts. His bedroom, tiny, next to his big office, under the peaked roof. The armchair in which he died. The portrait of his son August, who died two years before his father, in Rome. The portrait of his wife Christiane, who died fifteen years before him. Christiane's bedroom, with its curios: a beautiful fan, a pack of cards, a few perfume flasks, a blue cup with a rather touching inscription in gilt letters, To the Faithful One. *A feather. Two little portraits, one young and one less young. It's a strange feeling to walk through that house where, they say, everything has remained as it was in 1832. A little like visiting a tomb, mummies included.*

The most surprising thing is Weimar's relationship to the Orient—through Goethe, of course, but also Herder, Schiller, and India as well as Wieland and his Djinnistan *collection. Not to mention the ginkgoes (unrecognizable in this season) that have populated the city for over a century, so much so that they've even devoted a museum to them. But I imagine you know all this—I didn't. The Oriental side of German classicism. Once again, you realize how much Europe is a cosmopolitan construction . . . Herder, Wieland, Schiller, Goethe, Rudolf Steiner, Nietzsche . . . You feel as if all you have to do is lift a stone in Weimar for a link to the distant East to appear. But you remain firmly planted in Europe—destruction is never very far. The Buchenwald concentration camp is a few kilometers from here, I've heard the visit is terrifying. I don't have the courage to go.*

Weimar was bombed massively three times in 1945. Can you imagine? Bombing a city of sixty thousand inhabitants without any military stakes, when the war was almost won? Pure violence, pure vengeance. Bombing the symbol of the Parliamentary German first republic, trying

*to destroy Goethe's house, Cranach's house, Nietzsche's archives . . . with
hundreds of tons of bombs dropped by young pilots fresh out of Iowa or
Wyoming, who would die in turn burned alive in the cabins of their
planes, hard to see the sense in that, I'd rather keep quiet.*

*I have a souvenir for you; remember my article on Balzac and the
Arabic language? Well I could write another one, look at this beautiful
page, which you must know:*

It's from the original edition of the Divan. *Here too there's Arabic,
here too there are differences between Arabic and German, as you can
see: in Arabic, it's* The Eastern Divan by the Western Writer. *I find
that title very intriguing, maybe because of the appearance of the "Western" writer. It's no longer a mixed object, as in the German original,
a "west-eastern" divan, but an Oriental collection composed by a man
from the Occident. On the Arabic side of things, it's not a question of a
mingling, a fusion of one and the other, but an Oriental object separate*

from its author. Who translated this title for Goethe? His professors at Jena? At the Goethe museum, I saw a page of exercises in Arabic — the master was apparently entertaining himself by learning (with a pretty beginner's calligraphy) words taken from the book by Heinrich von Diez, one of the first Prussian Orientalists, Denkwürdigkeiten von Asien in Künsten und Wissenschaften. *(Good Lord how difficult German is, it took me five minutes to copy out that title.)*

There is always the other in the self. As in the greatest novel of the nineteenth century, Leg over Leg, or, The Life and Adventures of Fariac — *by Faris al-Shidyaq about whom I spoke this afternoon, that immense Arabic text printed in Paris in 1855 at the expense of Raphael Kahla, an exile from Damascus. I can't resist showing you the title page:*

كتاب
الساق على الساق في ما هو الفارياق

او
ايام وشهور واعوام في عجم العرب والاعجام

تأليف العبد الفقير الى ربه الرزاق فارس بن يوسف الشدياق

تأليف زبد وهند في زمانك ذا   اشهى الى الناس من تأليف سفرين
ودرس لورين قدشدّا الى قرن   اقنى وانفع من تدريس حبرين

طبعه بنفقته العبد الفقير الى رحمة ربه الموفى رافائيل كحلا الدمشقى
وذلك في مدينة باريس المحمية سنة ١٨٥٥ مسيحية ١٢٧٠ هجرية

LA VIE ET LES AVENTURES

DE FARIAC

RELATION DE SES VOYAGES

AVEC SES OBSERVATIONS CRITIQUES

SUR LES ARABES ET SUR LES AUTRES PEUPLES

Par FARIS EL-CHIDIAC

PARIS
BENJAMIN DUPRAT, LIBRAIRE DE L'INSTITUT,
DE LA BIBLIOTHÈQUE IMPÉRIALE, DES SOCIÉTÉS ASIATIQUES DE PARIS, DE LONDRES, DE MADRAS
ET DE CALCUTTA, etc.
Rue du Cloître-Saint-Benoît, n° 7.
1855

Seen from here, the mixed nature of al-Shidyaq's title calls to mind that of Goethe; you feel as if the 150 years following that have sought only to divide up patiently what the two great men had gathered together.

In Weimar one can also find (in no particular order) a reredos by Cranach with a magnificent misshapen, greenish demon; Schiller's house, and Liszt's house; the Bauhaus school; some pretty Baroque palaces; a castle; the souvenir of the Constitution of a fragile Republic; a park with beech trees that are hundreds of years old; a little ruined church that (covered in snow) looks straight out of a painting by Schinkel; a few neo-Nazis; sausages, hundreds of Thuringian sausages, in every form imaginable — raw, dried, grilled, and fond regards from Germany.

Yours,

Sarah

— to forget, rereading it, that death will no doubt take me before the age of Goethe or Faris al-Shidyaq the great Lebanese writer, at least there's not much chance I'll die at the controls of a bomber, hit by a DCA shell or shot down by a fighter plane, that's more or less out of the question, even though a plane accident is always possible: in this day and age you can get hit by a Russian missile in mid-flight or be blown up by a terrorist attack, it's not very reassuring. The other day I learned in the *Standard* that a fourteen-year-old jihadist had been arrested as he was preparing an attack in a train station in Vienna, a baby jihadist from Sankt Pölten, a den of terrorists, that's well-known, and this news would be amusing if it were not a sign of the times — soon hordes of Styrians will rush onto Viennese infidels shouting "Jesus is great!" and will start a civil war. I can't remember an attack in Vienna since the Schwechat airport and Abu Nidal's Palestinians in the 1980s, God forbid, God forbid, but you can't say God is giving the best of Himself, these days. Nor are Orientalists — I heard a specialist in the Middle East recommend we let all jihadist aspirants go to Syria, get themselves hanged elsewhere; they'd die under the bombs or in skirmishes and we'd hear no more about them. We'd just have to prevent the survivors from returning. This charming suggestion still poses a moral problem, can we reasonably send our regiments of bearded men to take revenge on Europe by killing the innocent civilian populations of Syria and Iraq? It's a little like throwing your trash into the neighbor's garden, it's not very nice. Practical, true, but not very ethical.

5:33 A.M.

Sarah's wrong, I've never been to Weimar. A condensation of Germany indeed. A miniature for collectors. An image. What strength Goethe had. To fall in love at the age of sixty-five with Hafez's *Divan* and with Marianne Willemer. To read everything through the glasses of love. Love generates love. Passion as driving force. Goethe a desiring machine. Poetry as fuel. I'd forgotten that bilingual frontispiece in the *Divan*. We've all forgotten these dialogues, in a hurry to forget the books on nationhood without glimpsing the space that opens up between languages, between German and Arabic, in the gutter of the binding, in the spines of books, in the turning white page. We should take more interest in the musical adaptations of the *East-Western Divan*, Schubert, Schumann, Wolf, dozens of composers probably, up to the moving *Goethe Lieder* for mezzo-soprano and three clarinets by Luigi Dallapiccola. It's beautiful to see how much Hafez and Persian poetry have irrigated bourgeois European art, Hafez and of course Omar Khayyam — Khayyam the irreverent scholar even has his statue not far from here, in the middle of the Vienna International Center, a statue offered a few years ago by the Islamic Republic of Iran, not at all spiteful against the poet of wine who was angry with God. Someday I'd like to take Sarah to the Danube to see this monument that sits in state in the midst of the UN buildings, those four white marble scholars under their brown stone canopies, framed by columns reminiscent of those of the Apadana in Persepolis. Khayyam, propelled by Edward Fitz-Gerald's translation, invaded literary Europe; the forgotten mathematician from the province of Khorassan became a leading European poet in 1870 — Sarah studied Khayyam through Sadegh Hedayat's commentary and edition, a Khayyam reduced to the essential, reduced to quatrains stemming from the oldest recensions. A Khayyam who was more skeptical than mystical. Sarah explained Omar Khayyam's immense worldwide fame by the universal simplicity of the quatrain form, first of all, and then by the diversity of the corpus: by turns atheist/agnostic or Muslim/hedonist or contemplative lover/inveterate drunkard or mystical drinker, the scholar from Khorassan, as he appears in the some thousand quatrains that are attributed to him, has something to please everyone — even Fernando Pessoa, who would compose, throughout his life, almost two hundred quatrains inspired by his reading of FitzGerald's translation. Sarah openly admitted that what she preferred about Khayyam was Hedayat's introduction and Pessoa's poems; she'd have happily gathered both together, making a rather beautiful monster, a centaur or a sphinx, Sadegh Hedayat introducing Pessoa's quatrains, in the shadow of Khayyam. Pessoa too liked wine,

> *Joy follows pain, and pain joy.*
> *We drink wine to celebrate, sometimes*
> *We drink wine in great suffering.*
> *But from either glass, what remains?*

and was at least as skeptical and despairing as his Persian ancestor. Sarah spoke to me of the taverns in Lisbon where Fernando Pessoa went to drink, listen to music or poetry, and in fact, in her story those taverns resembled the Iranian *meykhaneh*, so much so that Sarah would add ironically that Pessoa was a heteronym for Khayyam, that the Westernmost, Atlantic poet in Europe was actually an avatar of the god Khayyam,

> *After the roses, wine-bearer, you poured*
> *Wine into my cup and moved away.*
> *Who is more of a flower than you, who have fled?*
> *Who is more wine than you, who refused yourself?*

and during interminable conversations with our friend Parviz, in Tehran, she took pleasure in retranslating Pessoa's quatrains into Persian, to rediscover, they said, the taste of what had been lost — the spirit of drunkenness.

Parviz had invited us to a private concert where a young singer, accompanied by *tar* and *tombak* players, sang quatrains by Khayyam. The singer (maybe thirty, white shirt with a round collar, black trousers, handsome, somber, serious face) had a very beautiful tenor voice whose nuances were highlighted by the narrow living room we were sitting in; the percussionist shone — richness of clean, clear sounds, in both the low and high registers, impeccable phrasing in the most complex rhythms, his fingers rang against the skin of the *zarb* with surprising precision and speed. The *tar* player was an adolescent, sixteen or seventeen, and it was one of his first concerts; he seemed carried away by the virtuosity of his two elders, exalted by the audience; in the instrumental improvisations, he explored the *gousheh* (melody) of the chosen mode with a knowledge and expressiveness that, to my beginner's ears, compensated greatly for his lack of experience. The brevity of the words sung — four poems by Khayyam — allowed the musicians, quatrain after quatrain, to explore different rhythms and modes. Parviz was delighted. He scrupulously wrote the texts of the quatrains down for me in my notebook. My voice recorder would allow me later to train in that terrifying exercise of transcription. I had already notated instruments, *setar* or *tombak*, but never voice, and I was curious to see, calmly, on paper, how the alternation of short and long syllables in Persian meter is skillfully organized into song; how the singer transposes the meter or syllables of the verse to include them in a rhythm, and how the traditional musical phrases of the *radif* were transformed, revivified by the artist according to the poems sung. The encounter between a twelfth-century text, an age-old musical heritage, and contemporary musicians who actualize, in their individuality, faced with a given audience, the ensemble of these possibilities.

> *Pour me this wine, so I may say farewell to it*
> *Farewell to the nectar red as your fiery cheeks.*
> *Weary, my remorse is honest and sincere*
> *As the arabesque of the curls of your hair.*

The musicians were, like the rest of us, sitting cross-legged on a red Tabriz rug with a dark-blue central medallion; the wool, the cushions, and our bodies made the acoustics very clear, warm without any reverberation; to my right Sarah was sitting on her heels, her shoulder touching mine. The perfume of the song carried us away; the muted, deep waves of the drum, so close, seemed to fill our hearts made tender by the trills of the *tar*; we were breathing with the singer, holding our breath to follow him in the heights of those long strings of linked notes, clear, without vibrato, without hesitations, until suddenly, having reached the middle of that sonorous sky, he launched into a series of dizzying figures, a sequence of melismata and tremolos so nuanced, so moving, that my eyes filled up with held-in tears, shamefully choked back as the *tar* replied to the voice by taking up the phrase the singer had just sketched among the clouds, modulating it again and again.

You drink wine, you are faced with the truth,
Facing the memories of your days gone by,
The seasons of the rose, the drunken friends.
In this sad cup, you drink eternity.

I could feel the warmth of Sarah's body next to me, and my drunkenness was twofold—we were listening in unison, as synchronous in our heartbeats and our breath as if we were singing ourselves, touched, carried away by the miracle of the human voice, a profound communion, shared humanity, in those rare instants when, as Khayyam says, you drink eternity. Parviz too was delighted—when the concert was over, after a long applause and an encore, when our host, Reza, a music-loving doctor friend of Parviz's, invited us to move on to more earthly nourishment, Parviz emerged from his habitual reserve and shared his enthusiasm with us, laughing, dancing from one foot to the other to wake up his legs that had gone to sleep from sitting cross-legged for so long, he too half-intoxicated by the music and still reciting those poems we had just heard sung.

Reza the doctor's apartment was near Vanak Square, on the twelfth floor of a brand-new tower from which you could see all of Tehran as far as Varamin on a clear day. A reddish moon had risen above what I imagined to be the Karaj highway, which snaked, flanked with its rosary of buildings, between the hills until it disappeared into them. Parviz was speaking Persian with Sarah; exhausted by the emotion of the music, I had no more strength to follow their conversation; I was dreaming, my eyes gazing into the night, hypnotized by the carpet of yellow and red lights south of the city, dreaming of the caravanserais of long ago, those that Khayyam had frequented; between Nishapur and Ispahan, he had probably stopped in Ray, first capital of his Seljuk protectors, long before the Mongolian conquest transformed it into a pile of stones. From the lookout tower where I stood, you could have seen the poet-mathematician passing by, in a long caravan of horses and Bactrian camels, escorted by soldiers to counter the threat of the Ismailis of Alamut. Sarah and Parviz were talking about music, I understood the words *dastgah, segah, chahargah*. Khayyam, like many philosophers and mathematicians of classical Islam, also composed an epistle on music, which uses his theory of fractions to define the intervals between notes. Humanity in search of harmony and the music of the spheres. The guests and musicians conversed over drinks. Pretty, colorful carafes contained all sorts of drinks; the buffet was overflowing with stuffed vegetables, herb cakes, huge pistachios with beautiful dark-pink kernels; Parviz initiated us (without much success on my part) to the "White Iranian," a cocktail of his own invention consisting of mixing liquid yogurt with arak and a dash of pepper. Parviz and our host the doctor were complaining about the absence of wine — it's too bad, Khayyam would like wine, a lot of wine, said Parviz; wine from Urmia, from Shiraz, from Khorassan . . . What a world, the doctor sighed, living in the country that has sung most about wine and the vine, and being deprived of it. You could make some, I replied, thinking about the diplomats' "Neauphle-le-Château" vintage. Parviz looked at me in a disgusted way — we respect the Nectar too much to drink the putrid grape juices vinified in Tehran kitchens. I'll wait for the Islamic Republic to authorize its consumption, or at least officially tolerate it. Wine is too expensive on the black market, and often poorly preserved. The last time I went to Europe, our host went on, as soon as I arrived I bought myself three bottles of Australian shiraz that I drank alone, over the course of an afternoon, watching the Parisians walking by underneath my balcony. Paradise! Paradise! *Ferdows, Ferdows!* When I finally collapsed, even my dreams were perfumed.

I could easily imagine the effects that ingesting three bottles of red from the Antipodes could have on a Tehranese who had never drunk it. Even I was a little buzzed after just one screwdriver and one White Iranian. Sarah seemed to appreciate Parviz's horrible mixture, in which the yogurt was coagulating a little because of the arak. The doctor was telling us about the glorious 1980s, when the shortage of alcohol was so great that he embezzled fabulous quantities of 90 percent ethanol to make all sorts of mixtures, with cherries, barley, pomegranate juice, etc. Then, to prevent theft, they added camphor to it, which made it impossible to drink, Reza added with an air of sadness. And do you remember, Parviz interrupted, when the Islamic Republic began censoring the dubbing of movies and foreign serials? That was great. All of a sudden when you were watching a Western a guy would enter a saloon, Colts on his hips, and would say in Persian to the bartender: "A lemonade!" And the bartender would serve him a tiny glass of amber liquid that the cowboy would down in one gulp, and then repeat: "Another lemonade!" It was hysterical. Now we don't even notice it, Parviz added. I don't know, it's been ages since I watched Iranian TV, Reza confessed.

After these considerations on alcohol and after availing ourselves of the buffet, we went home; I was still reeling from the concert — in a sort of altered state. Musical phrases kept coming back to me, in snatches; the beat of the drum was still in my ears, the flashes of the lute, the interminable oscillations of the voice. I thought with melancholy about those who were lucky enough to give birth to such emotions, who possessed a musical or poetic talent; Sarah, on her side of the back seat in the taxi, must have been dreaming of a world where they would recite Khayyam in Lisbon and Pessoa in Tehran. She was wearing a dark-blue Islamic cloak and a white polka-dot scarf from which

a few locks of her red hair emerged. She was leaning against
the door, turned to the window and the night of Tehran which
was streaming past around us; the driver was shaking his head
to ward off sleep; the radio was blaring some slightly sinister
cantilenas about dying for Palestine. Sarah's right hand lay flat
on the artificial leather of the seat, her skin was the only brightness in the compartment, as I took it in mine I was able to catch
hold of the heat and light of the world: to my great surprise,
without immediately turning toward me, it was she who held
my fingers tight in hers, and drew my hand toward her — and
didn't let it go, not even when we arrived at our destination, not
even, hours later, when the red dawn set fire to Mount Damavand and invaded my bedroom and lit up, in the midst of the
sheets crisscrossed with flesh, her face made pale from fatigue,
her infinitely naked back where there lazed, rocked by the waves
of her breath, the long dragon of vertebrae and the traces of its
fire, those freckles that flowed up to the back of her neck, like
so many stars whose fire has been quenched, the galaxy that I
journeyed across with my finger outlining imaginary voyages
while Sarah, from the other side of her body, clutched my left
hand below her breasts. And I stroked her neck illuminated
by a thin pink ray of light sharpened by the venetian blinds; as
the dawn hummed, still surprised by this total intimacy, by her
breath made sweet from fasting and hints of alcohol, astonished
by the eternity, by the eternal possibility of finally burying myself in her hair, of traveling at leisure across her cheekbones, her
lips, stunned by the tenderness of her kisses, lively and laughing,
brief or profound, short of breath, at having been able to let her
undress me without any shame or embarrassment, blinded by
her beauty, by the reciprocal simplicity of nudity after minutes
or hours of cloth, friction of cotton, of silk, of clasps, of tiny
clumsy gestures, attempts at oblivion in the unison of body, of

heart, of the Orient, in the great ensemble of desire, the great chorus of desire where so many landscapes are found, past and future, I glimpsed in the night of Tehran Sarah naked. She caressed me, I caressed her, and nothing in us sought to reassure ourselves with the word "love," so deep were we in the murkiest beauty of love, which is absolute presence next to the other, in the other, desire satisfied at every instant, renewed at every second, for every second we found a new color to desire in this kaleidoscope of light and shade — Sarah sighed and laughed, she sighed and laughed and I was afraid of this laughter, I was afraid of it as much as I desired it, as much as I wanted to hear it, just like now, in the night of Vienna, as I seek to catch hold of the memories of Sarah as an animal tries to catch shooting stars. In vain I search through my memory, nothing but flashes remain from that night next to her. Flash of the first contact of our lips, clumsily after our cheeks, lips that were numb and greedy, that get lost too on the fingers that travel over our faces, lips that make up for foreheads bumped together, by surprise, by that strange clumsiness of the surprise of discovering yourself in the process of kissing, finally, without anything, a few minutes before, really preparing you for this clenching of the heart, this lack of air, neither the years spent envisioning it, nor the dreams, the many startling dreams devoted to this carnal topic, faded, erased by the flashes of a beginning of reality, the taste of a breath, a gaze so near that you close your eyes to it, reopen them, close the eyes that are observing you, with your lips, you kiss those eyes, you close them with your lips and you realize the true size of a hand when the fingers finally meet, no longer holding each other but intertwining.

Flash illuminating her upright torso, backlit, barred horizon of the white marble of her chest, under which the circles of her belly swim; flash of a thought, B major, I thought B major, and having lost myself for a moment far from the present, having seen myself, in B major, author of another's gestures, witness, for a few seconds, of my own questionings, why B major, how to escape from B major, and this thought was so incongruous, so frightened, that I was paralyzed for a minute, far from everything, and Sarah perceived (slower rhythm, gentle caress on my chest) my hesitations before drawing me simply away from them, by the miracle of her tenderness.

Flash of whisperings in the night, harmony increased by the friction of voices against bodies, vibrations of the tense air of Tehran, of sweet drunkenness prolonged by the music and by company—what did we say to each other that night that time has not erased, the dark brilliance of a smiling eye, the languor of a breast, the taste of skin slightly rough under the tongue, the smell of sweat, the provocative acidity of folds devoured, aqueous, sensitive, where the slow waves of pleasure overflow; the palp of beloved fingers in my hair, on my shoulders, on my penis, which I tried to hide from her caresses, before abandoning myself as well, offering myself up so that union could continue, as night advanced toward the inevitable dawn: each of us in profile, not knowing which liquids accompany which breaths, in a pose of intertwined statues, my hands clutched to her chest, knees in the hollows of knees, the riveted, twisted gazes of the caduceus, burning tongues made cold by bites, on the neck, on the shoulder, trying to maintain as much as possible this adhesion of our bodies that a murmured name loosens, unties into open syllables, spreads into phonemes, stifled by the power of the embrace.

Until the red dawn of warriors from the Book of Kings descends on Damavand: in the breathless silence, while I am still stunned, amazed by Sarah's presence beside me, the call to prayer—which you forget in Tehran, never hear, discreet, drowned as it usually is in the sounds of the city—resounds, a fragile miracle from an unknown source, a neighboring mosque or an apartment nearby, the *adhan* falls on us, envelopes us, judgment or blessing, sonorous ointment, "As my heart pounds up to my throat in excited love for this city and its sounds, I begin to feel that all my wanderings have always had but one meaning: to grasp the meaning of this call," said Muhammad Asad, and finally I understand its meaning, a meaning, the one of the sweetness of sharing and love, and I know that Sarah, like me, is thinking of the verses of the troubadours, of the sad alba, the aubade; the call is mingled with the song of the first birds, urban sparrows, our nightingales of the poor ("*Sahar bolbol hekayat ba Saba kard*, At dawn the nightingale speaks to the breeze"), with the gliding automobiles, the smells of tar, rice, and saffron that are the odor of Iran, forever associated, for me, with the salty, rainy taste of Sarah's skin: we remain motionless, bewildered, listening to the sonorous layers of this blind moment, knowing it signifies both love and separation in the light of day.

6:00 A.M.

No reply yet. Is there internet in Kuching, capital of Sarawak? Of course. There's no place left on earth without internet. Even in the midst of the most terrible wars, fortunately or unfortunately, you can find a connection. Even in her monastery in Darjeeling, Sarah had an internet café nearby. Impossible to escape the screen. Even in catastrophe.

In Tehran, at the end of the day after that incredibly sweet night, she hopped onto the first plane to Paris, the red-eye with Air France, trembling with suffering and guilt, after spending the day, without having closed her eyes for a minute, rushing from police station to police station to settle those sordid visa matters Iranians excel in, armed with a piece of paper sent urgently by the French Embassy, attesting to the extremely serious state of her brother's health and begging the Iranian authorities to facilitate her departure, even though she had the intuitive sensation, at the sound of her mother's voice, that Samuel had already died, regardless of what they told her, faced with this announcement she was destroyed by shock, distance, incomprehension, incredulity and, that very night, as she was fidgeting sleeplessly on her seat high up in the midst of the impassive stars, I rushed to go online and send her letters, letters and letters that she would read, I stupidly hoped, when she arrived. I too spent the night without closing my eyes in an enraged, incredulous state.

Her mother had called her without success all evening and into the morning, desperate, had contacted the Institute, the consulate, moved heaven and earth and finally, when Sarah, throwing me a kiss from afar, had modestly closed the bathroom door for privacy, they had come to inform me — the accident had occurred on the previous afternoon, the accident, the event, the discovery, no one knew anything yet, Sarah had to call her mother back *at home*, and it was the words *at home*, rather than at the hospital, or God knows where, it was the words *at home* that had made her sense the worst. She had rushed to the phone, I can see the dial and her hands hesitating, getting the number wrong, I slipped away, I went out too, as much out of decorum as cowardliness.

That last day, I wandered with her through the lower depths of the Iranian legal system, to the passport office, that kingdom of tears and injustice, where illegal Afghans, their clothes stained with cement and paint, handcuffed, defeated, filed in front of us surrounded by Pasdaran and looked for a little consolation in the gazes of those present; we waited for hours on the worn wooden bench, under the portraits of the first and second Guides of the Revolution, and every ten minutes Sarah would get up to go to the counter, always repeating the same question and the same argument, "*bayad emshab beravam*, I have to leave tonight, I have to leave tonight," and each time the functionary would reply "tomorrow," "tomorrow," "you'll leave tomorrow," and in the selfishness of passion I hoped in fact she wouldn't leave till the next day, that I could spend one more evening, one more night with her, consoling her, I imagined, for the catastrophe we had only just glimpsed, and the most terrible thing, in that dilapidated antechamber, under the wrathful gaze of Khomeini and the big myopic glasses of Khamenei, was that I could not take her in my arms, not even hold her hand or dry the tears of rage, anguish, and powerlessness on her face, fearing that this mark of indecency and offense to Islamic morality might diminish her chances of obtaining her exit visa even more. Finally, when all hope of a wave from the magic wand seemed lost, an officer (fifties, short gray beard, generous stomach in an impeccable uniform jacket) passed by us to go to his office; this kind family man listened to Sarah's story, took pity on her, and, with that magnanimous grandeur that belongs only to powerful dictatorships, after initialing an obscure document, he summoned his subordinate to request him to kindly affix the theoretically inaccessible seal on the passport of the lady in question, upon which the subordinate — the same unwavering functionary who had unceremoniously kept us waiting all morning — complied immediately, with a slight smile of irony or compassion, and Sarah flew to Paris.

B major — the dawn that brings an end to the love scene; death. Does Szymanowski's *Song of the Night*, which so skillfully links the verses of Rumi the mystic to the long night of Tristan and Isolde, shift into B major? I don't remember, but it's likely. One of the most sublime symphonic compositions of the last century, without a doubt. The night of the Orient. The Orient of night. Death and separation. With those choruses as brilliant as clusters of stars.

Szymanowski also set poems by Hafez to music, two song cycles composed in Vienna, not long before the First World War. Hafez. You feel as if the world spins around his mystery, like the mystical Firebird around the mountain. "Hafez, shh! No one knows the divine mysteries, be quiet! Whom will you ask what has happened in the cycle of days?" Around his mystery and his translators, from Hammer-Purgstall to Hans Bethge, whose adaptations of "Oriental" poetry are so often set to music. Szymanowski, Mahler, Schönberg, Viktor Ullmann — they all use

Bethge's versions. Bethge, an almost motionless traveler who knew no Arabic, no Persian, no Chinese. The original, the essence, remains between the text and his translations, in a land between languages, between worlds, somewhere in the *nakodjaabad*, the nowhere-place, that imaginal world where music also takes its source. There is no original. Everything is in flux. Between languages. Between times, the time of Hafez and that of Hans Bethge. Translation as metaphysical practice. Translation as meditation. It's very late to be thinking of these things. The memory of Sarah and music pushes me to these melancholies. These wide spaces of the vacuity of time. We didn't know the pain the night was hiding; what sort of long, strange separation was opening up then, after those kisses — impossible now to go back to sleep, no bird yet or muezzin in the dark of Vienna, heart beating with memories, with a lack as powerful as lack of opium possibly, lack of whispers and caresses.

Sarah has had a brilliant career; she's constantly invited to the most prestigious conferences, while she's still an academic nomad, has no "post," as they say, unlike me, who has exactly the opposite: security, indeed, in a comfortable campus, with pleasant students, in the city where I grew up, but a reputation close to nil. At best I can count on a gathering from time to time at the University of Graz, or even Bratislava or Prague to stretch my legs. It's been years since I've been to the Middle East, I haven't even been to Istanbul recently. I could stay for hours in front of this screen skimming through Sarah's articles and public appearances, reconstituting her travels, conferences in Madrid, Vienna, Berlin, Cairo, Aix-en-Provence, Boston, Berkeley, as far as Bombay, Kuala Lumpur, or Jakarta, that map of global scholarship.

Sometimes I feel as if night has fallen, that Western darkness has invaded the Orient of enlightenment. That spirit and learning, the pleasures of the spirit and of learning, of Khayyam's and

Pessoa's wine, have not been able to stand up to the twentieth century; I feel that the global construction of the world is no longer carried out by the interchange of love and ideas, but by violence and manufactured objects. Islamists fighting against Islam. The United States, Europe, at war against the other in the self. What's the use of pulling Anton Rubinstein and his *Persian Love Songs of Mirza Schaffy* from oblivion. What's the use of remembering Friedrich von Bodenstedt, his *Thousand and One Days in the Orient* and his descriptions of evenings around Mirza Schaffy the Azeri poet in Tiflis, getting plastered on Georgian wine, his wobbly praises of the Caucasian nights and Persian poetry, poems the German shouted out, dead drunk, in the streets of Tbilisi. Bodenstedt, one more forgotten translator. A traveler. A creator, especially. The book of the *Lieder von Mirza Schaffy*, though, was one of the great successes of "Oriental" literature in nineteenth-century Germany. As well as the musical adaptation by Anton Rubinstein in Russia. What's the use of remembering the Russian Orientalists and their beautiful encounters with the music and literature of Central Asia? You have to have Sarah's energy to constantly reconstruct yourself, always look mourning and illness in the face, have the perseverance to continue searching through the sadness of the world to draw beauty or knowledge from it.

Dearest Franz,

I know, I haven't been writing to you these days, I don't send much news, I'm drowning in travel. I've been in Vietnam for a little while, in Tonkin, Annam, and Cochin China. I'm in Hanoi in 1900. I can see your surprise: Vietnam? Yes, a project on the colonial imagination, can you believe it. Without leaving Paris, unfortunately. A project on opium. I've been diving into the stories of the addict Jules Boissière, the poor civil servant from Languedoc who died from his passion at the age of thirty-four after smoking many pipes and confronting the jungles of Tonkin, the cold, the rain, violence and illness, his sole companion the somber light of the opium lamp. The story of the imagery of opium in colonial literature is extraordinarily interesting. The process of the essentialization of opium as "Extreme-Oriental," belonging to the Far East, all the mysticism and clarity, the "good, sweet drug" concentrates, as Boissière says, in the heart of colonial violence. For Boissière, opium is the link to the Vietnamese; they share not only pipes and cots, but also the suffering from lack of opium and the violence of the times. The smoker is a being apart, a wise man who belongs to the community of seers: a visionary and a fragile beggar. Opium is the luminous blackness that is the opposite of the cruelty of nature and the ferocity of men. You smoke after having fought, after having tortured, after having witnessed heads cut off by sabers, ears hacked off by machetes, bodies ravaged by dysentery or cholera. Opium is a common language, a shared world; only the pipe and the lamp have the power to make us penetrate "the soul of Asia." The drug (precolonial scourge introduced by imperialist commerce and a formidable weapon of domination) becomes the key to a strange universe one must penetrate, so it becomes the image that best represents this world, that displays it most perfectly for the Western masses.

Here for example are two postcards sent from Saigon in the 1920s. The youth of the models gives the impression that opium is a practice that is not only extraordinarily widespread, but also accepted, eternal, rural, natural; the black, padlocked box no doubt encloses all the secrets of those so exotic countries where people devote themselves to this child-like passion. Portrait of the native as a drug-addicted child.

"There is always a need for intoxication: this country has opium, Islam has hashish, the West has women. Perhaps love is above all the means which the West uses to free itself from man's fate," writes Malraux in Man's Fate; *this phrase, which is curious to say the least, shows clearly how opium becomes the commodity of the Far East, the Extreme Orient, and how our representations are fabricated; it is not, of course,*

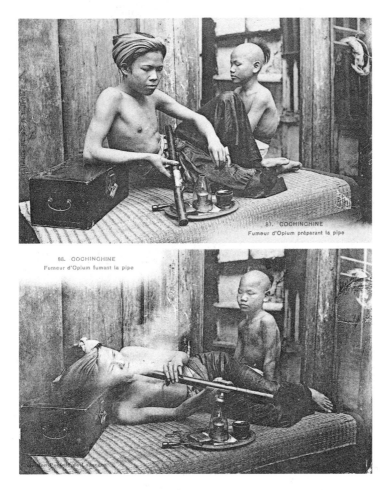

87. COCHINCHINE
Fumeur d'Opium préparant la pipe

86. COCHINCHINE
Fumeur d'Opium fumant la pipe

a question of denying the reality of the ravages of opium in China or Vietnam, but of seeing how this imagination is constructed, and how it serves colonial propaganda.

I remember Marc lost in opium in Tehran and I wonder if he succumbed to a great dream, if all his scientific justifications are actually unconscious excuses to plunge, like all of us, into dreamlike territories where you can escape yourself.

I explain all this to you, but actually I'd mostly like to stretch out on a mat, resting my head on a suitcase, to breathe in the vaporous oblivion, confide my soul to Nepenthes and forget all the pains of loss. My opium is these texts and images that I go to find every day in Parisian libraries, these butterflies of words that I collect, that I observe without thinking of anything else, this sea of old books in which I'm trying to drown — unfortunately, despite everything, I think of my brother, I feel as if I'm limping, as if I'm perpetually wobbly, and sometimes, when I come across a text that's too violent or too moving, I have a lot of trouble holding back my tears, so I lock myself in my bedroom, take one of those modern pills that no doubt have neither the charm nor the power of opium, and I sleep for twenty-four hours straight.

> You who suffer, here is the treasure that is left to you:
> Smoke. And may you, indulgent gods, be blessed
> Who place happiness at the mercy of a gesture.

That's the epitaph that Albert de Pouvourville wrote for his friend Jules Boissière in Hanoi, in the Pagoda of the Lake. I would like happiness to be at the mercy of a gesture. I know you think of me; I read your letters every day, I try to answer without managing to, I'm afraid you're mad at me, so I bury myself in my research like a child hiding under her blanket.
Write to me all the same, with love,

Sarah

Sarah reconstructed herself by going further east, more profoundly into herself, advancing in that spiritual and scientific quest that allowed her to escape her own unhappiness — I prefer to stay in my Viennese apartment, even if it means suffering from insomnia, illness, and Gruber's dog. I don't have her courage. War has never been the best time for our congregation. Archaeologists transformed into spies, linguists into propaganda experts, ethnologists into disciplinarians. Sarah does well to exile herself into those mysterious, distant lands where they're interested in the pepper trade and philosophical concepts, and very little in cutthroats and bomb-makers. *East of the East*, as Pessoa says. What would I find, in distant China, in the kingdom of Siam, among the martyred peoples of Vietnam and Cambodia or in the Philippines, old islands conquered by the Spaniards who seem, on the map, indecisive as to which side of the world to pick, fixated on the immensity of the Pacific, the last barrier closing the Sea of China, or on Samoa, the point farthest east from the German language, or the westernmost, the peaceful colony of Bismarck's empire buying from the Spaniards the last crumbs of their southern possessions — what will we find west of the West, where the planet's belt is looped, a few trembling ethnologists administering sweating colonies who drown their melancholy in alcohol and violence under the despairing eye of the natives, import-export companies, offshore banks, tourists, or else in knowledge, music, love, encounters, exchanges — the last trace of German colonialism is a beer, as it should be, Tsingtao, a beer named for the capital of the trading post of Zhan Qiao, in the northeastern part of mysterious China; a few thousand Germans lived in that territory rented from the Celestial Empire for ninety-nine years, which the Japanese troops assisted by a British contingent eventually took by assault in the autumn of 1914, drawn perhaps by its great brick brewery that continues, even today, to export millions of bottles all over the world — one more circle closed, an ex-colonial beer that colonizes in turn, a century later, the capitalist planet. I imagine the machines and the master brewers arriving from Germany in 1900 and coming ashore on the magnificent bay between Shanghai and Peking that the German gunboats had just wrenched from a Manchu dynasty overwhelmed by Western powers like a wound by worms: the Russians gave themselves Port Arthur, the French Fort-Bayard, the Germans Tsing-Tao, not counting the concessions in the cities of Tientsin and Shanghai. Even our poor Austria-Hungary would obtain a piece of land in Tientsin that it would hurry, they say, to cover in Viennese-style buildings — a church, a few residential buildings, some shops. Tientsin, 160 kilometers from Peking, must have looked like a European World's Fair, with its French, English, German, Russian, Austrian, Belgian, and even Italian neighborhoods, in a few kilometers you felt as if you'd traveled across haughty, colonizing Europe, that Europe of brigands and adventurers who'd pillaged and set fire to the Summer Palace of Peking in 1860, concentrating on the garden pavilions, the faience, the gold ornaments, the fountains, and even the trees, the English and French soldiers tore away the treasures of the palace like vulgar misers before setting fire to it, and imperial Chinese dishes and bronze receptacles would be found as far away as the markets of London or Paris, products of pillage and violence. Peter Fleming, brother of the creator of James Bond and traveling companion of Ella Maillart in Asia, writes in his book on the famous "55 Days at Peking," when the representatives of eleven European nations withstood the Siege of the Legations by the Boxers and the Imperial Army, that an Orientalist would cry, inconsolable, when fire destroyed the only complete copy of the *Yongle Dadian*, the immense encyclopedia of the Ming Dynasty, compiled in the fifteenth century and encompassing all the knowledge in the world, eleven thousand volumes, twenty-three thousand chapters, millions and millions of handwritten ideograms gone up in smoke in the hissing of the flames of the Imperial library, which as bad luck would have it was situated right next to the British legation. An unknown Sinologist cried: one of the rare beings conscious, in the tumult of war, of what had just disappeared; he happened to be there, in the middle of the catastrophe, and his own death suddenly became a matter of indifference to him, he had seen knowledge go up in smoke, the legacy of ancient scholars being erased — did he pray, full of hatred, to an unknown god for the flames to annihilate the English as well as the Chinese or, stunned by pain and shame, did he merely watch the sparks and glowing paper butterflies invade the summer night, his eyes protected from the smoke by his tears of rage, we have no idea. The only thing that's clear, Sarah would have said, is that the victory of the foreigners over the Chinese gave rise to massacres and pillages of unprecedented violence, the missionaries themselves, apparently, tasting the pleasure of blood and the joys of vengeance in the company of the soldiers of the glorious allied nations. Apart from the unknown Sinologist, no one sobbed over the destroyed encyclopedia, apparently; it was added to the list of war victims, victims of economic conquest and imperialism faced with a recalcitrant empire that obstinately refused to let itself be taken apart.

East of the East you don't escape the conquering violence of Europe either, its merchants, its soldiers, its Orientalists or its missionaries — Orientalists are the variation on the theme, the missionaries; while scholars translate and import foreign knowledge, the religious export their faith, learn local languages in order to make the Gospels intelligible there. The first Tonkin, Chinese or Khmer dictionaries were written by missionaries, Jesuit, Lazarist, Dominican. These missionaries paid a heavy tribute to the propagation of Faith — we should devote a volume of my great work to them:

On the Divers Forms of Lunacie in the Orient
Volume the Fourth
Encyclopedia of the Decapitated

The emperors of China and Annam, among others, martyred a considerable number of peddlers of Jesus, many of them subsequently beatified and even canonized by Rome, martyrs in Vietnam, China, or Korea, whose sufferings were no less terrible than the Roman martyrs, like Saint Théophane Vénard the ill-named — it took five saber blows to decapitate him not far from Hanoi: the young Frenchman testified to his faith by the shores of the Red River, in the 1850s, when the French offensive in Annam forced the Emperor to toughen persecutions against Christians. He is shown calmly kneeling facing the river, executioner at his side: the first saber blow, too swift and poorly aimed, misses the neck and only nicks his cheek; Théophane continues to pray. The second blow, perhaps because the executioner is even more tense from his initial failure, touches the side of his throat, spreads a little of the missionary's blood but does not interrupt his prayers; the executioner (I picture him tall, fat, bald, like in the movies, but he could have been small, hairy, and especially, they say, drunk, which would explain his misses in an entirely plausible way) would have to lift his arm five times for the martyr's head to roll, his body collapse and his prayers fall silent. His head would be placed on a pike, as an example, on the bank of the Red River; his body buried in the silt — catechumens would steal both body and head under cover of night, they would offer the torso a real burial in a Christian cemetery and the head a glass dome so it could be preserved as a relic by the diocese of Hanoi, and 150 years later the young priest from the Foreign Missions of Paris would be canonized, along with a number of his torn-apart, strangled, burned, or decapitated brothers.

Type of death: head cut off with a saber, crucifixion, dismemberment, evisceration, drowning, various tortures—that's what the files on missionaries in Asia would read.

What saint will I ask for comfort in my agony, Saint Théophane Vénard or some other massacred saints, or simply Saint Martin, the saint of my childhood, of whom I was so proud, in Austria, during the torchlit processions on November 11, his name day—for my fellow-citizens of Vienna, Saint Martin is not Saint Martin *of Tours*, whose tomb I had seen as a child with Grandmother and Mother in the basilica of the same name (gilt, more Oriental than Gallic), which, in my childlike religiosity, gave me a privileged closeness to the Roman legionary with the divided cloak, a closeness associated for me with the reeds on the shores of the Loire, the sandbanks, the porphyry columns of the underground, silent sepulchre where this so charitable saint lay who, according to my Grandmother, could be asked for his intercession for any purpose, which I didn't fail to do, clumsily no doubt, demanding sweets, biscuits, and toys. My devotions to the soldier-bishop were entirely self-interested, and in Vienna, when we went to the country in the middle of autumn to eat the Saint Martin's day goose, this slightly dry fowl was for me directly linked to Tours; it no doubt arrived from there by flying—if a bell were capable of returning from Rome to announce the Resurrection, a goose could easily fly from the Touraine to Austria to pay homage to the saint by lying down, completely roasted, between the chestnuts and the *Serviettenknödel*. Strangely, although Grandmother's village bore his name, Saint Benedict was never anything to me but phonemes: probably because, in the mind of a child, a legionary sharing his cloak with a poor man is much more attractive than an Italian monk, important as he may have been for medieval spirituality—Saint Benedict however is the patron saint of the dying, there's my intercessor, I could perhaps invest in an image of

Saint Benedict, be unfaithful to my icon of Saint Christopher. The giant from Chananea also died decapitated, on Samos; he's the saint of passage, the one who helps you cross rivers, who carried Christ from one shore to the other, patron saint of travelers and mystics. Sarah loved the Eastern saints. Saint Andrew of Constantinople or Saint Simeon the Holy Fool, she would tell the stories of these fools in Christ who used their madness to hide their holiness — madness, at the time, signifying the otherness of customs, the inexplicable difference of actions: Simeon who, finding a dead dog on the road at the entrance to Emesa, tied a rope around its neck and dragged it behind him as if it were alive; Simeon still, who played at putting out the church candles by throwing nuts at them and then, when they tried to chase him away, climbed onto the rostrum to bombard the congregants with his dried fruit, until he chased the faithful out of the church; Simeon dancing, beating with his hands and feet, making fun of monks, and eating lupines like a bear.

Bilger could be a saint, who knows. The first archaeologist saint, who hides his holiness beneath an impenetrable madness. Perhaps he experienced enlightenment in the desert, on the digs, confronting the traces of the past that he pulled from the sand, their Biblical wisdom penetrating him little by little until it became, one day that was clearer than the others, an immense rainbow. Bilger in any case is the most sincere of us all; he is not content with a slight rift, with insomnia, with indecipherable illnesses like mine, or with the spiritual thirst of Sarah; today he is the explorer of his profound otherness.

Sarah was also very fond of missionaries, martyred or not; they are, she said, the underground wave, the mystical, scholarly counterpart to the gunboat — both advance together, the soldiers following or shortly preceding the missionaries and the Orientalists, who sometimes are the same. Sometimes all three at once: member of a religious order, Orientalist, and soldier, like Alois Musil, the Dominican Father Jaussen, and Louis Massignon, the holy trinity of 1917. The first crossing of Tibet, for example (and I was happy to be able to teach Sarah this exalted fact of ecclesiastical nationalism) was the work of an Austrian Jesuit from Linz, Johannes Grueber, possibly an ancestor of my neighbor: this holy man from the seventeenth century, a mathematician in his spare time, and a missionary, was, on his way back from China, the first European to visit Lhasa. Sarah, in her long exploration of the lands of Buddhism, met other missionaries, other Orientalists, whose histories she often told me, at least as fascinating as the desert spies — Father Évariste Huc for example, whose benevolence as a man from the South (if my memory serves me right he was from Montauban by the Tarn River, rosy homeland of the painter Ingres so cherished by Orientalists and Halil Pasha) cheered up a Viennese tea that was otherwise rather tense and gloomy, during a visit from Sarah, the first after Samuel's death. She was studying Darjeeling, at the time. Horrible Viennese museums, memories of Orientalists, and a strange distance that we tried to fill with bouts of scholarship and learned discourse. Her visit had seemed very long to me. Sarah irritated me. I was both proud of showing her my Viennese life and terribly disappointed at not immediately rediscovering the intimacy of Tehran. It was all awkwardness, impatience, squabbles and misunderstandings. I'd have liked to take her to the Belvedere Museum or show her the traces of my childhood in Mariahilf, and she was interested in nothing but horrors or Buddhist centers. I had spent those months remembering her, investing so much in the wait, constructing an imaginary character, so perfect that it would, all of a sudden, fulfill my life — what selfishness, when I think about it. I never realized the extent of her mourning, the pain, the feeling of

injustice that the sudden loss of such a close being can represent, despite her letters:

*Dear Franz, thank you for this diplomatic note, which managed to
make me smile — not an easy thing for me to do right now. I miss you a
lot. Or rather I miss everything a lot. I feel as if I'm outside the world,
floating in mourning. I just have to meet my mother's gaze for us both to
start crying. Crying for the other's sadness, that void we each see on our
exhausted faces. Paris is a tomb, tatters of memories. I continue my in-
cursions into the literary territories of opium. I don't really know where
I am anymore.*
  With sad kisses, till soon,

Sarah

Franz Ritter wrote:

Dearest Sarah,

  *Ah if you knew how hard it is to live up to one's pretensions when
one doesn't have the luck of being French, how laborious it is to raise
oneself by the mere strength of one's intelligence to the summits of your
compatriots and understand their sublime motivations, their preoccupa-
tions and their emotions!!! The other night I was invited to dinner by the
cultural attaché of your great country, and I was able to take the measure
of the great distance I still had to travel to reach his ankle. The attaché is
a musician — you remember that he never missed an opportunity to talk
to me about the Opera or the Vienna Philharmonic. A bachelor, he hosts
a lot of parties, in his beautiful villa in Niavaran. I was very flattered by
the invitation. Come, he said to me, I've invited some Iranian friends,
we'll play some music and have dinner. An informal dinner, potluck.*
  *I arrive at the appointed time, around eight p.m., after walking for a
quarter of an hour in the snow because the Paykan taxi spun its wheels*

and refused to climb any higher. I reach the gate, ring the bell, wait, ring again: nothing. So I decide to take advantage of the occasion to take a little walk in the freezing night, especially, I must admit, because remaining motionless meant exposing myself to certain death. I stroll for a few minutes at random and, passing in front of the house again, I meet the employee of the house who is emerging: I rush over, question her, and she says:

"Oh, you're the one who rang. Monsieur is playing music with his friends, he never answers when he's playing."

Probably because the music room is on the other side of the villa and you can't hear the bell. OK OK OK. I hurry inside and walk into the entrance hall with its imposing Doric columns, its classic lighting like the music floating in, harpsichord, flute, Couperin? I cross the large living room taking great care not to walk on the precious rugs. I wonder if I should wait there, and you know me, I'm pretty polite, so I wait, standing, for a pause to enter the music room, as at the Musikverein. I have time to take a good look at the paintings, the bronze sculptures of ephebes and — horror! — the traces of snowy mud my poorly wiped shoes have left everywhere on the marble. Shame. A Teuton disembarks in this haven of beauty. You could easily follow my hesitant trajectory, skirting round the rugs, going from one statue to the other. Even greater shame. No matter: I notice a pearly box that looks as if it contains tissues, I grasp it, hoping the sonata will last long enough for me to perform my lowly task, kneel down, box in hand, and hear:

"Oh, you're there? What are you doing, playing marbles? Come in, come in."

In fact, the box contained porcelain marbles, don't ask me how I could mistake it for a box of tissues, I couldn't answer: aesthetic emotion no doubt, you say to yourself that in such a setting a box of Kleenex must of course be nacreous. Ridiculous, I made myself an object of ridicule, here I am suspected of wanting to play marbles on the rug while they're playing great music. A philistine. The Austrian musicologist plays marbles on the Oriental rugs instead of listening to Couperin.

I sigh, carefully set down the box and follow the attaché into said music room: a sofa, two armchairs, a few Orientalist paintings, more sculptures, a spinet, the musicians (the attaché seated at the keyboard, an Iranian flutist) and the audience, a young man with a very kind smile.

"Let me introduce you: Mirza, Abbas. Franz Ritter, Austrian musicologist, student of Jean During."

We shake hands; I sit down, and they start playing again, which gives me time to forget my shame for a bit and laugh at myself. The attaché was humming a little as he played, eyes closed in concentration. The music was beautiful, I must say, with the vibrating profundity of the flute, the fragile crystal of the harpsichord.

After five minutes, they finish the piece, I applaud. The attaché gets up: "Good, it's time to start on that fondue. This way, epicures."

Oh yes, I forgot to point out that I was invited for a Savoyard fondue, such a rare dish in Tehran that one wouldn't want to miss it. When the attaché had suggested it to me, I had replied:

"A fondue? I've never had one."

"Never? There's no fondue in Austria? Well, this is the time to invite you over. It's much better than raclette, even Swiss raclette. More refined. Yes, more refined. And with this snow, it's the ideal dish."

The cultural attaché is interested in all the arts, culinary included.

So, all four of us head for the kitchen. I had been envisioning, despite the attaché's precautions and his reference to pot luck, a rather snobbish dinner with large and small dishes served at the table, and I find myself with an apron around my waist, à la bonne franquette, as you say, home-style.

The task of slicing the bread falls upon me. Fine. I slice, under the careful supervision of the chef, who inspects the thickness of the slices. The chef is Mirza, also President of the Gourmet Club, which, I learn, meets once a week at the attaché's place.

"Last week, oh, quails, sublime quails," he tells me. "Succulent. Of course, tonight is simple, no comparison. Fondue, charcuterie, white wine. *All the originality lies in the Iranian bread and the* sabzi, *obviously. It'll be delicious."*

The attaché observes his guests bustling around with a delighted air, he likes animation in his kitchen, you sense. He delicately slices the ham and the salami, places some rounds on a large Iranian blue china dish. I haven't eaten pork in months, and I feel as if I'm committing an extraordinary transgression. We set the table, talk while we finish the aperitifs, and it's time to sit down. We take out the skewers and prepare the sabzi, *which, along with the* sangak *flatbread, gives a multicultural air to this pagan dinner. And the attaché exclaims, in a way that's not at all diplomatic:*

"Good, strip-fondue, whoever loses his piece of bread takes off his shirt." And he bursts out laughing, which makes him lift his eyes to the sky, shaking his head from right to left. Shocked, I cling to my fondue fork.

Wine is served, delicious, a white Graves. Mirza begins, plunges his bread into the melted cheese, and takes it out without any trouble, drawing little strands along with it. I try in turn: I have to admit it's excellent.

The conversation revolves around wine.

The attaché announces, with a satisfied air:

"I would like to announce that I am now a shareholder in a Côtes-du-Rhône vineyard. Yes, my dear friends."

I can read the envy on the faces of the two other sybarites.

"Oh, that's excellent." They nod their heads in unison. "The Côtes-du-Rhône!"

They talk about saccharimeters, vats, and fermentation. I'm pretty occupied with battling the fondue — I notice that, when it cools down, it's no piece of cake, if you'll excuse the expression, especially with a piece of Iranian bread, since it's soft and permeable, thus not supporting prolonged immersion in the warm liquid without disintegrating dangerously. Several times I almost lost my shirt.

In short, I did not eat very much.

Finally, the fondue ends without incident, with no one losing

anything but their illusions in the pot. Next comes dessert, coffee, digés-
tif, and talk about art, in precisely this order: candied chestnuts from
Provence, Italian espresso, Cognac, and "content and form." I drink in
the attaché's words, helped by the VSOP Cognac:
   "I am an aesthete," he says. "Aesthetics is in everything. Sometimes,
form even creates meaning, at bottom."
   "Which brings us back to the fondue," I say.
   I receive a black look from the two assistant aesthetes, but the attaché,
who has a sense of humor, makes a little nervous hiccup, ho-ho, before
continuing, with an inspired air:
   "Iran is the land of forms. A country that is aesthetically formal,"
he says, lingering over every syllable.

You see, this sort of thing leaves me with a lot of time to think about
you. I hope I've made you smile in these desperate times.

With much love,

                                 Franz

Paris is a tomb and I tell her humorous society stories, sketch
caricatures of people that she couldn't care less about, what an
idiot, what shame — sometimes absence and desperate powerlessness give you the confused gestures of a drowning man.
What's more this attaché allied a deep liking for Iran with immense cultural knowledge. Plus I lied, I didn't tell her about
those long weeks in Tehran without her, spent almost exclusively with Parviz reading poetry, the great Parviz, the friend
who patiently listened to everything I didn't say.

Except for Parviz, I had no friends left in Tehran. Faugier
had finally gone back, physically destroyed, morally lost in his
subject of study, in an opiated dream. He said farewell to me
as if he were leaving for the other world, gravely, with a sober

gravity that was quite frightening in that formerly exuberant dandy—I remembered the man from Istanbul, the seductive Gavroche, the prince of night in Istanbul and Tehran, and he had dissolved, almost faded away. I don't know what's become of him. Sarah and I talked about him many times, and one thing is more or less certain: Marc Faugier, despite all his expertise, all his publications, no longer belongs to the world of academia. Even Google yields no more news of him.

New researchers had arrived, among others a compatriot, an Austrian student of Bert Fragner, director of the Institute of Iranian Studies at the Academy of Sciences in Vienna, that same Academy of Sciences that had been founded, in his time, by dear Hammer-Purgstall. This historian wasn't a bad fellow, he just had one defect, which was to talk while walking—he would pace up and down the corridors thinking out loud in a low voice, for hours, kilometers of corridors traveled, and this monody as knowledgeable as it was unintelligible got on my nerves terribly. When he wasn't strolling back and forth, he would launch into endless Go parties with another newcomer, this one a Norwegian: an exotic Norwegian who played flamenco guitar at such a high level that every year he took part in a festival in Seville. Everything the world could offer in the way of absurd encounters: a philatelist Austrian passionate about the history of Iranian stamps playing Go with a gypsy Norwegian guitarist who specialized in research on oil administration.

Those last few weeks I lived at Parviz's house or as a recluse, aside from one or two social gatherings like that invitation to the music-loving cultural attaché's, surrounded by the objects that Sarah hadn't been able to take with her in her hurried departure for Paris: a lot of books, the prayer rug from Khorassan, of a magnificent mauve color, which I still have next to my bed, a silver-plated electric samovar, a collection of copies of ancient miniatures. Among the books, the works of Annemarie Schwarzenbach, of course, especially *The Happy Valley* and *Death in Persia*, in which the Swiss writer describes the valley of the Lahr, at the foot of Mount Damavand. Sarah and I had planned on going there, to that high arid valley where the streams from the highest summit in Iran flow, a valley where the Comte de Gobineau had also set his tent 150 years earlier — the majestic snow-capped cone streaked with basalt in the summer, the image, along with Mount Fuji or Kilimanjaro, of the perfect mountain, standing solitary in the middle of the sky, surpassing, from its height of 5,600 meters, the surrounding peaks. There was also a voluminous book of images based on Annemarie's life; many photos which she had taken herself in the course of her travels and portraits taken by others, especially her husband Claude Carac the embassy secretary — in one of them we see her half-naked, narrow shoulders, short hair, the water of the river up to her knees, arms alongside her body, wearing only a pair of black shorts. The nudity of her breasts, the position of her hands, hanging alongside her thighs, and her surprised face give her a fragile look, with a sad or vulnerable inexpressiveness, in the grandiose landscape of the high valley lined with rushes and thorn bushes and overhung by the dry, rocky slopes of the mountains. I spent entire nights of solitude leafing through this book of photographs, in my room, and regretted I didn't own any images of Sarah, any album to leaf through to find myself in her company again — I made up for it with Annemarie Schwarzenbach; I read the story of her journey with Ella Maillart from Switzerland to India. But it was in the two texts of passionate fever and narcotic melancholy that Annemarie sets in Iran — of which one is a more distanced reflection of the other, very intimate one — where I sought something of Sarah, for something that Sarah might have told me, the profound reason for her passion for the life and work of this "inconsolable angel." Both books were underlined and annotated in ink; you could retrace, according to the color of the annotations, the passages that had to do with anguish, the unspeakable fear that took hold of the narrator at night, the passages relating to drugs and illness and those concerning the Orient, the young woman's vision of the Orient. Reading her notes (spidery scrawls, black marginalia I had to decipher more than read) I could glimpse, or I thought I could glimpse, one of the basic questions that not only underlay Sarah's work, but that made Annemarie Schwarzenbach's so engaging—the Orient as resilience, as quest for a cure for an obscure illness, a profound anguish. A psychological quest. A mystical search without any god or transcendence other than the depths of the self, a search that, in the case of Schwarzenbach, resulted in a sad failure. There is nothing in this region to facilitate her cure, nothing to alleviate her pain: the mosques remain empty, the mihrab is only a niche in a wall; the landscapes are dried out in the summer, inaccessible in the winter. She moves forward in a deserted world. And even when she finds love, with a half-Turkish, half-Cherkess young woman and thinks she's filling with life the desolate surroundings she left near the slopes of blazing Damavand, what she discovers is death. Illness of the beloved and a visit from the Angel. Love lets us share the sufferings of the other no more than it cures our own. At bottom, we are always alone, said Annemarie Schwarzenbach, and I feared, as I deciphered her marginal notes to *Death in Persia*, that it was also Sarah's deep belief, a belief that no doubt, at the time I was reading those lines, was amplified by mourning, as it was for me by solitude.

Her interest in and passion for Buddhism are not just a search for a cure, but a profound conviction, which I knew was present long before her brother's death—her departure for India after her detours through the Far East of Parisian libraries was not a surprise, even though I took it as a slap, I have to admit, as if she'd abandoned me. It was me she was leaving along with Europe and I had every intention of making her pay for it, I must confess, I wanted to avenge myself on her suffering. It took this particularly touching email, talking about Darjeeling and Andalusia:

Darjeeling, June 15

Dearest Franz,

Here I am, back in Darjeeling, after a quick visit to Europe: Paris, two days for family, then Granada, two days for a boring conference (you know how it is) and two days to come back here, via Madrid, Delhi, and Calcutta. I'd have liked to go through Vienna (seen from here Europe is so small one can easily imagine crossing it on a whim) but I wasn't sure you were there. Or that you really wanted to see me.

Every time I go back to Darjeeling I feel as if I'm rediscovering calm, beauty, peace. The tea plantations devour the hills; they're little round shrubs with long leaves, planted close together: seen from above, the fields look like a mosaic of dense green buttons, mossy balls invading the Himalayan slopes.

Soon it will be monsoon season, in one month it will rain more than in your country in a year. The great cleansing. The mountains will sweat, drip, disgorge themselves; every street, every alleyway, every footpath will be transformed into a wild torrent. The stones, the bridges, sometimes even the houses are carried away.

I'm renting a little room not far from the monastery where my teacher teaches. Life is simple. I meditate in my room early in the morning, then I go to the monastery to receive teachings; in the afternoon I read or write a little, meditate again in the evening, then sleep, and so on. The routine suits me well. I'm trying to learn a little Nepalese and Tibetan, without much success. The vernacular, here, is English. Oh, guess what? I discovered that Alexandra David-Néel had been a singer, a soprano. And even began a career: can you believe, she was booked at the operas of Hanoi and Haiphong . . . Where she sang Massenet, Bizet, etc. The program from the Hanoi opera would interest you! Orientalism in the Orient, exoticism in exoticism, it's your field! Then Alexandra David-Néel was one of the first explorers of Tibet and one of the first Buddhist women in Europe. See, I'm thinking of you.

Someday we should talk about Tehran, even Damascus. I am aware of my share of responsibility in this whole story, which we could call "our story," if that weren't so grandiloquent. I'd very much like to come see you in Vienna. We could talk, a little; we could take walks—I still have a bunch of horrible museums to see. The Funeral Museum, for example. Just kidding. This is all a little incoherent . . . Probably because I'd like to tell you things I don't dare write, return to episodes one doesn't want to go back to—I never thanked you for your letters when Samuel died. The warmth and compassion I found there still shine today. No word of comfort has touched me as much as yours.

Two years soon. Two years already. Buddhists don't speak of "conversion," you don't convert to Buddhism, you take refuge in it. You take refuge in the Buddha. That's exactly what I did. I took refuge here, in the Buddha, the Dharma, and the Sangha. I'll follow the direction shown by those three compasses. I feel a little consoled. I'm discovering, inside me and around me, a new energy, a strength that doesn't require me at all to abdicate my reason, quite the contrary. What counts is experience.

I can see you smiling . . . It's hard to share. Picture me getting up at dawn with pleasure, meditating for an hour with pleasure, listening to and studying very old, wise texts that reveal the world to me much more naturally than anything I was able to read or hear before now. Their truth imposes itself very rationally. There is nothing to believe. There is no question of "faith." There is nothing but sentient beings, lost in suffering, there is nothing but the very simple, very complex awareness of a world where everything is connected, a world without substance. I'd like to show you all that, but I know that everyone travels this path on his own — or not.

Let's change the subject — in Granada I heard a fascinating talk, in the midst of torrents of boredom, a spark of beauty in the rivers of yawns. It was a paper on the Hebraic lyric poetry of Andalusia in relation to Arabic poetry, through the poems of Ibn Nagrila, a combatant-poet (he was a vizier) who they say composed even on the battlefield. How beautiful these poems were, and their Arabic "brothers"! Still full of those entirely earthly love songs, descriptions of faces, of lips, of gazes, I went for a stroll in the Alhambra. It was very beautiful out, and the sky contrasted with the red walls of the buildings, the blue color framed them, like a photograph. I was caught up in a strange feeling; I felt as if I had in front of me all the tumult of Time. Ibn Nagrila died long before the splendor of the Alhambra, and yet he sang of fountains and gardens, roses and springtime — these flowers in the Generalife Palace are no longer the same flowers, the stones in the walls themselves are no longer the same stones; I was thinking of the detours of my family, of history, which brought me there where, probably, my distant ancestors had lived, and I had the very strong sensation that all roses are only a single rose, all lives a single life, that time is a movement as illusory as the tide or the journey of the sun. A question of perspective. And perhaps because I was emerging from that conference of historians bent on patiently writing down the story of existences, I had a vision of Europe as indistinct, as multiple, as diverse as those rose bushes in the Alhambra that plunge their roots, without realizing it, so deeply into the past and the future, to such a point that it's impossible to say from where they're actually growing. And this dizzying sensation was not unpleasant, on the contrary, it reconciled me for a bit with the world, revealed to me for an instant the woollen ball of the Wheel.

I can hear your laughter from here. But I can assure you it was a sin-

gular, very rare moment. Both the experience of beauty and the sensation
of its emptiness. OK, on these fine words I'll have to leave you, it's getting
late. Tomorrow I'll go to the internet café to "send" this missive. Answer
me soon, tell me a little about Vienna, your life in Vienna, your plans . . .
  With love,
  Yours,

                                                              Sarah

for me to find myself entirely disarmed, surprised, as in love as
I was in Tehran, even more, perhaps—what had I done during
those two years, I'd buried myself in my Viennese life, in academia; I had written articles, pursued some research, published a book in an obscure collection for scholars; I had felt
the beginnings of illness, the first nights of insomnia. To take
refuge. That's a beautiful expression, a beautiful practice. To
fight against suffering, or rather to try to escape this world, this
Wheel of Fate, which is nothing but suffering. When I received
this Andalusian letter I collapsed: Tehran came flooding back
to me, the memories of Damascus too, Paris, Vienna, suddenly
tinted, the way a simple ray of light is enough to give its tonality to the immense sky of evening, sadness and bitterness. Dr.
Kraus didn't think I was in very good shape. Mother was worried
about my thinness and my apathy. I was trying to compose, a
practice (aside from my tinkering with the poems by Levet in
Tehran) I had abandoned for many years, to write, put down on
paper, or rather the ether of the screen, my memories of Iran,
to find a music that would resemble them, a song. In vain I was
trying to discover, around me, at the university or at a concert,
a new face on which to impose these cumbersome, rebellious
feelings that wanted no one but Sarah; I ended up fleeing (like
the other night with Katharina Fuchs) what I myself had sought
to initiate.

Fine surprise: when I was struggling in the past, Nadim came to give a recital in Vienna, with an ensemble from Aleppo; I bought a seat in the third row of the orchestra — I hadn't warned him of my presence. They played the *rast, bayati,* and *hedjazi* modes, long improvisations sustained by percussion, dialogue with a *ney* — and this reed flute, long and grave, married wonderfully well with Nadim's lute, so brilliant. Without a singer, Nadim relied on traditional melodies; the audience (the entire Arabic community of Vienna was there, including the ambassadors) recognized the songs before they got lost in the variations, and you could almost hear the hall humming these tunes in a low voice, with a concentrated fervor, vibrant with respectful passion. Nadim smiled as he played — the shadow of his short beard gave, by contrast, even more luminosity to his face. I knew he couldn't see me, blinded by the glare of the footlights. After the encore, during the very long applause, I thought about slipping away, going home without greeting him, fleeing; when the lights came back on, I was still hesitating. What would I say to him? What would we speak about, aside from Sarah? Did I really want to hear what he said?

I found out where his dressing room was; the hallway was full of officials waiting to greet the artists. I felt a little ridiculous, in the midst of these people; I was afraid — of what? That he wouldn't recognize me? That he'd be as embarrassed as I was? Nadim is much more generous — scarcely had he crossed the threshold of his dressing room than without even those few seconds of hesitation that separate a stranger from an old comrade he strode through the crowd to embrace me, saying, I hoped you'd be here, *old friend.*

During the dinner that followed, surrounded by musicians, diplomats, and VIPs seated opposite each other, Nadim told me he didn't hear much from Sarah, that he hadn't seen her since

Samuel's funeral in Paris; she was somewhere in Asia, nothing more. He asked me if I knew they had gotten divorced long ago, and this question wounded me terribly; Nadim was unaware of our closeness. Despite himself, by this simple phrase he tore me away from her. I changed the subject, we talked about our memories of Syria, the concerts in Aleppo, my few lute classes in Damascus with him, our evenings, the *ouns*, that beautiful Arabic word used for gatherings of friends. I didn't dare mention the civil war that was just beginning.

A Jordanian diplomat (impeccable dark suit, white shirt, gold-rimmed glasses) suddenly interrupted the conversation, he had known the Iraqi oud master Munir Bashir in Amman, he said—I have often noticed, in these sorts of musical dinners, that those present easily mention the Great Performers they have met or heard, without it being apparent if these implicit comparisons are praises or humiliations; these evocations often provoke, among the musicians, annoyed smiles, marked with suppressed anger faced with the boorishness of the so-called admirers. Nadim smiled to the Jordanian with a weary, knowing, or blasé air, yes Munir Bashir was the greatest and no, he had never had the luck to meet him, even though they had a friend in common, Jalaleddin Weiss. The name of Weiss brought us immediately back to Syria, to our memories, and the diplomat finally turned to his neighbor on the right, a UN official, abandoning us to our reminiscences. With the help of the wine and fatigue, Nadim, in that exhausted state of exaltation that follows great concerts, confided to me point-blank that Sarah had been the love of his life. Despite the failure of their marriage. If only life had been easier for me, in those years, he said. If only we'd had that child, he said. That would have changed things, he said. The past is the past. And tomorrow it's her birthday, he said.

I looked at Nadim's hands, I could see again his fingers sliding over the walnut of the oud or handling the plectrum, that eagle's feather you have to hold without strangling it. The tablecloth was white, there were green squash seeds fallen from the crust of a piece of bread next to my glass, in which bubbles were rising slowly to the surface of the water; tiny bubbles, which formed a thin vertical line, without it being apparent, in the absolute transparency of the whole, where they could be coming from. Suddenly these same bubbles were in my eye, I shouldn't have looked at them, they rose and rose — their needle-like thinness, their sourceless obstinacy, with no other goal but ascendency and disappearance, their slight burning made me squeeze my eyelids shut, incapable of raising my eyes to Nadim, to long ago, to that past whose name he had just uttered — the longer I kept my head lowered, the more the burning, at the corners of my eyes, intensified, the bubbles grew and grew, they sought, as in the glass, to reach the outside, I had to keep them from doing so.

I made up an urgent excuse and fled in a cowardly way, after having summarily excused myself.

Darjeeling, March 1

Dearest François-Joseph,

Thank you for this magnificent birthday gift. It's the most beautiful jewel anyone has ever given me — and I'm delighted that you're the one who discovered it. It will find a prize place in my collection. I know neither this language, nor this music, but the story of this song is absolutely magical. Sevdah! Saudade! *I will include it, with your permission, in an upcoming article. Always these shared constructions, these round-trips, these superimposed masks.* Vienna, Porta Orientis; *all the cities of Europe are gates to the Orient. Do you remember that Persian literature of Europe that Scarcia talked about in Tehran? All of Europe is in the Orient. Everything is cosmopolitan, interdependent. I imagine that* sevdalinka *resounding between Vienna and Sarajevo like the* saudade *of the fados of Lisbon, and I'm a little . . . A little what? I miss you, you and Europe. I can feel very strongly the* sankhara dukkha, *omnipresent suffering, which is perhaps the Buddhist name for melancholy. The movement of the wheel of samsara. The passage of time, the suffering of the awareness of impermanence. I must not give in to it. I will meditate; I always include you in my visualizations, you are behind me, with all the people I love.*

With love, say hello to the Strudlhofstiege for me,

S.

Franz Ritter wrote:

Dearest Sarah,

Happy birthday!
I hope all's well at the monastery. You're not too cold? I picture you sitting cross-legged facing a bowl of rice in a freezing cell, and it's a little worrisome, as visions go. I suppose your Lamasery isn't like the one in Tintin in Tibet, *but maybe you'll have the luck of seeing a monk levitating. Or hearing the* radong, *the great Tibetan horn, I think they make a din of all the devils. Apparently, they come in different lengths, according to the tonalities; these instruments are so large that it's very difficult to modulate the sound with the breath and the mouth. I looked for some recordings in our sound library, but there isn't much on the "Tibetan music" shelf. But enough chatter. I'm allowing myself to disturb you in your contemplation because I have a little birthday present for you.*
Bosnian folklore includes traditional songs called sevdalinke. *The name comes from a Turkish word,* sevdah, *borrowed from the Arabic* sawda, *which means "the black mood." In Avicenna's* Canon of

Medicine, *it's the name for the dark mood, the* melan kholia *of the Greeks, melancholy. So it's the Bosnian equivalent for the Portuguese word* saudade, *which (unlike what etymologists assert) also comes from the Arabic* sawda *— and from the same black bile.* Sevdalinke *are the expression of melancholy, like* fados. *The melodies and the accompaniment are a Balkan version of Ottoman music. End of etymological preamble. Now, your gift:*

I'm giving you a song, a sevdalinka: Kraj tanana šadrvana, *which tells a little story. The daughter of the sultan, as night falls, listens to the clear water of her fountain tinkling; every evening, a young Arab slave watches the magnificent princess in silence, fixedly. Each time, the slave's face turns even paler; finally he becomes pale as death. She asks him his first name, where he comes from, and what his tribe is; he simply replies that his name is Mohammed, that he comes from Yemen, from the tribe of the Asra: it's those Asra, he says, who die when they fall in love.*

The text of this song with the Turkish-Arab motif is not, as one might think, an old poem from the Ottoman era. It's a work by Safvet-beg Bašagić — a translation of a famous poem by Heinrich Heine, "Der Asra." (Remember the tomb of poor Heine at the Montmartre cemetery?)

Safvet-beg, born in 1870 in Nevesinje in Herzegovina, studied in Vienna at the end of the nineteenth century; he knew Turkish, and learned Arabic and Persian from Viennese Orientalists. He wrote an Austro-Hungarian thesis in German; he translated Omar Khayyam into Bosnian. This sevdalinka *joins Heinrich Heine to the ancient Ottoman Empire — the Orientalist poem becomes Oriental. It rediscovers (after a long imaginary journey, which passes through Vienna and Sarajevo) the music of the Orient.*

It's one of the most well-known and most often sung sevdalinke *in Bosnia, where few among those who hear it know that it comes from the imagination of the poet of the* Lorelei, *a Jew who was born in Düsseldorf and died in Paris. You can listen to it easily (I recommend the versions by Himzo Polovina) on the internet.*

I hope this little gift pleases you,
With much love,
Soon I hope,

Franz

I wanted to tell her about my meeting with Nadim, the concert, the fragments of their intimacy he had confided in me, but I couldn't bring myself to, and this strange birthday gift took the place of a difficult confession. A seven a.m. thought: my cowardliness is unprecedented, I abandoned an old friend there for the matter of a woman, as Mother would say. I left those doubts inside me, those idiotic doubts that Sarah would have swept aside with one of her definitive gestures, at least I think so, I didn't ask her about these things. She never talked to me again about Nadim in terms that were anything but respectful and distant. My thoughts are so confused that I don't know if Nadim is my friend, my enemy, or a distant ghostly memory whose Shakespearean appearance in Vienna only confused my contradictory emotions even more, the trail of that comet that illuminated my sky in Tehran.

I say to myself "it's time to forget all that, Sarah, the past, the Orient" and yet I am still obsessed, a compass pointing always toward the inbox of my email, still no news from Sarawak, it's one p.m. over there, is she getting ready for lunch, the weather's fine, between 73 and 80 degrees, according to the illusory world of the computer. When Xavier de Maistre published *A Journey Around My Room*, he didn't imagine that 150 years later this kind of exploration would become the norm. Farewell colonial pith-helmet, farewell mosquito nets, I visit Sarawak in my bathrobe. Then I'll do a tour of the Balkans, listen to a *sevdalinka* while watching images from Višegrad. Then I'll cross Tibet, from Darjeeling to the sands of the Taklamakan, desert of deserts, and I'll reach Kashgar, city of mysteries and caravans—in front of me, to the west, stand the Pamirs; behind them Tajikistan and the Wakhan corridor that stretches out like a hooked finger, you could glide on its phalanges as far as Kabul.

It's the hour of abandonment, of solitude and agony; the night is holding firm, it hasn't yet decided to veer into day, nor has my body agreed to veer into sleep—tense, my back stiff, arms heavy, the beginnings of a cramp in my calf, my diaphragm painful, I should lie down, why go back to bed now, with dawn just around the corner.

This should be the time for prayer, the time to open the *Horologion,* the Book of Hours for those still awake, and to pray; Lord have pity on those, like me, who have no faith and await a miracle they won't be able to see. But the miracle has been close to us. Some have smelt the perfume of incense in the desert, around the monasteries of the Fathers; they have heard, in the immensity of stones, the memory of Saint Macarius, the hermit who, one day, in the evening of his life, crushed a flea with his hand: he was sad about his revenge and to punish himself stayed naked in the desert for six months, until his body was nothing but an open wound. And he died in peace, "leaving the memory of great virtues to the world." We have seen the column of St. Simeon Stylites, the eroded rock in its great pink basilica, St. Simeon man of the stars, whom the stars discovered naked, on summer nights, on his immense pillar, in the hollow of Syrian valleys; we have seen St. Joseph of Cupertino, aerial fool, transformed into a dove in the midst of churches by his cowl and levitation; have followed the footsteps of St. Nicholas the Alexandrine, who also left to rejoin the desert sands, which are God powdered in the sun, and the traces of those less illustrious saints which are slowly being covered by the pebbles, the gravel, footsteps, bones caressed in turn by the moon, friable in winter and oblivion: the pilgrims who drowned in front of Acre, lungs full of the water eroding the Promised Land, the barbarous, cannibalistic knight who had infidels roasted in Antioch before converting to divine unicity in Oriental aridity, the Cherkess sapper of the ramparts of Vienna, who dug by hand the fate of Europe, he betrayed and was forgiven, the little medieval sculptor endlessly sanding a wooden Christ while singing lullabies to it as if to a doll, the Kabbalist from Spain buried in the Zohar, the alchemist in purple robes of the elusive mercury, the magi of Persia whose dead flesh never sullied the Earth, the crows who popped out the eyes of hanged men like cherries, the wild beasts tearing apart the condemned in the arena, the sawdust, the sand that absorbs their blood, the shouts and ashes of the pyre, the twisted, fertile olive tree, the dragons, the griffons, the lakes, the oceans, the endless sediments where age-old butterflies are imprisoned, the mountains disappearing into their own glaciers, pebble after pebble, second after second, until the liquid magma sun, all things singing the praises of their creator—but faith rejects me, even in the depths of night. Aside from my satori of the lifeguard's flip-flops in the mosque of Süleyman the Magnificent, no ladder to watch the angels climbing, no cave to sleep in for two hundred years, well guarded by a dog, near Ephesus; only Sarah found, in other grottos, the energy of tradition and its path to enlightenment. Her long path toward Buddhism began with a scholarly interest, with the discovery, in Masudi's *Golden Prairies*, of the story of Budasaf, when she was working on the idea of the marvelous at the beginning of her career: her journey to the East crossed classical Islam, Christianity, and even the mysterious Sabeans of the Koran, whom Masudi, from the depths of his eighth century, thought were inspired by that same Budasaf, the first Muslim image of the Buddha whom he associates with Hermes the Wise. She patiently reconstituted the transformations of these stories, up to their Christian counterpart, the life of the saints Barlaam and Josaphat, the Syrian version of the story of the bodhisattva and his path toward awakening; she developed a passion for the life of Prince Siddhartha Gautama himself, the Buddha of our era, and his teachings. I know she has *love* for the Buddha and for the Tibetan tradition whose meditation practices she has adopted, for the characters of Marpa the Translator and his disciple Milarepa, the black magician who succeeded, around the year 1100, by bending himself to the terrifying discipline imposed by his master, at attaining enlightenment within a single lifetime, which makes all aspirants to awakening dream—including Sarah. She soon abandoned colonial opium to concentrate on the Buddha; she became enthusiastic about the exploration of Tibet, about the scholars, missionaries and adventurers who, in modern times, revealed Tibetan Buddhism to Europe before, in the 1960s, great Tibetan teachers settled in the four corners of the West and themselves began transmitting spiritual energy. Like an annoyed gardener who, thinking he's destroying a weed, ends up disseminating the seeds to the four winds, China, by occupying Tibet, burning down the monasteries and sending countless monks into exile, spread Tibetan Buddhism throughout the world.

Even to Leopoldstadt: emerging from our visit to the Museum of Crime, museum of cut-up women, executioners, and brothels, in one of those little streets where Vienna wavers between low houses, nineteenth-century buildings, and modern apartment houses, a stone's throw from the Carmelite market, as I was looking at my feet, so as to avoid looking at her too much, and as she was thinking out loud about the Viennese soul, crime, and death, Sarah stopped suddenly and said, Look, a Buddhist center! And she began reading the programs in the window, waxing ecstatic over the names of the Tibetan Rinpoches who sponsored this *gompa* in exile — she was surprised that this community belonged to the same Tibetan school as she did, red or yellow hats, I forget, I never bothered to remember the color of the hat or the names of the great Tulkus she reveres, but I was happy at the auspiciousness she saw in this encounter, the bright glints in her eyes and her smile, even secretly envisaging that she might, perhaps, someday, make this center in Leopoldstadt her new cave — there were many auspicious signs that day, a strange mixture of our shared past: two streets lower down, we encountered Hammer-Purgstall Street; I had forgotten (if I had ever known it) that a street in Vienna was named after the old Orientalist. The plaque mentioned him as "founder of the Academy of Sciences," and it's certainly this quality, more than his passion for Oriental texts, that had earned him this distinction. The Hainfeld conference was revolving in my head as Sarah (black trousers, red turtleneck sweater, black coat under her flamboyant locks) kept talking about fate. A mixture of erotic images, memories of Tehran and Hammer-Purgstall's castle in Styria was devouring me, I took her arm and, so as not to leave the neighborhood right away, not to cross the canal again, I veered off toward the Taborstrasse.

In the pastry shop where we stopped, a swanky establishment with a neo-Baroque décor, Sarah was talking about missionaries and I felt, as she was talking about Huc the Lazarist from Montauban, as if this ocean of words had no other aim than to hide her embarrassment; even though the story of this Father Huc — so fascinated by his trip to Lhasa and his debates with Buddhist monks that during the next twenty years he dreamed of returning there — was more or less interesting, I had trouble giving it the necessary attention. Everywhere I saw the ruins of our failed relationship, the painful impossibility of rediscovering the same tempo, the same melody, and then, as she was wearing herself out inculcating me in the rudiments of philosophy, the Buddha, the Dharma, the Sangha, while drinking her tea, I couldn't help but miss those blue-veined hands wrapped around her cup, those lips painted with the same red as her sweater that left a slight stain on the porcelain, her carotid beating under the angle of her face, and I was sure that the only thing that united us now, beyond the memories melted around us like stained snow, was this shared embarrassment, this awkward chatter that sought only to fill the silence of our confusion. Tehran had disappeared. The complicity of bodies had vanished. The complicity of souls was in the process of disappearing. This second visit to Vienna was opening up a long winter that the third visit only confirmed — she wanted to work on Vienna as *Porta Orientis* and didn't even sleep at my place, which, at bottom, kept me from languishing, motionless and solitary in my bed, hoping all night she would come join me; I could hear the pages of her book turning, then could see her lamp go out, under my door, and I would listen for a long time to her breathing, only renouncing at dawn the hope that she would appear against the light on the threshold to my bedroom, even just for a kiss on my forehead, which would have chased away the monsters of darkness.

Sarah didn't know that Leopoldstadt, where this pastry shop was, had been the headquarters of Jewish life in Vienna in the nineteenth century, with the greatest temples in the city, including the magnificent, they say, Turkish synagogue in the Moorish style — all those buildings were destroyed in 1938, I explained, and all that was left were commemorative plaques and a few images of the time. Near here Schoenberg, Schnitzler, and Freud had grown up — the names that came to my mind, among so many others, like the name of a school friend, my only Jewish friend in Vienna: his name was Seth, but his first name was actually Septimus, since he was the seventh and final child of a very kind couple of professors from Galicia. His parents were not religious: as a cultural education, they forced their son to cross the entire city two afternoons a week to Leopoldstadt to take lessons in Yiddish literature from an old Lithuanian master who had miraculously escaped catastrophe and whom the storms of the twentieth century had finally deposited in the Taborstrasse. These teachings were a real chore for Septimus; they consisted, between studies of eighteenth-century grammarians and dialectical subtleties, of reading pages and pages of Isaac Bashevis Singer and commenting on them. One day my friend complained to his master:

"Master, would it be possible to change authors, even just once?"

The master must have had a sense of humor, for Septimus was inflicted, as punishment, the task of memorizing a very long short story by Israel Joshua Singer, big brother of the former; I can see him again reciting that story of betrayal for hours on end, until he knew it by heart. His Roman first name, his open friendliness, and his classes on Yiddish culture made him an exceptional being in my eyes. Septimus Leibowitz later became one of the greatest historians of Yiddishland before the Destruction, pulling, in long monographs, an entire material and linguistic world out of oblivion. It's been too long since I've seen him, even though our offices are less than two hundred meters away from each other, in one of the courtyards of that miraculous campus of the University of Vienna that the whole world envies — during her last visit Sarah thought our *cortile*, which we share with art historians, was absolutely magnificent: she gushed over our patio, with its two big porticos and the bench where she waited quietly, book in hand, for me to finish my class. I hoped, bringing to an end my lecture on Debussy's *Pagodes*, that she hadn't gotten lost and had followed my directions to find our porte-cochère in the Garnisongasse; I couldn't help but look out the window every five minutes, so much so that the students must have been wondering what meteorological bug had bitten me, to search the Viennese sky so anxiously, which moreover was of an entirely customary gray. At the end of the seminar I devoured the stairs four at a time, then tried to resume a normal gait as I reached the ground floor; she was reading calmly on the bench, a big orange scarf around her shoulders. Since early that morning, I had been in doubt: should I show her around the department? I wavered between my childlike pride at showing her my office, the library, the classrooms, and the shame that would seize me if we met colleagues, especially female ones: how to introduce her? Sarah, a friend, and that's it, everyone has friends. Except no one had ever seen me in this department with anyone other than honorable colleagues or my mother, and even then, very rarely. Exactly, maybe it's time for that to change, I thought. To come with a world-renowned star of research, a charismatic woman, that's something that would polish up my image, I thought. But maybe not, I thought. Maybe they'd think I want to cause a sensation, with this sublime red-head with the orange scarf. And at bottom, did I really want to fritter away a precious asset in hallway conversations? Sarah's staying too short a time to waste it with colleagues who might find her to their taste. Already she isn't sleeping at my place, with the doubtful excuse of taking advantage of God knows what luxury hotel, so I shouldn't abandon her to the hands of smutty professors or jealous harpies.

Sarah was immersed in an enormous paperback and was smiling; she was smiling at the book. The day before I had found her in a café in the center of town, we'd strolled along the Graben, but just as a carpenter's plane takes a while to lay bare the warmth of wood under an old varnish, seeing her there, absorbed in her reading, her scarf around her shoulders, in this familiar, quotidian setting, I was submerged in an immense wave of melancholy, movement of water and salt, tenderness and nostalgia. She was forty-five and could pass for a student. A dark comb held back her hair, a silver fibula shone on her shawl. She wasn't wearing make-up. She had a childlike joy on her face.

Finally she noticed I was watching her, got up, closed her book. Did I rush over to her, did I cover her with kisses until she disappeared into me, no, not at all. I kissed her clumsily on the cheek, from afar.

"So, you've seen it, it's not bad here, is it?"

"How are you? Did your lecture go well? This place is magnificent, really, what a wonder of a campus!"

I explained to her that this immense ensemble used to be the general hospital of Vienna, founded in the eighteenth century, enlarged throughout the nineteenth, and donated to scholarship just a few years ago. I showed her around the site — the big square, the bookshops; the former Jewish oratory of the hospital (*healing for souls*) which today is a monument to the victims of Nazism, a small dome-shaped construction reminiscent of the mausoleums of saints in Syrian villages. Sarah kept repeating "What a beautiful university." "Another kind of monastery," I replied, which made her smile. Crossing the successive courtyards we arrived at the wide, clumsy, cracked round brick tower of the former asylum for the mad, which with its five floors dominates a little park where a group of students, sitting in the grass despite the threatening weather, were talking and eating sandwiches. The long, very narrow windows, the graffiti on the façade, and the fencing round an endless renovation worksite gave the building an absolutely sinister air — perhaps because I knew what sorts of horrors the Narrenturm contained, the

Museum of Pathological Anatomy, a jumble of jars of formaldehyde full of atrocious tumors, congenital malformations, bicephalous creatures, deformed fetuses, syphilitic chancres, and bladder stones in rooms with peeling paint, dusty wardrobes, uneven floors where you stumble over missing tiles, guarded by white-smocked medics who make you wonder if, for fun, they get drunk on the alcohol from the medical preparations, one day testing the juice of a phallus afflicted with gigantism and the next that of a megalocephalous embryo, naively hoping to acquire their symbolic properties. All the horror of nature in its pure state. The pain of dead bodies replaced that of insane minds and the only shouts you hear there, these days, are the screams of terror of a few tourists who walk through these circles of affliction that are as bad as those of Hell.

Sarah took pity on me: my description was enough for her, she didn't insist (a sign, I naively thought, that her Buddhist practice had calmed down her passion for horrors) on visiting that immense dump of medicine from long ago. We sat down on a bench not far from the students; fortunately Sarah couldn't understand the subject of their conversation, not very scholarly. She was dreaming out loud, she talked about that Narrenturm, compared it to the big novel she was reading: it's the tower of Don Quixote, she said. The Tower of the Mad. *Don Quixote* is the first Arabic novel, you know. The first European novel and the first Arabic novel, look, Cervantes attributes it to Sayyid Hamid Ibn al-Ayyil, which he writes as Cide Hamete Benengeli. The first great madman in literature appears from the pen of a Mudejar historian from La Mancha. They should take over that tower and make it into a museum of madness, which would begin with the Eastern saints mad for Christ, the Don Quixotes, and would include quite a few Orientalists. A museum of integration and bastardy.

"They could even offer an apartment to our friend Bilger, on the top floor, with windows to be able to observe him."

"How mean you can be. No, on the top floor there would be the Arabic original of *Quixote*, written 240 years later, *The Life and Adventures of Fariac*, by Faris al-Shidyaq."

She continued her explorations of the lands of dream. But she was probably right, that might not be a bad idea, a museum for the other in the self in the Tower of the Mad, both an homage to and an exploration of otherness. A vertiginous museum, as vertiginous as that round asylum with cells overflowing with the debris of corpses and deadly juices worthy of her article on Sarawak—how long has she been there, a few months at most, when was the last email she sent me,

Dearest Franz,

Soon I'll leave Darjeeling.

A week ago, my teacher spoke to me, after the teachings. I should return to the world, he said. He thinks my place is not here. It's not a punishment, he said. It's hard to admit. You know me, I feel wounded and discouraged. It's pride speaking, I know that. I feel as if I'm a child who's been unfairly scolded, and I suffer from seeing how powerful my ego is. As if, in disappointment, everything I've learned here disappears. Suffering, dukkha, is the strongest thing. The prospect of going back to Europe—that is, Paris—exhausts me in advance. I've been tentatively offered a post in Calcutta at the French School of the Far East. Nothing official, just an associate researcher, but at least that gives me a starting point. Some new territories. Working on India would fascinate me—on the representations of India in Europe, on images of Europe in India. On the influence of Indian thought in the nineteenth and twentieth centuries. On Christian missionaries in India. Just as I've done for two years on Buddhism. Of course none of that puts bread on the table, but I could

*possibly find a few classes to give here and there. Life is so easy in India.
Or so hard.*

*I can imagine your reaction (I can hear your earnest, sure-of-yourself
tone): Sarah, you're running away. No, you'd say: you're fleeing. The
Art of Flight. After all these years, I don't have many attachments in
France — a few colleagues, two or three old high school friends whom I
haven't seen in ten years. My parents. Sometimes I imagine myself going
back to their apartment, my room as a teenager, next to Samuel's full
of relics, and I tremble. The few months I spent there after his death,
immersed in colonial opium, still send shivers up my spine. My teacher
is the person who knows me better than anyone, and he no doubt is right:
a monastery is not a place to hide. Nonattachment is not a flight. At
least that's what I understood. Yet, even if I think about it deeply, I have
trouble seeing the difference . . . This command is so brutal to me that it's
incomprehensible.*

With love, I'll write more very soon,

S.

*P.S. Upon rereading this letter I see only the confusion of my own
emotions, the product of my pride. What an image you'll have of me!
I don't know why I write all this to you — or rather, yes, I do know.
Forgive me.*

Since last spring, no other signs of life despite my many letters, as usual — I kept her up to date on my slightest actions and
thoughts, my musical investigations; I worried about her health
without bothering her with the difficulties of mine, my countless appointments with Dr. Kraus ("Ah, Dr. Ritter, happy to see
you here. When you're cured or dead I'll be terribly bored") to
find sleep and reason, and finally I grew weary. Silence comes
after everything. Everything is enclosed in silence. Everything
is extinguished there, or falls asleep there.

Until the new installment of her thoughts on symbolic cannibalism I received yesterday morning. The wine of the dead
of Sarawak. She compares this practice to a medieval legend,
a tragic love poem, which first appears in Thomas of Britain's
Roman de Tristan—Iseult sighs for Tristan, and from her sadness
a somber song is born, which she sings to her ladies in waiting;
this lyric lay tells of the fate of Guirun, surprised by a ruse of his
beloved's husband, and killed immediately. The husband then
removes Guirun's heart, and makes the woman Guirun loved
eat it. This story is then transposed many times; many women
condemned to swallowing their lovers' hearts, in terrifying ban-
quets. The life of the troubadour Guillem de Cabestan ends in
this way, with him killed and his mistress forced to devour his
heart, before she leaps out of her tower window. Sometimes
the most extreme violence has unsuspected consequences; it
allows the lovers to be inside each other once and for all, to
overcome the abyss that separates self from other. Love is realized in death, Sarah argues, which is very sad. I wonder which
is the least enviable role, the eaten or the eater, despite all the
culinary precautions medieval tales surround themselves with
to describe the horrible recipe of the heart in love.

Look, the night is beginning to turn light. I can hear a few
birds. Obviously I'm starting to be sleepy. My eyes are closing.
I didn't correct that paper, but I had promised that student—

Dearest Franz,

*Forgive me for not sending you news earlier—it's been so long since
I wrote to you that I don't know anymore how to break this silence; so I
sent you that article—I did well.*

*I've been in Sarawak since early summer, after a brief stay in Calcutta
(an even crazier city than you can imagine) and Java, where I met the*

ghosts of Rimbaud and Segalen. In Sarawak I knew nothing and no one other than the saga of the Brooke family, and it's good sometimes to abandon yourself to novelty and discovery. I followed a very nice anthropologist into the forest, she's the one who put me on the trail (if I can put it that way) of the wine of the dead and let me spend some time with the Berawans.

How are you? You can't imagine how happy your (short) email made me. I've thought a lot about Damascus and Tehran, these last few days. About time passing. I pictured my article in a canvas sack in the bottom of a boat, then on board a train, in a bicyclist's saddlebag, in your mailbox, and finally in your hands. Quite a journey for a few pages.

Tell me a little about yourself . . .

With much love, soon I hope,

Sarah

Franz Ritter wrote:

Dearest, I received your offprint yesterday morning, I didn't know they were still printing those . . . Thank you very much, but how horrible, that wine of the dead! I'm worried, all of a sudden. Are you doing well? What are you doing in Sarawak? Here it's everything as usual. The Christmas market has just opened in the middle of the university. Atrocious odors of mulled wine and sausages. Do you plan on coming back through Europe soon?

Send me news.

Much love.

Franz

The heart hasn't been eaten, it's still beating—of course she doesn't realize I'm also sitting in front of the screen. Reply. But is she doing well? What's this story of the Berawans, I was so worried I couldn't get any sleep. Nothing much new in my old city. How long is she staying in Sarawak? Lie: what a coincidence, I'd just gotten up when her email arrived. Love, sign and send quickly, so as not to give her the possibility of setting off for God knows what mysterious lands.

And wait.

And wait. No, I can't stay here rereading over and over her emails waiting for

Franz!

It's strange and wonderful to know you're there, on the other side of the world, and to think that these emails travel much faster than the sun. I feel as if you're listening to me.

You tell me my article on the Berawans of Sarawak worries you — I'm happy you're thinking of me; in fact I don't feel so great, I'm a little sad, right now. But that has nothing to do with Sarawak, it's the hazards of the calendar: suddenly the day comes round again and I plunge into commemoration — then everything is slightly tinged with mourning, despite myself, and this little fog takes a few days to dissipate.

As you read, the Berawans place the bodies of their dead in earthen jars on the verandas of "longhouses," those collective habitations equivalent to our villages where up to a hundred families can live. They let the corpse decompose. The liquid from the decomposition flows through a hollow bamboo placed at the bottom of the jar. Like for rice wine. They wait for this life to stop flowing from the body to declare it dead. Death, for them, is a long process, not a single instant. This liquid residue from putrefaction is a sign of the life that's still present. A fluid, tangible, drinkable life.

Beyond the horror that this tradition might provoke in us, there is a great beauty in this custom. It's death that escapes from the body, not just life. Both together, always. It's not just a symbolic cannibalism, like that of Dik el-Jinn the Mad from love who got drunk from the cup shaped from the ashes of his passion. It's a cosmogony.

Life is a long meditation on death.

Remember the Death of Isolde, *which you spoke to me about at such length? You heard in that a total love, of which Wagner himself wasn't aware. A moment of love, of union, of unity with the All, unity between the Eastern enlightened ones and Western darkness, between text and music, between voice and orchestra. As for me, I hear in it the expression of compassion,* karuna. *Not just Eros seeking eternity. Music as the "universal expression of the suffering of the world," said Nietzsche. This Isolde loves, at the instant of her death, so much, that she loves the entire world. Flesh allied with spirit. It's a fragile instant. It contains the seed for its own destruction. Every work contains the seeds of its own destruction. Like us. We are equal neither to love nor to death. For that we need enlightenment, awareness. Otherwise we just make corpse juice, everything that goes out of us is nothing but an elixir of suffering.*

I miss you. I miss laughter. A little lightness. I'd very much like to be near you. I've had enough of travel. No, that's not true — I'll never have enough of travel, but I've understood something, maybe along with Pessoa:

> They say that the good Khayyam rests
> In Nishapur among the fragrant roses
> But it's not Khayyam who lies there,
> It's here he is, he is our roses.

I think I can guess now what my teacher meant to tell me, in Darjeeling, when he recommended that I leave. The world needs integration, diasporas. Europe is no longer my continent, so I can go back to it. Be part of the networks that intersect there, explore it as a stranger. Bring something to it. Give, in my turn, and bring to light the gift of diversity.

I'll come to Vienna for a little, what do you think of that? I'll come find you at the university, I'll sit on the bench in the pretty courtyard, I'll wait for you, looking by turns at the light from your office and the readers in the library; a teacher will have left the window of his lecture room open; music will fill the patio, and I will have, like the last time, the sensation of being in a friendly, reassuring world, of pleasure and knowledge. I'll laugh in advance at your sullen surprise of seeing me there, you'll say, "You could have warned me, all the same," and you'll have that tender, half-embarrassed gesture, a little stilted, that makes you stick your chest toward me to kiss me while stepping back a little, hands behind your back. I like these hesitations very much, they remind me of Aleppo, Palmyra, and especially Tehran, they're sweet and tender.

We are not enlightened beings, unfortunately. We form a notion of difference, the other, at times, we glimpse ourselves struggling in our hesitations, our difficulties, our mistakes. I'll come find you at the university, we'll walk by the Tower of the Mad, our tower, you'll inveigh against the building's state of dilapidation and abandon and about the "museum of horrors" it contains; you'll say "it's absolutely inadmissible! The university should be ashamed of itself!" and your rantings will make me laugh; then we'll walk down the Strudlhofstiege to deposit my suitcase at your place and you'll be a little embarrassed, you'll avoid looking at me. You know, there's something I never told you: the last time I went to Vienna, I agreed to stay in that luxury hotel they had offered me, remember? Instead of sleeping at your place? That had made you terribly angry. I think it was in the secret, slightly childlike hope that you'd accompany me there, that we'd resume, in a beautiful unknown room, what we had begun in Tehran.

All of a sudden, I pine for you,
How beautiful Vienna is,
How far away Vienna is,

S.

She's got some nerve. *Guindé*, "stilted," according to my French dictionary, means "lacking naturalness, trying to appear dignified," how shameful. She's going too far. She really knows how to make herself detestable, sometimes. If only she knew my state, my terrifying state, if she knew the throes I'm struggling in, she wouldn't make fun of me in that way. It's dawn; it's at daybreak that people die, says Victor Hugo. Sarah. Isolde. No, not Isolde. Let's avert our eyes from death. Like Goethe. Goethe who refused to see corpses, to come close to illness. He refused death. He averted his eyes. He thought he owed his longevity to flight. Let's look elsewhere. I'm afraid, I'm afraid. I'm afraid of dying and afraid of replying to Sarah.

How beautiful Vienna is, how far away Vienna is, that's a quotation, but from what, by whom, an Austrian? Grillparzer? Or Balzac? Even translated into German it says nothing to me. Good Lord good Lord what to say, what to say, let's summon the Google djinn like the genie of the lamp, Genie are you there, ah, far from literature, it's an extract from a horrible French song, a horrible French song, there's the complete text, found in 0.009 of a second — good Lord, these words are long. Life is long, life is very long sometimes, especially listening to this Barbara, "If I write to you tonight from Vienna," what an idea, really, Sarah what came over you, with all the texts you know by heart, Rimbaud, Rumi, Hafez — this Barbara has an unsettling face, impish or demonic, good Lord I hate French songs, Édith Piaf with her rasping voice, Barbara sad enough to uproot an oak, I've come up with a response, I'll copy out another passage from a song, Schubert and winter, there, half-blinded by the dawn that's pointing to the Danube, the atonal light of hope, you have to see everything through the spectacles of hope, cherish the other in the self, recognize it, love this song that is all songs, ever since the *Songs of Dawn* by the troubadours, by Schumann and all the ghazals of creation, you're always surprised by what always comes, the answer of time, suffering, compassion, and death; the sun, which keeps rising; the Orient of the enlightened, the

East, the direction of the compass and the Purple Archangel,
you're surprised by the marble of the World veined with suffering and love, at daybreak, go on, there is no shame, there hasn't
been any shame in a long time, it is not shameful to copy out this
winter song, not shameful to let yourself give in to your feelings

> I close my eyes,
> My heart still beats fervently.
> When will the leaves at the window turn green again?
> When will I hold my love in my arms?

and to the warm sunlight of hope.

ENVOI

To Peter Metcalf and his "Wine of the Corpse, Endocannibalism and the Great Feast of the Dead in Borneo," published in *Representations* in 1987, which inspired the article on "The Wine of the Dead of Sarawak"—a much more profound and scholarly contribution in reality than what Franz and Sarah say about it.

To the Berliner Künstlerprogramm of the DAAD (Deutscher Akademischer Austauschdienst), which welcomed me to Berlin and allowed me to immerse myself in German Orientalism.

To all the researchers whose work has nourished me, Orientalists from long ago and modern scholars—historians, musicologists, literary specialists; when their names are mentioned, I have tried as much as possible not to betray their points of view.

To my old teachers, Christophe Balay and Ricardo Zipoli; to the Circle of Melancholy Orientalists; to my friends in Paris, Damascus, and Tehran.

To the Syrian People.